開企,

是一個開頭,它可以是一句美好的引言、
未完待續的逗點、享受美好後滿足的句點,
新鮮的體驗、大膽的冒險、嶄新的方向,
是一趟有你共同參與的奇妙旅程。

一本掌握易混淆

英文文法

文法常見錯誤與用法精論

User's Guide 使用說明

文法不可怕！
只要跟著本書學習，有任何文法細節上的疑問，答案都能隨找即查；不論是想要閱讀／口說齊頭並進，或是考試拿高分，一本全掌握。

01 有系統地規劃八大文法及寫作培訓章節，強力訓練句構、詞彙用法，助突破學習盲點，提升文法實力

全書依「文法常見錯誤」和「寫作用法精論」兩大部分來策劃，只要按章節循序漸進學習，不論是寫作或口說能力，都能同步提升；同時，內容也針對學測、指考、中級英檢寫作評分標準設計，定能一舉突破考試分數，輕鬆拿高分。

Contents

Part I 文法常見錯誤

Chapter 1 句子結構 ....

例如：
- All of the + 名詞中的 of 是贅字
- Neither of ≠ Both (of) + not
- Taller than I 還是 Taller than m

Chapter 2 字彙和片語 ....

例如：
- All 還是 whole 呢？
- As 還是 like 呢？
- At the beginning
- At the end 還是 i

Part II 寫作用法精論

Chapter 1 句子結構 ....

例如：
- 6123 結構
- 分裂句 (cleft sentences) ……等等。
- 如何強調句中的元素

Chapter 2 字彙和片語 ....

例如：
- After 和 behind 的用法差異
- Do 和 make 後接名詞片語當受詞時的用
- Enough 的用法

3 拼字 ....

02 高效學習三大步驟，化繁為簡地幫助理解重點文法

只要跟著三步驟學習，即使再複雜的文法觀念，都能清晰地快速理解，有條理的完整學習。

步驟 1
重要觀念 非學不可
先理解重要文法觀念

步驟 2
必閃陷阱 非學不可
再釐清容易混淆的文法陷阱

步驟 3
好用 Tips 非學不可
利用 100 個搶分祕訣拿高分

Unit 20 Get 還是 go 呢？

重要觀念 非學不可

在表示「移動，行進」的意思時，get 和 go 是
達。例如：
- ◆ I'll call you as soon as I **get** to Seoul. (O)
- ◇ I'll call you as soon as I **go** to Seoul. (✕)
（我一到首爾就會打電話給你。）
- ◆ The thing is, he **got** to work late and miss
- ...ing is, he went to work late

必閃陷阱 非學不可

Get 和 **go** 都有「變成，變得，變為」的意思
別與不同的形容詞連用。
Get 通常與 late、dark、light、hot、cold、hu
容詞連用，而 **go** 則跟**顏色**（如 go grey/red）
crazy、mad、wild、bad、rotten、sour、nake
面聯想的形容詞連用，通常指變壞。例如：
- ◆ It's **getting** late—I have to go. (O)
- ◇ It's **going** late—I have to go. (✕)
（晚了，我該走了。）
- ...ing dark. (O)

好用 Tips 非學不可

然而，**angry**、**old**、**sick**、**tired**、**ill**、**wet** 和
則與 **get** 連用。例如：
- ◆ It was raining and we all **got wet**. (O)
- ◇ It was raining and we all **went wet**. (✕)
（下雨了，我們都被淋濕了。）
- ◆ Our boss often **gets angry** about trivial things.
- ◇ Our boss often **goes angry** about trivial things.
（我們老闆常因瑣碎小事動怒。）
- ...**got tired** after studying all day. (O)
- ...t tired after studying all day.（...我很累了）

03 70 篇易混淆文法精準解析

學習時常見的文法錯誤，全書以正誤例句的鮮明對照方式，一目了然地助你釐清易犯錯的文法概念，學習記憶更深刻，還能避免誤入考試陷阱，快速作答不失分。

Unit 22 Pick 還是 pick up 呢？

重要觀念 非學不可

Pick 的動詞用法有好幾個常用的意思，包括「（用手）採、選，選擇」、「（用手指或尖形工具）挖，剔」、「搶起或類似的動作」等。然而，這些意思無一可⋯⋯代。**Pick up** 主要意為「（用手從某⋯⋯「（用車子）接載（某人）⋯⋯起」的意思，但含意不同（P⋯⋯**Pick** 意為「（用手）採、⋯⋯

We spent the summer hol⋯⋯
spent the summer hol⋯⋯
⋯⋯

Unit 30 使用 marry 時常見的錯⋯⋯

重要觀念 非學不可

Marry（結婚）可當及物和不及物動詞⋯⋯詞。**Divorce**（離婚）的用法亦同。例如：

1. Amy married a wealthy old man last month.
（艾美上個月嫁給一個有錢的老頭。）
2. Last year he divorced his second wife.
（去年他跟他第二任太太離婚了。）

⋯⋯在**正式文體**中，它們都用作不及⋯⋯

Unit 12 如何強調句中的元素(二)

重要觀念 非學不可

The thing, the one/only/first thing, something
The thing
我們可以用 the thing l⋯⋯
was) 來強調 BE 動⋯⋯
用一樣，但比較⋯⋯

The thing I love⋯⋯
我喜歡約翰的⋯⋯
I love a⋯⋯

Unit 22 Many 的形容詞用法

必閃陷阱 非學不可

Many 是個大家所熟知的字，當形容詞時意為「（⋯⋯多的，很多的」，通常**用於否定句和疑問句**。例如⋯⋯

1. How many sisters do you have?
（你有幾個姊妹？）
2. I don't have many relatives.
（我的親戚不多。）

⋯⋯的前面可以加上 not 來表示⋯⋯

04 90 則寫作概念精論，強化正確觀念，文法不再是夢魘！

寫作時，如何寫正確的句子結構、用字如何更精準⋯⋯用 90 則寫作精論，讓你學會準確地使用寫作常用詞彙，同時深入瞭解各字詞的正確用法。全方位有效提升寫作實力。

05 100 個語用法搶分祕訣，學習深入簡出更有效

將複雜的文法化為 100 個好記好用的小提醒，學習有撇步，不僅能融會貫通也記更牢。

⋯⋯y picking up your clo⋯⋯
⋯⋯y in the closet?（O）
⋯⋯老是在收拾你散落在地板上的衣服。你不能把⋯⋯

好用 Tips 非學不可

Pick up 意為「（用車子）**接載**（某人）」。我們亦可用⋯⋯from）來表達相同的意思。例如：

◆ He'll **pick me up** after the party.（O）
◇ He'll pick me after the party.（×）
（聚會後他會開車來接我。）
◆ I will **pick up** Sam at the airport and take him to his hotel.
◇ I will pick Sam at the airport and take him to his hotel.（×
（我會開車到機場接山姆，載他到他下榻的旅館。）
◆ I'll **collect** you **from** the station.（O）
（我會去車站接你。）
⋯⋯hat time do you **collect** the kids **from** school?
⋯⋯時候去接孩子放學呢？）

Preface 作者序

　　談到「文法」，相信絕大多數的人都會搖搖頭地說：「文法好難啊！」可是，面對考試或真心想要提升英文能力的人，文法卻是至關重要的一環。有鑑於此，這本文法書誕生了。

　　本書分為「常見錯誤」和「用法精論」兩個部分，但兩者皆以語法的正確性為主要訴求，主要差異在於前者還提供對錯例句的對比。兩者的敘述均力求精闢與詳盡，**是一本適合不同程度使用的英文文法與用法學習書籍。**讀完本書後，相信您的英文能力會獲得顯著的精進與提升。

　　本書的第一部份旨在探討使用英文時經常發生的錯誤，並提出正確的用法和例句，在對與錯的鮮明對比之下，讓讀者從此不會再犯相同的錯誤。事實上，這些錯誤經常被忽視、似是而非，抑或用錯而不自知，實在有加以匡正之必要。

　　例如：I slipped on a banana skin and fell. 和 All the Mayday concert tickets were sold out soon. 這兩句都是錯誤的，但錯在哪裡呢？請看本書的說明：

◆ I slipped on a banana skin and fell down.（○）

　（我踩到香蕉皮滑倒摔了一跤。）

◇ I slipped on a banana skin and fell.（×）

→ Fall 指的是從較高的位置掉落到地面，而 fall down 則是指人或物從其正常的位置掉落到地面。不論身高，人走路時的姿態是個正常位置。

◆ Soon all the Mayday concert tickets were sold out.（○）

（五月天演唱會門票瞬間秒殺。）

◆ All the Mayday concert tickets were soon sold out.（○）

◇ All the Mayday concert tickets were sold out soon.（×）

→ 在指過去某個時間點之後不久的句子中，soon 不可用在句末。

　　從上述例子可以看出，經由鮮明的正確與錯誤的示範比對以及精準的解析後，學習思路能更加清晰，也不用再擔心被模糊不清的觀念所混淆，文法這次可以學得好。

　　本書的第二部份旨在針對一些經常用到的字詞或其相關語法觀念加以精闢的闡述，讓讀者能鉅細靡遺地瞭解到各該字詞的文法功能及正確用法。

　　例如：「At、on 和 in 後接地點的用法」一文會告訴讀者 work at Google、work for Google 跟 work with Google 之間有何不同；再者，許多人都想瞭解 Here you are、there you are、Here you go、There you go、Here it is、There he is、Here I am、Here we are、Here we go 在不同情境下的意思和用法，但卻找不到完整資料。現在只要看完本書的「Here 和 there 的用法」一文，讀者就能融會貫通這些幾乎每天都會用到、但語意一直無法精準掌握的用語如何使用。

　　任何書籍都無法十全十美，本書亦然，若有疏漏之處，歡迎批評指正。最後，希望透過有系統的整理，讓讀者學習感受煥然一新，同時更有實效，文法程度能突飛猛進。

俞亨通

目錄
Contents

Part I 文法常見錯誤

例如：
- All of the ＋ 名詞中的 of 是贅字
- Neither of ≠ Both (of) ＋ not ⎱……等等。
- Taller than I 還是 Taller than me 呢？

例如：
- All 還是 whole 呢？
- As 還是 like 呢？
- At the beginning 還是 in the beginning？ ⎱……等等。
  At the end 還是 in the end 呢？

例如：
- Altogether 還是 all together 呢？
- Cannot 還是 can not 呢？ ⎱……等等。
- Content 還是 contents 呢？

例如：
- E.g. 和 i.e. 的差異
- East, west, south, north 不大寫 ⎱……等等。
- 用引號來表示「所謂的」概念

Part II 寫作用法精論

特別收錄

Part I
文法常見錯誤

Chapter 1

句子結構

Chapter 1 | 句子結構

Unit 01 All of the ＋ 名詞中的 of 是贅字

重要觀念 非學不可

在「all of the／these／those／所有格 ＋ 名詞」的句型中，all 是不定代名詞（indefinite pronoun），如：All of these students live in Taipei.（這些學生全都住在台北）；All of his money is spent on food.（他的錢全都花在食物上。）由於 **of 可以省略**，上述句型就變成「**all the／these／those／所有格 ＋ 名詞**」，此時 all 變成（前置）限定詞（determiner or pre-determiner），如：All these students live in Taipei.；All his money is spent on food.。雖然 all 後面有沒有 of 都可以，文法都沒有錯，但許多人認為 all of ... 的寫法不夠簡潔，因為 of 一點作用都沒有，是不折不扣的贅字。所以，

◆ All my students are female.（○）
◇ All of my students are female.（欠佳）
→ of 是贅字。
（我的學生全都是女生。）
◆ I want to hear all the details.（○）
◇ I want to hear all of the details.（欠佳）
→ of 是贅字。
（我想要聽所有的細節。）

必閃陷阱 非學不可

然而，如果將「**all of the／these／those／所有格 ＋ 名詞**」中的「the／these／those／所有格 ＋ 名詞」換成**人稱代名詞的受格（us, you, them, it）**，那麼 **of 不能省略**，否則就犯了大錯。例如：

1. All of us must attend the meeting.
（我們全都要參加這項會議。）

2. All of you need to buy me a coffee.
（你們全都要請我喝杯咖啡。）

3. All of them can speak Japanese.
（他們全都會講日語。）

4. He'd like all of us to get there.
（他希望我們全都去那裡。）

5. I've invited all of them to my birthday party.
（我已邀請他們全都來參加我的生日派對。）

好用 Tips 非學不可 🔍

不過，若「all of ＋ 人稱代名詞」當主詞用，那麼它可改寫為不用 **of** 的「**人稱代名詞主格 ＋ all**」；若「all of ＋ 人稱代名詞」當受詞用，那麼它可改寫為不用 **of** 的「**人稱代名詞受格 ＋ all**」。茲將上面 5 句改寫如下，上下對應句之間的意思完全一樣，且都是標準英語：

1. We all must attend the meeting.

2. You all need to buy me a coffee.

3. They all can speak Japanese.

4. He'd like us all to get there.

5. I've invited them all to my birthday party.

Unit 02 Neither of ≠ Both (of) + not

重要觀念 非學不可

Neither 可當連接詞、副詞、限定詞和代名詞用,這裡要談的是 **neither 當限定詞和代名詞**的用法,表示兩者中沒有任何一個,即「兩者都不」。例如:

1. Neither answer is correct.

(兩個答案都不對。)

→ neither 在此當限定詞用,後接**單數可數名詞**。

2. Neither of the answers is/are correct.

(兩個答案都不對。)

→ neither 在此當代名詞用。用作代名詞的 neither 後接複數名詞時,在正式書面文件中,**動詞通常用單數形式**,但在口語或非正式文件中,**動詞通常用複數形式**。Either 的代名詞用法亦同。

Both 可當形容詞和代名詞用,前者表示「**兩者**」,如:Both children can speak English.(兩個小孩都會講英語),後者表示「**兩者都**」,如 Both (of) his parents are doctors.(他的父母親都是醫生。)用作代名詞的 both 的句型為「**Both (of) + the, these, those, my, his, our 或 their 等限定詞 + 複數名詞**」,其中 of 可以省略,但 of 後面若接**受格代名詞**,則 **of 不可省略**。例如:

1. Both (of) these books are new.
(這兩本書都是新的。)

2. Both of them speak Japanese.
(他們倆都會講日語。)

必閃陷阱 非學不可

然而，當我們要表達「**兩者都不**」的意思時，**只能用 neither of**，而**不能用 both（of）+ not**，因為 both 只能用於肯定句。例如：

◆ Neither of these shirts is/are dry yet.（O）
（這兩件襯衫都還沒乾。）

◇ Both（of）these shirts aren't dry yet.（×）

◆ Both（of）these shirts are still wet.（O）
（這兩件襯衫都還是濕的。）

◆ Neither of them was/were interested in going to university.（O）

◇ Both of them were not interested in going to university.（×）
（他們兩個都對上大學不感興趣）

Neither of 亦不能用 none of 來代替，因為 none of 是表示三者（或三者以上）中沒有任何一個。例如：

◆ I have two sisters. **Neither of** them is/are teachers.（O）

◇ I have two sisters. None of them is/are teachers.（×）
（我有兩個姊妹。她們都不是老師。）

好用 Tips 非學不可

用作代名詞的 none，意為「沒有任何人（或物）」，後接複數名詞時，它的動詞亦可以是單數或複數形式。例如：

1. None of the earphones are/is working.
（所有耳機都壞了。）

2. None of them speak(s) English.
（他們都不會講英語。）

最後要提的是，neither 有兩種發音：/ˈniðɚ]/ 或 /ˈnaɪð•(r)/；同樣地，either 亦有兩種發音：/ˈiðɚ / 或 /ˈaɪð•(r)/。

No doubt 還是 without doubt 呢？

重要觀念 非學不可

當我們認為我們所說的事情是**真的或可能發生**時，可以用 no doubt 來表示。儘管字典給 **no doubt** 下的定義幾乎都是「毫無疑問，毋庸置疑，肯定」，但其實它的意思類似於 **"I imagine"** 或 **"I suppose"**（**我想，我認為**）。例如：

1. No doubt Amy was the most beautiful girl in her class.
（我認為艾美是她班上最漂亮的女生／艾美很可能是她班上最漂亮的女生。）
2. Tom will no doubt visit us if he comes to Taipei.
（如果湯姆來台北，他很可能會來我們家作客。）

當我們**非常肯定**我們的看法時，**可以用 there is no doubt that ...**（毫無疑問，毋庸置疑，肯定）來表示，但**不可用 no doubt**。There is no doubt that ... 係用於正式場合。例如：

◆ **There is no doubt that** she is the best badminton player in the country.（○）
（無庸置疑地，她是全國最優秀的羽球選手。）
◇ No doubt she is the best badminton player in the country.（×）
（她很可能是全國最優秀的羽球選手。）

必閃陷阱 非學不可

Without doubt（或 without a doubt）比 there is no doubt that ... 更正式。當我們絕對或十分肯定我們的看法時，**可以用 without（a）doubt**（毫無疑問，毋庸置疑，肯定）來表示，但**不可用 no doubt**。例如：

◆ John is **without（a）doubt** the best student I have ever taught.（○）
（毫無疑問地，約翰是我教過最優秀的學生。）

◇ John is no doubt the best student I have ever taught.（×）
（約翰很可能是我教過最優秀的學生。）

Unit 04　Taller than I 還是 Taller than me 呢？

重要觀念 非學不可

這兩者都對，但不是每個人都同意這兩者都對，這就是問題所在。儘管 Tom is taller than me. 這樣的說法比較自然，但許多人認為這是錯的；相對地，有些人則認為 Tom is taller than I. 的說法顯得做作。所以，最安全的作法就是將句子展開為 **Tom is taller than I am.**。這樣的結構殆無疑義，不會引起任何爭議。

爭議的根源在於 **than 這個字既可當連接詞**，亦可**當介系詞用**。當 than 用作連接詞時，句子寫成：

◆ Tom is taller **than** I am.（O）
◆ Tom is taller **than** I.（O）
→（只是比較簡潔。）當 than 用作介系詞時，句子寫成：
◆ Tom is taller **than** me.（O）
（湯姆比我高。）

文法學者已為 than 到底是連接詞還是介系詞爭論了好幾百年。對大多數人來說，"than me" 的說法比較自然，但這種說法被認為錯誤的機率也是最高的。這是因為 "than I" 的說法比較早出現，而且在文法上似乎也比較正確。然而，"than I" 的說法聽起來顯得做作，所以公說公有理，婆說婆有理。

必閃陷阱 非學不可

此外，還有另一個問題要考慮：**"than me"** 有時會引發歧義。請看下面的例句：

Tom likes John more than me.

這一句可能意為——

Tom prefers John to me.

（湯姆喜歡約翰更甚於我。換言之，在約翰和我之中，湯姆比較喜歡約翰。）

也可能意為——

Tom likes John more than I like John.

（湯姆比我更喜歡約翰。換言之，湯姆喜歡約翰，我也喜歡約翰，但湯姆喜歡約翰的程度大於我。）

避免引發這種模稜兩可情況的最佳方法，就是**把 than 當作連接詞並將句子完整地寫出**。例如：

1. Tom likes John more than he likes me.
（湯姆喜歡約翰更甚於我。）
2. Tom likes John more than I do.
3. Tom likes John more than I like John.
（湯姆比我更喜歡約翰。）

好用 Tips 非學不可

然而，當 than 後面接代名詞 who 時，than 必須用作介系詞，所以 who 要變成 whom；簡言之，**"than whom" 是唯一正確的版本**。例如：

◇ Blanche likes you more than who?（×）
◆ Blanche likes you more **than whom**?（○）
（布蘭奇喜歡你更甚於誰？）

Unit 05 They, their 和 themselves 都可用作單數

重要觀念 非學不可

當單數的人可能是男性或女性時，他們的代名詞可以使用主格的 he, he or she 或 they、所有格的 his, his or her 或 their 以及受格的 him, him or her 或 themselves。許多婦女不喜歡使用「雌雄莫辨」、不分性別的 he 來指人，她們往往使用 **he or she, she or he** 或者在口語中使用 **they** 來代替。例如：

◆ Anyone can solve the problem if **he** tries.（○）
（如果大家都肯試試，任何人都能解決這問題。）
◆ Anyone can solve the problem if **he or she** tries.（○）
（如果大家都肯試試，任何人都能解決這問題。）→ 在書寫中，he or she 經常寫成 he/she 或 s/he。
◆ Anyone can solve the problem if **they** try.（○）
（如果大家都肯試試，任何人都能解決這問題。）
◆ Each person gave **his** opinion.（○）
（每個人都發表了意見。）
◆ Each person gave **his or her** opinion.（○）
（每個人都發表了意見。）→ 在書寫中，his or her 經常寫成 his/her。
◆ Each person gave **their** opinion.（○）
（每個人都發表了意見。）
◆ Each person must introduce **themselves** before performing.（○）
（每個人在表演之前必須先自我介紹。）

從上面例句可以看出，這樣的用法最常出現在 **each, every, everyone（everybody）, someone（somebody）, anyone（anybody）** 或 **no one（nobody）** 的句子中。它們雖然都接單數動詞，但除了在非常正式的演講或文章中，其後經常接**複數代名詞**。再來看下面的例句：

Chapter 1 ｜ 句子結構

1. Each of them expressed their opinion.
（他們每個人都發表了意見。）

2. Has everyone finished their drinks/his or her drink?
（每個人都把酒喝光了嗎？）

3. Someone's stood you up, haven't they?
（有人放你鴿子，不是嗎？）

必閃陷阱 非學不可

不過，要注意的是，everyone 或 everybody 僅能用來指人，其後絕不可接 of，而 every one 可以指每個人或每件事，其後通常接 of。例如：

1. Everyone in the class wants to take a day trip.
（班上的每個人都想一日遊。）

2. There are 30 students in the class and every one of them wants to go on a day trip.
（這一班有 30 個學生，每個人都想一日遊。）

Unit 06　You and I or you and me

重要觀念 非學不可

不少人經常在 you and I 或 my husband and I 等應該用 me 的情況中使用 I，簡單的文法卻犯了大錯，令人遺憾！

◆ It is a gift from my husband and **me**.（O）
（那是我先生跟我送的禮物。）→ 介系詞 from 後面要使用 I 的受格 me。

◇ It is a gift from my husband and I.（×）
→ 這跟說 from I 一樣是錯誤的。

◇ Between you and I, I think his wife is rather ugly. （ ✕ ）
（這是我們私下說的話，我認為他太太長得有夠抱歉。）
→ 這跟說 between I and the gatepost 一樣是錯誤的。

註：Between you and me = between ourselves = between you, me, and the gatepost / bedpost（你我私下說說，不可讓其他人知道。）

必閃陷阱 非學不可

記住，介系詞（from, between, by, for, in, at, on ...）後面要用受格，所以**當 I 位在介系詞的後面做為介系詞的受詞時，I 要變成 me**。這與 I 的前面是否有 you 或 my husband 無關。
只有 you and I 或 my husband and I 在句中當動詞的主詞時，才使用 I。
例如：

◆ **You and I** often argue on this subject. （ O ）
（你我經常吵這個話題。）→ You and I 是動詞 argue 的主詞。
◆ **My wife and I** accept your invitation. （ O ）
（我太太和我接受你的邀請。）→ My wife and I 是動詞 accept 的主詞。

好用 Tips 非學不可

如果你還搞不懂到底要用 you and I 還是 you and me，這裡提供一個簡單的方法讓大家嘗試一下，以後應該就會用對了。首先**把 I 以外的元素全部拿掉，然後再決定要用 I 還是 me**。

● It is a gift from my husband and I/me.
問題：I 或 me 呢？
步驟 1：把 "my husband and" 拿掉。
步驟 2：再重新檢視句子。
步驟 3a：It is a gift from I. （ ✕ ）
步驟 3b：It is a gift from **me**. （ O ）

所以：

◆ It is a gift from my husband and **me**.（O）
◇ It is a gift from my husband and I.（×）.

Unit 07　介系詞的受詞

重要觀念 非學不可

介系詞後面所接的字被稱為介系詞的受詞。**介系詞都是以名詞類當受詞**，包括名詞（片語）、代名詞、動名詞（片語）和名詞子句。

名詞（片語）當介系詞的受詞時通常不會發生文法上的問題，如：

He borrowed a lot of money from the bank.

（他向銀行借了許多錢。）

→ 這句中的名詞（片語）the bank 是介系詞 from 的受詞。

必閃陷阱 非學不可

然而，其他名詞類在當介系詞的受詞時，或多或少都會有文法錯誤的情況發生。茲將可能發生錯誤的情況說明如下：

就代名詞而言，既然是受詞，那麼就必須用受格形式，單純的受格代名詞應該也不太會發生文法錯誤，如 Mary sent an email to me yesterday.（瑪麗昨天傳電子郵件給我。）這句中的 me（I 的受格）是介系詞 to 的受詞。然而，當介系詞的受詞為**名詞 + 代名詞、代名詞 + 名詞或代名詞 + 代名詞**時，文法錯誤的情況不時會發生。例如：

◇ My brother is going to Japan tomorrow with his wife and I.（×）

（我哥哥跟他太太和我明天要去日本。）

→ 由於 his wife 和 I 都是介系詞 with 的受詞，**所以 I 要用受格的 me**。如果將 his wife and 拿掉，使句子變成 My brother is going to Japan tomorrow with me.，應該就不會用錯了。

◇ Between you and I, I think her husband has extramarital affairs.（×）

（你不要告訴別人，我認為她先生有婚外情。）

→ 由於 you 和 I 都是介系詞 between 的受詞，所以 **I 要用受格的 me**；這裡的 you 是受格。

主格要用做主詞。例如：

◆ **My brother and I** are going to Japan tomorrow.（O）

（我哥哥和我明天要去日本。）→ My brother 和 I 是動詞 are 的主詞。

在所有代名詞當中，只有人稱代名詞的 I/me、he/him、she/her、we/us 和 they / them 以及**關係代名詞的 who / whom** 有不同的主格和受格型態。在當介系詞的受詞時，人稱代名詞因為主格和受格型態不同而發生的文法錯誤如上述，所在多有。同樣地，關係代名詞 who/whom 往往也會發生這樣的錯誤，而且發生的頻率甚至更高。例如：

◆ **With whom** did you see Amy?（O）

（你看到艾美跟誰在一起？）

◇ John gave the Jody Chiang's farewell concert tickets to who?（×）

（約翰把江蕙的封麥演唱會門票給誰？）

→ **介系詞 to 的受詞須用受格的 whom。**

◆ You have a child **by whom**?（O）

（妳是跟誰有個孩子的？）

◇ Helen is the lady who I made the promise to.（×）

（海倫就是那位我對她做出承諾的女士。）

→ **lady 是句末介系詞 to 的受詞，所以須用受格的 whom。**雖然我們盡量不要將介系詞放在句末，但有時卻是不得不然的作法。

◇ Who did you stay with?（×）
（你跟誰住在一起？）

→ **介系詞 with 的受詞須用受格的 whom**。然而，口語往往使用 who 而不用 whom，這是口語相當常見的說法，所以這句其實並沒有錯。這就是 whom 被許多人視為已奄奄一息、時日不多的原因。

Who 為主格，要用做主詞。例如：

◆ **Who** is that girl over there?（O）
（在那邊的那個女孩是誰？）

→ Who 是動詞 is 的主詞。

◆ I have not seen the man **who** lives over the road for a month.（O）
（我已經有一個月沒有看見那位住在馬路對面的男子。）

→ who 是動詞 lives 的主詞。

介系詞若接動詞，須將動詞變成動名詞。例如：

◇ Cindy earns her living by sell insurance.（×）
（辛蒂靠賣保險為生。）→ **sell 須改為 selling**。

◆ Thank you for **being** here with us to discuss this problem.（O）
（感謝您蒞臨跟我們討論這個問題。）

◇ I am looking forward to see that singer.（×）
（我盼望見到那位歌手。）

→ **to 並非不定詞而是介系詞，其後須用動名詞 seeing**。

好用 Tips 非學不可 🔍

最後，就介系詞接名詞子句的情況而言，這種情況的名詞子句，指的是由 whether 或 if 所引導的名詞子句。雖然**引導名詞子句的 whether （意為「是否」）可用 if 來代替，但在介系詞之後只能用 whether，不能用 if**。例如：

◆ I am unsure **whether** I will be attending his birthday party.（O）

◆ I am unsure **if** I will be attending his birthday party.（〇）
（我不確定我是否會參加他的生日派對。）

◆ There was a big argument **about whether** we should move to Taipei.（〇）

◇ There was a big argument about if we should move to Taipei.（✕）
（我們曾為是否應搬到台北而發生嚴重爭吵。）

◆ Benjamin has yet to make the decision on **whether** he will study abroad.
（〇）

◇ Benjamin has yet to make the decision on if he will study abroad.（✕）
（班傑明還沒決定是否出國唸書。）

Unit 08 主詞中含有 or 或 nor 的單複數問題

重要觀念 非學不可

當主詞是由 or 或 nor 所連接的兩個元素所構成，**若這兩個元素都是單數，則主動詞為單數**。若其中有個**元素為複數**，則**主動詞變成複數**。例如：

1. Taylor or his wife is going to pick up his parents at the airport.
（泰勒或者他太太將到機場接他的父母親。）

2. The twin brothers or their sister are going to pick up their parents at the airport.
（這對雙胞胎兄弟或是他們的姊姊將到機場接他們的父母親。）

兩個元素都是單數時接單數動詞

若主詞中的兩個元素是用相關字組或相關連接詞（correlative or correlative conjunction）**either ... or**（either 經常省略）或 **neither ... nor** 來連接，**其後接單一動詞，且兩個元素都是單數，那麼該動詞也必須為單數**。例如：

◆ Neither **Paul** nor **Peter is** in the library.（O）
（保羅和彼得都不在圖書館。）

→ 由於 Paul 是單數，而 Peter 也是單數，所以動詞用 is 是正確的，若用複數 are 就錯了。

◆ Neither **Dickens** nor **Gary was** a nice guy.（O）
（狄更斯和蓋瑞都不是好人。）

→ Dickens 和 Gary 都是單數，所以動詞用 was（不是 were）。

◆ Either **Mr. Chen** or **his wife has** the keys to the Lexus.（O）
（陳先生或者他太太有這部凌志的鑰匙。）

→ Mr. Chen 和 his wife 都是單數，所以動詞用 has（不是 have）。

◇ Neither Tracy nor Gina do as they are told.（×）
（崔西和吉娜都沒有按照指示去做。）

→ Tracy 和 Gina 都是單數，所以動詞應該用單數的 does（不是複數的 do）。

◆ Either **Mary** or **her sister plays** the piano at night.（O）
（不是瑪麗就是她姊姊在晚上彈鋼琴。）

必閃陷阱 非學不可

兩個元素有一是複數時接複數動詞

若主詞中的兩個元素是用 either ... or（either 經常省略）或 neither ... nor 來連接，其後接單一動詞，且**兩個元素至少有一個是複數**，那麼該**動詞也必須為複數**。例如：

◆ Neither **the teacher** nor **the students are** able to solve the math problem.（O）
（老師和學生都解不出這個數學問題。）→ teacher 是單數，students 是複數，所以動詞用 are（不是 is）。

◆ There **were** neither **cakes nor ice cream** at the birthday party.（O）
（生日聚會上既沒有蛋糕也沒有冰淇淋。）

◆ Neither **the detectives** nor **the policemen** know him.（O）
（警探和警察都不認識他。）→（不是 knows）。

◇ Either Amy and Sarah or Kevin has to go there.（×）
（不是艾美和莎拉就是凱文必須去那裡。）

好用 Tips 非學不可 🔍

靠近規則（Proximity Rule）

顯然地，若由 or 或 nor 所連接的兩個元素都是單數，動詞用單數，若兩個元素都是複數，動詞用複數，殆無疑義。然而，若兩個元素一為單數、一為複數，那麼動詞該用單數還是複數，仍有爭議；換言之，上述的規則並非放諸四海皆準，也不完全符合所有文法慣例。事實上，**英文有一個所謂的「靠近規則」**，根據此規則，**動詞的單複數是由最靠近動詞的元素來決定**。例如：

1. There was neither ice cream nor cakes at the birthday party.
（生日聚會上既沒有冰淇淋也沒有蛋糕。）

→ 根據一般慣例，這句不對，因為 cakes 為複數字，即主詞的兩個元素中有一為複數，動詞應為 were。但**根據靠近規則**，這句是正確的，因為最靠近動詞的元素 ice cream 是單數，動詞用 was 自是無誤。

2. Either Amy and Sarah or Kevin has to go there.
（不是艾美和莎拉就是凱文必須去那裡。）

→ 根據一般慣例，這句不對，因為主詞的兩個元素中有一為複數，即 Amy and Sarah，動詞應為 have。但**根據靠近規則**，這句是正確的，因為最靠近動詞的元素 Kevin 是單數，動詞用 has 自是無誤。

Unit 09 使用 both 時常見的錯誤

重要觀念 非學不可 ●

Both 可當（前置）限定詞和代名詞用，意為「兩個；兩者；雙方」。
在所有格 + 名詞的前面可以使用 both 或 both of；換言之，**both of 跟 all of 和 half of 一樣，of 可以省略**。例如：

1. Both （of） her parents are doctors.
（她的父母親都是醫生。）

2. Both （of） his sisters are living in Japan.
（他的兩個姊姊都住在日本。）

Both 可修飾名詞。例如：

1. There are five cars on both sides of the road.
（路的兩邊各有五輛汽車。）

2. Both children went.
（兩個孩子都去了。）

Both 與代名詞連用時，無論代名詞是主格還是受格，both 都位在它們的後面。例如：

◆ They **both** need some money.（O）
（他們兩人都需要一些錢。）

◇ Both they need some money.（×）

◆ I like them **both.**（O）
（他們兩人我都喜歡。）

◇ I like both them.（×）

但我們可以用 **both of ＋ 受格代名詞來當主詞或受詞**。例如：

◆ **Both of them** （= They both） need some money.（O）

◆ I like **both of them** （= them both）.（O）

不過，雖然「both of ＋ 受格代名詞」等於「受格代名詞 ＋ both」，但**在介系詞後面，通常使用「both of ＋ 受格代名詞」**。例如：

1. Mary looked at both of us.
（瑪麗看著我們兩個。）

→ 優於 Mary looked at us both.。

2. This plan is beneficial for both of you.
（這項計畫對你們兩人都有利。）

→ 優於 This plan is beneficial for you both.。

Both ... and ... 與名詞連用時，both 可位在名詞的前面或後面。例如：

◆ We all like **both** Tom **and** Cindy.（○）
（湯姆和辛蒂兩個我們都喜歡。）

= We all like Tom and Cindy both.（○）

◆ **Both** Teresa **and** Amy have pixie cut hairstyle.（○）
（泰瑞莎和艾美都留了一頭俏麗短髮。）

= Teresa and Amy both have pixie cut hairstyle.（○）

◆ **Both** men **and** women like the movie.（○）
（男人和女人都喜歡這部電影。）

= Men and women both like the movie.（○）

必閃陷阱 非學不可

當 both 指的是主詞時，亦即**當 both 是主詞的一部份時，它在句中通常位在副詞慣常的中間位置**，即主詞和主動詞之間、語氣助動詞或第一個助動詞之後，或當主動詞用的 BE 動詞之後。例如：

1. We both wanted to live abroad.
（我們兩人都想住在國外。）

→ both 位在主詞和主動詞之間。

2. They have both been working for that company for five years.
（他們兩人都已在那家公司工作了五年。）

→ both 位在語氣助動詞或第一個助動詞之後。

◆ They were **both** very generous and friendly.（○）

→ both 位在當主動詞用的BE 動詞之後。

◇ They both were very generous and friendly.（×）
（他們兩人都很大方和友善。）

Who are you like in your family?
（你在家中像誰？）

◆ My father I suppose, we're **both** quite moody.（O）
（我想是像我爸爸，我們兩人都很情緒化。）
→ both 位在當主動詞用的 BE 動詞之後。
◇ My father I suppose, we both are quite moody.（×）

在否定句中，我們不可使用 both，必須改用 **either**（兩者之中任何一個）。例如：

◆ John studied chemistry and physics, but he had **little** interest in **either** subject.（O）
（約翰唸的是化學和物理，但他對這兩門學科都沒有什麼興趣。）
→ little 為否定詞。
◇ John studied chemistry and physics, but he had little interest in both subjects.（×）
◆ I **don't** agree with **either** of you on these issues.（O）
◇ I don't agree with both of you on these issues.（×）
（在這些問題上，你們兩個我都不同意。）
◆ A: Are Paul and his girlfriend both coming to my birthday party?（O）
（A：保羅和他女友會來參加我的生日派對嗎？）
◆ B: I **don't** know if **either** of them are coming.（O）
◇ B: I don't know if both of them are coming.（×）
（B：我不知道他們兩人是否會來？）

好用 Tips 非學不可 🔍

必須說明的是，在上句中，either 雖然是個單數字，但在非正式的口說英語中，它通常接複數動詞。不過，**在比較正式的情況，either 係接單數動詞**，即 ... **if either of them is coming.**。

最後，我們要特別注意 both 這個字所表達的意義；在**使用 both 的句子中，動詞所表示的狀態或動作分別及於該兩者中的每一個**。所以，

Both volleyball teams have 20 members.

這個句子的意思是「每支排球隊都有 20 個隊員」，而不是兩支球隊加起來共有 20 個隊員（亦即每支球隊只有 10 個隊員）。

Unit 10 使用 either 時常見的錯誤

重要觀念 非學不可

Either 可當限定詞、代名詞、副詞或連接詞用。這個字其實有兩種發音，國內大多教美式發音 /ˈiðɚ/，但英式英語亦發成 /ˈaɪð•(r)/。

Either 用作限定詞、位在名詞之前時意為「兩者之中任何一個的；兩者的」。在此用法中，**either 後面的名詞必須是單數可數名詞**（雖然 either + 單數可數名詞可用 both + 複數可數名詞來替代，但 **both 只能用在肯定句**）。例如：

◆ I don't like **either** color. （○）

◇ I don't like either colors. （×）

◇ I don't like both colors. （×）

（這兩種顏色 [中任何一種] 我都不喜歡。）

◆ John studied chemistry and physics, but he had little interest in **either** subject. （○）

◇ John studied chemistry and physics, but he had little interest in either subjects. （×）

◇ John studied chemistry and physics, but he had little interest in both subjects. （×） little 為否定詞。

（約翰唸的是化學和物理，但他對這兩門學科都沒什麼興趣。）

◆ **Either** candidate would be ideal for the job. （○）

（這兩個人中的任何一個都是做這項工作的理想人選。）

◇ Either candidates would be ideal for the job. （×）

◆ **Both** candidates would be ideal for the job. （○）

◆ There are three cars on **either** side of the river. （O）
（河的兩邊各有三輛汽車 總共有六輛車子。）

= There are three cars on each side of the river. （O）

= There are three cars on **both** sides of the river. （O）

Either 用作代名詞時意為「兩者之中任何一個」。例如：

1. A: What color footbeds/insoles do you want, gray or brown?
（A：你想要哪種顏色的鞋墊，灰色還是棕色？）

  B: Either. It doesn't matter.
（B：任何一種都可以。無所謂。）

2. John: Do you prefer beef or pork?
（約翰：你喜歡吃牛肉還是豬肉呢？）

  Jack: I don't like either.
（傑克：任何一樣我都不喜歡。）

必閃陷阱 非學不可

在 the、these、those 及所有格 + 複數名詞的前面須使用 either of，其中 of 不可省略。例如：

◆ I don't agree with **either of** my parents on these issues. （O）
（在這些問題上，我父母親的意見我都不同意。）

◇ I don't agree with either my parents on these issues. （×）

◆ **Either of** the students can do this part-time job. （O）
（這兩個學生中的任何一個都可以做這項兼職工作。）

◇ Either the students can do this part-time job. （×）

Either 用作副詞時，意為「（用於否定句）**也**」。例如：

1. There's no answer to that question either.
（那個問題也沒有答案。）

2. I don't eat mutton and my wife doesn't either.
（我不吃羊肉，我太太也不吃。）

3. If Amy doesn't go, I won't either.
（如果艾美不去，我也不去。）

> ### 好用 Tips 非學不可 🔍
>
> **Either 用作連接詞時通常與 or 連用來連接兩個字、片語或子句**，意為「（兩種可能性的選擇）要麼……要麼，不是……就是，或者……或者……」。必須注意的是，與 "both ... and ..."、"neither ... nor ..."、"not only ... but also ..." 等一樣，**"either ... or ..." 也是一種相關字組（correlative），亦即與其兩個元素連用的詞類和結構必須平行對稱、對仗工整**。例如：

1. Her leggings are either **red** or **yellow**.
（她的緊身褲不是紅色就是黃色。）
→ 連接兩個形容詞。

2. Mary's going on a business trip to Japan either **today** or **tomorrow**.
（瑪麗不是今天就是明天去日本出差。）
→ 連接兩個副詞。

3. You can stay either **with me** or **at/in a hotel**.
（你可以住我這裡或者住飯店。）
→ 連接兩個介系詞片語。

4. Either **you leave now** or **I call the police**!
（要麼你現在離開，要麼我就報警！）
→ 連接兩個子句。

◇ We can either eat now or after the concert.（×）
（我們可以現在吃飯，也可以在演唱會後吃。）

◆ We can eat either **now** or **after the concert**.（○）
→ Either 和 or 必須平行對稱，連接相同詞類（在此為副詞）。

◆ We can either **eat now** or **eat after the concert.**（○）
→ Either 和 or 必須平行對稱，連接相同詞類（在此為動詞）。

◆ Either **you** or **your father** can make a large donation in your mother's name.（○）
（你或是你父親可以用你母親的名義做大筆捐款。）
→ Either 和 or 必須平行對稱，連接相同詞類（在此為代名詞和名詞，屬於名詞類）。

◇ Either you can get there by train or by bus. (×)
（你可以搭火車或坐巴士去那裡。）

◆ Either **you can get there by train** or **you can take the bus**. (O)

→ Either 和 or 必須平行對稱、對仗工整，連接子句結構。

Unit 11　使用 suggest 時常見的錯誤

重要觀念 非學不可

Suggest 是個及物動詞，主要意為「建議，提議」。這個動詞使用頻率之高自不待言，幾乎可以說是「無日無之」。**Suggest 後面可以接名詞（片語）、動名詞、that 子句**（由連接詞 that 所引導的名詞子句）或 **what/who/where 等 wh-字所引導的名詞子句**。

Suggest 可接名詞（片語）當受詞。例如：

1. John suggested an inexpensive restaurant near the school for the party.
（約翰建議在學校附近一家平價餐廳舉行聚會。）

2. He suggests a little walk.
（他建議去散步一下。）

Suggest 可接動名詞當受詞，但不可接不定詞。這種句型意為「**建議做某事**」，但不必提及行動或動作的執行者，因為行動或動作的執行者在上下文中不言可喻。但若在動名詞的前面加上所有格，即可明確指出行動或動作的執行者。例如：

◆ Phil **suggested going** in his car. (O)
（菲爾提議坐他的車子去。）

◇ Phil suggested to go in his car. (×)

◆ Phil **suggested our going** in his car. (O)
（菲爾提議我們坐他的車子去。）

◆ I **suggest going** to the library on Sunday.（○）
（我建議禮拜天上圖書館。）

◇ I suggest to go to the library on Sunday.（✕）

◆ I **suggest our going** to the library on Sunday.（○）
（我建議我們禮拜天上圖書館。）

◆ I **suggested putting** the matter to the school.（○）
（我提議把這件事交給學校處理。）

◇ I suggested to put the matter to the school.（✕）

◆ If there is a mechanical problem, I **suggest contacting** the manufacturer directly.（○）
（若發生機械故障，我建議直接與製造廠商聯繫。）

◇ If there is a mechanical problem, I suggest to contact the manufacturer directly.（✕）

> **Suggest 不可接雙受詞（間接受詞 ＋ 直接受詞）**，亦即 suggest 不可接間接受詞當受詞。當我們需要提到被建議或接受建議的對象時，我們須使用「**suggest ＋ 直接受詞（事物）＋ to ＋ 間接受詞（人）**」。例如：

◇ If this happened to your daughter, what would you suggest her?（✕）
（如果這件事發生在你女兒身上，你會給她什麼建議？）

◆ If this happened to your daughter, what would you **suggest to** her?（○）

◇ The specialist suggests parents that they should adopt a different way of bringing up their children.（✕）

◆ The specialist **suggests to** parents that they should adopt a different way of bringing up their children.（○）
（這位專家建議父母應採取不同的教養子女方式。）

> 在上述 suggest 接動名詞當受詞的句型中，顯然地 suggest 的主詞和動名詞的主詞（即行動或動作的執行者）是不同人。這種句型可以改寫為 suggest ＋ that 子句（在非正式情況中，that 通常省略）。**Suggest 後接動名詞**的意思是「**建議做某事**」，而 **suggest 後接 that 子句**的意思則是「**建議某人做某事**」。例如：

◆ I **suggest having** dinner first and then watching the film.（O）
（我建議先吃晚飯再看電影。）

◆ I **suggest**（that）**we have dinner first, and then watch the film**.（O）
（我建議我們先吃晚飯再看電影。）

◆ I **suggest going** there around five o'clock. They usually go for a jog at six o'clock.（O）
（我建議五點左右去那裡。他們通常六點去慢跑。）

◆ I **suggest**（that）**you go there around five o'clock**. They usually go for a jog at six o'clock.（O）
（我建議你五點左右去那裡。他們通常六點去慢跑。）

必閃陷阱 非學不可

在 suggest 接 that 子句的句型中，**如果 suggest 為過去式**，而 that 子句是要表示應該做但還未做的意思，那麼該子句要用假設語氣，即**主詞 +（should）原形動詞 + ……**。Demand、insist 和 order 等表示要求或命令的動詞亦有相同的用法。例如：

◆ The company **suggested that she**（**should**）**resign.**（O）
◇ The company suggested that she resigned.（×）
（公司建議她辭職。）

◆ He **suggested that we**（**should**）**accept these gifts**.（O）
◇ He suggested that we accepted these gifts.（×）
（他建議我們收下這些禮物。）

◆ Mary **suggested that John be present.**（O）
◇ Mary suggested that John was present.（×）
（瑪麗建議約翰要出席。）

◆ Helen **suggested**（that）**I should try the shop on Nanjing East Road**.（O）
◇ Helen suggested（that）I tried the shop on Nanjing East Road.（×）
（海倫建議我去南京東路的那家店看看。）

所以，若要表達「建議某人做某事」的意思，則用 suggest ＋ that 子句，亦即 suggest（that）somebody（should）do something，但千萬不可使用 suggest somebody to do something（上面已說過，**suggest 不可接間接受詞當受詞！**）。例如：

◇ The company suggested her to resign.（×）
◇ He suggested us to accept these gifts.（×）
◇ Mary suggested John to be present.（×）
◇ Helen suggested me to try the shop on Nanjing East Road.（×）

好用 Tips 非學不可 🔍

Suggest 可接 wh- 子句當受詞。例如：

1. Can anyone suggest what we should do to improve computer performances?
（有人能給個建議，要如何提升電腦效能嗎？）

2. Can anyone suggest how we might attract more customers?
（有人能給個建議，要如何才可以吸引更多的顧客嗎？）

3. Could you suggest where I might be able to buy a high-end engagement ring?
（哪裡可以買到高檔的訂婚戒指，你能給個建議嗎？）

Unit 12 雙重否定並非文法錯誤，但應避免表錯意

重要觀念 非學不可 🔍

雙重否定（double negative）並非文法錯誤，但它**可能改變寫作者或說話者原本想要表達的意思**，尤其是在使用 neither ... nor 這個相關字組或相關連接詞（correlative or correlative conjunction）時，必須謹慎，**別使用雙重否定**，因為 **neither ... nor ... 在句中已經扮演否定的角色。**

◇ Duke did not find the key neither on nor under his desk.（×）
→ 這是雙重否定，意思跟原意相反。

◇ We didn't have neither money nor food.（×）
→ 這是雙重否定，意思跟原意相反。

◆ We had **neither** money **nor** food.（O）
◆ We didn't have **either** money **or** food.（O）
（我們沒有錢也沒有食物。）

必閃陷阱 非學不可

由於「負負得正」，兩個否定等於肯定，因此儘管雙重否定並非文法錯
誤，但**它的意思可能跟原本要表達的意思正好相反**。例如：

◇ Edward doesn't know nothing.（×）
（愛德華無所不知。）
→ 原意是「愛德華一無所知」。

◇ Stanley doesn't believe in no God.（×）
（史丹利相信有上帝。）
→ 原意是「史丹利不相信有上帝」。

◇ I haven't got no money.（×）
（我有錢。）
→ 這幾乎肯定不是原意。

◆ My wife is not unattractive.（O）
（我太太很漂亮。）
→ 這一定是原意。

Note

Part I
文法常見錯誤

Chapter 2
字彙和片語

Chapter 2 │ 字彙 & 片語

Unit 01 According to me, on my opinion, in my point of view

🔍 重要觀念 非學不可

這幾個片語都是在表達「根據我的看法」、「依我看」、「在我看來」的意思，但它們的用字或寫法都錯了。正確版本敘述如下：

According to 後面只能接別人的意見、看法或說法。若要表示我或我們的意見，則必須使用 "in my opinion/view" 或 "in our opinion/view"。例如：

◆ According to **the students**, Mary's a good teacher.（O）
（根據學生的說法，瑪麗是個好老師。）

◆ In my opinion/view, **Mary's a good teacher.**（O）
（依我看，瑪麗是個好老師。）

◇ According to me, Mary's a good teacher.（×）

從上述可知，**in my opinion/view 是正確的寫法**，on my opinion/view 或 to my opinion/view 都是錯的。例如：

◆ **In my opinion/view** it was a waste of time.（O）
（依我看，那是浪費時間。）

◇ On my opinion/view it was a waste of time.（×）

◇ To my opinion/view it was a waste of time.（×）

◆ **In my humble opinion**, the government made a big mistake.（O）
（依我個人淺見/依拙見，政府犯了一個重大的錯誤。）

🔍 必閃陷阱 非學不可

另外，要注意的是，**in my opinion 不可跟 I think 連用**。例如：

◆ **In my opinion**, it was a waste of time. （〇）

（依我看，那是浪費時間。）

◇ In my opinion, I think it was a waste of time. （×）

（依我看，我認為那是浪費時間。）

好用 Tips 非學不可 🔍

至於 my point of view，其前的介系詞**只能用 from**，in my point of view

或 on my point of view 都是錯的。例如：

◆ **From my point of view**, the president hasn't done enough to deal with tricky problems. （〇）

（在我看來，總統在處理棘手問題方面做得還不夠。）

◇ In my point of view, the president hasn't done enough to deal with tricky problems. （×）

◇ On my point of view, the president hasn't done enough to deal with tricky problems. （×）

Unit 02 Agenda, criteria, data 和 media 是單數還是複數呢？

重要觀念 非學不可 🔍

Agenda, criteria, data 和 **media** 這四個字分別為拉丁字 agendum, criterion, datum 和 medium 的複數。然而，在現代英語中，它們**並非都被視為複數字**。

Agenda 是單數還是複數呢？

Agenda 這個字主要意為「（會議的）議程，待議事項；待辦事項」，是拉丁字 agendum 的複數。然而，隨著時間的演進，它已去掉所有「複數」的成分。

在現代英語中，它**被視為單數字**，而它的**複數為 agendas**。例如：

◆ There is **a** hidden/secret **agenda** in the government's tax break.（O）
（政府減稅優惠的背後有秘密的動機。）

◆ All the **agendas** are listed in the e-mail I sent to you.（O）
（所有待辦事項都列在我寄給你的電子郵件中。）

Criteria 是單數還是複數呢？
Criteria 意為「（判斷、決定的）標準，準則」，是 criterion 的複數。
由於 criterion 這個字現今仍被廣泛地使用著，因此 **criteria 一直保留複數的地位**。然而，我們仍經常在口語和寫作中見到 **criteria 被用作單數的情況**。例如：

◆ Dora's **criteria** for selecting her future husband **is** very simple. He has to be tall, rich, and handsome.（O）
（朵拉挑選未來老公的標準非常簡單。他必須高富帥。）
→ 現今這是可以接受的，但可能惹惱一些人。由於 criteria 被用作單數，句子看起來怪怪的，因為前後句不是很匹配。

◆ Dora's **criterion** for selecting her future husband **is** very simple. He has to be tall, rich, and handsome.（O）
→ 這當然可以接受，但句子看起來同樣不自然，因為前後句不是很匹配。

◆ Dora's **criteria** for selecting her future husband **are** very simple. He has to be tall, rich, and handsome.（O）
→ 這句就對了，沒有可挑剔的瑕疵。

最安全的作法是，若為單一標準則使用 criterion，**若是兩個或兩個以上的標準，那麼只能使用 criteria，而且要將 criteria 視為複數**。例如：

◆ What **are** your **criteria** for judging the quality of a student's work?（O）
（你用什麼標準來衡量學生的課業？）

◆ What **is** your main **criterion**?（O）
（你的主要標準為何？）

必閃陷阱 非學不可

Data 是單數還是複數呢？

Data 意為「資料」，是 datum 的複數。以前 data 被視為複數（事實上，現今一些科學機構仍是如此）。例如：

◇My data were corrupted.（×）（我的資料毀損了。）（已經過時）

◇My data are being collated by three professionals.（×）（我的資料正由三位專業人士核對校勘中。）（不合時宜）

現今 data 被視為單數名詞。例如：

◆ **My data was** corrupted.（O）
◆ **My data is** being collated by three professionals.（O）

在現代英語中，data 被歸類為抽象名詞，接單數動詞，就像 information 這個字一樣。

好用 Tips 非學不可

Media 是單數還是複數呢？

Media 意為「（新聞）媒體，傳媒」，這包括電視台、電台、報紙、雜誌及電子傳媒（即網際網路）。這個字來自拉丁字 medium 的複數型。職是之故，許多人會認為 media 是複數名詞。然而，即使 media 可被視為複數名詞，因為它是 medium 的複數，但這也只對了一半而已。事實上，**media 現在可以被視為單數或複數名詞**。這是因為它是個集合名詞，就跟 family, jury, orchestra, team 等字一樣。例如：

◆ The **media have** a lot of influence today.（O）
（現今大眾傳播媒體有很大的影響力。）

◆ The **media has** a lot of influence today.（O）
（現今大眾傳播媒體有很大的影響力。）

因此，**句子的意思才是決定 media 應被視為單數還是複數的主要依據**。
不過，要注意的是，美式英語將所有集合名詞都視為單數，而英式英語
則以句意來做判斷，但傾向於將它們視為複數。

Unit 03　All 還是 whole 呢？

重要觀念 非學不可 🔍

All 和 whole 皆可用作限定詞（形容詞）和代名詞（名詞）。 當限定詞
用時，它們係用在名詞之前或與其他限定詞連用來表示「全部的；所有
的」、「整個的；完全的」等意思。它們的基本句型分別為 **「all ＋ 限定
詞 ＋ 名詞」** 和 **「限定詞 ＋ whole ＋ 名詞」**。例如：

1. All his family are waiting for him.
（他的一家人都在等他。）
2. His whole family are waiting for him.
（他的一家人都在等他。）

All 和 whole 當代名詞和名詞用時意為「全部」，經常與 of 連用。 例
如：

1. It rained all of the time we were there.
（我們在那裡時一直下雨。）
2. It rained the whole of the time we were there.
（我們在那裡時一直下雨。）

Whole 可與 a/an 連用，但 all 則不行。 例如：

◆ Sandy ate **a whole** bag of potato chips all by himself!（O）

◇ Sandy ate all a bag of potato chips all by himself!（×）
（桑迪一個人把一整包洋芋片全吃光了！）

必閃陷阱 非學不可

All 和 whole 的其他用法差異

一、單數可數名詞的情況之一：**若該單數可數名詞指的是單一完整的（不能分開的、不能細分的）事物或事件，則只能使用 the whole 或 the whole of**。例如：

The whole match was awesome from start to finish.
= The whole of the match was awesome from start to finish.
（整場比賽從頭至尾都令人驚嘆。）

The whole 或 the whole of 經常與時間名詞連用來**強調該段時間**。例如：

They spent the whole summer/the whole August/the whole school holidays abroad.
（他們整個夏天／整個八月／整個學校假期都在國外度過。）
= They spent the whole of the summer/August/the school holidays abroad.（月份前面不可有 the）

必須注意的是，**whole 修飾單數可數名詞時，其前的定冠詞 the 不可省略**。例如：

◆ The most important person in **the whole** (wide) world/country/school/class is you.（○）
◇ The most important person in whole (wide) world/country/school/class is you.（×）
（全世界／全國／全校／全班最重要的人就是你。）

二、單數可數名詞的情況之二：**若該單數可數名詞指的是可以分成幾個部分的一個東西或一個事件，那麼可以使用 whole 或 all，意思一樣**。例如：

1. We don't have to pay the whole （of the） bill at once.
= We don't have to pay all （of） the bill at once.
（我們不必馬上支付整筆帳單。）

2. Tom ate the whole orange.
= Tom ate all of the orange.
（湯姆吃了整顆橘子。）

三、不可數名詞的情況：不可數名詞只能跟 all （of） the 連用，不可跟 the whole 連用，亦即 **whole 不可直接修飾不可數名詞**。例如：

◆ **All the equipment** has been checked.（○）
（所有設備都檢查過了。）
◇ The whole equipment has been checked.（×）
◆ I gave Mary **all the advice** she needed.（○）
◇ I gave Mary the whole advice she needed.（×）
（我給了瑪麗需要的所有意見。）

四、複數可數名詞的情況：**複數可數名詞通常與 all the 和 all of the 連用**（事實上，all 的一項重要文法觀念就是後接不可數名詞和複數可數名詞）。例如：

1. No one can solve all the problems.
（沒有人能解決所有這些問題。）

2. I want to hear all the details.
（我想聽所有的細節。）

3. All of the tickets had been sold.
（所有的票都賣完了。）

好用 Tips 非學不可 🔍

複數可數名詞亦可與 whole 連用，亦即用 whole 來修飾，但意思不同。
試比較下面兩句：

1. Whole cities **were devastated**.
（整座整座的城市被摧毀了。）
→ Whole 與複數名詞連用時意為「整個的」（entire）。
2. All cities **were devastated**.
（所有的城市都被摧毀了。）
→ All 與複數名詞連用時意為「每個；各個」（each and every）。

Unit 04　As 還是 like 呢？

重要觀念 非學不可

事實上，as 和 like 幾乎是風馬牛不相及的兩個字，但偏偏卻有不少人把它們當作同義詞，還三不五時將它們互換一下。必須注意的是，**as 和 like 只有當連接詞且用作比較時才可互換，此時它們意為「像，好像，就像；如同（……那樣），正如（……那樣）」**。誠如大家所知，as 還有幾個很常見的連接詞用法和意思，與 like 更是毫無關聯。雖然 as 和 like 當連接詞且用作比較時是同義詞，但 like 僅能用於非正式的上下文中，因為迄今傳統的文法書仍將 like 的這項用法視為錯誤。例如：

1. Like I said, I enjoy reading novels.
= As I have already said, I enjoy reading novels.
（就像我說過的，我喜歡看小說。）
2. Nobody understands her as I do.
= Nobody understands her like I do.
（沒有人像我這樣瞭解她。）
3. John got divorced, （just） as his parents had done years before.
= John got divorced, like his parents had done years before.
（約翰離婚了，重蹈了多年前他父母婚姻破裂的覆轍。）

4. Like any good grammar books will tell you, cleft sentences are very important structures.

= As any good grammar books will tell you, cleft sentences are very important structures.

（正如／就像任何好的文法書會告訴你的一樣，分裂句是非常重要的結構。）

必閃陷阱 非學不可

As 和 like 除了當連接詞且用作比較時才可互換外，其他用法都不相關。 然而，令人遺憾地，還是有人把它們的介系詞用法當作同義詞。As 當介系詞用後面接名詞時意為「以……的身份；作為」，而 like 當介系詞用後面接名詞時意為「像；與……相似，與……近似」，可見**兩者的意思完全不同**。例如：

1. As your father, I'll help you as much as I can.
（身為你的父親，我會竭盡所能幫你。）

→ 說這句話的人是聽者的父親。

2. Like your father, I'll help you as much as I can.
（就像你的父親，我會竭盡所能幫你。）

→ 說這句話的人並非聽者的父親。

◆ I've got a shirt just **like** that.（O）
◇ I've got a shirt just as that.（×）
（我有一件和那件一模一樣的襯衫。）

◆ Mary looks **like** her mother.（O）
◇ Mary looks as her mother.（×）
（瑪麗長得像她媽媽。）

◆ The little girl sings **like** an angel!（O）
◇ The little girl sings as an angel!（×）
（那位小女孩的歌聲宛如天使一般！）

◆ Do you suffer from migraines **like** me?（O）
◇ Do you suffer from migraines as me?（×）
（你像我一樣患有偏頭痛嗎？）

◆ **Like** most people, I'd prefer not to live in Taipei.（O）
◇ As most people, I'd prefer not to live in Taipei.（×）
（和大多數人一樣，我寧願不住在台北。）
◆ 但 **As** most people **would**, I'd prefer not to live in Taipei.（O）
◆ Amy works **as** a waitress.（O）
◇ Amy works like a waitress.（×）
（艾美是個服務生。）
◆ She's worked for a long time **as** an interpreter in that company.（O）
◇ She's worked for a long time like an interpreter in that company.（×）
（她長期以來一直在那家公司擔任口譯員。）

Unit 05 At the beginning 還是 in the beginning？At the end 還是 in the end 呢？

重要觀念 非學不可 🔍

At the beginning（of something） 意為「在（某事物）開始時；開頭部分；開端」，其後**經常接介系詞 of**。**In the beginning** 意為「起初，當初；開始時，一開始（用來與時間上的「後來」相對）」，與 at first 和 at the start 同義（beginning 和 start 的前面皆可用 very 來修飾），其後**不接介系詞 of**。例如：

◆ **At the beginning of** every lesson, the teacher gave us a quiz.（O）
（每堂課開始時，老師都會給我們小考。）
◇ In the beginning of every lesson, the teacher gave us a quiz.（×）
◆ I'll go abroad for two weeks **at the very beginning of** May.（O）
（五月初我會出國兩個禮拜。）
◇ I'll go abroad for two weeks in the very beginning of May.（×）
◆ Children are still **at the beginning of** their lives.（O）
◇ Children are still in the beginning of their lives.（×）
（兒童仍處於他們生命的初期。）

◆ **In the beginning** the main energy source was wood.（ **O** ）
（最初主要能源是木材。）

◇ At the beginning the main energy source was wood.（ × ）

◆ **In the beginning** I didn't know what had happened.（ **O** ）
（起先我不知道發生了什麼事。）

◇ At the beginning I didn't know what had happened.（ × ）

◆ If **at first** you don't succeed, try, try again.（ **O** ）
（一次不成功，那就再接再厲。）

◆ He was a bit shy **at the（very）start.**（ **O** ）
（他開始時有點害羞。）

必閃陷阱 非學不可

At the end（of something） 意為「最後部分，末尾」，其後**經常接介系詞 of**。**In the end** 意為「最後，終於」，與 **at last** 和 **at length** 同義，其後**不接介系詞 of**。例如：

◆ My room was situated **at the end of** the corridor.（ **O** ）
◇ My room was situated in the end of the corridor.（ × ）
（我的房間位在走廊的盡頭。）

◆ **At the end of** the movie, everyone was crying.（ **O** ）
◇ In the end of the movie, everyone was crying.（ × ）
（電影結束時，每個人都哭了。）

◆ I'm going on holiday **at the end of** this month.（ **O** ）
◇ I'm going on holiday in the end of this month.（ × ）
（這個月底我要去度假。）

◆ **In the end**, we decided to move to Taipei.（ **O** ）
◇ At the end, we decided to move to Taipei.（ × ）
（最後我們決定搬到台北。）

◆ Everything will turn out all right **in the end**.（ **O** ）
◇ Everything will turn out all right at the end.（ × ）
（最後一切都會好轉的。）

◆ **At last** I succeeded.（ **O** ）
（最後我成功了。）

◆ **At length** they reached Bangkok.（ **O** ）
（他們終於抵達曼谷了。）

Unit 06　Being 和 been 的差異

重要觀念 非學不可 🔍

Being 是 BE 動詞的現在分詞，而 Been 是 BE 動詞的過去分詞。有些人還是三不五時會被這兩個看似簡單的分詞所搞混。這裡提供一個規則讓大家參考，**been 一定用在 have（及其他 have 形式，如 has, had, will have 等）之後**，而 **being 絕不會用在 have 之後**。

Being 是用在 BE 動詞（及其他 be 形式，如 are, were, is, was 等）之後。例如：

◆ She **is being** very clever today.（○）
◇ She has being very clever today.（×）
（她今天表現得很聰明。）

◆ They **have been** busy.（○）
◇ They are been busy.（×）
（他們一直很忙）

◇ Sophia has being working at that big company.（×）
（蘇菲亞一直在那家大公司工作。）

→ being 不可位在 have 或 has 的後面。

Being 可用作名詞。例如：

1. A human being
（人；人類）

2. A strange being stepped out of the spaceship.
（一個奇怪的人步出了太空船。）

Being 亦可用作動名詞（動名詞也是名詞類，用法與名詞相同）。例如：

1. Do you like being so careless?
（你喜歡這麼粗心大意嗎？）

2. The accident was caused by his being so clumsy.
（這起事故肇因於他太笨手笨腳了。）

3. I live in terror of not being misunderstood.
（我活在不被誤解的恐懼中。）

→ 這句話語出英國大文豪王爾德（Oscar Wilde），竟然有人希望被誤解，以被誤解為榮。

必閃陷阱 非學不可

一般而言，**現在分詞和過去分詞都可以當形容詞來修飾名詞**，但 **being 和 been 不行**。例如：

◆ **Broken** vase（○）
（破碎的花瓶）

◆ **Deleted** file（○）
（刪除的檔案）

◆ **Cooking** oil（○）
（烹飪油）

◆ **Jogging** girl（○）
（慢跑的少女）

◇ The been car（×）
（無意義）

◇ The being flower（×）
（無意義）

Unit 07　Below 還是 under 呢？

重要觀念 非學不可 🔍

本文將就 below 和 under 與測量單位和數字連用來表示「低於；少於；小於」（less than）的意思時常見的錯誤，做一說明。

年齡

在**指年齡時要用 under，不用 below**。然而，有些字典亦使用 below，讓人感到困惑，殊不知「未成年」的英文是 underage 而不是 belowage（沒這個字）。例如：

◆ We have three children **under** the age of six.（O）
（我們有三個不到六歲的孩子。）
◆ The nursery is open for children **under** 4.（O）
（這家托兒所收 4 歲以下的兒童。）

必閃陷阱 非學不可 ●

測量單位

在**指時間和重量時要用 under**，不用 below。例如：

◆ The sports car can get from standstill up to 100 kilometers per hour in **under** five seconds.（O）
◇ The sports car can get from standstill up to 100 kilometers per hour in below five seconds.（✕）
（這部跑車從靜止加速到時速 100 公里還不到五秒。）
◆ A visa is not required for a stay of **under** six months.（O）
◇ A visa is not required for a stay of below six months.（✕）
（停留六個月以內不需要簽證。）
◆ This type of schoolbag was just **under** two kilos, so they could not hinder development in schoolchildren.（O）

◇ This type of schoolbag was just below two kilos, so they could not hinder development in schoolchildren.（ ✕ ）
（這款書包重量不到兩公斤，所以它們不會妨礙學童的發育。）

◆ The newborn baby weighed **under** three kilos.（ O ）
◇ The newborn baby weighed below three kilos.（ ✕ ）
（這個新生兒重量不到三公斤。）

在指**高度**時要用 below，不用 under。例如：

◆ The roof of my new house is just **below** the height of the library.（ O ）
◇ The roof of my new house is just under the height of the library.（ ✕ ）
（我新房子的屋頂比圖書館的高度稍微低一點。）

在**指溫度時可用 below 或 under，但 below 是主流**。例如：

◆ Last night it was two degrees below（zero）in Taipei.（ O ）
◇ Last night it was two degrees under（zero）in Taipei.（ ✕ ）
（昨晚台北只有零下二度。）
◆ The water must be kept below ten degrees Celsius.（ O ）
（這水必須保持在攝氏十度以下。）
→ 這句亦可使用 under，但並不建議這樣做。

好用 Tips 非學不可 🔍

數字、數量、金額或水平通常與 below 連用；部分情況使用 under 也可以，但並不多見。例如：

1. If you get below 50%, you fail the exam.
（如果你考不到一半的分數，那麼就不及格。）

2. All items are/cost below ten NT dollars.
（所有物品的價格均低於台幣十元。）

3. Jack's test scores have been well below average.
（傑克的考試分數遠低於平均水平。）

4. The company's profits in 2016 were below what they had expected.
（這家公司 2016 年的獲利比他們預期的來得低。）

Unit 08 Consider 還是 regard 呢？

重要觀念 非學不可 🔍

當 consider 意為「認為；把……當作，把……視為」而 regard 意為「認為，看待；把……看作，將……認為」時，兩者皆不可使用進行式（consider 意為「考慮」時才可使用進行式）。例如：

◆ I **consider** her irresponsible.（○）
◇ I am considering her irresponsible.（×）
（我認為她不負責任。）

◆ Mary **regards** Jack's achievement as unique.（○）
◇ Mary is regarding Jack's achievement as unique.（×）
（瑪麗認為傑克的成就獨一無二。）

必閃陷阱 非學不可 🔍

就上述意思而言，consider 有下列幾種句型：
Consider + 受詞（+ to be）+ 名詞或形容詞片語。例如：

1. Randy is currently considered（to be）the best actor in Taiwan.
（藍迪目前被認為是台灣最出色的演員。）
2. I consider Cindy to be right for the position.
（我認為辛蒂適合這個職位。）

這個句型是 consider 最常發生錯誤的地方，許多人用 as 來代替 to be，這是一項重大錯誤。切記：**Consider 不可跟 as 連用**（regard 才可與 as 連用）。例如：

◆ Brant is **considered to be** an expert in horticulture.
= Brant is considered an expert in horticulture.（○）
◇ Brant is considered as an expert in horticulture.（×）
（布蘭特被認為是園藝專家。）

◆ We all **consider** him **to be** the most successful businessman in Taiwan.（O）

= We all consider him the most successful businessman in Taiwan.（O）

◇ We all consider him as the most successful businessman in Taiwan.（×）

（我們都認為他是台灣最成功的商人。）

Consider ＋（that）子句。例如：

1. We consider that Professor Chen is not competent.

（我們認為陳教授不適任。）

2. Teresa considers（that）she should not help him.

（泰瑞莎認為她不應該幫他。）

Consider ＋ 受詞 ＋ 不定詞；BE ＋ considered ＋ 受詞 ＋ 不定詞。

例如：

1. Most people consider the company to have the most advanced mobile technology.

（大多數人都認為這家公司擁有最先進的行動技術。）

2. It is considered bad manners to talk loudly in public transportation.

（在大眾交通工具上大聲交談被認為是不禮貌的。）

好用 Tips 非學不可 🔍

Regard 經常與 as 連用來構成「**regard（＋ 受詞）＋ as ＋ 名詞或形容詞片語**」的句型。例如：

1. He is generally/widely regarded as an expert on criminal law.

（他被普遍認為是刑法專家。）

2. Professor Lin is generally regarded as one of the best teachers in the school.

（林教授被普遍認為是該校最優秀的老師之一。）

3. The government regards pay raise for the working class as a main priority.

（政府把勞工加薪視為主要優先考慮事項。）

4. Do you regard their customer services as good or bad?

（你認為他們的客戶服務好還是不好？）

Unit 09　Different from、different to 還是 different than 呢？

重要觀念 非學不可

許多人認為 **different（不同的）**後面僅能接介系詞 from，不可接 to 或 than。事實上，**這個形容詞無論接 from 或接 to，甚至接 than，都是正確的用法**。Different 可用來說明兩個人或事物之間的差異，其後通常接 from，但我們亦可使用 different to，尤其是在說話時。例如：

◆ Our school is very **different from** theirs.（O）
◆ Our school is very **different to** theirs.（O）
（我們學校跟他們學校有很大的不同。）

◆ The incumbent president is so **different from** the former president.（O）
◆ The incumbent president is so **different to** the former president.（O）
（現任總統迥異於前任總統。）

◆ These results are a bit **different from** the ones we got three days ago.（O）
◆ These results are a bit **different to** the ones we got three days ago.（O）
（這些結果和我們三天前得到的結果有點不同。）

◆ My opinion could hardly be more **different from** hers.（O）
◆ My opinion could hardly be more **different to** hers.（O）
（我的觀點正好和她的完全相反。）

　　在美式英語中，口語也經常使用 different than。例如：

◆ Amy is completely/entirely **different than** her elder sister.（O）
= Amy is completely/entirely different from her elder sister.
= Amy is completely/entirely different to her elder sister.
= Amy and her elder sister are completely/entirely different.
（艾美跟她姊姊截然不同。）

◆ American English is slightly/somewhat/subtly **different than** British English. （O）

= American English is slightly/somewhat/subtly different from British English.

= American English is slightly/somewhat/subtly different to British English.

= American English and British English are slightly/somewhat/subtly different

（美式英語與英式英語略有差異。）

必閃陷阱 非學不可

在英式英語中，人們說話時經常將 **different than** 中的 **than** 用作連接詞 **（甚至也把 from 當連接詞用）**，後接子句，但許多人認為這是不正確 的。例如：

◆ My younger brother is significantly/markedly/radically/vastly **different than me.** （O）

◇ My younger brother is significantly/markedly/radically/vastly different than I am. （？）

（我弟弟跟我大不相同。）

◇ His attitude to life is different now than before he got married. （？）

◇ His attitude to life is different now from before he got married. （？）

（他現在的人生觀與婚前有所不同。）

Unit 10　Due to 還是 because of 呢？

重要觀念 非學不可

Due to 和 because of 均意為「由於，因為」，所以有些人、甚至有些字典，都認為這兩個介系詞片語可以互換，或者對它們被互換使用並不以為意。然而，其他人，包括筆者在內，則不以為然。根據既定的規則，**它們的用法並不相同**，如果互換使用，就不合語法，也就是文法錯誤。

當句子的主動詞為 **am, is, are, was, were 等 BE 動詞**時，我們要用 **due to**，此時 due to 可以用 caused by 來替換。例如：

◆ The serious accident was **due to** his careless driving.（O）
→ 主動詞為 was。

= The serious accident was caused by his careless driving.
◇ The serious accident was because of his careless driving.（×）
（這起嚴重意外事故是由於他駕駛疏忽所造成。）

◆ Mary's coming to class late was **due to** the rain.（O）
= Mary's coming to class late was caused by the rain.
◇ Mary's coming to class late was because of the rain.（×）
（瑪麗因雨而上課遲到。）

必閃陷阱 非學不可

當句子的主動詞為 BE 動詞以外的其他動詞，即**普通動詞時，我們要用 because of**，此時 because of 可以用 on account of 或 in view of 來替換。例如：

◆ Robert cannot go to work **because of** sickness.（O）
→ 主動詞為普通動詞 go。

= Robert cannot go to work on account of sickness.

◇ Robert cannot go to work due to sickness.（×）
（羅伯特因病不能上班。）

◆ The prices are rising **because of** the government's inability to control inflation.（O）

→ 這句是陷阱題，因為句中有 BE 動詞 are，但**這個 are 是助動詞**而非主動詞，真正的主動詞為 rising。

= The prices are rising in view of the government's inability to control inflation.

◇ The prices are rising due to the government's inability to control inflation.（×）

（由於政府無力控制通貨膨脹，物價正在上揚中。）

好用 Tips 非學不可 🔍

有人可能會自然而然地把 because of、on account of 和 in view of 歸為同一類，因為這三個同義詞都以 of 做結尾且都與普通動詞連用，而另一個常用的同義詞 **owing to 應該是跟 due to 同一類**，因為它們都以**介系詞 to 做結尾**，所以應與 BE 動詞連用。非也！**Owing to 的用法跟 because of 完全一樣**。例如：

◆ Poverty is **due to** laziness.（O）
◇ Poverty is owing to laziness.（×）
（懶惰是貧窮之源。）

◆ **Because of** the weather, we will cancel anniversary celebrations.（O）
= Owing to the weather, we will cancel anniversary celebrations.（O）
（由於天氣的關係，我們要取消週年慶。）

Unit 11　Each 和 every 你完全分得清楚嗎？

重要觀念 非學不可

不少人迄今仍無法把 each 和 every 分得一清二楚！**Each** 可用作代名詞和形容詞（限定詞），**指兩個或兩個以上之中的每一個；著重個別的情況**，指若干固定數目中的每一個。**Every** 僅能用作形容詞，**僅可指三個或三個以上之中的每一個，不能指兩個之中的每一個；著重整體的全部情況**，指任何一個（其中沒有一個例外）。例如：

◆ **Each** of you has a job to do.（O）
（你們每個人都有工作要做。）

◇ Every of you has a job to do.（×）
（你們每個人都有工作要做。）

◆ John had a cut on **each** hand/**each of** his hands.（O）
（約翰每隻手上都有傷口。）

◆ John had a cut on **every one of** his toes.（O）
（約翰的每根腳指都有傷口。）

◇ Japan, China, and South Korea every won two gold medals.（×）
（日本、中國和南韓各得兩面金牌。）

◆ **Each** boy gets a prize.（O）
（每個男孩都得到一份獎品。）

◆ **Every** boy gets a prize.（O）
（所有男孩都得到獎品。）

◆ I have read **every** book in the school.（O）
（我已讀過學校裡的所有書籍。）

◆ **Each dog** has a name.（O）
（每一隻狗都有牠自己的名字。）

◆ **Every dog** has a name.（O）
（所有狗都有名字。）

值得注意的是，「**each ＋ 名詞**」和「**every ＋ 名詞**」都**表單數**，所以要**用單數動詞**。但「every ＋ 名詞 ＋ and every ＋ 名詞」也表單數，換言之，主詞不管是由幾個「every ＋ 名詞」（中間以 and 連接）所構成，都看作單數主詞，所以要接單數動詞。同樣地，**each and every ＋ 名詞**也是單數。此外，each 可放在複數主詞之後或與 other 構成片語 **each other（互相）**，但 every 則不行。然而，every 與 not 連用，即「every ... not」或「not ... every」是部分否定，表示「並非每一個」的意思，但 each 則無此結構。例如：

1. Every boy and every girl likes to go to party.
（每個男孩和每個女孩都喜歡參加聚會。）

2. Each and every one of us has the responsibility to protect the environment.
（我們每個人都有責任保護環境。）

3. Not every student has a new book.
（並非每個學生都有新書。）

Unit 12　Elder, eldest 還是 older, oldest 呢？

Elder 和 eldest 都可當形容詞和名詞用。Elder 用作形容詞時意為「（尤指家庭兩個成員中）年紀較大的；較年長的」，與 older 同義。Eldest 用作形容詞時意為「（尤指家庭三個或三個以上的成員中）年紀最大的；最年長的」，與 oldest 同義。**Elder 和 eldest 只能用在名詞之前，亦即僅能當定語形容詞**（attributive adjectives）用。例如：

◆ His **elder** sister has a beautiful face.（○）
◆ His **older** sister has a beautiful face.（○）
（他姊姊有一張漂亮的臉蛋。）

◆ My **eldest** daughter is in college.（○）
◆ My **oldest** daughter is in college.（○）
（我的長女正在上大學。）

◆ He's my **elder/eldest** brother.（○）
◆ He's my **older/oldest** brother.（○）
（他是我哥哥／大哥。）

必閃陷阱 非學不可

Elder 和 eldest 亦可當名詞用，前者意為「長者，長輩；（尤指家庭兩個成員中的）年長者，年齡較大者」，而後者意為「（尤指家庭三個或三個以上的成員中）年齡最大者；長子；長女」。例如：

◆ Of the two sisters Mary is the **elder**.（○）
◆ Of the two sisters Mary is the **older**.（○）
→ 從 older 前面有定冠詞可以得知，older 後面省略了名詞。
（兩姊妹中瑪麗是姊姊。）

◆ John was **the eldest** of four brothers.（○）
◆ John was **the oldest** of four brothers.（○）
→ 從 oldest 前面有定冠詞可以得知，oldest 後面省略了名詞。
（約翰是四個兄弟中的老大。）

◆ I am your **elder** by ten years.（○）
◇ I am your older by ten years.（×）
（我比你大十歲。）

◆ Her **eldest** is at college.（○）
◇ Her oldest is at college.（×）
（她最大的小孩正在上大學。）

英美父子同名者所在多有，最顯著的例子就是美國總統唐納‧川普（Donald Trump）父子。由於川普在當總統之前就已因美國房地產大亨的身份而舉世聞名，所以他的兒子被固定叫做 Donald Trump Jr.（小唐納‧川普），否則我們就可以稱川普為 Donald Trump Sr. 或 Donald Trump the elder（老唐納‧川普）。

Older 和 oldest 除了用作**定語形容詞來修飾名詞**外，**亦可用作表語形容詞**（predicative adjectives），**放在連綴動詞的後面**。此外，older 和 oldest 還分別意為「較舊的；較古老的」和「最舊的；最古老的」，而 elder 和 eldest 並沒有這樣的意思，亦即 **elder 和 eldest 只能指人，不能指事物**。例如：

◆ His wife **is older** than he (is).（○）
◇ His wife is elder than he (is).（×）
（他太太的年齡比他大。）

◆ The museum is by far **the oldest** building in that country.（○）
◇ The museum is by far the eldest building in that country.（×）
（那座博物館是該國最古老的建築。）

 Unit 13

Fall 還是 fall down 呢？

Fall 可當名詞和動詞用，意思少說也有一、二十個之多，但本文僅就其「落下，倒下，摔倒，跌倒；下降」的意思來討論相關的用法錯誤。**Fall 是個不規則動詞**，時態變化為 fall, fell, fallen。它**僅當不及物動詞用，所以不需要受詞**。例如：

◆ Robert had a bad **fall** yesterday.
（羅伯特昨天重重地摔了一跤。）
→ fall 當名詞用。

◆ Many trees **fell** in the storm.
（許多樹在暴風雨中被吹倒了。）
→ fall 當動詞用。

◆ House prices **have fallen** recently.
（房價最近下跌。）
→ fall 當動詞用。

必閃陷阱 非學不可 🔍

由於 fall 僅當不及物動詞用，再加上其「向下」的含意，許多人乃把 **fall 和 fall down** 當作同義詞，**用錯而不自知。Fall 指的是從較高的位置掉落到地面，或從較高的水平或價位降下來，**而 **fall down 這個片語動詞則是指人或物從其正常的位置掉落到地面**。因此，當你認為既然「摔倒；跌倒」的名詞是 fall，那麼動詞當然也是用 fall 時，錯誤於焉發生。例如：

◆ I slipped on a banana skin and **fell down**.（○）
→ 不論身高，人走路時的姿態是個正常位置。
◇ I slipped on a banana skin and fell.（×）
→ 我可不是從高處掉下來。
（我踩到香蕉皮滑倒摔了一跤。）
◆ The clock **fell down** last night.（○）
→ 從牆上掉到地上（除非時鐘不是掛在牆上）。
◇ The clock fell last night.（×）
（時鐘昨晚掉了下來。）

好用 Tips 非學不可 🔍

根據上述，樹木落葉或價格滑落要用 fall，不可用 fall down。例如：

◆ In early autumn, the leaves begin to **fall** from/off the trees. （〇）
◇ In early autumn, the leaves begin to fall down from/off the trees. （×）
（初秋，樹葉開始凋落。）

◆ Gold prices have **fallen** a lot since last year. （〇）
◇ Gold prices have fallen down a lot since last year. （×）
（自去年以來金價大幅滑落。）

Unit 14　Far 還是 a long way 呢？

重要觀念 非學不可

Far 和 a long way 都可用來表示距離遠的。例如：

1. A lot of people can't see very far without their glasses on.
（許多人沒戴眼鏡就不能看得很遠。）

2. Taiwan is a long way from Canada.
（台灣與加拿大距離遙遠。）

Far 大多用在否定句和疑問句。例如：

1. There's a Korean restaurant not far from here.
（離這裡不遠處有一家韓式餐廳。）

2. How far is her house from the airport?
（她家離機場多遠？）

必閃陷阱 非學不可

A long way 大多用在肯定句，但亦可用在否定句和疑問句。例如：

1. It's a long way to Taipei from here.
（這裡離台北很遠。）

2. A: How long will it take you to drive to the airport from your house?
（A：從你家開車到機場要多久的時間？）

  B: About three hours.
（B：大約三小時。）

 A: That's a long time, isn't it?
（A：時間很長，不是嗎？）

◆ B: Yeah. It's **a long way.**（O）
（B：沒錯。路途遙遠。）

◇ B: Yeah. It's far.（×）

3. A: I have to go to Randy's dormitory first to pick him up.
（A：我必須先到藍迪的宿舍去接他。）

 B: Is it a long way from here?
（B：離這裡很遠嗎？）

◆ A: No, it's not far.（O）
（A：不，不遠。）

好用 Tips 非學不可 🔍

不過，當 **far** 與 **as, so, too**（far 位在後面）和 **enough**（far 位在前面）**連用時**，則可**用在肯定句**。這些片語既**可指距離，亦可指時間。**例如：

1. The old woman had got as far as the riverside before the rescuers found her.
（在救援人員找到該名老婦人之前，她已經走到河邊。）

2. There have been 20 deaths in the train crash so far.
（截至目前已有 20 人死於這起火車撞車事故。）

3. Six months is too far ahead. The restaurant only takes bookings for up to three months in advance.
（提前六個月預定太早了。那家餐廳最多只接受提前三個月預定。）

4. His house is far enough away from his downtown office.
（他的住家離他的市區辦公室夠遠。）

Far 亦可用來修飾比較級，意為「非常；很多」。例如：

1. The President is far more interested in the vote.
（總統對選票更感興趣得多。）

2. The roads in Taiwan are far better than in the Philippines.
（台灣的道路比菲律賓好得多。）

形容詞最高級的前面可用 **by far** 來加強語氣。例如：

1. The restaurant is by far the most expensive in Taipei.
（這家餐廳是台北最貴的。）

2. This is by far the quickest way.
（這是最快捷的路徑。）

在由 a long way 所構成的片語中，**have come a long way** 和 **have a long way to go** 用得頗為頻繁，前者意為「大為進步；獲得重大的成就」，後者意為「還有很長的路要走；（在成功之前）還要多多努力」。此外，**be a long way off**（後接名詞或動名詞）亦相當常用，意為「（離某時間）還早」。例如：

1. The development of weapon technology has come a long way since World War II.
（自第二次世界大戰以來，武器科技的發展已有長足的進步。）

2. We've recruited 10 professionals so far, but we still have a long way to go.
（我們迄今已招聘 10 位專業人才，但還需招聘更多的專業人才。）

3. I'm a long way off retiring.
（我離退休還早。）

Unit 15　Finally、at last、lastly 還是 in the end 呢？

重要觀念 非學不可

Finally、at last、lastly 和 in the end 這四個字或片語都當副詞用，除了 lastly 外，finally、at last 和 in the end 均意為「最後；終於」，但用法並不相同。

Finally 意為「最後；終於」，通常是指在一段長時間或遭遇一些困難之後。就此意思而言，**finally 通常位在句子的中間**，亦即位在主詞和主動詞之間（即普通動詞之前），或位在語氣助動詞或第一個助動詞之後，或位在當主動詞的 BE 動詞之後。例如：

1. We finally got home at midnight.
（我們終於在午夜時分回到了家。）

2. After months of looking John finally found a job.
（找了好幾個月之後，約翰終於找到了一份工作。）

Finally 還意為「最終地」，指事情已經不可改變。就此意思而言，**finally 在句中的位置與上述同**。例如：

1. The plan hasn't been finally approved.
（該計畫還沒有獲得最終批准。）

2. The exact amount has not been finally decided.
（確實的數量尚未底定。）

Finally 亦可用來表示所說的事物中的最後一項，意為「最後」。此時它**通常位在句首**。例如：

1. Finally, I'd like to say many thanks for your assistance.
（最後，我要說多謝你們的協助。）

2. Finally, I'd like to thank everyone for coming along this evening.
（最後，我要感謝各位今晚光臨。）

At（long）last 意為「終於，最終」，通常是指在一段長時間的等待、延宕（而出現不耐煩的情緒）之後。**At last 除了可放在上述 finally 的位置外，亦經常置於句首或句末。**例如：

1. My father has at last bought me the bicycle he promised me.
（我父親終於把他答應送我的腳踏車買給我了。）

2. At last they reached Hanoi.
（他們終於到達河內。）

3. At long last the government is starting to listen to our problems.
（政府終於開始關注我們的問題了。）

4. The president is here at last !! We've been waiting one and a half hours.
（總統終於到達！！我們已經等候一個半小時了。）

5. Fiona's finished her essay at last !
（費歐娜終於把論文寫完了！）

必閃陷阱 非學不可 🔍

Lastly 係用來指列舉的最後一項，意為「最後（一點、一項等）」。例如：

◆ And **lastly**, remember that you arrive at the airport right on time tomorrow.（○）
◆ And finally, remember that you arrive at the airport right on time tomorrow.（○）
◇ And at last, remember that you arrive at the airport right on time tomorrow.（×）
（最後我要提醒大家明天要非常準時到達機場。）

◆ We need to learn subjects, verbs, objects and, **lastly**, complements.（○）
◇ We need to learn subjects, verbs, objects and complements in the end.（×）
（我們必須學習主詞、動詞、受詞，還有補語。）

◆ In accepting this award, I would like to thank the producer, the director, the scriptwriter, and, **lastly**, the film crew.（○）
◇ In accepting this award, finally（or at long last or in the end）I would like to thank the producer, the director, the scriptwriter, and the film crew.（×）
（獲得這個獎項，我要感謝製片人、導演、編劇，還有全體拍攝人員。）

好用 Tips 非學不可 🔍

In the end 意為「最後；終於」，通常是指在一個冗長的過程或經過許多的討論、考慮或修正之後的結論。**In the end 通常置於句首或句末，主要用於口語**。例如：

1. In the end, she decided not to marry him.
（最後她決定不嫁他。）

2. Everything will be all right in the end.
（最終一切都會好的。）

3. Cindy was thinking about going to Japan, but in the end she went to South Korea.
（辛蒂一直打算要去日本，但最後卻去了南韓。）

4. And then, in the end, after months of discussion Mr. Smith decided to sell his mansion.
（然後，經過數個月的討論之後，史密斯先生終於決定出售他的豪宅。）

Unit 16　First、firstly 還是 at first 呢？

重要觀念 非學不可 🔍

First 可當形容詞和副詞用，前者意為「第一的；最早的；最初的；最先的」，而後者意為「第一；首先；首次；最先；最初」。例如：

形容詞

1. Your first year at university can be quite frightening and exciting at the same time.
（你上大學的頭一年可能恐懼和刺激兼而有之。）

2. Why didn't you seek help from the police in the first place?
（你為何不先求助於警方呢？）

副詞

1. You（go）first!
（你先請！）

2. When did the idiom first appear?
（這個成語首次出現在什麼時候？）

3. He finished first in math, second in English, and third in fine arts.
（他獲得數學第一名、英文第二名、美術第三名。）

必閃陷阱 非學不可

Firstly 僅當副詞用，意為「第一；首先」，與當副詞用的 first 同義，但 firstly 比 first 來得正式。**寫作時，我們經常使用 first 或 firstly 來做列舉**，即第一、第二、第三……等等，英文為 first, ... second, ... third ... 或 firstly, ... secondly, ... thirdly ...（美式英語還使用 first of all, ⋯ second of all, ... thirdly ...）。例如：

◆ **First** let us discuss the most important issue.（O）
◆ **Firstly** let us discuss the most important issue.（O）
◇ At first let us discuss the most important issue.（×）
（首先讓我們來討論最重要的問題。）

◆ There are three diseases to take into account——**firstly** hyperthyroidism, secondly glaucoma, and thirdly osteoporosis.（O）
◇ There are three diseases to take into account——at first hyperthyroidism, secondly glaucoma, and thirdly osteoporosis.（×）
（有三種疾病要考慮——第一是甲狀腺機能亢進，第二是青光眼，第三是骨質疏鬆症。）

◆ Every employee wants two things from their boss: **Firstly,** a good salary, and secondly, a large year-end bonus.（O）
◆ Every employee wants two things from their boss: **First** a good salary, and second a large year-end bonus.（O）
◇ Every employee wants two things from their boss: At first a good salary, and second a large year-end bonus.（×）
（每個員工都想從他們老闆那裡得到兩樣東西：第一，可觀的薪水，第二，一大筆年終獎金。）

好用 Tips 非學不可 🔍

從上面的例句可知，**at first 與 first 或 firstly 不能劃上等號**。這個片語意為「**起初，起先，當初**」（= at/in the beginning），係**用於對比**。例如：

1. At first, I thought she was shy, but then I discovered she was a lively, talkative person.
（起初我還以為她很靦腆，後來才發現她是個活潑健談的人。）

2. At first John thought I was joking but then he realized I meant it.
（起初約翰以為我在開玩笑，後來他才意識到我是認真的。）

3. The old man fell down and cried for help. No one was interested in him at first, but eventually two girls came to help him.
（那個老人跌倒後呼救。起初沒有人理他，但最後有兩個女生前來幫他。）

Unit 17　Following 還是 the following 呢？

重要觀念 非學不可 🔍

Following 可當介系詞、形容詞和名詞用。這個字並非動詞 follow（聽從，遵循，遵從；理解，明白；[社群媒體上的] 追蹤，關注）的現在分詞，而是**單獨存在的一個字**。

Following 用作介系詞時，意為「**在……之後**」，後接名詞片語，**其前不可有定冠詞 the 或所有格代名詞**。例如：

◆ The team blossomed **following** the selection and recruitment of the new players.（○）
（球隊在遴選和招募新球員後大放異彩。）

◆ **Following** the banquet, there will be a costume party.（○）
→ costume party 為美式英語。英式英語的化裝舞會叫做 fancy-dress party。

◇ The following banquet, there will be a costume party.（×）
（宴會之後將有一場化裝舞會。）

◆ **Following** my teaching career, I'd like to be a writer of children's books.（○）
◇ My following teaching career, I'd like to be a writer of children's books.（×）
（教書生涯結束後，我想當兒童文學作家。）

必閃陷阱 非學不可

Following 用作形容詞時，意為「接著的；接下來的」，僅用於名詞之前，亦即其後須接名詞（通常是時間名詞），而且**其前一定要有定冠詞 the**，即 **the following (= the next) ＋ 名詞**。例如：

◆ The problem will be discussed in **the following** chapter.（○）
（這問題將在下一章討論。）
◆ They married **the following** June.（○）
（他們在翌年六月結婚了。）
◆ John only stayed with his grandparents one night and left early **the following morning.**（○）
◇ John only stayed with his grandparents one night and left early following morning.（×）
（約翰僅在他爺爺奶奶家住了一個晚上，第二天早上就提前離開了。）
◆ Unfortunately, the Prime Minister died **the following day.**（○）
◇ Unfortunately, the Prime Minister died following day.（×）
（不幸地，總理第二天就過世了。）

Following 用作名詞時，意為「下列的人事物；下述的人事物」，用於列舉，**其前一定要有定冠詞 the**。Following 本身恆為單數，若 **the following** 當主詞，則動詞視其所列舉的人事物來決定單複數。例如：

◆ I don't like eating any of the following: cauliflower, onions, green peppers, and bean sprouts.（○）
（我不喜歡吃下列任何一種蔬菜：花椰菜、洋蔥、青椒和豆芽菜。）
◆ The recipe needs **the following**: brown sugar, flour, and eggs.（○）
（這道食譜需要下列配料：紅糖、麵粉和雞蛋。）
◆ **The following is an extract** from his novel.（○）

◇ The following are an extract from his novel. （×）
（下面是摘錄自他小說中的一段。）

◆ **The following have** given me some good advice on which web hosting plan to use: Bill Gates, Jeff Bezos, and Elon Musk.（O）

◇ The following has given me some good advice on which web hosting plan to use: Bill Gates, Jeff Bezos, and Elon Musk.（×）

（下列人士都給了我一些有關採用何種網頁主機方案不錯的建議：比爾・蓋茲、傑夫・貝佐斯和伊隆・馬斯克。）

好用 Tips 非學不可 🔍

不過，這裡的 **the following 其實亦可當形容詞用**，與上述的 the following 形容詞用法完全一樣，只是它的意思並非「接著的；接下來的」，而是**「下列的；下述的」**。例如：

◆ I don't like eating any of **the following** vegetables: cauliflower, onions, green peppers, and bean sprouts.（O）
（我不喜歡吃下列任何一種蔬菜：花椰菜、洋蔥、青椒和豆芽菜。）

◆ The recipe needs **the following** ingredients: brown sugar, flour, and eggs.（O）
（這道食譜需要下列配料：紅糖、麵粉和雞蛋。）

Part I 文法常見錯誤

Unit 18　For free 的文法對嗎？

必閃陷阱 非學不可

嚴格的文法學家堅稱 for free 的文法錯誤，所以下句的文法有誤：
She got her new book for free.（她免費獲得新書。）
他們抱持的理由是，for 是 in exchange for 的簡寫，而 free 是 free of charge 的簡寫。所以，兩者若完整地寫出，那麼就變成 in exchange for free of charge，如果這不是文法錯誤，什麼才是文法錯誤呢？

事實上，這項主張太嚴苛了。雖然**我們可以用 for nothing, free, free of charge, gratis, without charge, without cost 和 without payment 等同義詞來代替 for free** 以避免不必要的困擾，但這樣做似乎因噎廢食，而且昧於事實。眾所周知，語言會隨時間變化，**for free 早已被廣泛接受和使用**，我們沒有理由說它文法錯誤，所以**想用就用吧**！

Unit 19　Forget 還是 leave 呢？

重要觀念 非學不可

有人可能納悶，forget 和 leave 有何關連呢？怎麼可以相提並論？如果你去查字典、詳細看它們的定義，你會發現這兩個動詞有個意思是一樣的，那就是「忘記帶」。**Forget 僅指忘了帶某物**，而 **leave 則可指忘了帶某人或某物**，前者一定是**無意的**，但後者也可能是**有意的**。由於 **leave 必須用在有地點或場所的句子中**，一般幾乎都以「留在，遺留在，遺忘在（某個地點）」來表示 leave 的意思，讓我們未去探究它**真正的含意其實是「忘記帶」**。

由於 **leave 必須與地點連用，而 forget 則不可以**，因此經常發生用字錯誤，卻不自知或不知錯在哪裡的情況。現在我們就來舉例說明這兩個字在此意思上的正確用法。例如：

◆ I **forgot** my car keys.（○）
◇ I left my car keys.（×）
（我忘了帶車鑰匙。）

◆ I'll have to go back; I've **forgotten** my purse.（○）
◇ I'll have to go back; I've left my purse.（×）
（我必須回去；我忘了拿錢包。）

◆ John **left** his cellphone **on my desk**.（○）
◇ John left his cellphone.（×）
◇ John forgot his cellphone on my desk.（×）
（約翰把他的手機遺留在我的書桌上。）

◆ Mary **left** her son **on the bus**.（○）
◇ Mary forgot her son on the bus.（×）
（瑪麗把她兒子遺忘在公車上。）

◆ My daughter is always **leaving** her cellphone **at home**.（○）
◇ My daughter is always forgetting her cellphone at home.（×）
◇ My daughter is always leaving her cellphone.（×）
（我女兒老是把手機留在家裡。）

◆ They decided to **leave** the cat **at home**.（O）
（他們決定把貓留在家裡。）

→（有意的行為）

必閃陷阱 非學不可 🔍

如果你堅持要在沒有提到地點或場所的句子中使用 leave，而且用法要正確無誤，那也未嘗不可，也不是故意找碴，因為 leave behind 這個片語動詞可以符合這項要求。

Leave behind 也意為「忘記帶（某人或某物）；留下，遺留在，遺忘在」（無意或有意），受詞可以接在 leave 或 behind 的後面。 例如：

◆ I **left** my car keys **behind**.（O）
（我忘了帶車鑰匙。）

◆ We **left** in a hurry and I must have **left** my cellphone **behind.**（O）
（我們走得太匆忙，我一定是忘了拿手機。）

◆ He had to **leave behind** his wife and children.（O）
（他不得不拋下／丟下／留下他的妻兒。）

→（有意的行為）

好用 Tips 非學不可 🔍

Leave behind 可以用在沒有提到地點或場所的句子中，但這不表示它不**可用在有地點或場所的句子**。例如：

◆ Bill **left** his briefcase **behind on the train.**（O）
（比爾把他的公事包遺忘在火車上。）

◆ He was forced to **leave** his family **behind in North Korea.**（O）
（他被迫把他的家人留在北韓。）

Leave 和 leave behind 都還有其他常用的意思，但不在這裡的討論範圍內。

Unit 20 Get 還是 go 呢？

重要觀念 非學不可 🔍

在表示「移動，行進」的意思時，get 和 go 是近義詞，但 **get 著重於到達**。例如：

◆ I'll call you as soon as I **get** to Seoul.（○）
◇ I'll call you as soon as I go to Seoul.（×）
（我一到首爾就會打電話給你。）

◆ The thing is, he **got** to work late and missed part of the on-the-job training.（○）
◇ The thing is, he went to work late and missed part of the on-the-job training.（×）
（問題是，他上班遲到而且錯過了部分在職訓練。）

上下公車、巴士、火車和飛機要用 get on 和 get off，不能用 go on 和 go off。例如：

◆ When Jack **got on** the plane, there was someone sitting in his seat.（○）
◇ When Jack went on the plane, there was someone sitting in his seat.（×）
（傑克登上飛機時，有人坐在他的座位上。）

◆ I will be waiting for you when you **get off** the train.（○）
◇ I will be waiting for you when you go off the train.（×）
（你下火車時，我會在那裡等你。）

早上「起床」的英文是 get up，不是 go up，後者意為「上去，上升」等等。例如：

◆ I **got up** early today.（○）
◇ I went up early today.（×）
（今天我很早就起床了。）

必閃陷阱 非學不可

Get 和 go 都有「變成，變得，變為」的意思，為連綴動詞，但它們分別與不同的形容詞連用。

Get 通常與 late、dark、light、hot、cold、humid 和 interesting 等形容詞連用，而 **go** 則跟**顏色**（如 go grey/red）和 bald、blind、deaf、crazy、mad、wild、bad、rotten、sour、naked、topless 及**其他予人負面聯想的形容詞連用**，通常指變壞。例如：

◆ It's **getting late**—I have to go.（O）
◇ It's going late—I have to go.（×）
（太晚了，我該走了。）

◆ It's **getting dark**.（O）
◇ It's going dark.（×）
（天就要黑了。）

◆ It's been **getting colder** and colder all morning.（O）
◇ It's been going colder and colder all morning.（×）
（整個上午天氣變得越來越冷。）

◆ Tom tried to deny it, but he **went very red**.（O）
◇ Tom tried to deny it, but he got very red.（×）
（湯姆極力否認，但還是羞愧得滿臉通紅。）

◆ John's only 30, but he's **going bald.**（O）
◇ John's only 30, but he's getting bald.（×）
（約翰只有 30 歲，但就要童山濯濯了。）

◆ He **went mad** and tried to attack someone.（O）
◇ He got mad and tried to attack someone.（×）
（他發瘋了想攻擊別人。）

◆ The milk was left in the fridge too long and it's **gone bad**.（O）
◇ The milk was left in the fridge too long and it's got bad.（×）
（牛奶留在冰箱太久而變質了。）

然而，**angry、old、sick、tired、ill、wet 和 difficult 等負面形容詞**，
則與 get 連用。例如：

◆ It was raining and we all **got wet**.（ O ）
◇ It was raining and we all went wet.（ ✕ ）
（下雨了，我們都被淋濕了。）
◆ Our boss often **gets angry** about trivial things.（ O ）
◇ Our boss often goes angry about trivial things.（ ✕ ）
（我們老闆常因瑣碎小事動怒。）
◆ I **got tired** after studying all day.（ O ）
◇ I went tired after studying all day.（ ✕ ）
（唸了一整天的書，我很累了。）
◆ Things are starting to **get a bit difficult** in Taiwan.（ O ）
◇ Things are starting to go a bit difficult in Taiwan.（ ✕ ）
（台灣的情況開始變得有點艱難。）

Unit 21　Opposite 還是 in front of 呢？

重要觀念 非學不可 🔍

Opposite 用作介系詞時意為「與某人／某物相對；在某人／某物的對
面」，而介系詞片語 in front of 意為「在某人／某物的前面」。例如：

◆ The bank is **opposite** the post office.（ O ）
（銀行在郵局的對面。）
◇ The bank is in front of the post office.（ ✕ ）
→ 除非兩棟建築的位置是一前一後。
◆ They sat **opposite** each other.（ O ）
◇ They sat in front of each other.（ ✕ ）
（他們面對面坐著。）

◆ Jack sat **opposite** Monica in the restaurant. （O）
（傑克和莫妮卡在餐廳裡面對面坐著。）
→ 傑克和莫妮卡坐在同一張餐桌的不同邊，面對面。

◆ Jack sat **in front of** Monica in the restaurant. （O）
（傑克在餐廳裡坐在莫妮卡的前面。）
→ 傑克和莫妮卡坐在不同的餐桌，傑克坐在莫妮卡的前面。

◆ The bus stops right **opposite** my house. （O）
（公車都停在我家的對面。）

◆ The bus stops right **in front of** my house. （O）
（公車都停在我家的前面。）

◆ We parked **opposite** the restaurant. （O）
（我們把車子停在餐廳的對面。）

◆ We parked **in front of** the restaurant. （O）
（我們把車子停在餐廳的前面。）

◆ A crowd gathered **opposite** the movie theater. （O）
（電影院對面圍了一大群人。）

◆ A crowd gathered **in front of** the movie theater. （O）
（電影院前圍了一大群人。）

◆ The car **in front of** me stopped suddenly and I had to brake. （O）
→ 我的車開在那輛車的後面。

◇ The car opposite me stopped suddenly and I had to brake. （×）
（我前面那輛車突然停住，我只好煞車。）

◆ I keep my girlfriend's photos **in front of** me on the desk. （O）
◇ I keep my girlfriend's photos opposite me on the desk. （×）
（我把女友的照片放在書桌上，擺在我的面前。）

◆ There was a man **in front of** me in the queue for tickets who was as bald as a coot. （O）
◇ There was a man opposite me in the queue for tickets who was as bald as a coot. （×）
（排隊買票時，站在我前面的是個童山濯濯的男子。）

Unit 22　Pick 還是 pick up 呢？

Pick 的動詞用法有好幾個常用的意思，包括「（用手）採，摘」、「挑選，選擇」、「（用手指或尖形工具）挖，剔」、「撿起，拾起，拿起或類似的動作」等。然而，這些意思無一可以用片語動詞 pick up 來替代。Pick up 主要意為「（用手從某一表面）拿起、舉起（人或物）」及「（用車子）接載（某人）」。雖然 **pick 和 pick up 都有「拿起，撿起」的意思**，但含意不同（Pick 和 pick up 的其他意思請參閱字典）。**Pick 意為「（用手）採、摘」**。例如：

◆ We spent the summer holiday **picking** strawberries.（O）
◇ We spent the summer holiday picking up strawberries.（×）
（我們這個暑假都在採草莓。）
◆ John **picked** Mary a rose.（O）
= John picked a rose for Mary.（O）
◇ John picked up a rose for Mary.（×）
（約翰摘了一朵玫瑰花給瑪麗。）

Pick 意為「挑選，選擇」。例如：

◆ My classmates **picked** me to ask the teacher.（O）
◇ My classmates picked me up to ask the teacher.（×）
（我的同學挑選我去問老師。）
◆ He has yet to **pick** a name for his newborn baby.（O）
◇ He has yet to pick up a name for his newborn baby.（×）
（他尚未給他的新生寶寶取名。）

Pick 意為「（用手指或尖形工具）挖，剔」。例如：

◆ Don't **pick** your nose!（○）
◇ Don't pick up your nose!（×）
（不要挖鼻孔！）

◆ Albert was **picking** his teeth.（○）
◇ Albert was picking up his teeth.（×）
（艾伯特正在剔牙。）

Pick 意為「撿起，拾起，拿起或類似的動作」。例如：

◆ The students were on their knees **picking** crumbs off the carpet.（○）
（學生跪著撿拾地毯上的食物碎屑。）

◆ He **picked** a book off the shelf.（○）
（他從書架上取下一本書。）

◆ A helicopter **picked** a survivor off the sea.（○）
（一架直升機把一名生還者從海中吊起來。）

◆ The mother **picked** the baby out of the pram.（○）
（媽媽把嬰兒從嬰兒車裡抱了出來。）

◆ Jack **picked** all the cherries off the top of his birthday cake.（○）
（傑克把生日蛋糕上面的所有櫻桃都挑走了。）

必閃陷阱 非學不可

在上面這五個例句中，pick 同樣不能換成 pick up，否則就錯了。**Pick up 的「拿起，撿起」意思雖與 pick 重疊，但它有兩個構成要件，一是必須用手，二是必須有由下而上的動作**，至於句中是否有表示從某個表面拿起的介系詞片語（from/off/out of ＋ 名詞）則不重要。現在再回頭看這五個例句。它們都只滿足其中一個要件，有的是用手，但沒有由下而上的動作，有的是沒有用手，但有由下而上的動作，無一同時滿足兩個構成要件。

Pick up 意為「（用手從某一表面）拿起、舉起（人或物）」。例如：

◆ Tom **picked** the phone **up** and dialed.（○）
（湯姆拿起電話撥了號碼。）

◆ The mother rushed to **pick up** the baby as soon as it started to cry. （〇）
（嬰兒一哭，這位媽媽就衝過去把它抱了起來。）

◆ I'm tired of **picking up** the things the children leave lying around every day.
（〇）
（我厭煩每天收拾孩子們扔得到處都是的東西。）

◆ I am constantly **picking up** your clothes from the floor! Can't you hang them
up properly in the closet? （〇）
（我老是在收拾你散落在地板上的衣服。你不能把它們好好掛在衣櫥裡嗎？）

好用 Tips 非學不可 🔍

Pick up 意為「（用車子）**接載**（某人）」。我們亦可用 collect （⋯
from）來表達相同的意思。例如：

◆ He'll **pick me up** after the party. （〇）
◇ He'll pick me after the party. （✕）
（聚會後他會開車來接我。）

◆ I will **pick up** Sam at the airport and take him to his hotel. （〇）
◇ I will pick Sam at the airport and take him to his hotel. （✕）
（我會開車到機場接山姆，載他到他下榻的旅館。）

◆ I'll **collect** you **from** the station. （〇）
（我會去車站接你。）

◆ What time do you **collect** the kids **from** school? （〇）
（你什麼時候去接孩子放學呢？）

Unit 23 Such 還是 so 呢？

重要觀念 非學不可 🔍

Such 和 so 的用法都需要相當大的篇幅才能說明清楚。本文僅就這兩者同義的「**如此，這麼；很，非常**」（to this degree; very）的意思來說明一般使用上常見的錯誤。就此意思而言，**such 為限定詞，後接名詞片語，而 so 為副詞，後接形容詞**或**副詞片語**。

不過，在此有需要先說明一下**名詞片語的結構**。完整的名詞片語主要是由三個元素所構成：不定冠詞（a/an）＋ 形容詞 ＋ 名詞，其中名詞一定會有，但名詞若為複數可數名詞或不可數名詞，那麼該名詞片語就不會有不定冠詞，而形容詞可能存在、也可能不存在，所以最精簡的名詞片語可能只有名詞一個元素而已。

現在就來看看一般在**使用 such 或 so 時常見的錯誤**。例如：

◆ It was **such an interesting party**.（O）
（這是一場很有趣的聚會。）

◆ The party was **so interesting**.（O）
◇ It was so interesting party.（×）
◇ It was a so interesting party.（×）
（這場聚會很有趣。）

◆ Jessica's **such a smart woman**.（O）
◇ Jessica's so smart woman.（×）
◇ Jessica's a so smart woman.（×）
（潔西卡真是個聰明的女人。）

◆ It was **such a shock**.（O）
（那是非常令人震驚的事。）

◆ It was **so shocking**.（O）
（它使人大為震驚。）

◇ It was such shocking.（×）
→ shocking 為形容詞。

◆ They're **such snobs**!（○）
◇ They're so snobs!（×）
（他們真是自負傲慢的勢利鬼！）
→ snobs 為複數可數名詞。

◆ Those are **such cool earrings**. Where did you get them?（○）
◇ Those are so cool earrings. Where did you get them?（×）
（那些耳環很酷。你在哪裡買的？）

◆ We've had **such awful weather** lately.（○）
◇ We've had so awful weather lately.（×）
（最近的天氣非常糟糕。）
→ weather 為不可數名詞。

◆ I'm **so glad** to see you.（○）
◇ I'm such glad to see you.（×）
（我很高興見到你。）
→ glad 為形容詞。

◆ Tom sat there ever **so quietly**.（○）
◇ Tom sat there ever such quietly.（×）
（湯姆靜靜地坐在那裡。）
→ quietly 為副詞。

必閃陷阱 非學不可

然而，**當名詞前面是用 much, many, little 或 few 來修飾時**，該名詞片
語的前面要用 so，不可使用 such。例如：

◆ **So much food** was wasted every day.（○）
◇ Such much food was wasted every day.（×）
（每天都有很多食物被浪費掉了。）

◆ There were **so few doctors** in Taiwan fifty years ago.（○）
◇ There were such few doctors in Taiwan fifty years ago.（×）
（五十年前台灣的醫生很少。）

◆ We've had **such a lot of problems** with the new computer.（○）
= We've had so many problems with the new computer.（○）
◇ We've had such many problems with the new computer.（×）
（我們新電腦的問題真多／我們的新電腦問題太多了。）

◆ There were/was ever **such a lot of** people/money.（O）

◆ = There were/was ever **so many/much** people/money.（O）

◇ There were/was ever such many/much people/money.（×）

（超多的人／錢）

◆ Thanks (ever) **such a lot**.（O）

= Thanks so much.（O）

（太感謝了。）

好用 Tips 非學不可 🔍

在上面的例句中，such 和 so 的前面有時會加上 ever，這個副詞係用來加強 such 和 so 的語氣。**Ever such 的意思和用法跟 such 完全一樣，**而 **ever so 的意思和用法跟 so 亦無不同**。這與 never 在口語中經常用 ever 來加強語氣而說成 **never ever**（從不，絕不）的用法雷同。例如：

1. Hilary's ever such a nice girl.
（希拉蕊真是個好女孩。）

2. It's ever so cold.
（天氣很冷。）

3. I never ever drink beer.
（我從來不喝啤酒。）

Unit 24 Tall 還是 high 呢？

必閃陷阱 非學不可 🔍

Tall 和 high 這兩個形容詞都意為「高的」。但 **tall 是用來指人、建築物以及會長高的東西**，而 **high 則用來指高山以及離地面有一段頗長距離的東西**。例如：

◆ James is thin and **tall**.（○）
（詹姆斯又瘦又高。）

◇ James is thin and high.（×）

1. It's the world's tallest tower.
（那是世界最高的大樓。）

2. It's the highest mountain in the world.
（那是世界最高的山。）

3. The plants were two meters tall.
（這些植物有 2 公尺高。）

4. There are many tall trees in our school.
（我們學校有許多高樹。）

5. The light switch is too high for a child to use.
（電燈開關對小孩來說太高了，碰觸不到。）

6. There is a high ceiling in my office.
（我辦公室的天花板很高。）

7. John built a 3-meter-high wall around his house.
（約翰在他房子的四周築起了 3 公尺高的圍牆。）

8. How tall are they?
（他們身高有多高？）

9. How high are they?
（他們距地面有多高？）

Unit 25　Wait 還是 wait for 呢？

重要觀念 非學不可

Wait 意為「等，等候」，可當及物和不及物動詞用，**若受詞為時間，其後可接或不接介系詞 for**。例如：

◆ They **waited** hours to get the tickets **for** the exhibition. (O)
◆ They **waited for** hours to get the tickets for the exhibition. (O)
（他們等了好幾個小時才買到展覽會入場券。）
◆ I **waited** 30 minutes **for** the bus. (O)
◆ I **waited for** 30 minutes for the bus. (O)
（我等了三十分鐘公車。）

必閃陷阱 非學不可

然而，**當受詞為人事物時，wait 的後面須有 for**。例如：

◆ We're **waiting for** the bus. (O)
◇ We're waiting the bus. (×)
（我們在等公車。）
◆ **Wait for** me! (O)
◇ Wait me! (×)
（等我啊！）
◆ **Wait for** us outside the library. We'll be there at eight o'clock. (O)
◇ Wait us outside the library. We'll be there at eight o'clock. (×)
（在圖書館外面等我們。我們八點會到那裡。）
◆ The airport was full of anxious relatives, **waiting nervously for** news of the missing plane. (O)
◇ The airport was full of anxious relatives, waiting news of the missing plane nervously. (×)
（機場擠滿了焦急的家屬，他們緊張不安地等候失蹤飛機的消息。）

Wait 的後面亦可接不定詞，即 **wait to do something**，但 wait 後面若要接受詞，其後須有 for，其句型為 **wait for someone/something to do something**。例如：

◆ Amy is **waiting to tell** you a secret. (O)
（艾美正等著告訴你一個秘密。）
◆ He's **waiting to use** the computer. (O)
（他正等著用這台電腦。）

92

◆ I can't **wait to**（＝ I'm very eager to）**tell** my wife the good news!（○）
（我等不及／急著要告訴我太太這好消息！）
◆ I've been **waiting for Allen to change** his mind for several months.（○）
◇ I've been waiting Allen to change his mind for several months.（×）
（我等艾倫改變心意已等了好幾個月。）

好用 Tips 非學不可 🔍

然而，若 **wait 後面接 chance、opportunity 或 turn 等名詞，則 for 可有可無**。例如：

◆ Louis was just **waiting his chance/opportunity** to sneak away.（○）
◆ Louis was just **waiting for his chance/opportunity** to sneak away.（○）
（路易斯正伺機溜走。）
◆ You'll just have to **wait your turn** like everyone else.（○）
◆ You'll just have to **wait for your turn** like everyone else.（○）
（你必須跟別人一樣等候輪到你。）

Unit 26　With regard to 還是 with regards to 呢？

重要觀念 非學不可 🔍

With regard to 或 in regard to（＝ in connection with）意為「關於；至於」，其中 **regard 須用單數，不可用 regards**。儘管 with regards to 自 1990 年代以來有越來越多人使用的趨勢，但仍應被視為錯誤。例如：

◆ **With regard to** your suggestion I will consider it carefully.（○）
◇ With regards to your suggestion I will consider it carefully.（×）
（關於你的建議，我會好好考慮。）

不過，由於許多人認為 with regard to 和 in regard to 這兩個在商業書信中經常用到的片語不夠簡潔，因此往往使用**同義的 about、concerning 或 regarding 來代替**。例如：

1. There is no question with/in regard to his loyalty.
→There is no question about his loyalty.
（他的忠誠毋庸置疑。）
2. My sister asked me many questions with/in regard to study in Taipei.
→My sister asked me many questions concerning study in Taipei.
（我妹妹問我許多有關在台北唸書的問題。）
3. There is no problem with/in regard to the settings of the new software.
→There is no problem regarding the settings of the new software.
（新軟體的設定方面毫無問題。）

必閃陷阱 非學不可

在比較正式的情況中，我們亦可使用 **as regards** 來表示相同的意思。注意這裡的 **regards 須用複數**，不可使用 regard。例如：

◆ We have received your complaint **as regards** the noise.（O）
◇ We have received your complaint as regard the noise.（×）
（我們已收到您關於噪音的投訴。）

◆ **As regards** your request, we will consider the payment on Monday.（O）
◇ As regard your request, we will consider the payment on Monday.（×）
（關於你的要求，我們週一會考慮這項付款。）

Unit 27 使用 abroad 時常見的錯誤

必閃陷阱 非學不可 🔍

Abroad 與 go, live, study 等動詞連用時一定用作副詞，此時它意為「在國外；到國外」。例如：

◆ We intend to **go abroad** at least once a year from now on.（O）
◇ We intend to go to abroad at least once a year from now on.（×）
（我們打算從現在起一年至少出國一次。）

◆ My brother is still **living abroad**.（O）
◇ My brother is still living in abroad.（×）
（我哥哥仍住在國外。）

◆ Blanche would like to **study abroad**.（O）
◇ Blanche would like to study in abroad.（×）
（布蘭琪想要出國留學。）

◆ We're planning our first trip **abroad**/overseas.（O）
◇ We're planning our first trip to abroad/overseas.（×）
（我們正在規劃我們的首次出國旅遊。）

好用 Tips 非學不可 🔍

一般都認為 abroad 僅當副詞用，若干字典也抱持相同的看法，但若從文法觀點來看，這並不完全正確。事實上，**abroad 亦可用作名詞**（意為「國外，海外」），否則它怎可當介系詞的受詞呢！然而，儘管名詞（片語）可當介系詞的受詞，但 abroad 僅能當 from 的受詞，亦即 **from 是唯一可以用 abroad 當受詞的介系詞**。例如：

◆ Most of the luxury goods are imported **from abroad**.（O）
（這些奢侈品大多是從國外進口的。）

◆ My parents just returned **from abroad**.（O）
（我父母親剛從國外回來。）

Unit 28　使用 could 時常見的錯誤；釐清 could 和 can 易混淆之處

重要觀念 非學不可 🔍

能力

Could 和 can 皆可表示能力（意為「能，會」），前者表示過去的能力，後者表示現在和未來的能力。在此用法中，**could 為 can 的過去式**。例如：

1. When I was young, I could play the piano, violin, and cello.
（年輕時我會彈鋼琴、拉小提琴和大提琴。）
2. He can speak English, French, German, and Spanish.
（他會講英文、法文、德文和西班牙文。）
3. I can walk home after school tomorrow.
（明天放學後我能走路回家。）

必閃陷阱 非學不可 🔍

當 **could 用作 can 的過去式來表示過去有能力做某事**時，這是指過去某一段時間發生的事實。對於過去有能力去做某一偶發的單一事件而且做了，在肯定句中我們就不能使用 could，**必須使用 was/were able to 或 managed to** 或比較正式的 succeeded in（後接動名詞），意為「成功做到，順利完成」。例如：

◆ I **was able to** get the concert tickets I wanted.（O）
= I managed to get the concert tickets I wanted.（O）
= I succeeded in getting the concert tickets I wanted.（O）
◇ I could get the concert tickets I wanted.（×）
（我 [成功地] 買到了我想要的演唱會門票。）
◆ We **were able to** find the missing girl we were looking for.（O）
= We managed to find the missing girl we were looking for.（O）
= We succeeded in finding the missing girl we were looking for.（O）

◇ We could find the missing girl we were looking for.（×）
（我們 [成功地] 找到了我們要找的那個失蹤女孩。）

然而，在否定句中，我們卻可以使用 couldn't 或比較正式的 was/were unable to。例如：

◆ Paul **couldn't** pass the exam.（○）
= Paul was unable to pass the exam.（○）
（保羅未能 [成功地] 通過考試。）

可能性

Could 和 can 皆可表示可能性（意為「可能，可能會」），兩者都表示現在和未來的可能性。若要表示**過去的可能性**，則要使用 could have ＋ P.P.，但**過去否定式**卻可**使用 couldn't have ＋ P.P. 或 can't have ＋ P.P.**。例如：

1. It can be diamond.
（那可能是鑽石。）（現在）
2. My homework can be completed ahead of time.
（我的家庭作業可能提前完成。）（未來）
3. That could be my bus.
（那可能是我要搭乘的公車。）（現在）
4. The typhoon could get worse.
（颱風可能更加猛烈。）（未來）

→ 現今，肯定句已鮮少使用 can 來表示可能性，而是以 may、might 和 could（could 也越來越少用了）來代之；但在問句中，則可**用 can 來詢問可能性**，如 **Can this be true?**（這可能是真的嗎？）。

◆ I **couldn't** possibly **accept** the invitation.（○）
（我不可能接受邀請。）（現在）
◆ He **could have been** a lawyer.（○）
◇ He could be a lawyer.（×）
（他以前可能是個律師。）（過去）

◆ They **couldn't have taken** a taxi home last night.（O）

◇ They couldn't take a taxi home last night.（×）

（他們昨晚不可能搭計程車回家。）（過去）

◆ You can't have arrived here earlier than me.（O）

（你不可能比我早到這裡。）（過去）

雖然 **couldn't have ＋ P.P.** 或 **can't have ＋ P.P.** 現今仍可表示可能性，指過去某事「不可能」發生，但 **can't be** 和 **couldn't be** 則已不常用來表示現在或未來某事「不可能」發生。

這**四個否定動詞片語**現今在絕大多數的情況下都是用來**表示推測**，其中 **can't be 是 must be 的否定詞（或疑問形式），也就是 must 現在式的否定詞**，而 couldn't be、couldn't have ＋ P.P. 和 can't have ＋ P.P. 則是 must 過去式（must have ＋ P.P.）的否定詞。我們不可在 must 後面直接加 not，因為 must not 或 mustn't 是在表示「禁止，不准」，不是表示「推測」。在此用法中，must 意為「一定，肯定，想必，諒必」，而四個否定詞則意為「一定不；一定未；一定沒有」。例如：

1. If Tom didn't leave here until five o'clock, he can't be home yet.

（如果湯姆五點才離開這裡，那麼此時他一定還未到家。）

2. John: Whose shirt is this? It must be yours.

（約翰：這件襯衫是誰的？肯定是你的。）

　Jack: It can't be mine. It's too small.

（傑克：這件襯衫一定不是我的。它太小了。）

3. Mary must have made a mistake. It couldn't be true.

（瑪麗肯定搞錯了。那一定不是真的。）

→ 這句後半段似乎也可以譯為「那不可能是真的」，但從前半段可知，must have made 是過去式，所以 **couldn't be 是表推測**，不是表可能性。

4. David can't have found his car, for he came to work by bus this morning.

（大衛一定還沒有找到他的車，因為早上他是坐公車來上班的。）

5. Amy: Robert must have made a lot of money.

（艾美：羅伯特一定賺了很多錢。）

　Cindy: He couldn't have done. He doesn't even own a house.

（辛蒂：他肯定沒有。他連一間房子都沒有。）

好用 Tips 非學不可 🔍

許可

Could 和 can 皆可用來禮貌地請求許可（意為「可以，能」），而 **could 比 can 更正式且更有禮貌**。但 **can 可用來表示允許或不允許**，could 則不行；換言之，只有 can't 才有不許、不准的意思，couldn't 並無此意，亦即我們不可使用 couldn't 來表示不允許。例如：

1. Could I interrupt?
（能打斷一下嗎？）
2. Could I speak to Ms. Chen, please?
（我可以跟陳小姐通話嗎？）
3. Can I smoke here?
（我可以在這裡抽菸嗎？）
4. Can I help you?
（要我幫忙嗎？）

◆ We **can't** park there.（○）
◇ We couldn't park there.（×）
（我們不准在那裡停車。）

◆ Anyone **can't** smoke here.（○）
◇ Anyone couldn't smoke here.（×）
（任何人都不准在這裡抽菸。）

A: Could I ask you a personal question?
（A：我可以問你一個私人的問題嗎？）

◆ B: Yes, you **can**./No, you **can't**.（○）
◇ B: Yes, you could./No, you couldn't.（×）
（B：可以／不可以）

Unit 29　使用 largely 時常見的錯誤

重要觀念 非學不可 🔍

Largely 是個副詞，意為「主要地；大多；大部分地」。例如：

1. Mr. Chen runs a largely female company.
（陳先生經營一家員工大多為女性的公司。）

2. The company's success is largely due to our efforts.
（這家公司能成功主要是靠我們的努力。）

必閃陷阱 非學不可 🔍

Largely 並無 enormously、greatly 或 significantly 等字「極其，非常，大大地，巨大地」的意思。例如：

◆ The noise was **greatly** reduced.（O）
◇ The noise was largely reduced.（×）
（噪音大大地降低了。）

◆ Mary admired her professor **enormously.**（O）
◇ Mary admired her professor largely.（×）
（瑪麗對她的教授極為欽佩。）

Largely 也沒有「（人們）廣泛地」（widely）的意思。例如：

◆ The issue of transitional justice has been **widely** debated in recent years.
（O）
◇ The issue of transitional justice has been largely debated in recent years.
（×）
（近年來轉型正義的問題一直廣受爭論。）

◆ This set of regulations is no longer **widely** accepted.（O）
◇ This set of regulations is no longer largely accepted.（×）
（這套規定不再被人們廣泛接受。）

使用 marry 時常見的錯誤

重要觀念 非學不可 🔍

Marry（結婚）可當及物和不及物動詞用，但**通常用作及物動詞**，後接受詞。Divorce（離婚）的用法亦同。例如：

1. Amy married a wealthy old man last month.
（艾美上個月嫁給一個有錢的老頭。）
2. Last year he divorced his second wife.
（去年他跟他第二任太太離婚了。）

然而，在**正式文體中**，它們都**用作不及物動詞**。例如：

1. He did not marry until he was forty.
（他直到四十歲才結婚。）
2. John and Mary divorced two years ago.
（約翰和瑪麗兩年前離婚了。）

在非正式的口說英語中，若沒有受詞，我們係使用 **get married** 和 **get divorced** 來表示「結婚」和「離婚」。例如：

1. My son and his girlfriend are getting married in Hawaii.
（我兒子和他女友將在夏威夷結婚。）
2. The couple finally got divorced last year.
（那對夫妻去年終於離婚了。）

Be married 和 be divorced 可表示結婚和離婚的狀態。例如：

1. We've been married for nearly 40 years.
（他們已結婚快 40 年。）
2. They're divorced now.
（他們現在已離婚。）

必閃陷阱 非學不可

Marry 後面不可接 **to** 或 **with** 再接結婚對象當受詞。例如：

◆ Bert **married** Betty last year.（O）
◇ Bert married to Betty last year.（×）
◇ Bert married with Betty last year.（×）
（伯特去年和貝蒂結婚。）

但 **get married** 和 **be married** 後面可接 **to** 再接結婚對象當受詞，只是**仍不可接 with**。例如：

◆ Bert **got married to** Betty last year.（O）
◇ Bert got married with Betty last year.（×）
◆ Bert's **married to** Betty last year.（O）
◇ Bert's married with Betty last year.（×）

好用 Tips 非學不可

其實，**marry**、**get married** 和 **be married** 後面都可接 **with** 再接受詞，只是這裡的**受詞**並非結婚對象，而是**「結婚的產物」**，亦即**子女**。這裡的 with 並非意為「和……」，而是表示**「伴隨」**的意思。例如：

◆ Jennifer **married/got married/is married with** a boy.（O）
◆ Jennifer **married/got married/is married with** a child.（O）
◆ Jennifer **married/got married/is married with** a son.（O）
（珍妮佛已婚，有個兒子。）
→ 這句的意思並非「珍妮佛跟一位男生結婚。」

Unit 31 使用 soon 時常見的錯誤

重要觀念 非學不可 🔍

Soon 意為「不久」、「很快地」。就「不久」的意思而言，soon 可以指現在之後的不久（亦即**未來或過去的未來**）以及過去某個時間點之後的不久。與其他許多短副詞一樣，**soon 可用在句首、句中和句末**，但在**指過去某個時間點之後不久的句子中，soon 不可用在句末**。例如：

1. The winter is coming. Soon it will be Christmas.
（冬天來了。耶誕節很快就要到了。）（句首位置）

2. I soon realized the mistake.
（我很快就意識到了錯誤。）（句中位置）

3. Peter will soon be here./Peter will be here soon.
（彼得很快就到。）（句中或句末位置，指未來。）

4. Mom phoned to say she'd be home soon.
（媽媽打電話說她很快就回家。）（句末位置，指過去的未來。）

5. A: Bye for now!
（A：再見！）

B: Bye. See you soon!
（B：再見。一會兒見！）（句末位置，指未來）

◆ **Soon** all the Mayday concert tickets were sold out.（O）
◆ All the Mayday concert tickets were **soon** sold out.（O）
◇ All the Mayday concert tickets were sold out soon.（×）
（五月天演唱會門票瞬間秒殺。）

我們可以使用 **pretty、quite 或 very 來修飾 soon**，用法與上述相同。例如：

1. The novel will be published quite/very soon.
（這本小說很快就會出版。）

2. If Henry doesn't show up pretty soon, I'm leaving.
（如果亨利不能快點來，我就要走了。）

必閃陷阱 非學不可

就「很快」的意思而言，soon 的用法與 quickly 並不相同，兩者不能劃上等號。例如：

◆ How **soon** （= when） can we have dinner?（O）
◇ How quickly can we have dinner?（×）
（我們什麼時候能吃晚餐？／我們多快能吃晚餐？）

◆ How **soon** can John get here?（O）
◇ How quickly can John get here?（×）
（約翰多快能趕到這兒？）

◆ I hope to see you **soon**.（O）
◇ I hope to see you quickly.（×）
（我希望能很快見到你。）

Soon 可以用在 after 或 afterwards 的前面來表示「不久之後」的意思，但副詞 afterwards 的後面不可接子句或受詞。例如：

1. Tom supposedly showed up at the Christmas party soon after I left.
（湯姆大概是在我離開耶誕晚會後不久現身的。）
→ 不可用 afterwards。

2. They arrived soon after us.
（我們到了之後不久他們就到了。）
→ 不可用 afterwards。

3. Soon after agreeing to go out to eat with George, Mary realized she'd made a mistake.
（同意跟喬治一起出去吃飯之後不久，她就意識到自己犯了一個錯誤。）
→ 不可用 afterwards。

4. Teresa left first, and Emily left soon after/afterwards.
（泰瑞莎先離開，不久之後艾茉莉也離開了。）

As soon as ... 是個相當常用的片語，**其後可接形容詞 possible（as soon as possible 意為「盡快」）**或子句（as soon as ＋ 子句意為「一……就……」）。例如：

1. Teddy wants you to call him back as soon as possible.
（泰迪希望你盡快給他回電。）
2. Come and see me as soon as you can.
（盡快來看我。）
3. I'll tell him as soon as I see him.
（我一見到他就告訴他。）
4. As soon as I saw the babysitter, I knew there was something wrong with my baby daughter.
（我一看到保母，就知道我小女兒出事了。）

Unit 32 使用 without 時常見的錯誤

Without 為介系詞，意為「無，沒有，不」。例如：

1. Money is not everything but nothing can be done without money.
（錢不是萬能，但沒有錢卻萬萬不能。）
2. I like to drink coffee without sugar.
（我喜歡喝不加糖的咖啡。）

在上面的例句中，without 後面都是接不可數名詞。若 **without 後接單數可數名詞，則該名詞前面一定要有不定冠詞 a/an**。例如：

◆ Henry left us **without a word**.（O）
◇ Henry left us without word.（×）
（亨利一句話也沒說就離開我們了。）

◆ He can do mathematics **without a calculator.**（O）
◇ He can do mathematics without calculator.（×）
（他不用計算機就能做數學計算。）

◆ Don't go out **without an umbrella.** It's raining cats and dogs.（O）
◇ Don't go out without umbrella. It's raining cats and dogs.（×）
（沒帶傘不要外出。外面正下著傾盆大雨。）

好用 Tips 非學不可

Without 已經有否定的意思，其後不能再接任何否定字。 例如：

◆That girl stood me up and made me wait for two hours there **without** anything to eat or drink.（O）
◇That girl stood me up and made me wait for two hours there without nothing to eat or drink.（×）
（那個女孩放我鴿子，讓我在那裡沒有吃的也沒有喝的等了兩個小時。）

◆Allen walked past **without** saying anything.（O）
◇Allen walked past without saying nothing.（×）
（艾倫走了過去，什麼話也沒說。）

Unit 33　狀態形容詞和動態形容詞的差異

必閃陷阱 非學不可

顧名思義，**狀態形容詞**（stative adjectives）指的是表示狀態或狀況的形容詞。

大多數的形容詞都是狀態形容詞，它們通常**可以被視為永久性**，不會改變的，如 big, green, heavy 等。狀態形容詞不可用於祈使結構。例如：

◇ Be big!（×）
（大一點！）
◇ Be green!（×）
（綠一點！）
◇ Be heavy!（×）
（重一點！）

此外，狀態形容詞亦不可用於進行式。例如：

◇ He is being big.（×）
（他裝模作樣地大了起來。）
◇ He is being green.（×）
（他裝模作樣地綠了起來。）
◇ He is being heavy.（×）
（他表現得很重。）

相對地，**動態形容詞**（dynamic adjectives）指的是**表示個人特質的形容詞**，這些特質至少在某種程度上是受到擁有這些特質的人的控制，而表現在他們的動作或行為上。譬如說，brave（勇敢的）係表示一種可能永遠都不會比 big, green, heavy 等來得明顯的特質，但它在必要時或被要求時可能會表現出來、表現在動作或行為上。因此，它們可以用於祈使句。例如：

◆ Be **brave**! You can do it!（○）
（勇敢一點！你可以做得到的！）
◆ Be **careful**!（○）
（小心！）
◆ Don't be **cruel**!（○）
（別太殘忍！）

好用 Tips 非學不可 🔍

動態形容詞包括 brave, calm, careful, clever, cruel, disruptive, foolish, friendly, good, impatient, kind, patient, polite, rude, shy, stupid, suspicious, tidy, vacuous, vain 等等。

所有動態形容詞都可用於祈使句，亦皆可用於進行式。必須注意的是，這裡所指的進行式一定是狀態動詞 "BE" 的進行式 "be + being"，其後接動態形容詞來描述主詞。再者，雖然 **"be + being" 是進行式時態，但它卻沒有動作正在發生或進行的意義。當 "be + being" 後接動態形容詞時，主詞所表現的是一種與平時不同的故意行為或例外情況**。例如：

1. He is being polite.
（他裝模作樣地客氣起來了。）

→ 這是故意的行為，因為他平時待人處事並不是很有禮貌，也不是很客氣。

2. She is being very clever today.
（她今天表現得很聰明。）

→ 這是例外的情況，因為她平常給人的感覺是笨笨的，不是那種聰明的類型。

3. Mrs. Huang's son was being disruptive in class yesterday.
（黃太太的兒子昨天在課堂上搗蛋。）

→ 這是例外的情況，因為黃太太的兒子平常乖巧聽話，上課都專心聽講，但昨天卻一反常態，破壞課堂秩序。

Unit 34 盡量不要將介系詞放在句末

必閃陷阱 非學不可 🔍

事實上，這並不是規則，但許多人認為是，所以我們應盡量避免這種情況的發生。不過，若改寫句子後，反而使**句子變得不自然**，治絲益棻，那麼**就讓介系詞留在句末吧**！例如：

◇ That is a situation Ted has not thought of.（×）

（那是泰德沒有想到的情況。）

→ of 為介系詞，應避免出現在句末，因為介詞應位在名詞或代名詞之前。

◇ Mary is a person her husband cannot cope with.（×）

（瑪麗是個她先生無法應付的人。）

→ with 為介系詞，應避免出現在句末。

◇ It is behavior anyone will not put up with.（×）

（那是任何人都無法容忍的行為。）

→ 同樣地，with 為介系詞，應避免出現在句末。

因此，我們應將介系詞移位，以符合上述要求。例如：

◆ That is a situation **of which** Ted has not thought.（O）

◆ Mary is a person **with whom** her husband cannot cope.（O）

◆ It is behavior up **with which** anyone will not put.（O）

→ 這句顯得非常不自然，不改還比較好。

一般而言，對於介系詞出現在句末的情況，最佳的解決辦法就是改寫句子，**尤其是用同義字來取代含有句末介詞的片語動詞**。例如：

◆ That is a situation Ted has not **considered**.（O）

→ 這句已沒有介系詞，但意思一樣。

◆ It is behavior anyone will not **tolerate**.（O）

然而，若句子改寫後反而變得不自然，**那麼寧可讓介系詞留在句末**。例如：

◆ Helen is the lady I made the promise **to**.（O）

（海倫就是那位我對她做出承諾的女士。）

→ 雖然我們盡量不要將介系詞放在句末，但有時卻是不得不然的作法。

◆ There is only one thing in the world worse than being talked about, and that is not being talked **about**.（O）

（世上只有一件事比被人議論更糟，那就是無人議論你。）（王爾德）

Part I
文法常見錯誤

Chapter 3

拼字

Chapter 3 | 拼字

Unit 01 All right 還是 alright 呢？

必閃陷阱 非學不可

許多人習焉不察，總是把 alright 用來代替 all right，殊不知這樣的用法並非放諸四海皆準、人人可以接受，有些字典仍將 alright 列為錯字。所以，**寫作時應該使用 all right 而不要用 alright**。例如：

◆ Are you **all right**?（O）
（你還好吧？／你好嗎？）
◇ Everything is alright.（×）
（一切都好。）
◆ **All right**, calm down.（O）
（好，沒事，冷靜下來。）
◇ "Alright Anthony?" "Alright."（×）
（「你好，安東尼」「你好」。）

好用 Tips 非學不可

然而，從 alright 開始被用來表示 all right 至今已有一百年以上的歷史，而且用得越來越普遍。換言之，現在接受 alright = all right 的人越來越多。有趣的是，微軟文書處理軟體 Microsoft Word 的拼字檢查並未將 alright 列為錯字，但如果你拼錯字，如 alrigght，它也沒有把 alright 列在建議使用的字裡面。顯然地，微軟對於 alright 是否可以被接受為標準字，現在是騎牆派，仍在觀望。

由於現今電視節目名稱、影集名稱、歌名等大多使用 alright 來代替 all right，因此一些人認為 alright 比較有現代感。但不管如何，**在正式寫作中應避免使用 alright，因為十之八九會被當成錯字**。

Unit 02　Altogether 還是 all together 呢？

重要觀念 非學不可

Altogether 是個副詞，主要意為「完全，全然」（completely）或「總共，共計」（in total）。Altogether 意為「完全，全然」時旨在強調某事物完全停止、結束，或者強調某事物被完全遺忘或忽視，抑或強調對所說的話完全肯定；所以，**not altogether 意為「不完全是」（not completely）**。例如：

1. The government has decided to abolish the tax altogether.
（政府已決定完全取消這項稅收。）

2. Many people have stopped using their computers altogether.
（許多人已完全不用自己的電腦了。）

3. John seemed to have forgotten our quarrel altogether.
（約翰似乎已完全忘了我們吵過架。）

4. This is a new solution altogether.
（這完全是一種新的解決方案。）

5. I don't altogether agree with you.
（我不完全同意你的看法。）

6. I'm not altogether sure Mary will marry me.
（我不能完全肯定瑪麗會嫁給我。）

7. The speaker was $60 and the microphone was $30, so it was $90 altogether.
（喇叭 60 美元、麥克風 30 美元，所以總共是 90 美元。）

8. How many students will there be altogether?
（總共會有多少學生？）

必閃陷阱 非學不可

All together 亦當副詞用，意為「（每個人或每件事物）**一起**」，意思和用法皆近似於 together。例如：

◆ You must add all these numbers together.

= You must add these numbers all together.

（你必須把這些數字全部加起來。）

◆ The waiter asked if we were **all together**, so I said that we were two separate parties.（O）

◇ The waiter asked if we were altogether, so I said that we were two separate parties.（×）

（服務生問我們是不是一起的，我說我們是不同的兩組人。）

◆ They were still **all together** when I left.（O）

◇ They were still altogether when I left.（×）

（我走的時候，他們還在一起。）

◆ Put your books **all together** and I'll arrange them neatly along the shelf.（O）

◇ Put your books altogether and I'll arrange them neatly along the shelf.（×）

（把你的書籍集中在一起，我會把它們整整齊齊地排列在書架上。）

◆ Teacher: "Idiosyncrasy." **All together** now.（O）

（老師：idiosyncrasy。現在大家一起唸。）

◇ Teacher: "Idiosyncrasy." Altogether now.（×）

　Students: "Idiosyncrasy."（學生：idiosyncrasy。）

→ **All together now** 意為「**現在大家一起來**」，如「現在大家一起說」、「現在大家一起唱」、「現在大家一起唸」等等。

Unit 03　Cannot 還是 can not 呢？

重要觀念 非學不可

情態（或語氣）助動詞（modal or modal auxiliary）**can 的否定形式為 cannot**，而 cannot 的縮寫為 can't。反過來說，can't 的原形是 cannot，不是 can not。Can not 的寫法不僅極為少用，而且被視為錯誤。在寫作或書面文件中，cannot 是個正式用字，而 can't 並不適合用在這些場合；can't 大多用於口語。再強調一次，**cannot 要寫成一個字，不能寫成 can not**。

例句：

◇ You should tell your son what he can and can not do!（×）
（你應該告訴你兒子他什麼能做什麼不能做！）

◆ We **cannot** be too careful in choosing friends.（O）
（我們在擇友時愈謹慎愈好。／我們在擇友時無論多謹慎都不為過。）

→ 這一句是改寫自英國大文豪王爾德（Oscar Wilde）的 A man cannot be too careful in the choice of his enemies.
（一個人在選擇敵人時愈謹慎愈好。／一個人在選擇敵人時無論多謹慎都不為過。）

必閃陷阱 非學不可

Can not 現在僅被用於強調 not 的句子；問題是，喜歡用 can not （而不是 cannot） 來強調 NOT 的人還不在少數。不過，下句中的 can not 雖是兩個字，但卻是個完全正確、毫無爭議的句子，因為 **can not 並非 can't 的意思，這裡的 not 是 not only ... but (also) ... 這個相關字組的一部份**：Norma can not only sing but play the saxophone too.（諾瑪不僅能唱而且也能吹奏薩克斯風。）

茲將英文常見的縮寫字及其原形列表如下供大家參考：

縮寫	原形
aren't	are not
can't	cannot
couldn't	could not
didn't	did not
doesn't	does not
don't	do not
hadn't	had not
hasn't	has not
haven't	have not
he'd	he had, he would
he'll	he will, he shall
he's	he is, he has
I'd	I had, I would
I'll	I will, I shall
I'm	I am
I've	I have
isn't	is not
it's	it is, it has
let's	let us
mustn't	must not
shan't	shall not
she'd	she had, she would
she'll	she will, she shall
she's	she is, she has
shouldn't	should not
that's	that is, that has
there's	there is, there has
they'd	they had, they would
they'll	they will, they shall

Part I 文法常見錯誤

they're	they are
they've	they have
we'd	we had, we would
we're	we are
we've	we have
weren't	were not
what'll	what will, what shall
what're	what are
what's	what is, what has
what've	what have
where's	where is, where has
who'd	who had, who would
who'll	who will, who shall
who're	who are
who's	who is, who has
who've	who have
won't	will not
wouldn't	would not
you'd	you had, you would
you'll	you will, you shall
you're	you are
you've	you have

Unit 04　Content 還是 contents 呢？

必閃陷阱 非學不可

Content 主要當名詞和形容詞用，**用作名詞時有攸關對錯的單複數之分**，即 **content 和 contents**，因為兩者的意思和用法皆不同，使用時不**可不慎**。單數的 content 是個不可數名詞，意為「（文章、電影、電視節目、演講等的）內容）；（網站、光碟、隨身碟等的）內容」。例如：

◆ This film's adult **content** is not suitable for young children.（O）
◇ This film's adult contents are not suitable for young children.（×）
（這部電影的成人內容對兒童不宜。）

◆ Several well-known websites have closed down because of the high cost of producing original **content**.（O）
◇ Several well-known websites have closed down because of the high cost of producing original contents.（×）
（數個知名網站因製作原創內容的成本過高而關門大吉了。）

除上述意思外，**單數的 content 還意為「（物質）含量」**，但這個 content 卻是可數名詞，**只是要用單數，沒有複數型**。例如：

◆ Chocolate has a high fat **content**; it's not good for your health.（O）
◇ Chocolate has high fat contents; it's not good for your health.（×）
（巧克力的脂肪含量很高，對你的健康無益。）

◆ John usually eats a breakfast cereal with a high sugar **content**.（O）
◇ John usually eats a breakfast cereal with high sugar contents.（×）
（約翰經常吃含糖量很高的早餐麥片。）

◆ The vitamin and mineral **content** of fruit and vegetables is high.（O）
◇ The vitamin and mineral contents of fruit and vegetables are high.（×）
（蔬果的維生素和礦物質含量很高。）

複數型 contents 意為「（書籍或雜誌的）目錄；（書籍、雜誌、信件、文件等的）內容；所容納的東西，內容物」。例如：

◆ I can't find the chapter on K-pop in the **contents**. (○)

◇ I can't find the chapter on K-pop in the content. (×)

（我在目錄中找不到探討韓國流行音樂的那一章。）

◆ The **contents** of the document need to be revised substantially. (○)

◇ The content of the document needs to be revised substantially. (×)

（這份文件的內容需要大幅修訂。）

◆ The **contents** of the letter remain secret. (○)

◇ The content of the letter remains secret. (×)

（這封信的內容仍然保密。）

◆ Peter sold the apartment and its **contents**. (○)

◇ Peter sold the apartment and its content. (×)

（彼得把公寓和裡面的東西都賣了。）

◆ The **contents** of her handbag spilled all over the floor. (○)

◇ The content of her handbag spilled all over the floor. (×)

（她手提包裡的東西掉了一地。）

好用 Tips 非學不可 🔍

Content 亦可當形容詞用，意為「滿足的；滿意的」，但不可放在名詞之前修飾名詞，只能放在 BE 動詞及其他連綴動詞之後，其後通常接介系詞 with 或不定詞。例如：

1. Tom seems quite content with （his） life.
（湯姆似乎對生活很滿足。）

2. Benjamin was perfectly content with his work.
（班潔明對自己的工作十分滿意。）

3. Teresa seems fairly content to live with Bill.
（泰瑞莎好像相當滿意跟比爾生活在一起。）

Unit 05 Into, onto, up to

重要觀念 非學不可

有些人分不清楚 into 和 in to 的用法差異。**Into 有時等於 in to，但有時並不相等，須視其後的受詞而定**；onto 的情況亦然，而 up to 則比較容易處理，因為英文並無 upto 這個字。

當一個動詞與 in 所構成的片語動詞（phrasal verb）後接 to 時，in 和 to 要分開，如 hand in to, step in to, turn in to，因為這個 to 可能是不定詞，也可能是介系詞，但不管是不定詞還是介系詞，in 恆為副詞，而 into 和 onto 一定是介系詞。例如：

◆ John decided to hand the purse **in to** see if there was a reward.（O）
（約翰決定交出那個錢包，看看是否有獎賞。）
→ 就這句的 in to 而言，由於 to 後接動詞 see，所以 to 是不定詞。
◆ John decided to hand the purse **in to** the police.（O）
（約翰決定把那個錢包交給警方。）
→ 就這句的 in to 而言，由於 to 後接名詞 the police，所以 to 是介系詞。

必閃陷阱 非學不可

有些動詞既可接 in 亦可接 into，意思相似，如 dive in/into, fall in/into, put in/into；由此可知，這裡的 in 是介系詞而非副詞，因此其後往往不能再使用當介系詞用的 to。例如：

◆ Todd **dived in** the river to save a drowning girl.（O）
◆ Todd **dived into** the river to save a drowning girl.（O）
◇ Todd dived in to the river to save a drowning girl.（×）
（陶德跳入河中拯救一個快溺斃的女孩。）
◆ Todd **dived in** to test the water.（O）
（陶德跳入水中試水溫。）

◆ Fiona **put** the fruit **in** the basket.（O）
◆ Fiona **put** the fruit **into** the basket.（O）
◇ Fiona put the fruit in to the basket.（×）
（費歐娜把水果放入籃子裡。）

然而，turn into 有兩個意思，一為「（使）變成」（transform into），
如 The government is turning waste land into housing estates.（政府
正在使荒地變成住宅區）；另一為「進入」，即「走進，走入」（walk
into）或「駛入」（drive into），如 Jason turned into Avenue des
Champs-Élysées.（傑森走進了香榭麗舍大道。）這兩個意思有時會發
生模稜兩可的情況，以 The car turned into a garage. 為例，相信絕大多
數人都會理解為「車子開進車庫」，但如果有人堅持這句的意思是「車
子變成了車庫」，誰也不能說它錯了。為了避免 turn into 產生歧義，我
們往往把**表示「走進；駛入」意思的 turn into 寫成 turn in to**，但若句
意夠清楚，不改寫亦無妨。例如：：

◆ Jason **turned into** Avenue des Champs-Élysées.（O）
◆ The car **turned in to** a garage.（O）
（車子開進了車庫。）

◆ Jack **turned** the car **in to** the cul-de-sac.（O）
（傑克把車子開進了死胡同。）
→ 這裡用 turned into 也可以，不會產生歧義，因為車子不可能變成死胡同。
◆ The caterpillar **turned into** a butterfly.（O）
（毛毛蟲變成了蝴蝶。）

On to 和 onto 亦適用上述的規則，但必須注意的是，**onto 意為「到……
之上；向……之上」**。例如：

◆ The boy jumped **onto** the chair.（O）
（男孩跳到椅子上。）
◆ Sam walked **onto** the balcony slowly and then climbed onto the roof.（O）
（山姆慢慢地走到陽台上，然後爬到屋頂上。）

◇ More and more fans moved onto the concert.（×）
（越來越多的粉絲往演唱會的上方移動。）

◆ More and more fans moved **on to** the concert.（O）
（越來越多的粉絲往演唱會移動。）

好用 Tips 非學不可 🔍

Up to 和 upto 比較容易處理，因為**英文沒有 upto 這個字**；換言之，**up to 恆為兩個字**。例如：

◇ I can't afford upto 1,000 dollars.（×）
（我付不起多達 1,000 美元的金錢。）

→ upto 須改為 up to。

◆ Children are forced to work **up to** 16 hours a day, 7 days a week in that country.（O）
（那個國家的兒童被迫每週工作 7 天、每天工作長達 16 小時。）

Unit 06 No one 還是 no-one？

必閃陷阱 非學不可 🔍

No one 是正式拼法，沒有連字號。然而，近幾年來，no-one 的拼法變得越來越流行。一些文法學者和專家也許是審時度勢，也認為加連字號的 no-one 可消除在 No one person would take responsibility for bringing Mary home.（沒有一個人願意負責帶瑪麗回家。）這樣的句子中所造成的歧義。然而，這似乎言過其實，因為這種情況發生的可能性微乎其微。

儘管 no-one 不再被視為文法錯誤，但在此必須明確指出，正確的拼法是 no one。

此外，nobody 和 nowhere 都已變成單一個字，但 no one 還沒有。Noone 是錯誤的。

Unit 07　Who's 和 whose 的差異

必閃陷阱 非學不可

Who's 和 whose 的發音相同，但在英文中扮演截然不同的角色。不過，有些人還是三不五時會被這兩個常用詞所搞混，令人遺憾。**Who's 為 who is 或 who has 的縮寫，**而 **whose 為 who 的所有格**，通常位在名詞前面，但它還可用作關係代名詞。

Who's 的例句：

◆ **Who's** coming to fix the computer?（○）
（誰來修理電腦？）

→ Who's = who is。

◆ **Who's** Mary talking about?（○）
（瑪麗正在說誰？）

→ Who's = who is。

◆ **Who's** eaten the last apple?（○）
（誰吃了最後一個蘋果？）

→ Who's = who has。

◆ **Who's** John brought to my class?（○）
（約翰帶誰來上我的課？）

→ Who's = who has。

◇ Whose John brought to my class?（×）

◆ You'll soon know **who's** who in this department.（○）
（你很快就會知道這個部門裡面誰是誰。）

→ who's = who is。

註：Who's who 也是個片語，意為「名人錄；（總稱）名人」，用作單數，如 a who's who of the fashion industry（時裝界的名人錄）。

然而，在極為輕鬆的非正式場合或在隨意的書寫中，who's 還被用作 who does 的縮寫，如 Who's he mean?（他指的是誰？）。這與 What does that mean? 被說成或寫成 What's that mean? 的情況一樣。儘管這樣的說法或寫法不合文法（因為 Who's = Who is 或 Who has，而 What's = What is 或 What has），但卻是習慣用法。

Whose 的例句：

◆ **Whose** smartphone was stolen?（O）
（誰的智慧型手機被偷？）

→ Whose 位在名詞 smartphone 之前。

◇ Who's smartphone was stolen?（×）

◆ I know **whose** smartphone was stolen.（O）
（我知道誰的智慧型手機被偷。）

→ Whose 位在名詞 smartphone 之前。

◆ I know the girl **whose** smartphone was stolen.
（我認識那位智慧型手機被偷的女孩。）

→ Whose 位在名詞 smartphone 之前。

◆ **Whose** car is this?（O）
（這是誰的車子？）

→ Whose 位在名詞 car 之前。

◇ Who's car is this?（×）

◆ **Whose** is this car?（O）
（這是誰的車子？／這部車子是誰的？）

→ 在本例中，whose 為關係代名詞。

◆ I'm not quite sure **whose** Cindy will prefer.（O）
（我不是很確定辛蒂會比較喜歡誰的。）

→ 在本例中，whose 為關係代名詞。

Unit 08 句子開頭的數字

重要觀念 非學不可

句子若以阿拉伯數字做開頭，儘管沒有錯，但被視為凌亂、不整齊，應該避免。因此，我們須**改寫句子**或**將阿拉伯數字寫成英文字**。例如：

1. 93 people have been reported dead after a magnitude 7.2 earthquake hit the central Philippines.
（據報導，在菲律賓中部發生規模 7.2 的強震後，已經有 93 人死亡。）
→（句子沒有錯，但不整齊。）

2. It is reported that 93 people have been dead after a magnitude 7.2 earthquake hit the central Philippines.
→（改寫句子後變得比較整齊。）

3. Ninety-three people have been reported dead after a magnitude 7.2 earthquake hit the central Philippines.
→（用英文字來寫可避免句子以阿拉伯數字做開頭。）

好用 Tips 非學不可

若數字含有小數點後的位數，則不用英文拼寫。

如果**數字含有小數點**，若無法改寫句子，則**不必用英文拼寫出來**，否則情況會變得更糟。例如：

◆ **58.43**% of people add decimal places to make their statistics look more credible. （○）
◇ Fifty-eight point forty-three per cent of people add decimal places to make their statistics look more credible. （×）
（百分之五十八點四三的人會加上小數點後的位數來使其統計數字看起來更可信。）

Unit 09　複合名詞的複數

必閃陷阱 非學不可

當複合名詞（compound nouns）中的字是由連字號結合在一起（如 daughter-in-law, forget-me-not）或者當複合名詞是由兩個或以上的字（如 dry dock, lieutenant colonel）所構成時，該**複合名詞通常是以在其主要字後面加 s 的方式來構成複數**。若複合名詞中沒有主要字或者複合名詞為單一個字（如 banknote, paperclip），那麼**一般的規則是在該複合名詞的後面加 s 來構成複數**。例如：

1. Wendy now has two sons-in-law.
（溫蒂現有兩個女婿。）

→ son-in-law 的複數是在主要字 son 的後面加 s。

2. They were the Knights Templar.
（他們都是聖殿戰士。）

→ Knight Templar 的複數是在主要字 Knight 的後面加 s。

3. Their parents are all lieutenant colonels.
（他們的父母都是陸軍中校。）

→ lieutenant colonel 的複數是在主要字 colonel 的後面加 s。

4. There are now still some courts-martial in Taiwan.
（台灣現在仍有若干軍事法庭。）

→ court-martial 的複數是在主要字 court 的後面加 s（事實上，由於有不少人認為 martial 是 court-martial 的主要字，在其後加 s 來構成複數，因此 courts-martial 或 court-martials 都可以。）

5. There are seven forget-me-nots on the table.
（桌上有七朵勿忘草。）

6. Could you please pass me two paperclips?
（請遞給我兩支迴紋針好嗎？）

好用 Tips 非學不可 🔍

當複合名詞是以「字 of 字」（如 bottle of wine）的型態出現時，**第一個字永遠是該複合名詞的主要字**。例如：

◇ I bought Bruce two can of beers, but he only drank one.（✕）
（我買給布魯斯兩罐啤酒，但他只喝了一罐。）

→ 應為 two cans of beer。

◇ Diana drank three cup of coffees last night.（✕）
（戴安娜昨晚喝了三杯咖啡。）

→ 應為 three cups of coffee。

當複合名詞是以「[容器]ful」（如 bucketful, cupful, handful）的型態出現時，該複合名詞是在 -ful 的後面加 s 來構成複數。例如：

◇ There were three spoonsful of peanut butter left in the jar.（✕）
（瓶裡還剩下三匙花生醬。）

→ 應為 three spoonfuls。

◆ Two **spoonfuls** of sugar, please.（O）
（請放兩匙糖。）

◆ Please sprinkle two **handfuls** of corn on the porch for the chickens.（O）
（請在走廊撒兩把穀粒給雞吃。）

Unit 10 駕照是 driver's license、driver's licence、driving licence 還是 driving license 呢？

必閃陷阱 非學不可 🔍

◆ Your **driver's license** is invalid in Japan.（O）
◆ Your **driving licence** is invalid in Japan.（O）
◇ Your driver's licence is invalid in Japan.（✕）→ （在澳洲，這是正確的）
◇ Your driving license is invalid in Japan.（✕）
（你的駕照在日本無效。）

License 這個字可當名詞和動詞用，前者主要意為「許可證，執照，牌照」，後者意為「許可，准許；發許可證給」。**在美國，名詞和動詞都使用 license，但在英國，license 僅當動詞用，名詞是用 licence。在美國，licence 這個字是不存在的。**

駕駛執照在美國叫做 driver's license，在英國叫做 driving licence。所以，不管你是遵循美國還是英國的書寫慣例，driver's licence 和 driving license 都是錯誤的寫法。不過，在前英國殖民地的澳洲，駕照是叫做 **driver's licence**。

車輛牌照在美國是 **license plate**，在英國是 **licence plate** 或 number plate；牌照號碼或車牌號碼在美國通常用 license plate number 來表示，而英國是用 registration 或 registration number（口語叫做 reg）來表示。所以，當你在某一網路字典看到 licence plate 被注釋為「主美」（主要為美國用法）時，「你肯定會驚呆了」、「讓人笑噴了」。例如：

1. You can't get a driver's license until you're eighteen in this country.
（在這個國家，18 歲才能考駕照。）

2. Have you got any identification? A driving licence will do.
（你有什麼身份證明嗎？駕照就可以。）

3. Simon lost his driver's license after being caught drunk driving.
（賽蒙酒駕被抓到後被吊銷了駕照。）

4. Simon lost his driving licence after being caught drink-driving.
→「酒後駕車」在美國叫做 drunk driving，在英國叫做 drink-driving。

Note

Part I
文法常見錯誤

Chapter 4

其他文法
須注意事項

Chapter 4 | 其它文法須注意事項

Unit 01 E.g. 和 i.e. 的差異

必閃陷阱 非學不可

E.g. 是拉丁文 exempli gratia (= **for example** 的縮寫，意為「**例如；譬如說**」，而 **i.e.** 是拉丁文 id est (= that is, in other words) 的縮寫，意為「**亦即；換言之**」。由於它們都是用來引導補充資料來解釋或說明前面提到的事物，這兩個常用的縮寫字經常被搞混。

E.g. 是用來舉例說明。例如：

◆ Mary is so obese that she must avoid taking sweet foods, **e.g.**, cake, chocolate, and ice cream.（O）
（瑪麗過胖，她必需避免吃甜食，諸如蛋糕、巧克力和冰淇淋。）

◆ John was the school champion of many sports (**e.g.**, badminton, table tennis, javelin, and long jump).（O）
（約翰是學校許多運動（譬如說，羽毛球、桌球、標槍和跳遠）的冠軍。）

I.e. 是用來更清楚地、更明確地重述某個概念或提供更多資訊。例如：

◆ The traffic accident happened in May, **i.e.**, three months ago.（O）
◇ The traffic accident happened in May, e.g., three months ago.（×）
（這起車禍發生在五月，亦即三個月前。）

◆ Service charge is included in all prices; **i.e.**, you don't have to leave a tip.（O）
（服務費已含在所有價格中；換言之，你不必給小費。）

有時同一個句子**既可用 e.g. 亦可用 i.e.**，兩者的語法都正確，只是句意不同。例如：

◆All amphibians are thriving in the new pond; **e.g.**, the two bullfrogs were being very active yesterday.（O）
（新池塘裡的所有兩棲動物都生機盎然；譬如說，這兩隻牛蛙昨天活繃亂跳。）
→ 這句的文法毫無瑕疵。我們從這句推論出，池塘裡除了兩隻牛蛙外還有其他兩棲動物。

◆All amphibians are thriving in the new pond; **i.e.**, the two bullfrogs were being very active yesterday.

（新池塘裡的所有兩棲動物都生機盎然；也就是說，這兩隻牛蛙昨天活繃亂跳。）

→ 這句的文法也是一點問題都沒有。我們從這句推論出，池塘裡僅有的兩棲動物就是這兩隻牛蛙。

好用 Tips 非學不可 🔍

必須注意的是，e.g. 或 i.e. 有幾種廣為接受的格式。

E.g. 或 i.e. 之前使用逗點

◆ He has studied a variety of topics, **e.g.**, crime, disaster, hypnotism, black magic. （○）

（他已研究了各式各樣的主題，諸如犯罪、災難、催眠術、巫術。）

→ 注意：如果 e.g. 或 i.e. 之前使用逗點，那麼其後就不能接子句，否則就會犯了兩個句子之間沒有連接詞而是用逗點來當連接詞的「逗點謬誤」(comma fault or run-on error)。不過，只要將逗點換成分號，就可避免這種錯誤。

E.g. 或 i.e. 之前使用分號

◆ He has studied a variety of topics; **e.g.**, he has studied crime, disaster, hypnotism, and black magic. （○）

（他已研究了各式各樣的主題；譬如說，他已研究了犯罪、災難、催眠術和巫術。）

→ 當 e.g. 或 i.e. 後面接子句時，其前最常使用分號。

E.g. 或 i.e. 置於括號內

◆ He has studied a variety of topics (**e.g.**, crime, disaster, hypnotism, black magic). （○）

（他已研究了各式各樣的主題（諸如犯罪、災難、催眠術、巫術。））

E.g. 或 i.e. 之後是否使用逗點？

在美國，e.g. 或 i.e. 之後通常有逗點；在英國，e.g. 或 i.e. 之後往往不用逗點。這兩種寫法都可接受，但最高指導原則是：**整篇文章都要一致。**

E.g. 之後別使用 etc.

E.g. 之後所舉的例子通常是一份比較完整的實例清單中的幾個而已,所以在 **e.g. 之後使用 etc.(等等)被認為不恰當**,因為一般都知道它們只是其中部分例子而已。在下句中,e.g. 的用法正確,但 **etc. 是贅詞、是多餘的**:

He directed a lot of film genres, e.g., crime, science fiction, comedy, horror films, etc.

(他導演過許多電影類型,諸如犯罪片、科幻片、喜劇片、恐怖片等等。)

Unit 02 East, west, south, north 不大寫

必閃陷阱 非學不可

East, west, south 和 north 這四個方向字通常不大寫,除非它們是專有名詞的一部份,如 North Korea(北韓)、South Africa(南非)等等。例如:

◆ Go **west** then **south**.(O)
(向西走,然後往南走。)
→ 順便一提,go west 也是個片語,意為「完蛋;歸西,上西天」。
◇ Take ten paces North and then dig.(×)
(朝北走十步,然後挖下去。)
◆ Professor Park is from **South Korea**.(O)
(朴教授來自南韓。)
◇ There are no penguins at the north pole.(×)
(北極沒有企鵝。)
→ 北極為專有名詞,英文為 the North Pole。

值得注意的是，地理區域 **The East**（東方國家，亞洲國家；美國東部）、**The West**（西方國家，歐美國家；美國西部）、**The South**（南半球；南半球經濟不發達國家；南極地區；美國南部各州）和 **The North**（北半球；北半球經濟發達國家；北極地區；美國北部各州）**被視為專有名詞，應該大寫。**

The East, The West, The South 和 The North 中的 The 是否要大寫，意見並不一致。少數人認為它們指的地區就叫做 The East ... 不是 East ...，所以 The 要大寫，但許多人認為這跟一般的用法或習慣不一樣，The 看起來有些奇怪。例如：

◆ James comes from The **South**.（O）
◆ James comes from **the South**.（O）
（詹姆斯來自南半球國家。）

好用 Tips 非學不可

某個地名是否為正式名稱，有時會引發爭議，連帶地會使**是否大寫**的問題變得更複雜。譬如說，有些人認為「北高雄」並非被正式認可的地區，所以它不是專有名詞，英文不應該寫成 North Kaohsiung。問題是，「北高雄」的地理位置深植人心，North 大寫也沒有什麼不對。另外，純粹從美學的觀點來看，North Kaohsiung 比 north Kaohsiung 好看多了。不過，如果您謹小慎微，不想出任何差錯，那麼可以寫成 northern Kaohsiung，或者更保險地寫成 **the northern region of Kaohsiung**（高雄北區。）

Unit 03 句子開頭的副詞片語或子句應使用逗點與主要子句隔開

必閃陷阱 非學不可

一個句子若以副詞片語或子句做開頭，那麼**該副詞片語或子句的後面應使用逗點來與主要主句（即獨立子句）隔開**。儘管有人認為可以不用，但使用逗點的主要目的是要讓句子**易讀易懂**，對於句意的正確傳達有很大的助益。不過，若句子的開頭並非副詞片語或子句，而是**一個字的副詞**（如 Now, Today, Here 等），那麼它們的**後面通常不用逗點**。例如：

◆ **In the center of Taipei,** a lot of people fell victim to pickpockets.（O）
（在台北市中心，許多人遭到扒竊。）

◆ **On Wednesday 2nd December,** Jack broke up with his girlfriend.（O）
◇ On Wednesday 2nd December Jack broke up with his girlfriend.（×）
（12 月 2 日星期三，傑克跟他女友分手。）

◆ **When I was a kid,** I would always swim in the sea.（O）
（小時候我常常在海中游泳。）

◆ **After Jack had broken up with his girlfriend,** he suffered from depression.（O）
（傑克跟他女友分手後得了憂鬱症。）

◆ **Here** they disagree with us.（O）
（在這一點上，他們和我們看法不同。）

◆ **Yesterday** Jack saw his ex-girlfriend having dinner with a man **in a restaurant.**（O）
（昨天傑克看見他前女友和一名男子在一家餐廳共進晚餐。）

然而，若**副詞片語或子句位在句末**，則**無須使用逗點**。例如：

◆ A lot of people fell victim to pickpockets **in the center of Taipei**.（O）
◆ Jack broke up with his girlfriend **on Wednesday 2nd December**.（O）
◆ I would always swim in the sea **when I was a kid**.（O）
◆ Jack suffered from depression **after he had broken up with his girlfriend**.（O）

副詞片語亦可能位在**句子中間**，此時它們**前後都可使用逗點**，但通常不用。例如：

◆ I'm not my parents' biological son. My father, **on his deathbed**, told me the truth.（O）
◆ I'm not my parents' biological son. My father **on his deathbed** told me the truth.（O）
（我不是我父母親生的兒子。我父親臨終時告訴了我真相。）

好用 Tips 非學不可 🔍

值得注意的是，若**句子開頭是修飾主要子句主詞的分詞片語**，那麼其後**一定要有逗點**。例如：

◆ **Having read our petition**, the principal has decided to meet with us.（O）
◇ Having read our petition the principal has decided to meet with us.（×）
（看了我們的陳情書之後，校長已決定和我們會晤。）

◆ **Disappointed almost to the point of tears**, I have decided not to talk politics at all from now on.（O）
◇ Disappointed almost to the point of tears I have decided not to talk politics at all from now on.（×）
（失望到幾近落淚的程度，我已決定從此完全不談政治。）

Unit 04 四季不大寫

必閃陷阱 非學不可 🔍

四季的英文通常不大寫，除非它們是專有名詞的一部份。不過，根據一項古早的規則， spring, summer, autumn/fall, winter **若被擬人化，則它們應該大寫。** 例如：

◆ I enjoy the feeling of being kissed by **Winter**'s icy breath.（O）
（我喜歡被冬天冰冷氣息親吻的感覺。）

→ Winter 擬人化，所以大寫。

◆ Where are you going this **winter**?（O）
（今年冬天你要去哪裡？）

→ winter 未擬人化，應小寫。

◆ The closer **Autumn**'s step is, the more the falling leaves are.（O）
（秋天的腳步越近，落葉也越多。）

→ Autumn 擬人化，所以大寫。

◆ The trees were all the colors of **autumn**.（O）
（這些樹木一片秋色。）

→ autumn 未擬人化，應小寫。

◇ It was a cold, sunny day in early Spring.（×）
（那是早春裡寒冷而陽光燦爛的一天。）

→ spring 未擬人化，所以應小寫。

好用 Tips 非學不可 🔍

然而，不管是否擬人化，現今大多數人對於**春夏秋冬都不大寫，除非它們是專有名詞的一部份**。例如：

1. I came across a famous singer at the Summer Palace, a nightclub.
（我在一家名叫「夏宮」的夜店遇見一位名歌手。）

2. The Prague Spring refers to a period of political liberalization in Czechoslovakia.
（「布拉格之春」是指捷克斯洛伐克的一個政治自由化時期。）

→ Czechoslovakia 現已分為兩個國家：捷克共和國 (Czech Republic) 和斯洛伐克共和國 (Slovak Republic or Slovakia)。

Unit 05 用引號來表示「所謂的」概念

重要觀念 非學不可

引號 (quotation marks) 可用來表示「所謂的」、「聲稱的」或「據稱的」(so-called, alleged, supposed) 概念。在英式英語中，引號叫做 inverted commas（倒置或顛倒的逗號），包括雙引號和單引號。例如：

◆ Miranda's "boyfriend" got married to another girl a few days ago.（O）
（米蘭達所謂的男友幾天前和另一名女子結婚了。）

→ "boyfriend" = so-called boyfriend。

◆ Much to Mary's surprise, they offered her the "job."（O）
（令瑪麗甚為驚訝的是，他們竟然給了她那份所謂的工作。）

→ 在本例中，引號扮演兩個角色，一是對說話者的直接引述 (direct speech) 或引述原話 (quoted speech)；另一是表示「所謂的工作」(so-called job) 的概念。

◆ His "friends" all disappeared when he was in trouble.
= His friends, in quotation marks, all disappeared when he was in trouble.
= His friends, in inverted commas, all disappeared when he was in trouble.（O）
（當他陷入困境時，他那些所謂的朋友全都不見了。）

必閃陷阱 非學不可

「所謂的」是在表示用來描述某人或某物的字詞只是其通常的名稱，**並非一般所認為的意思**，因此，**引號亦可用來表示該字詞並非字面上的意思**。這經常用於擬人化的情況。例如：

◆ Tony's girlfriend wants him to dress as a superhero and "rescue" her.（O）
（東尼的女友要他穿得像超級英雄一樣來「拯救」她。）

→ rescue 並非真正的拯救。

◆ The breeze "kissed" my face when I was lying on the grass.
（當我躺在草地時，微風「親吻」我的臉。）

→ 顯然地，微風不會親吻。引號用來傳達「非字面意思」的概念。

由於**引號可用來表示「所謂的，聲稱的」(so-called, alleged)** 概念，所以**若使用引號來表示此一概念，那麼就無需再使用這些字**，否則疊床架屋，將**造成贅述 (tautology)**，應予避免。例如：

◇ Miranda's so-called "boyfriend" got married to another girl a few days ago.（×）

→ 在本例中，so-called 和引號連用是一種贅述；它們僅能擇一使用。

◆ Miranda's **so-called** boyfriend got married to another girl a few days ago.（O）

◆ Miranda's "boyfriend" got married to another girl a few days ago.（O）

好用 Tips 非學不可 🔍

切勿使用引號來做強調。例如：

◇ I enjoy "fresh" fish.（×）
（我喜歡吃所謂新鮮的魚。）

◇ This is a "very clean" Italian restaurant.（×）
（這是一家所謂非常乾淨的義大利餐廳。）

Unit 06　在書信稱呼中，Dear 後面不可有逗點，而 Hello 後面要有逗點

必閃陷阱 非學不可 ●

Dear 後面不可有逗點

若在書信或電子郵件的開頭使用 Dear 這個字，則其後不可有逗號或逗點 (comma)。但**在整個稱呼之後須用逗點**。例如：

1.

Dear Steven,

Thanks for buying me a coffee last night.
（感謝你昨晚請我喝咖啡。）

2.

Dear Sir,

Thank you for your sincere assistance.
（感謝您竭誠的協助。）

在非常正式的情況中，稱呼之後可以使用冒號 (colon)。例如：

1.

Dear Mr Chen:

I regret to inform you that your application has been declined.
（我遺憾地通知您，您的申請已遭到拒絕。）

2.

Dear Professor:

Thank you once again for hosting our seminar.
（再次感謝您主持我們的研討會。）

Hello 或 Hi 後面要有逗點

然而，**若書信或電子郵件的開頭是使用 Hello 或 Hi，則其後**——也就是你所稱呼的人名之前——**要有逗點**。而在你所稱呼的人名之後同樣也要有個逗點，這亦是標準慣例。例如：

1.
Hi, Steven,

Thanks for buying me a coffee last night.

2.
Hello, Sir,

Thank you for your sincere assistance.

在這種使用 Hello 或 Hi 的非正式情況中,使用冒號來代替逗點並沒有錯,但顯得很奇怪。你也可以使用驚嘆號 (exclamation mark) 來強調某種情緒(如驚訝)。

好用 Tips 非學不可

雖然你所稱呼的人名之後絕大多數情況是用逗點,**但信件內容第一句的開頭仍須大寫**(見上面的例句)。這似乎不合文法,但慣例就是這樣。這就是為什麼有些人比較喜歡**使用冒號而不用逗點**的原因。然而,使用逗點還是**目前**沛然莫之能禦**的主流**,不必因噎廢食。

Unit 07 在商業寫作中,company 和 manager 等普通名詞可以大寫

必閃陷阱 非學不可

根據英文規則,專有名詞 (proper nouns) 要大寫(如 Paul, Microsoft, Pacific Ocean, Taipei 101, One Direction),但普通名詞 (common nouns) 不可大寫(如 cat, dog, bus, ship, book, people, women),除非它們位在句子開頭第一個字。**即使某個普通名詞在句中特別重要,亦不可因此將該字大寫,否則就違反了這個規則**。例如:

◇ We value our Clients' opinions.(×)
(我們重視顧客的意見。)
→ client 為普通名詞,不可大寫。

◇ I have their latest Brochure on vacations abroad.（╳）
（我有他們最新的國外度假指南。）
→ brochure 為普通名詞，不可大寫。

然而，在**商業寫作中**，基於禮貌，將**若干普通名詞大寫**（如 Company, Manager 等）被視為**是一項很好的作法**。當然了，您亦**可選擇不大寫**。例如：

◆ The manager of your **company** placed an order in email on July 15.（○）
◆ The Manager of your **Company** placed an order in email on July 15.（○）
（貴公司經理七月 15 日在電子郵件中下了訂單。）

好用 Tips 非學不可 🔍

基本上，**職稱和部門名稱都可大寫**。至於其他在商業寫作中重要到足以讓我們給予大寫的普通名詞，還有 Director, President, Commanding Officer, Division, Court, Regiment 和 Unit 等。例如：

◆ The **director** will make the final decision.（○）
◆ The **Director** will make the final decision.（○）
◇ The Director will make the final Decision.（╳）
（這位董事將做最後的決定。）

Unit 08　時間名詞中的所有格符號

必閃陷阱 非學不可

當**時間名詞為單數時**，所有格符號 (apostrophe) (') 係加在 s 的前面，即 's，如 one day's wage（一天的工資），the week's proceeds（本週的收入），today's young people（今日的年輕人），this evening's storm（今晚的暴風雨）。若**時間名詞為複數，則所有格符號加在 s 的後面**，即 s'，如 two days' wage（兩天的工資），3 years' salary（三年的薪水）。例如：

◆ It's only about **an hour's drive** from here.（○）
（從這裡開車只要約一小時的路程。）

◆ The system crashed and Gordon lost **three hours' work**.（○）
（系統突然當機，戈登白幹了三個小時的工作。）

◆ Please give me **a week's notice** if you're planning to move to Taipei.（○）
（如果你打算搬到台北，請提前一週通知我。）

◆ The diamond engagement ring cost me **three months'** salary.（○）
（這個訂婚鑽戒花了我三個月的薪水。）

◇ Applicants should have at least three year's practical experience.（×）
（申請人至少要有三年的實務經驗。）

→ 所有格符號應放在 s 的後面。

◇ After a days' wait, I saw the doctor.（×）
（等了一天之後，我見到了醫生。）

→ 所有格符號應放在 s 的前面。

好用 Tips 非學不可

這種所有格亦可用 of 結構來表示，因此時間名詞為複數時的所有格符號 (') 或時間名詞為單數時的 's，可用 of 來代替，如 **5 days' leave = 5 days of leave**（五天的休假）；**a year's wait = a year of wait**（一年的等待）。

當時間名詞的後面沒有所屬的名詞時，**該時間名詞無論單複數都不可加上所有格符號**。例如：

◇ Shirley has worked for that big company for more than one year'. （×）
（雪莉已為那家大公司工作了超過一年。）
◇ I've been waiting here for two hours'. （×）
（我已在這裡等了兩個鐘頭。）
→ 這句若用 of 結構來代替就變成 I've been waiting here for two hours of. ，顯然錯得離譜。

除了時間名詞外，距離、長度、價值、重量等名詞亦可使用這種以 apostrophe 來表示的所有格結構，如 two hours' walk/flight/drive（兩小時的步行或路程／飛行／車程），a cable's length（電纜的長度），a dollar's worth (of apples)（價值一元的蘋果），two tons' weight（兩噸重）。

Unit 09 連接詞前面使用逗點的時機

重要觀念 非學不可

And, or 或 but 等連接詞 (conjunctions) 的前面何時使用逗點（或逗號），並無一定的規則可資遵循。

使用逗點來結合兩個獨立子句 (independent clauses)

當兩個獨立子句使用 and, or 或 but 等連接詞來結合時，該連接詞的前面應使用逗點。例如：

◆ Sophia loves music, **but** Mary loves dance. （○）
（蘇菲雅愛好音樂，但瑪麗喜愛舞蹈。）
→ Sophia loves music. 和 Mary loves dance. 這兩句使用連接詞 but 來結合成一句，but 前面應有逗點。

◆ I have called Cindy, **and** she has confirmed the date of the meeting. （○）
（我已打電話給辛蒂，而她已確認會議的日期。）
→ 連接詞 and 前面有逗點是正確的。

◇ I have called Cindy, and confirmed the date of the meeting. （ ✕ ）
（我已打電話給辛蒂並確認了會議的日期。）
→ 連接詞 and 前面不應有逗點，因為 "confirmed the date of the meeting" 不是句子。這只是將 "called Cindy" 和 "confirmed the date of the meeting" 這兩個項目列在一起。

◆ His sister's had an accident at work, **and** she's had to go to hospital. （○）
（他妹妹在工作時發生事故，必須去醫院治療。）

◆ We had dinner **and** then went to the movies. （○）
（我們吃了晚餐後就去看電影。）
→ 沒有逗點是正確的。

必閃陷阱 非學不可

別用逗點來結合兩個列在一起的項目
當有兩個項目被列在一起時，無須使用逗點來將它們分開。例如：

◆ Pajamas and slippers （○）
（睡衣和拖鞋）
◆ I want to eat pizza and ice cream now. （○）
（我現在想吃披薩和冰淇淋。）
◇ My wife has never been to Tokyo, or Seoul. （ ✕ ）
（我太太從未去過東京或首爾。）
→ 兩個項目列在一起無須使用逗點。

三個或三個以上的項目列在一起時，美國人會在連接詞的前面使用逗點，但英國人則不用逗點。

當有三個或三個以上的項目被列在一起時，情況會變得比較複雜，因為一般而言，**美國人習慣在連接詞的前面使用逗點，但英國人則否**。例如：

◆ Pajamas, slippers, and T-shirts（○）
（睡衣、拖鞋和 T 恤）（美國）
◇ Pajamas, slippers, and T-shirts（×）
（睡衣、拖鞋和 T 恤）（英國）
◆ Pajamas, slippers and T-shirts（○）
（睡衣、拖鞋和T恤）（英國）

My wife has never been to Tokyo, Seoul, or Bangkok.
（我太太從未去過東京、首爾或曼谷。）（美國──○）（英國──×）

然而，上述這兩個慣例在美英兩國都未受到嚴格的遵循。儘管這一逗點問題在文法學者之間引發頗大的爭論，但大多數專家或學者都建議，為了使文意更加清晰明白，在寫作時隨時可以打破自己所遵循的慣例，但要選擇一個最不會引起教授、老闆或讀者不快的慣例來遵循，而且**整篇文章從頭至尾都要一致**。

Unit
10

單引號和雙引號的用法

重要觀念 非學不可

在**使用引號時，美國人習慣使用雙引號** (double quotation marks)，而英國人使用單引號 (single quotation marks)。例如：

◆ John said that he was "very angry."（○）
◆ John said that he was 'very angry'.（○）
（約翰說他「很生氣」。）

因此，就**美式英語而言，一般都是先使用雙引號，若該引號內還需要引號，則使用單引號**。例如：

◆ Julian asked me: "Would you like to see 'Fast & Furious 7'?"（○）
（朱利安問我：「你想看《玩命關頭7》嗎？」）

◆ Mary asked Henry: "Do you have lyrics to 'Radioactive' by Imagine Dragons?"（○）
（瑪麗問亨利：「你有 Imagine Dragons 樂團所唱的《Radioactive》的歌詞嗎？」）

◆ The professor said: "This course uses two books. The first is Howard Jackson's 'Lexicography' and the second is 'Language Assessment' by H. Douglas Brown."（○）
（教授說：「本課程使用兩本書。第一本是 Howard Jackson 所著的《Lexicography》，第二本是 H. Douglas Brown 所著的《Language Assessment》」）

◇ The professor said: "This course uses two books. The first is Howard Jackson's "Lexicography" and the second is "Language Assessment" by H. Douglas Brown."（×）
→ 將這句標示錯誤是有點嚴苛，因為有些人認為這樣也可以。

必閃陷阱 非學不可

然而，大家一致公認的規則是，在**同一層級，單引號和雙引號不可混合使用**。例如：

◇ The professor said: "This course uses two books. The first is Howard Jackson's 'Lexicography' and the second is "Language Assessment" by H. Douglas Brown."（×）

註：在句子中，書籍、報紙、雜誌、報告、文學與藝術作品、詩詞、戲劇、電影和電視節目的名稱，通常以**引號**或**斜體字**來區隔。

因此，上述的 Fast & Furious 7、Lexicography 和 Language Assessment 亦可用斜體字而不用引號，即 *Fast & Furious 7*、*Lexicography* 和 *Language Assessment*。相對地，就英式英語而言，一般都是先使用單引號，若該引號內還需要引號，則使用雙引號。例如：

◆ Julian asked me: 'Would you like to see "Fast & Furious 7"?' （〇）
◆ Mary asked Henry: 'Do you have lyrics to "Radioactive" by Imagine Dragons?' （〇）

好用 Tips 非學不可 🔍

由於英美的引號用法並不一致，著名的文體指南有的建議雙引號內使用單引號，有的則建議單引號內使用雙引號。不過，**視寫作者的個人偏好而定**，不管採用何種寫法，整篇文章或**整份文件須保持一致**。例如：

◆Does anyone know what the difference between "soon" and "when" is? （〇）
◆Does anyone know what the difference between 'soon' and 'when' is? （〇）
◇Does anyone know what the difference between "soon" and 'when' is? （×）
（有人知道「soon」和「when」之間有什麼不同嗎？）

Unit 11　廣告中的大寫

重要觀念 非學不可 🔍

從文法觀點來看，普通名詞大寫是錯誤的，如果這是出現在商業書信中，有可能會嚇走您的客戶（請看下面的「文法錯誤可能讓您損失慘重」），但大寫可以吸睛、凸顯訴求，因此**在廣告（和招牌）中使用大寫是可以接受的**，因為它會使廣告更有效果。例如：

◆ Our company offers valuable **Mortgage Tips**.（O）
（本公司提供寶貴的房貸訣竅。）

→ 我們沒有任何文法理由可以將 Mortgage 的 M 及 Tips 的 T 大寫，只有在廣告中才可以這麼做。

◆ Eat our **Pineapple Cakes** and get **Thinner**.（O）
（吃我們的鳳梨酥可以變得更苗條。）

→ 只有在廣告中，P、C 和 T 才可以大寫。

◆ Kids **Eat FREE**.（O）
（兒童免費吃。）

→ 只有在廣告中，E 和 FREE 才可以大寫。

文法錯誤可能讓您損失慘重

根據一項對美國商務人士所做的調查，三分之一的受調者表示，他們不會跟拼寫和文法差勁的公司做生意。

在美國，因為書寫不佳所造成的營收損失，估計一年高達 2,000 億美元以上。在英國，據「皇家郵政」(Royal Mail) 公司表示，寫得「零零落落」的商業書信使企業一年損失逾 400 億英鎊的營業額。

Unit 12

複合主詞可用逗點跟主動詞分開

重要觀念 非學不可

在英文中，**主詞跟動詞之間不可用逗點分開**，尤其是短句，否則就犯了大錯。例如：

◇ John, is such a lazybones.（✕）
（約翰真是個懶骨頭。）

→ 主詞 John 跟動詞 is 之間不可有逗點。

即使是**不定詞或動名詞片語當句子的主詞，該主詞及其主動詞之間也不可有逗點**。例如：

◇ To believe in one's self, is a good thing.（×）
（相信自己是件好事。）
◇ Believing completely and positively in oneself, is essential for success.（×）
（完全且堅決地相信自己，對成功至關重要。）

必閃陷阱 非學不可

然而，當句子的主詞含有兩個或多個名詞、代名詞、名詞片語和名詞子句時，有時為了協助讀者閱讀，我們可以在這種所謂的**「複合主詞」(compound subject) 後面加上逗點**，使其跟主動詞分開。

但要注意的是，複合主詞有長有短，即使是**短的複合主詞**，或者謂語（predicate，指一個句子中，主詞以外的其餘部分）太短，亦**不能有逗點**。例如：

◇ My wife and I, cannot go to your birthday party tomorrow.（×）
（我太太跟我明天不能參加你的生日派對。）
◇ Cats and dogs, are animals.（×）
（貓和狗都是動物。）
◇ A clean driver's license, working 12 hours a day and team spirit, are essential.（×）
（無違規記錄的駕照、一天工作 12 小時及團隊精神至關重要。）
→ 這句謂語部分 "are essential" 太短，不適合用逗點跟主詞分開。

只有長複合主詞才適合使用逗點來告訴讀者主詞結束的地方。不過，並非所有文法學者都認為這項作法是必要的。例如：

◆ **A clean driver's license, working 12 hours a day and 5 years' sales experience**, are the only criteria stipulated by the selection panel.（O）

（無違規記錄的駕照、一天工作 12 小時及 5 年的行銷經驗，是選拔小組規定的唯一遴選標準。）

◆ **Increasing your life insurance, listing Internet passwords and making a will**, will give you peace of mind while you are on operations.（O）

（提高壽險保額、列出網路密碼及立下遺囑，會讓你在動手術時心平氣和。）

◆ **Armed robbery, murder, assault and battery, disorderly conduct, larceny, theft, rape, sexual assault and other misdemeanors and felonies**, have increased dramatically in recent years.（O）

（近年來，武裝搶劫、殺人、暴力攻擊、擾亂治安、竊盜、偷竊、強暴、性侵及其他輕罪和重罪，都急遽增加。）

Unit 13　複合形容詞

重要觀念 非學不可

複合形容詞 (compound adjectives) 是由至少兩個字所組成的形容詞；**複合形容詞中的字通常用連字號 (hyphen) 連接起來以表示其為形容詞。**

例如：

1. I bought a five-foot table yesterday.
   （昨天我買了一張五英尺的桌子。）

→ five-foot 為形容詞，修飾名詞 table。連字號用來連結 five 和 foot 以表示 five-foot 為形容詞。複合形容詞中的名詞須用單數。

2. This is a 10-page document.
   （這是一份 10 頁的文件。）

3. Fiona worked as a part-time librarian.
   （費歐娜兼差當圖書館管理員。）

4. That is an all-too-common mistake.
   （那是一項十分常見的錯誤。）

專有名詞所構成的複合形容詞

複合形容詞往往由必須**大寫的專有名詞** (proper nouns) 所構成。在這些情況中，**專有名詞中的字無須使用連字號來連結**。例如：

1.Did you manage to get the Bruno Mars tickets?
（你成功買到「火星人」布魯諾・馬爾斯的門票了嗎？）

→ Bruno Mars 這個專有名詞亦可當形容詞用，修飾 tickets；其他專有名詞亦同。由於大寫字母具有字的「群組」功能，所以無須使用連字號。

2.Sarah Wayne Callies is a *The Walking Dead* star.
（莎拉・維恩・考麗絲是《陰屍路》的女星。）

→ The Walking Dead 是由專有名詞所構成的複合形容詞，修飾 star。

注意：**專有名詞當複合形容詞用時，其後的名詞不可大寫，除非它是該專有名詞的一部份。**

◇ Did you manage to get the Bruno Mars Tickets?（×）

引號和斜體字所構成的複合形容詞

雖然這是一項比較不常見的慣例，但**引號 (quotation marks)、斜體字 (italics) 或兩者的組合**亦可用來將幾個字群組起來做為**複合形容詞**。（斜體字往往用於**外來語**。）例如：

1.It is a *bona fide* commercial transaction.
（那是一項真正的商業交易。）

2.Eric looked at the handbag in the water, looked Bonnie in the eye and then turned away, giving her a "get it yourself" look.
（艾立克看一看水中的手提包，再直視邦妮的眼睛，然後轉身就走了，給了邦妮一個「妳自己去拿」的眼色。）

→ 引號具有複合形容詞的群組功能。

3.For more than three years, Lance claimed to be part of the "*Aquitaine D-650*" crew before admitting to his cousin at a party that he was not.

（三年多來，蘭斯一直宣稱他是法國巡防艦《阿基坦號》的船員，直到在一場派對中才向他的表弟承認他不是。）

→ 句中的複合形容詞使用了大寫字母、斜體字和引號。

副詞與複合形容詞

誠如大家所知，形容詞的前面經常使用 very, completely, extremely 等副詞 (adverbs) 來修飾。在絕大多數的情況中，**副詞和形容詞之間無須使用連字號來連結**。例如：

1. Malala is an extremely brave girl.
（馬拉拉是個非常勇敢的女孩。）

→ 副詞 extremely 修飾形容詞 brave，但不是形容詞的一部份，因此無須使用連字號來將它與 brave 連結在一起。

2. It was a beautifully painted self-portrait in a skillfully carved frame.
（那是一幅畫工精美的自畫像，嵌在一個精雕細琢的畫框中。）

→ 副詞 beautifully 修飾形容詞 painted，但不是形容詞的一部份。skillfully 和 carved 的情況亦同。它們均無須使用連字號。

好用 Tips 非學不可 🔍

模稜兩可的副詞

然而，**well 和 fast**（這兩者皆可當副詞和形容詞）**等字則可使用連字號以避免歧義**。例如：

1.Hank took the well-fatted calf to the riverside.
（漢克牽著小肥牛到河邊。）

→ well-fatted calf 意為「肥滋滋的小牛」。

2.Hank took the well fatted calf to the riverside.

→ well fatted calf 可能被理解為 "well (= healthy) and fatted calf " （健康的小肥牛）。在上例中，**well-fatted calf 可能有病**。

因此，在大多數情況中，當**形容詞前面使用副詞 well 來修飾時，須使用連字號**。例如：

◆ Mayday is a **well-known** band. （〇）
（「五月天」是個眾所周知的樂團。）

→ well 須使用連字號。

◆ Mayday is a **widely known** band. （〇）
（「五月天」是個廣為人知的樂團。）

→ **其他副詞則無需連字號。**

Unit 14 縮略字的句點

必閃陷阱 非學不可

僅在縮略字 (contractions) 的最後一個字母與整個字的最後一個字母不同時，該縮略字才須使用句點或句號（[英] full stop／[美] period）。雖然這不是確定的規則，事實上也沒有確定的規則，但卻是一項有用的參考依據，有助於我們決定縮略字是否使用句點。例句：

◆ Mr（〇）
→（Mister 的縮略）
◆ Revd（〇）
→（Reverend 的縮略）
◆ Rev.（〇）
→（也是 Reverend 的縮略）

◆ para.（○）
（paragraph 的縮略）

◆ paras（○）
（paragraphs 的縮略）

◇ Dr.（×）
（Doctor 的縮略；r 都是 Dr 和 Doctor 的最後一個字母）

◇ para（×）
（paragraph 的縮略；最後一個字母不同——須用句點）

◆ The course is supported by **Prof**. White.（○）
（這項課程受到懷特教授的支持。）

這裡所述的規則並非不容改變。過去所有的縮略字都會使用句點，但現今本文所述的規則則被廣泛接受。這項規則合乎邏輯，且提供明確的指導原則。但遺憾的是，這一規則並未受到充分地遵守，尤其是**在美國，所有縮略字往往都會加上句點**，以 Ms, Mr 和 Mrs 為例，美國的用法是都加句點（英國的用法則都不加句點）。

是故，現在的情況是，縮略字後面是否加上句點，隨個人喜好而定，沒有人會因此而被扣分。然而，儘管如此，瞭解這規則還是值得的，因為它讓我們明確地知道什麼情況要用句點，又什麼情況不用句點。這規則需要大力推廣。如果你確切知道 "Para. 1" 和 "Paras 2-4" 這樣寫的原因，那不是一件很棒的事嗎！

Unit 15　縮寫字是否一定要加句點

必閃陷阱 非學不可

縮寫字可加句點，亦可不加句點，只要上下文保持一致即可。在一篇文章中，如果有些縮寫字加句點，另有些縮寫字不加，就會顯得凌亂、不整齊。下面前兩例都正確，因為加不加句點保持一致。例如：

◆ Doris and Grace moved to **USA** and **UK** respectively last year.（○）
◆ Doris and Grace moved to **U.S.A.** and **U.K**. respectively last year.（○）
（多麗絲和葛蕾絲去年分別搬到美國和英國。）
◇ The program was only shown on NBC not C.B.S.（×）
◇ The program was only shown on N.B.C. not CBS.（×）
（這節目僅在美國國家廣播公司播出，不在哥倫比亞廣播公司播出。）
→ 加不加句點不一致，顯得凌亂、不整齊。

縮寫字加不加句點的趨勢

由**大寫字母**所構成的**縮寫字**現今傾向於**不加句點**，而由**小寫字母**所構成的**縮寫字**則傾向於**加句點**。注意：這只是一項趨勢，不是規則。例如：

1. BBC / CNN / NBC

2. a.m. / i.e. / e.g. / p.m. / p.p.

一般而言，吾人可以選擇縮寫字加不加句點，但若公司行號或組織機構的名稱有其固定的縮寫形式，那麼我們只能複製該縮寫形式，不可任意更動，如 CNN 不可寫成 C.N.N.。

Part II
寫作用法精論

Chapter 1

句子結構

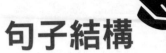

Chapter 1 | 句子結構

Unit 01 「6123」結構

必閃陷阱 非學不可

這是一種句型的俗稱，由於這種句型實在太重要、太常用了，大家一定要把它學會，而且要運用自如。這種句型的基本結構為「**find, make 等 6 個常用動詞 ＋ it（形式受詞）＋ 形容詞／名詞（受詞補語）＋ that 子句／不定詞片語／動名詞片語（真正受詞）**」。

在此結構中，"6" 是指主句中常用的 6 個動詞 (think, believe, make, find, consider, feel)，"1" 是指形式受詞 it，"2" 是受詞補語的兩種形式（形容詞或名詞），而 "3" 則是指真正受詞的 3 種形式（不定詞片語、動名詞片語或 that 所引導的受詞子句──這個 **that 不能省略**）。請看下面的例句：

1. We think it our duty to clean our classroom every day.

（我們認為每天打掃教室是我們的責任。）

→ 句中 it = to clean our classroom ...。

2. He felt it very important learning English well.

（他覺得把英文學好很重要。）

→ 句中 it = learning English ...。

3. They found it difficult that they would finish their work in two days.

（他們覺得要在兩天內完成他們的工作是有困難的。）

→ 句中 it = that they would finish ...。

Unit 02　Ever 的用法

Ever 是個副詞，主要意思為「在（過去、現在或未來）**任何時候；從來**」，通常用於疑問句，否定句以及表示比較和條件的附屬子句。

疑問句

1. Have you ever been to New York?
（你去過紐約嗎？）

2. Have you ever heard of the word "dotard"?
（你聽過「老番癲」這個字嗎？）

3. Do you ever dream about winning the lottery?
（你夢想過中樂透嗎？）

否定句

Ever 用於否定句時，通常與 not、no、none、no one、nobody、nothing 和 hardly 等否定詞連用。例如：

1. No such animal ever existed.
（這樣的動物從來就沒有存在過。）

2. None of my friends have ever heard of that guy.
（我的朋友當中從來就沒有人聽說過那個傢伙。）

3. No one ever told me John had moved to Taipei.
（從來就沒有人告訴我約翰已搬到台北。）

4. It hardly ever rains here in the summer.
（這裡夏天幾乎從不下雨。）
→ hardly ever = almost never
（幾乎從不）

Not (...) ever 與 never 同義，兩者可以互換，但 **never 比 not ever 要來得常用許多**。例如：

1. Never do that again.
（千萬不要再做那樣的事了。）

= Don't ever do that again.
→ 較不常用。

2. Tom has never been a friend of mine.
（湯姆從來就不是我的朋友。）

= Tom hasn't ever been a friend of mine.
→ 較不常用。

必閃陷阱 非學不可

然而，我們可以將 **never 放在句首形成倒裝句來加強語氣**，但 not ever 卻不行。例如：

◆ **Never** will we give up the struggle for freedom and peace.（○）
◇ Not ever will we give up the struggle for freedom and peace.（×）
（我們絕對不會放棄為自由與和平而奮鬥。）
◆ **Never** have I seen such a wicked man.（○）
◇ Not ever have I seen such a wicked man.（×）
（我從未見過這樣邪惡的人。）

我們亦可將 never 和 ever 放在一起來加強語氣。**Never ever** 意為「**絕不，從不**」，是個相當常用的片語。例如：

1. When there's a K-pop show on TV, my sister never ever misses it.
（只要電視上播出韓國流行音樂節目，我妹妹從不錯過。）

2. We must never ever forget what our parents have done for us.
（我們絕對不能忘記父母親為我們所做的一切。）

比較句

Ever 用來強調與過去的比較。主要句型為：**As + 原級 + as ever**（像往常一樣……）；**比較級 + than ever**（比以前任何時候都……）；**the + 最高級 + ever**（有史以來或歷來最……）。例如：

1. I'm as busy as ever.
（我仍像往常一樣忙碌。）

2. I thought Gary might be angry, but he was as polite and friendly as ever.
（我原本認為蓋瑞可能會生氣，但他卻和以前一樣客氣與友善。）

3. He's worse than ever.
（他的病情比以前更嚴重了。）

4. The government is spending less than ever on education.
（現在政府的教育支出比以前任何時候都要來得低。）

5. Mary was more confident than she had ever been.
（瑪麗比以前任何時候都更有信心。）

6. These are our best results ever.
（這些是我們歷來所得到的最好的結果。）

= These are our best-ever results.
→ 最高級 best 和 ever 之間有時不加連字號。

7. This is the worst disaster ever.
（這是有史以來最嚴重的災難。）

= This is the worst-ever disaster.

8. She is one of the very best girls I have ever met.
（她是我遇過的最好的女孩之一。）

條件句

Ever 用在 if 所引導的條件句時，ever 可緊接在 if 之後或位在句子的中間位置，亦即位在主詞和主動詞之間（即普通動詞之前）、語氣助動詞或第一個助動詞之後，或當主動詞用的 BE 動詞之後。例如：

1. If ever you're in Taipei, do give me a call.
（如果你有到台北，一定要打個電話給我。）

= If you're ever in Taipei, do give me a call.

2. If you ever see Robert, give him my kind regards.
（如果你見到羅伯特，請代我向他致以問候之意。）

3. If Tony had ever worked harder, he would have earned more money.
（如果東尼以前更努力工作的話，他會賺更多的錢。）

4. I seldom/rarely, if ever, watch television.
（我難得看電視。）

5. His wife seldom/rarely, if ever, does any cleaning.
（他太太難得打掃一次。）

→ seldom, if ever 或 rarely, if ever = probably never（難得；可能從不）。

6. Now there's a great challenge, if ever there was one.
（現在確實有一項重大的挑戰。）

7. That was a fine dinner if ever there was one!
（那確實是一頓豐盛的晚餐！）

8. It was a difficult job if ever there was one.
（毋庸置疑地，那是一項艱難的工作。）

9. If ever there was an opportunity for you to see the president, this was it.
（如果說有一個可以讓你見到總統的機會，那就是這個機會了。）

→ if ever there was one/something 意為「（用來強調所說情況的真實性）不容置疑，確實」。不管主句的時態為何，if ever there was one/something 中的 there was 為固定用語。

Ever since

Ever since 是 since 的加強語氣版，意為「從此；自從（……以來／以後就一直……）」。 它所引導的附屬子句使用過去簡單式，而主要子句大多使用現在完成式，但亦可使用現在簡單式。例如：

1. I've known him ever since Paul was a boy.
（從保羅孩提時代起，我就已認識他了。）

2. Ever since his wife left him, he's been depressed.
（他太太離他而去之後，他一直很消沈。）

3. I first met Carl at high school and we've been such great friends ever since.
（我和卡爾初識於中學，從此我們就成了非常要好的朋友。）

4. He doesn't take walks on his own ever since he fell.
（他摔倒後就無法獨自散步了。）

Ever so, ever such

So 和 such 的前面可以加上 ever 來加強語氣。Ever so 和 ever such 為英國口語，兩者皆意為「很，非常」(= very, a very)。

前者的句型為：**Ever so ＋ 形容詞／副詞（後面不接名詞）**。後者的句型為：**Ever such a/an ＋ 形容詞 ＋ 單數可數名詞**；ever such ＋ 形容詞 ＋ 複數可數名詞或不可數名詞。例如：

1. He's ever so rich.
（他很有錢。）

2. He walked ever so fast.
（他走得非常快。）

3. It was ever so kind of you to help the poor.
（你救濟窮人，你人真好。）

4. She's ever so pretty.
（她很漂亮。）

= She's very pretty.

5. She's ever such a pretty girl.
（她是個很漂亮的女孩。）

= She's a very pretty girl.

6. You're ever such nice people.
（你們人真好。）

7. My pet dog is in ever such good condition.
（我的寵物狗健康狀況非常好。）

Ever 還意為「永遠，一直」。例如：

1. The situation is the same as ever.
（情況一如往常。）

2. As ever, Kevin refused to admit that he was wrong.
（跟往常一樣，凱文拒絕承認他錯了。）

3. The prince and princess got married and lived happily ever after.
（王子和公主結婚後，從此一直過著幸福快樂的生活。）

在比較正式的情況中，**ever 可以跟形容詞連用**或用作**複合形容詞的字首**來表示「總是，始終；永遠」、「一直，不斷，持續」的意思。例如：

1. John is ever ready to help other people.
（約翰總是樂意幫助別人。）

2. The government's foreign policy seems to be ever-changing.
（政府的外交政策似乎不斷地在改變。）

3. The danger is ever present.
（危險總是存在的。）

4. Nuclear devastation was an ever-present threat.
（核子毀滅是個一直存在的威脅。）

5. The university cannot sustain ever-decreasing numbers of students.
（這所大學無法承受不斷減少的學生人數。）

6. Ben Affleck is an ever-popular movie star.
（班・艾佛列克是個一直廣受歡迎的電影明星。）

Unit 03　Here 和 there 的用法

Here 和 there 都是副詞。Here 意為「這裡；在這裡；到這裡」，通常是指**說話者所在的地方**。例如：

1. We stay here in summer and live in another city in winter.
（我們夏天留在這裡，冬天則住在另一城市。）

2. Could you bring the novel here?
（你把那本小說拿過來好嗎？）

There 意為「那裡；在那裡；到那裡」，通常是指**聽者或另一人所在的地方**。例如：

1. You had better stand there.
（你最好站在那兒。）

2. You must go there and back in an hour.
（你必須去那裡並在一個小時內回來。）

Here 和 there 分別與 this, these 和 that, those 連用

Here 通常與使用指示形容詞 **this** 或 **these** 來修飾的名詞連用，而 **there** 通常與使用指示形容詞 **that** 或 **those** 來修飾的名詞連用。Here 和 there 用在名詞之後具有加強語氣的作用。例如：

1. **These** paragraphs **here** need to be corrected.
（這幾段需要改正。）

2. **That** machine **there** is very powerful.
（那部機器非常強大。）

Here 和 there 分別與 bring 和 take 連用

Here 通常與 **bring**（拿來，帶來）連用，而 **there** 通常與 **take**（帶去）連用。例如：

1. What brings you here?
（什麼風把你吹來了？）

2. I can't take you there!
（我不能帶你去那裡！）

Here 和 there 位在介系詞後面

Here 和 there 可用在介系詞的後面。例如：

1. We're over here.
（我們在這裡。）

2. They're over there.
（他們在那裡。）

3. I live near here.
（我住在這附近。）

4. He lives near there.
（他住在那附近。）

5. It's so cold in here. Shut the door!
（這裡面／屋內好冷。把門關上！）

6. Put the key in here, please.
（請把鑰匙放在這裡面。）

7. Put the key in there, please.
（請把鑰匙放在那裡面。）

8. Put your bag up here.
（把你的包包放在這上面。）

9. Put your bag on there.
（把你的包包放在那上面。）

10. There are two restaurants around here.
（這附近有兩家餐廳。）

11. How far is her house from there?
（她家離那裡多遠？）

Here 和 there 位在句首

Here 和 there 可以用於句首，此時主詞和動詞要倒裝。這種用法最常見的句型是 **Here is** ＋ 主詞、**Here comes** ＋ 主詞、**There is** ＋ 主詞、**there goes** ＋ 主詞。**Here 和 there 用於句首**旨在加強語氣及引起注意。例如：

1. Here's the grammar book I said I'd lend you.
（這就是我說要借你的文法書。）

2. Here comes your taxi.
（你叫的計程車來了。）

3. Here comes James on his new bike.

（詹姆斯騎著他的新腳踏車來了。）

4. There's the restaurant where that kind of delicacy is served only once every week.

（那就是那家每週僅供應一次那種美味佳餚的餐廳。）

→ 這裡的 There's 或 There is 並不是「有」的意思。

5. There goes my brother on his motorbike.

（我弟弟騎著他的機車離開了。）

6. There goes the bus.

（公車走了。）

必閃陷阱 非學不可 🔍

然而，**當主詞為代名詞時，主詞和動詞不倒裝**。例如：

A: Has anyone seen my purse?

（A：有人看到我的錢包嗎？）

◆ B: **Here it is**, right by the phone.（○）

◇ B: Here is it, right by the phone.（✕）

（B：在這裡呀，就在電話機旁邊。）

A: Where's the remote control?

（A：遙控器在哪裡？）

◆ B: **There it is**, on the little table.（○）

◇ B: There is it, on the little table.（✕）

（B：在那裡呀，就在那張小桌子上。）

好用 Tips 非學不可 🔍

Here you are, there you are

當我們要把東西遞給或拿給某人時，我們可以使用 **here you are** 或 **there you are**（或者在非正式情況中使用 here you go 或 there you go）來表示「拿去吧」、「來，給你」的意思。**在此用法中，here 和 there 同義**。例如：

1. Jim: Did you get my pearl milk tea?
（吉姆：你有買我的珍珠奶茶嗎？）

Jill: Yes. Here you are.
（吉兒：有。拿去吧。）

2. Mary: Can you pass me the salt?
（瑪麗：把鹽巴遞給我好嗎？）

John: There you go.
（約翰：來，給你。）

Mary: Thank you.
（瑪麗：謝謝。）

Here it is! / There he is!

在找到或看到／遇見我們正在找或正在等的某人或某物時，我們經常使用 **here ＋ 主格代名詞 ＋ BE 動詞**或 **there ＋ 主格代名詞 ＋ BE動詞**來表示「在這裡呀」、「在那裡呀」、「你來了呀」、「他來了呀」等意思。例如：

1. A: Has anyone seen my purse?
（A：有人看到我的錢包嗎？）

B: Here it is, right by the phone.
（B：在這裡呀，就在電話機旁邊。）

2. A: Where's the remote control?
（A：遙控器在哪裡？）

B: There it is, on the little table.
（B：在那裡呀，就在那張小桌子上。）

3. Look (over) there! There he is!
（瞧那兒！他來了呀！）

4. Cindy! There you are! Everyone's waiting for you!
（辛蒂！你來了呀！大家都在等妳啊！）

Here I am! / Here we are!

我們經常使用 **here ＋ 主格代名詞 ＋ BE 動詞**來表示「我來了！／我到了！」、「我們來了！／我們到了！」、「他／她來了！／他／她到了！」、「他們來了！／他們到了！」等意思。例如：

1. David: Hello! Here I am! I hope I haven't missed dinner!
（大衛：你好！我來了！我希望沒有錯過晚餐！）

Kevin: Hello. No, you're right on time.
（凱文：你好。沒有，你來得正是時候。）

2. Here we are!
（我們到了！）

3. Here he is! Let's get started!
（他到了！我們開始吧！）

Here we go

我們經常使用 **Here we go** 來表示「（某事）開始了」、「（不好的事情）又來了」的意思。例如：

1. A: When are the fireworks going to start? We've been waiting here for over an hour!
（A：煙火何時開始施放？我們已經在這裡等超過一小時了！）

　B: Here we go, the first one just went off.
（B：開始了，第一枚煙火剛剛施放了。）

2. Oh, here we go (again)! Simon's just asked to borrow some more money from me.
（唉，又來了！賽蒙剛才又向我借錢了。）

3. Here we go again, another one of grandpa's boring stories!
（又來了，又是一個老掉牙的無聊故事！）

Unit 04 Prefer 的用法

重要觀念 非學不可

Prefer 是個及物動詞，意為「更喜歡，較喜歡；寧願，寧可，更願意，更希望」。由於是狀態動詞，prefer 本身不用進行式，**其後可接名詞（片語）、不定詞或動名詞當受詞。Prefer 經常與介系詞 to 所引導的介系詞片語連用**來比較兩個事物或兩個動作。例如：

1. Do you prefer summer or winter?
（你比較喜歡夏天還是冬天？）

2. He prefers his daughter to live near him.
（他更希望他女兒住在他附近。）

3. Do you prefer to exercise indoors or outdoors?
（你比較喜歡在室內還是戶外運動？）

4. She prefers living in Kaohsiung.
（她比較喜歡住高雄。）

5. I prefer white wine to red.
（比起紅葡萄酒，我更喜歡白葡萄酒。）

6. A lot of people prefer the quiet countryside to the noisy cities.
（許多人喜歡寧靜的鄉村更勝於喧囂的城市。）

7. Most people prefer watching television to reading books.
（比起看書，大多數人更喜歡看電視。）

必閃陷阱 非學不可

必須注意的是，**prefer ... to ... 是固定搭配**，不可使用 than 來替代介系詞 to。例如：

◆ Mary **prefers** coffee **to** tea.（O）
◇ Mary prefers coffee than tea.（×）
（瑪麗喜歡咖啡更勝於茶。）

◆ Mary **prefers** drinking coffee **to** tea.（○）
◇ Mary prefers drinking coffee than tea.（×）
（瑪麗喜歡喝咖啡更勝於喝茶。）

然而，我們可以使用略具強調作用的 **rather than 來代替 to**。但這就會
出現 rather than 後面要接何種詞類的問題。這是個經常被討論且困擾許
多人的問題。如果 prefer 後接動名詞，那麼 rather than 後面可接動名
詞，但這並不常用；如果 prefer 後接不定詞，那麼 **rather than 後面要
接省略 to 的不定詞，即原形動詞**。例如：

◆ Most people **prefer** watching television **to** reading books.（○）
→ 佳

◆ Most people **prefer** watching television **rather than** reading books.（○）
→ 不常用

◆ Most people **prefer** to watch television **rather than** read books.（○）
→ 最佳

◆ Most people **prefer** to watch television **rather than** reading books.（○）
→ 不常用

如上所述，與 like（喜歡）、love（喜歡）和 hate（討厭，不喜歡）等
表示喜歡或不喜歡的動詞一樣，prefer 亦可接不定詞或動名詞，但不定
詞型態比較常用，尤其在美式英語中，不定詞型態比動名詞型態來得常
見許多。這兩種型態的意思基本上並無區別，但含意略有差異。**動名詞
型態強調動作或經驗**，是在**表達一般的偏好**，而**不定詞型態比較強調動
作或事件的結果**，是在**表達一種習慣**。例如：

1. I prefer going to the movies.
（我比較喜歡看電影。）

2. He prefers working on his own.
（他比較喜歡獨自工作。）

3. I prefer to solve a computer problem as soon as possible.
（我寧可盡快解決電腦問題。）

4. I prefer not to wear a tie to work.
（我寧願不打領帶上班。）

同樣地，與 like、love 和 hate 的前面可加上 would（或縮寫 'd）來表示想要、不想要、寧願或不願等意思一樣，prefer 的前面亦可加上 would 或 'd，但此時這些動詞的後面僅**能接不定詞**，不可接動名詞。例如：

◆ **I would like/love to buy** this car.（O）
◇ I would like/love buying this car.（×）
（我想買這部車。）
◆ **I'd hate (= would not like) to cause** a problem.（O）
◇ I'd hate causing a problem.（×）
（我不想製造問題。）
◆ **I'd prefer not to live** in Taipei.（O）
◇ I'd prefer not living in Taipei.（×）
（我寧願不住在台北。）

Would prefer 主要用來**表示我們比較喜歡、寧願或更希望某人做某事**，其後可接**受格代名詞 + 不定詞、that 子句**或 **if 子句**，其中以不定詞結構和 if 子句最常用，that 子句比它們少用多了，但 that 子句若省略連接詞 that，則又變成這三種句型中最常用的。這**三種句型都是指現在或未來的事件**。
Would prefer + that 子句的句型是一種假設語氣，用來表示**「與現在事實相反」**或「未來不太可能發生的事件或不太可能實現的願望」。That 子句的動詞有三種型態，最常用的是**過去簡單式**，其次是 **should + 原形動詞**，最少見的型態是**省略 should 後的原形動詞**（這種型態不可用於否定句）。例如：

1. I would prefer that John told me the truth.
I would prefer that John should tell me the truth.
I would prefer that John tell me the truth.
（我希望約翰對我說實話。）

2. I'd prefer that the job were a little closer to my home.

→ 這裡不可使用 was。

I'd prefer that the job should be a little closer to my home.

I'd prefer that the job be a little closer to my home.
（我希望工作地點離家更近一點。）

3. Party leaders would prefer that the election did not take place in the next six months.

Party leaders would prefer that the election should not take place in the next six months.
（政黨領導人希望這項選舉不要在未來六個月內舉行。）

好用 Tips 非學不可 🔍

Would prefer it ＋ if 子句 ＋ 過去簡單式（BE 動詞用 were）的句型是一種現在和未來條件句，句中的 it 不可省略。例如：

1. I would prefer it if John told me the truth.
（我希望約翰對我說實話。）

2. I'd prefer it if the job were a little closer to my home.
（我希望工作地點離家更近一點。）

3. I would prefer it if you didn't smoke in here.
（麻煩你不要在這裡抽菸。）

Would prefer ＋ 受格代名詞 ＋ 不定詞的句型其實是 **would prefer it ＋ if 子句的減化**。例如：

1. They'd prefer me to drive.
（他們比較想讓我來開車。）

= They'd prefer it if I drove.

2. I'd prefer you not to smoke in here.
（麻煩你不要在這裡抽菸。）

= I'd prefer it if you didn't smoke in here.

3. Would you prefer him to come on Monday instead of Tuesday?
（你更希望他星期一來，而不是星期二來？）

= Would you prefer it if he came on Monday instead of Tuesday?

Unit 05　Rather 的用法

重要觀念 非學不可

Rather 可用來表示「相當，尚可，頗，有幾分」以及「不是……而是……」和「寧願」等意思。

Rather 用作程度副詞

Rather 當程度副詞用時意為「相當，尚可，頗，有幾分」，與後接可分等級形容詞或副詞（有比較級和最高級形式的形容詞或副詞）時的 **quite** 同義，但 **rather 比 quite 來得正式**。它通常用來指想不到、出乎意料或令人吃驚的事情。例如：

1. I'm afraid to say I found the novel rather dull.
（抱歉，我得說我覺得這本小說相當無聊。）

2. They walked rather slowly.
（他們走得相當慢。）

3. Although Robert is poor, he leads/lives a rather happy life.
（羅伯特雖窮，但卻過著相當快樂的生活。）

Rather 用作前置限定詞

Rather 當前置限定詞 (pre-determiners) 用時，後面接不定冠詞 a/an（在英文中，冠詞亦經常被稱為中間限定詞）再接形容詞 + 名詞，即「rather + a/an + 形容詞 + 名詞」。

不過，在此結構中，我們亦可將 a/an 挪到 rather 的前面，使其變成「a/an + rather + 形容詞 + 名詞」（這種結構比較不常用）。然而，當 rather 與其他限定詞（some, those 等）連用時，rather 只能放在它們的後面。例如：

1. It's rather a cold day.
（相當寒冷的一天。）

= It's a rather cold day.
2. They had to wait (for) rather a long time.
（他們得等相當長的一段時間。）

= They had to wait (for) a rather long time.

◆ They have some **rather** expensive wine.（O）
◇ They have rather some expensive wine.（×）
（他們擁有一些相當昂貴的葡萄酒。）

◆ The boss has decided to sack those **rather** indolent employees.（O）
◇ The boss has decided to sack rather those indolent employees.（×）
（老闆已決定解雇那些相當懶散的員工。）

Rather + a/an + 名詞

Rather + a/an + 名詞這種結構在正式場合比非正式場合來得常見，尤其是在書寫時。例如：

1. Neil was rather a fool to do such stupid things.
（尼爾相當傻，竟然做了這麼愚蠢的事情。）

2. It was rather a surprise to know him to be a coward/liar.
（知道他是個懦夫／愛撒謊的人，令人相當驚訝。）

= It was rather a surprise to know that he was a coward/liar.

Rather a lot

Rather 經常與 a lot 連用來表示「大量，許多」的意思。例如：

1. Peter earns rather a lot of money.
（彼得賺的錢相當多。）

2. You've given me rather a lot.
（你已經給了我相當多。）

Rather a lot 亦可表示「經常，常常」的意思。例如：

1. We went there rather a lot.
（我們經常去那裡。）

2. Does Bruce come here rather a lot?
（布魯斯常來這裡嗎？）

3. We'll be seeing rather a lot of our new CEO in the coming days.
（在未來幾天，我們將會常常見到我們新的執行長。）

Rather ＋ 動詞

Rather 亦可用來加強動詞的語氣，它最常與 enjoy, hope, like 等動詞連用。例如：

1. John was rather hoping his wife had forgotten about his cheating.
（約翰相當希望他太太已經把他出軌的事情忘得一乾二淨。）

2. I rather like these new types of smartphones.
（我相當喜歡這些新式的智慧型手機。）

3. I rather liked that girl next door.
（我相當喜歡鄰家那個女孩。）

Rather like

我們亦可使用 **rather like** 來表示「相當類似；頗為相似」(quite similar to) 之意。但必須注意的是，這裡的 like 為介系詞，意為「像；相像」，與上面提到的 rather like 中的 like 不一樣，後者為動詞，意為「喜歡」。例如：

1. It's rather like an ET.
（那頗有幾分像外星人。）

2. He spoke rather like a professor.
（他說起話來頗像個教授。）

Rather + 比較級

Rather 可與形容詞或副詞的比較級連用，在正式寫作中做兩事物之間的比較。例如：

1. The problem was rather more complicated than we had expected.
（這問題比我們預期的要複雜得多。）

2. Mary's feeling rather better.
（瑪麗現在覺得好些了。）

3. I'm now writing blog posts rather more frequently than in the past.
（我現在比以前更常一些寫部落格文章。）

必閃陷阱 非學不可

Not ... rather ..., rather than

我們經常使用 not ... rather ... 或 **rather than** 來表示「沒有……反而……」、「不是……而是……」或「是……而不是……」的意思。就 rather than 而言，當它位在句子中間時，其左右必須平行對稱，使用相同的詞類。例如：

1. The situation didn't improve, but rather deteriorated.
（情況沒有好轉，反而惡化了。）

2. Our aim was not to punish the students. Rather, it was to make them know the importance of being honest.
（我們的目的不是要懲罰這些學生，而是要他們知道誠實的重要性。）

3. His decision was taken for political rather than humanitarian reasons.
（他做出的決定是出於政治需要而不是基於人道因素。）

4. The development project will take years rather than months.
（這項開發計畫需要幾年才能完成，而不是幾個月。）

5. I want to marry sooner rather than later.
（我想盡快結婚，不想拖到以後。）

Rather than 通常位在句中兩個被比較的事物之間，但它亦可用於句首。

當 rather than 後接動詞時，該動詞須用原形或動名詞（動名詞比較不常見）。例如：

◆ **Rather than cause** trouble, Paul left.（○）
◆ **Rather than causing** trouble, Paul left.（○）
◇ Rather than to cause trouble, Paul left.（×）
（與其惹麻煩，保羅寧可離去。）

◆ **Rather than pay** the taxi fare, Cindy walked home.（○）
◆ **Rather than paying** the taxi fare, Cindy walked home.（○）
◇ Rather than to pay the taxi fare, Cindy walked home.（×）
（辛蒂不願意花計程車資，寧可走路回家。）

好用 Tips 非學不可

Or rather

Or rather 意為「說得更確切些；說得更準確點」，可用來更正我們前面說過的事情或剛剛說過的話。例如：

1. Her husband came home very late last night, or rather very early this morning.
（她先生昨天夜裡很晚才回家，說得更準確點，是今天凌晨才回家。）

2. The teacher couldn't help us, or rather he didn't want to.
（老師不能幫助我們，或者更確切地說，他不想幫我們。）

3. We stayed at my son's friend's house, or rather at his friend's parents' house.
（我們住在我兒子朋友家裡，說得更確切些，是住在我兒子朋友的父母家。）

Unit 06　Seem 的用法

必閃陷阱 非學不可

Seem 意為「**似乎，好像，看起來**」，僅能當連綴動詞用，**其後接形容詞**（或名詞——接名詞的情況比較少見）來做主詞補語，**本身通常不用進行式**。例如：

1. Tom seemed slightly embarrassed to see me in the nightclub.
（湯姆在夜店看到我好像有點尷尬。）
→ 接形容詞。

◆ Mary **seems** very **happy** with her new boyfriend.（O）
→ 接形容詞。

◇ Mary is seeming very happy with her new boyfriend.（×）
→ 不可使用進行式。
（瑪麗對她的新男友似乎很滿意。）

2. Buying a new computer seems a complete waste of money to me. A used one would be just as good.
（買新電腦對我來說完全是浪費金錢。二手電腦就好了。）
→ 接名詞（片語）。

Seem 後面經常接「**to + 原形動詞**」的不定詞結構，或者接「**to + have + P.P.**」的完成式不定詞結構來表示該完成式動作或狀態比 seem 還要早發生或出現。例如：

1. She would always seem to offend people.
（她過去似乎老是得罪人。）

2. Teresa seems to know more about me than my wife.
（泰瑞莎似乎比我太太更瞭解我。）

3. Cindy seems to have gone out.
（辛蒂似乎已經外出了。）

4. The professor seemed to have mistaken me for someone.
（教授看來好像把我誤認為某人。）

Seem 的否定形式有兩種，一是將**否定詞放在 seem 之前**，另一是**將否定詞放在 seem 後面的不定詞之前**，但意思一樣。例如：

1. The president seems not to like the plan.
（總統似乎不喜歡這項計畫。）

= The president doesn't seem to like the plan.

2. They seem not to be at the dormitory.
（他們似乎不在宿舍。）

= They do not seem to be at the dormitory.

好用 Tips 非學不可 🔍

除上述外，seem 還有下列幾種常見的句型：

There seem (s) to be 或 there seemed to be ＋ 名詞（片語)）

→ 注意：Seem 的單複數與名詞一致

1. There seem to me to be two possibilities.
(= I think there seem to be two possibilities.)
（我覺得有兩個可能性。）

2. There seems to be something wrong with her.
（她似乎有點不對勁。）

3. There seemed to be a mistake in these calculations.
（這些計算似乎有錯。）

Seem ＋ as if/as though/like 所引導的子句（like 後面亦可接名詞或名詞片語）

1. Dad seemed (as if/as though/like he was) tired.
（爸爸好像累了。）

2. It seems as if they're no longer in love.
（他們似乎不再相愛了。）

3. Sam seemed as though he was a bit detached.
（山姆似乎有些心不在焉。）

4. It seems like their marriage is over.
（他們的婚姻好像結束了。）

→ 這句與 It seems that their marriage is over. 的意思相同，但大多用於非正式場合或口說英語。

5. It doesn't seem like a good idea to lend money to John.
（借錢給約翰似乎不是個好主意。）

> **It seems 或 it seemed ＋ that** 所引導的**名詞子句**（連接詞 that 可以省略）。在此一句型中，**seem 後面可接介系詞 to ＋ 人**來表示「某人感覺好像，某人覺得似乎」的意思。例如：

1. It seems (that) he is a good guy.
（他似乎是個好人。）

2. It seemed (that) he had changed his mind.
（他似乎已改變心意。）

3. It seemed to everyone (that) Linda was wrong.
（大家都覺得琳達似乎是錯了。）

= Everyone thought (that) Linda was wrong.

4. It seems to me (that) it will rain tonight.
（在我看來，今晚會下雨。）

= I think (that) it will rain tonight.

> 在 **it seems 或 it seemed ＋ (that) 名詞子句**的句型中，名詞子句的否定詞可轉移到主句中；進一步而言，主句的否定詞係否定名詞子句的動詞，不是否定 seem。例如：

1. It seems that they don't know how to deal with the situation.
（他們似乎不知道如何處理這種情況。）

= It doesn't seem that they know how to deal with the situation.

2. It seems (that) Peter can't come.
（彼得好像不能來了。）

= It doesn't seem (that) Peter can come.

3. It seems to me (that) Richard isn't the right person for the job.
（在我看來，理查不是這項工作的合適人選。）

= It doesn't seem to me (that) Richard is the right person for the job.

= I don't think (that) Richard is the right person for the job.

→ think、believe 等動詞後面的名詞子句也是否定轉移。

Unit 07 So that 和 in order that 的用法

重要觀念 非學不可 🔍

So that 和 in order that 都是用來表示目的，意為「為了；以便；目的在於」，當連接詞用，通常與語氣助動詞（can、will、could、would 等）連用。So that 比 in order that 來得常用許多，在非正式情況中，**so that 中的 that 往往省略**。In order that 是個正式用語，通常用於正式場合。例如：

1. John lowered his voice to tell me the secret so that no one would hear.
（約翰壓低嗓音告訴我這個秘密，這樣就沒有人能聽到。）

2. Mary got up early in order that she should/would/might be on time for school.
（瑪麗一早就起床以便準時上學。）

3. I'll go there so that I can talk to the president.
（我要去那裡，這樣我才能跟總統談話。）

4. In order that you can sign the contract, please give me your address and I will mail it to you.
（為了讓你能夠簽約，請給我你的地址，我會把合約寄給你。）

5. Thomas worked hard so (that) he would earn one million dollars before the age of 25.
（湯瑪斯努力工作俾在 25 歲之前能賺到 100 萬。）

6. I've made some sushi so (that) you can have a snack with your girlfriend.
（我做了一些壽司，這樣你就能跟你女朋友一起吃點心。）

在表示未來時，**so that 的後面可以使用現在簡單式**或 **will/'ll**，而 **in order that 的後面通常使用現在簡單式**。例如：

1. I'll sign and mail the contract so that you get it by Monday.
（我今天會簽署並寄出合約，這樣你在週一前就能收到。）
= I'll sign and mail the contract so that you will get it by Monday.
2. Monica will leave early in the morning in order that she arrives on time for a stress-management workshop.
（莫妮卡明天一大早就要動身，以便準時參加一場壓力管理研討會。）
= Monica will leave first thing in the morning so that she arrives on time for a stress-management workshop.
= Monica will leave first thing in the morning so that she'll arrive on time for a stress-management workshop.

必閃陷阱 非學不可

So that 還可表示前因後果 (cause and effect)（但 in order that 則無此用法），其主要句型為 **so ... that ...**，意為「**如此……以致於……；（因為……）所以……**」，so 在此當副詞用，後面通常接形容詞或副詞，而 **that 有時亦可省略**。然而，**當 so 的後面沒有接形容詞或副詞時，無論表示目的或因果，兩者都是寫成或說成 so that**，此時我們只能從上下文判斷屬於何者。表示因果關係的 so that 省略 that 後，so 就從副詞直接變成連接詞。例如：

1. The manager fixed the meeting for 10 so that all employees could come.
（經理把會議時間定在 10 點，為的是讓所有員工都能參加。）（表目的）
2. Gary was so surprised that he remained speechless for a few minutes.
（蓋瑞驚訝得好幾分鐘說不出話來。）（表因果）
3. An almost 50-year-old mom looks so young that people think she's her son's girlfriend.
（一位近 50 歲的凍齡媽媽看起來是如此的年輕，以致於大家都認為她是她兒子的女朋友。）（表因果）

4. I was so thirsty I drank up the whole bottle of water.
（我很渴，把整瓶水都喝光了。）（表因果）

5. Everything's changed so much I can scarcely recognize the place.
（一切都變化得如此之大，我幾乎認不出這個地方了。）（表因果）

→ 這兩句都省略了連接詞 that，而 so 還是當副詞用，但可別因此認為這是兩個子句沒有用連接詞連接的 run-on sentence。這是 so ... (that) 句型的特色。

6. Nothing more was heard from Amy so that we began to wonder if she moved to Japan.
（由於再也沒聽到艾美的消息，因此我們便開始懷疑她是否搬到日本了。）(表因果)

7. These bushes flower in the spring, so that March is a good time to view the booming flowers.
（這些灌木春天開花，所以三月是賞花的好時機。）（表因果）

8. His wife was ill so he did the washing on his very own.
（他太太生病了，所以他自己洗衣服。）（表因果）

9. My blood pressure was getting higher and higher so I quit smoking.
（我的血壓越來越高，因此我戒菸了。）（表因果）

→ 這兩句的 so 本身就是連接詞。

Unit 08　Would rather 的用法

重要觀念 非學不可

Would rather 或 'd rather 係用來表示「寧願，寧可」的意思。Would rather 有兩種不同的句型或結構，一是 **S + would rather (not) + 原形動詞**（亦即主詞相同），另一是 **S1 + would rather + S2 + 過去簡單式**（亦即主詞不同）。例如：

1. We'd rather stay at home than go out tonight.
（我們寧願今晚待在家裡，也不想外出。）

We'd rather you stayed at home tonight.
（我們寧願你今晚待在家裡。）

2. We'd rather not go out tonight.
（我們寧願今晚不外出。）

We'd rather you didn't go out tonight.
（我們寧願你今晚不外出。）

根據上面的例句，在主詞不同的句型中，**否定詞是加到「S2 + 過去簡單式」的子句**，而不是加到 would rather。例如：

◆ **I'd rather** you **didn't** phone after 10 o'clock.（○）
◇ I wouldn't rather you phoned after 10 o'clock.（✕）
◇ I'd rather not you phoned after 10 o'clock.（✕）
（我寧願你 10 點之後不打電話。）

必閃陷阱 非學不可

在主詞相同的句型中，**would rather (not) 係接原形動詞**，不可接帶 to 的不定詞或動名詞。例如：

◆ We **would rather try** it again.（○）
◇ We would rather to try it again.（✕）
◇ We would rather trying it again.（✕）
（我們寧願再試一次。）

◆ **I'd rather not fly**. I hate planes.（○）
◇ I'd rather not to fly. I hate planes.（✕）
◇ I'd rather not flying. I hate planes.（✕）
（我寧可不搭飛機。我討厭飛機。）

Would rather + have + P.P.

Would rather + 原形動詞是 would rather 的現在式或未來式，指的是現在或未來的事件。它的過去式為 **would rather + have + P.P.**，係用來表示過去寧願做某事但卻沒有做，或寧願某事發生但卻沒有發生的情況。例如：

1. Linda would rather have studied abroad.
（琳達寧願出國留學 。）

→ 但事實上她並沒有出國。

2. I'd rather have seen the movie at the movie theater than on DVD.
（我寧願在電影院看這部電影，而不是看 DVD。）

→ 但事實上我是看這部電影的 DVD。

主詞不同的句型其實是一種假設語氣用法。當 S2 後接過去簡單式時，該子句是表示「與現在事實相反」或「未來不太可能發生的事件或不太可能實現的願望」；當 S2 後接過去完成式時，該子句是表示「與過去事實相反」。例如：

1. My mother would rather we caught the bus, rather than walk home after the party.
（我媽媽寧願我們在派對後搭公車而不是走路回家。）

→ 事實上，我們是走路回家的。

2. Would you rather I wasn't honest with you?
（你寧願我不對你說實話嗎？／你寧願我不對你開誠布公嗎？）

◇ Would you rather I'm not honest with you?（×）

◇ Would you rather I won't be honest with you?（×）

3. I'd rather Tom hadn't called me at the office this afternoon.
（我寧願湯姆今天下午沒有打電話到我辦公室來。）

→ 事實上，湯姆今天下午打電話到我辦公室找我。

好用 Tips 非學不可

Much rather

Much 可以跟 would rather 連用來加強 would rather 的語氣。在講話時，much 必須唸重音（重讀）。例如：

1. He'd much rather make a phone call than send an email.
（他寧願打電話，也不願寄電子郵件。）

2. I'd much rather they didn't know about what had happened.
（我寧願他們不知道已經發生的事。）

I'd rather not 可用作簡答
我們經常將 **I'd rather not（我寧願不）用作簡答來對提議或要求說
「不」**。例如：

A: Shall we go out for dinner tonight?
（今晚我們外出吃晚餐好嗎？）
B: No, I'd rather not, if you don't mind.
（不，如果你不介意的話，我寧可不。）

Would sooner, would (just) as soon
我們亦可用 **would sooner 和 would (just) as soon 來表達與 would
rather 相同的意思**。這兩個在口語中亦頗為常用的片語，不僅與 would
rather 同義，它們的用法亦完全一樣。例如：

1. A: Do you want to go out to eat?
（A：你想出去吃飯嗎？）
   B: I'd sooner stay in—I'm not feeling very well.
（B：我寧願待在家裡——我有些不舒服。）
2. I'd sooner my sister married no one than marry a fool like him.
（我寧願我妹妹不嫁人，也不願她嫁給像他那樣的笨蛋。）
3. He'd just as soon live in Penghu.
（他寧願住在澎湖。）
4. I'd as soon have a beer.
（我寧可喝杯啤酒。）

就使用頻率而言，would sooner 比 would (just) as soon 來得常用，而
would rather 又比這兩個片語更常用。

Unit 09 分裂句 (cleft sentences)

必閃陷阱 非學不可

Cleft 意為 divided。在分裂句中，一項資訊被分成兩個子句來敘述，這也就是它們被稱為**分裂句**的原因。我們使用分裂句（尤其是在說話時）來使聽者已經知道的事情（舊資訊）和不知道的事情（新資訊）產生關連，藉此來**強調聽者不知道的事情**，也就是**新的資訊。英文的分裂句可分為 It- 分裂句和 Wh-分裂句。**

It-分裂句 (句型為 It is/was ... that ...)

It- 分裂句是最常見的分裂句。要強調的新資訊是位在 **it is/was 的後面**，而舊資訊則位在 that 子句中，使 it 子句和 that 子句產生關連。在非正式情況中，當 that 為該子句之動詞的受詞時，**that 通常省略**。例如：

1. Cindy: Did you find your handbag, Monica?

(辛蒂：莫尼卡，妳找到妳的包包了嗎？)

　Monica: It was my purse that I'd lost. I found it under the sofa.

（莫尼卡：我遺失的是錢包。我在沙發下面找到了。）

→ 這裡強調的新資訊是「我的錢包（不是我的包包）」。已經知道的舊資訊是：「我遺失某樣東西。」

2. John: Professor Chen's Spanish lesson is very interesting, isn't it?

（約翰：陳教授的西班牙文課很有趣，不是嗎？）

　Mary: It is English that Professor Chen teaches us.

（瑪麗：陳教授教我們的課程是英文。）

→ 這裡強調的新資訊是「英文課（不是西班牙文課）」。已經知道的舊資訊是：「我有上陳教授的語文課。」

3. Is it November that you are going to get married?

（你要結婚的月份是十一月嗎？）

→ 這裡強調的新資訊是「十一月這個月份嗎？」。已經知道的舊資訊是：「你將要結婚。」

在 **It- 分裂句中，若被強調的元素是人，那麼我們可以用 who 來代替 that**，但這僅限於被強調的元素是人，其他情況只能用 that，不能用其他關係代名詞。同樣地，在非正式情況中，**當 who 為該子句之動詞的受詞時，who 通常省略**。例如：

1. It was Jack who/that cleaned the classroom yesterday.
（昨天打掃教室的人就是傑克。）

2. It was my wife who/that you talked to in the hospital yesterday.
（昨天在醫院跟你交談的人就是我太太。）

或 It was my wife you talked to in the hospital yesterday.

若被強調的元素為複數，那麼 that 或 who 子句須用複數動詞，而 it 後面的 BE 動詞仍維持單數的 is 或 was。例如：

It's the young people who/that have suffered severe job losses in the region.
（該地區遭遇嚴重失業問題的人就是年輕人。）

It 子句可以使用否定結構。例如：

It isn't Allen who plays an important role in that matter.
（在該事件中扮演重要角色的人不是艾倫。）

好用 Tips 非學不可 🔍

Wh- 分裂句（句型為 What ＋ S ＋ V ＋ is …）
Wh- 分裂句最常使用 what 來引導，但我們亦可使用 why、where、how 等 wh-字。Wh-子句中的資訊是已經知道的舊資訊，而 is 後面的資訊則是要強調的新資訊。例如：

1. A: I don't know what Henry needs now.
（A：我不知道約翰現在需要什麼。）

B: What he needs most now is **a wife**.

（B：他現在最需要的是太太。）

→ 這裡已經知道的舊資訊是：我們正在談論約翰現在需要什麼，而強調的新資訊是他需要太太。

2. A: My motorbike won't start.

（A：我的機車發不動。）

 B: What you need to do is **get a new battery for it**.（B：你需要做的是給它換個新的電瓶。）

→ 這裡已經知道的舊資訊是：你需要做某事來修復機車，而強調的新資訊是你要換個新電瓶。

3. Where you can find a lot of English learning materials is **a quality website** addressed blog.cybertranslator.idv.tw.

（你能找到許多英文學習資料的地方，是個網址為 blog.cybertranslator.idv.tw 的優質網站。）

Unit 10　分詞介系詞

重要觀念 非學不可 🔍

分詞介系詞 (participial prepositions) 是指**當介系詞用的現在分詞或過去分詞**。英文中常用的分詞介系詞包括 barring（除非；除……以外）、considering（考慮到；就……而論)、given（考慮到；鑑於）、expecting（除……以外）、judging by/from（根據……來判斷，由……來看）和 regarding（關於，有關）──具有現在分詞字尾 -ing 的 during（在……期間）和 notwithstanding（儘管）亦屬之。

由於長期且普遍的使用習慣，這些**現在分詞或過去分詞**現今都是不折不扣的**介系詞**，與其他分詞係分屬不同的詞類。

職是之故，**分詞介系詞**所引導的分詞構句，其文法上、邏輯上或意義上的主詞雖然不是主要子句的主詞，**但它們並非** dangling modifiers 或 dangling participles（**不連結的分詞或虛懸的分詞**）。

茲舉兩例說明 dangling participles。例如：

◇ Having followed a strict high-protein diet, Helen's weight dropped off rapidly. （×）

（在恪遵嚴格的高蛋白質飲食之後，海倫的體重快速滑落。）

→ 分詞構句與主要子句的主詞不同，這是 dangling participle，因為 Having followed a strict high-protein diet 修飾的對象是 Helen，不是 Helen's weight；反過來說，是 Helen，不是 Helen's weight 恪遵嚴格的高蛋白質飲食。

◆ **Having followed** a strict high-protein diet, **Helen lost** weight rapidly. （O）

（在恪遵嚴格的高蛋白質飲食之後，海倫快速地減重了。）

◇ Upon entering the classroom, a big balloon caught my eye. （×）

（一進入教室，一個大氣球就吸引了我的目光。）

→ 分詞構句與主要子句的主詞不同，這是 dangling participle，因為 Upon entering the classroom 修飾的對象是 I，不是 a big balloon。

◆ **Upon entering** the classroom, I immediately **noticed** a big balloon. （O）

（一進入教室，我就注意到一個大氣球。）

必閃陷阱 非學不可

然而，**分詞介系詞的分詞構句即使主詞與主要子句的主詞不同，亦非 dangling participles**。例如：

◆ **Barring any** (= If there are no) unexpected delays, I should be able to arrive at eight o'clock. （O）

（除非有任何意外的延誤，否則我應該在八點鐘就能到達。）

◆ **Considering** the distance, we got here quite quickly. （O）

（考慮到路程較遠，我們到這裡算夠快的了。）

◆ **Given** his experience, John's done a good job. （O）

（鑑於約翰缺乏經驗，這工作他算是做得不錯了。）

◆ **Judging** by what everyone says about him, I'd say he has a good chance of winning.（O）

（根據大家對他的評價來判斷，我想他獲勝的機會很大。）

◆ **Notwithstanding** the poor weather, we still went skateboarding.（O）

（儘管天氣惡劣，但我們仍去溜滑板。）

從上面的例句可以看出，分詞介系詞所引導的分詞構句與主要子句的關連性並不強。顯然地，它們不是一般的分詞構句，或許可把它們視為一種**獨立的分詞結構**。

Unit 11 如何強調句中的元素(一)

重要觀念 非學不可

英文使用下列結構和句型來強調句中的元素。

間接受詞與介詞片語

若要表示某人接受某物，我們可以使用典型的詞序：**間接受詞 (indirect object) ＋ 直接受詞 (direct object)**。但若要**強調接受者**，則可**使用介系詞片語**來代替間接受詞。例如：

1. I gave my daughter an iPhone 7.
（我送我女兒一支 iPhone 7 手機。）

→ 典型的詞序：間接受詞 ＋ 直接受詞。

2. I gave an iPhone 7 to my daughter.
（我送一支 iPhone 7 手機給我女兒。）

→ 非典型詞序：直接受詞 ＋ 介詞片語。將介詞片語置於句末可對接受者（間接受詞）起強調作用。

在正式的上下文中，我們有時會**將介詞片語置於句首以便強調直接受詞**。例如：

For his wife, he bought a Mercedes Benz.
（他買了一部賓士給他太太。）
→ 這句係用來強調直接受詞 Mercedes Benz。

主動態與被動態

主動態是典型的詞序，即**主詞（動作的執行者）位在句子的最前面**，主詞後面的部分是句中被強調的元素。例如：John passed his exams with flying colors.（約翰以優異的成績通過考試。）

若使用被動態，我們**可以省略動作執行者**，但句中被**強調**的元素仍是**主詞後面的部分**。例如：

The car was washed.
（車子被洗好了。）
→ 沒有動作執行者。

我們可以將**動作執行者置於動詞後面的介詞片語中**，此時我們**強調的是動作的執行者**。例如：

1. The car was washed by his son.
（車子被他兒子洗好了。）
2. The restaurant was run by a young couple.
（這家餐廳是由一對年輕夫妻所經營。）

必閃陷阱 非學不可

動詞的名詞化

在正式寫作，尤其是在學術寫作中，我們可以**使用動詞的名詞型態做為主詞**，藉此來特別**強調主動詞後面的元素**。例如：

1. The successful implementation of the plan brought immense profit to the company.
（該計畫之成功執行帶給這家公司巨大的利潤。）

→ 強調 "immense profit to the company"。

<試比較：The plan was implemented successfully and this brought immense profit to the company.>

2. Germany's invasion of Poland in 1939 was the immediate cause of the outbreak of the Second World War.
（德國 1939 年侵略波蘭是二次世界大戰爆發的直接致因。）

→ 強調 "the immediate cause of the outbreak of the Second World War"。

<試比較：Germany invaded Poland in 1939 and this was the immediate cause of the Second World War breaking out.>

動詞（或形容詞）的名詞化，英文叫做 nominalization。如上述，**正式寫作，尤其是學術寫作，經常使用動詞的名詞化來強調句中的元素。但在其他情況中應避免過度使用動詞的名詞化，因為這往往會造成句子不夠簡潔**。例如：

1. The police conducted their investigation of the crime scene.
（警方進行犯罪現場的調查。）

2. The police investigated the crime scene.
（警方調查犯罪現場。）

→ 這句比上句來得言簡意賅，符合一般寫作的簡潔原則。

3. As an indication of her support for the cause, Mary presented a donation of 10,000 dollars.
（瑪麗遞交一萬元的捐款，以示她對這個目標的支持。）

4. Mary donated 10,000 dollars to demonstrate her support for the cause.
（瑪麗捐獻一萬元以示她對這個目標的支持。）

→ 這句比上句來得言簡意賅，符合一般寫作的簡潔原則。

Unit 12 如何強調句中的元素(二)

重要觀念 非學不可 🔍

The thing, the one/only/first thing, something

The thing

我們可以用 **the thing（＋ 形容詞子句）當主詞，後接 BE 動詞 (is 或 was) 來強調 BE 動詞後面的元素（即主詞補語）**。這與 Wh- 分裂句的作用一樣，但比較不是那麼正式。例如：

The thing I love about John is his loyalty to his wife.
（我喜歡約翰的一點是，他對他太太的忠誠。）
= What I love about John is his loyalty to his wife.

即使被強調的元素為複數，BE 動詞亦用單數，因為 the thing 是單數名詞。例如：

The thing I like most about Penghu is the historic sites.
（我最喜歡澎湖的地方是歷史古蹟。）
= What I like most about Penghu is the historic sites.

必閃陷阱 非學不可 🔍

BE 動詞後面要強調的元素也可以是**連接詞 that 所引導的名詞子句**。在非正式情況中，**有人會將 that 省略，但筆者期期以為不可，因為這是錯誤的文法**。例如：

◆ **The thing** you need to remember is **that you've lent James 50,000 dollars**. （O）
= **What** you need to remember is **that you've lent James 50,000 dollars**. （O）
◇ The thing you need to remember is you've lent James 50,000 dollars. （×）
（你必須記住的是，你已借給詹姆斯五萬元。）

BE 動詞後面要強調的元素亦可以是帶 to 或不帶 to 的不定詞或不定詞片語。若形容詞子句有動詞 do，則當**主詞補語用的不定詞或不定詞片語可以省略 to**，若是 do 以外的其他動詞，則 to 不省略。下面所討論的強調句型，若 BE 動詞後面被強調的元素是不定詞或不定詞片語，都適用這項規則。例如：

1. The thing I have to do is (to) marry her.
（我必須要做的就是跟她結婚。）

= What I have to do is (to) marry her.

2. The thing Megan plans is to study abroad.
（梅根所計畫的就是到國外留學。）

= What Megan plans is to study abroad.

One thing, the one thing, the only thing, the first thing

我們可以**用 one 來加強 thing 的語氣**，而 the one thing、the only thing 和 the first thing 的語氣更強烈。BE 動詞後面要強調的元素與上述相同。例如：

1. One thing I admire most about Peter is his diplomatic tact.
（我最欣賞彼得的一點就是他的外交手腕。）

2. The one thing you should know is that your husband has extramarital affairs.
（妳應該要知道的一件事就是妳先生有外遇。）

3. The only thing I want is to win the lottery.
（我唯一想要的就是中樂透。）

4. The first thing we must do is (to) deal with all of the documents from before 2015.
（我們首先必須要做的就是處理 2015 年之前的所有文件。）

Something

我們還可使用 **something（＋形容詞子句）當主詞**，後接 **BE 動詞**（is 或 was）來強調 BE 動詞後面的元素（即主詞補語）。

同樣地，這與 Wh- 分裂句的作用一樣，但沒有 the thing 那麼特定和直接，它的含意相當於「除了別的以外的另一件事」。例如：

1. Something you must never do is give your cellphone number to a complete stranger.

（你絕對不能做的另一件事就是，把你的手機號碼給一個完全陌生的人。）

或 What you must never do is give your cellphone number to a complete stranger.

2. Something I love about John is that he frequently lends money to me.

（我喜歡約翰的另一點是，他常常借錢給我。）

或 What I love about John is that he frequently lends money to me.

3. Something you need to remember is that you mustn't yawn in class.

（你還必須記住的是，千萬不要在課堂上打哈欠。）

或 What you need to remember is that you mustn't yawn in class.

用 it 做假主詞或形式主詞來強調真正的主詞

這種**以 it 做假主詞或形式主詞**來代表其後的動名詞或動名詞片語、帶 to 的不定詞或不定詞片語或 that 所引導的名詞子句的句型，在英文中用得很多。例如：

1. It was very dangerous having a foot in both camps.

（腳踏兩條船是很危險的。）

→ 這句真正的主詞是 having a foot in both camps。

2. It is my hobby to play computer games.

（玩電腦遊戲是我的嗜好。）

→ 這句真正的主詞是 to play computer games。

3. It is generally believed that mice are afraid of cats.

（一般認為老鼠怕貓。）

→ 這句真正的主詞是 that mice are afraid of cats。

若要強調句中的時間副詞 (如 yesterday, in the morning, at 8 pm)，我們可以使用 it is/was not until、it is/was only when 等句型。它們的意思都是「到某時才（做某事）」。例如：

1. It wasn't until I read your email yesterday that I understood the true reason.
（我直到昨天看了你的電子郵件才瞭解真正的原因。）

→ 強調 "yesterday"。但這個句型可改成更具強調作用的倒裝句：Not until I read your email yesterday did I understand the true reason.

<試比較：Until I read your email yesterday, I didn't understand the true reason.>

2. It was only when I met him in the afternoon that I realized his true intention.
（我直到下午跟他會面才明白他真正的意圖。）

→ 強調 "in the afternoon"。但這個句型可改成更具強調作用的倒裝句：Only when I met him in the afternoon did I realize his true intention.

<試比較：When I met him in the afternoon, I realized his true intention.>

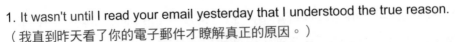

好用 Tips 非學不可

用 there 做假主詞或形式主詞來強調真正的主詞

這種**以 there 做假主詞或形式主詞並與 BE 動詞連用的結構**，可對其後的真正主詞起強調作用。例如：

1. There's a strange sound coming from behind the door.
（有個奇怪的聲音從門後傳來。）

→ 強調 "a strange sound coming from behind the door"。

<試比較：A strange sound is coming from behind the door.>

2. There were many people attending his wedding.
（有許多人參加他的婚禮。）

→ 強調 "many people attending his wedding"。

<試比較：Many people were attending his wedding. >

Unit 13 如何閱讀長句

必閃陷阱 非學不可

長句 (long sentences) 就是讓我們感到很困難的句子，**長句的明顯特徵就是句子比較長，一個句子往往有三、四行**，甚至一個句子就是一段。許多人在閱讀英文文章時經常會陷入一個很長的句子中，不知道它到底講什麼。長句之所以長，主要有下列幾個原因：

一、附屬子句又多又長：一個主句帶多個子句，子句中又有子句

應對之道：首先找到主句的主體部分（即主詞、動詞和受詞），然後再確定子句的主體部分，如果子句中還有子句，再確定下一層子句的主詞、動詞和受詞。注意：閱讀時要一層一層進行，先把同一層的內容看完，再看下一層的內容。例句：

"A survey of new stories in 1996 reveals that the anti-science tag has been attached to many other groups as well, from authorities who advocated the elimination of the last remaining stocks of smallpox virus to Republicans who advocated decreased funding for basic research."

在連接詞 that 所引導的名詞子句（當受詞用）中，又有兩個由 who 所引導的關係子句（形容詞子句）。這個句子的主句的主體是 a survey ... reveals that...。子句的結構比較複雜，主詞是 the anti-science tag（反科學的標籤），動詞（片語）是 has been attached to（被貼到），受詞是 many other groups，後面用了一個 from sb. who ... to sb. who ... 的結構來舉例解釋這些 groups 包括什麼人。這句的意思是「1996 年對新報導所做的一項調查顯示，反科學標籤也被貼在其他許多族群身上，包括提倡根除殘餘天花病毒的權威人士，以及提倡削減基礎科學研究經費的共和黨人士」。

二、長長的插入成分

英文長句的一大特點就是喜歡用**插入語**，譬如說，用插入語交代某句話是誰說的，說話者是什麼身份；或是用插入語來修飾、解釋、補充前面的內容等等。**插入語使作者能更靈活地表達自己的意思，但插入語過長或是過多往往使讀者找不到閱讀的重點。** 從形式上看，插入語的出現有明顯標誌：**用雙破折號與主句隔開或者用雙逗號與主句隔開。**

應對之道：讀句子時，先不要理會插入語，先把主句的意思看完。然後再看插入部分。 例如：

"Today, stepladders carry labels several inches long that warn, among other things, that you might — surprise! — fall off."

顯然地，這句的插入語比較多，首先我們要**找出主句，即 stepladders carry labels （梯子上貼有標籤）**，這個 labels 有兩個修飾語：several inches long 和一個由關係代名詞 that 所引導的關係子句。子句的主詞是關代 that（也就是先行詞 labels），動詞是 warn，其受詞是連接詞 that 所引導的名詞子句，在 warn 及其受詞子句之間插入 among other things，表示此受詞子句的內容只是 labels 所警告的多個內容中的一項而已。這個被列舉出來的內容就是 fall off（摔下來），但在 fall off 之前又插入了一個 surprise!，插入這個詞是因為作者認為梯子警告 fall off 是件令人吃驚的事，因為爬梯子本來就有摔下來的危險，但商家為了怕消費者控告，竟然將這麼顯而易懂的事情也寫進了警語。

這個句子的閱讀順序應該是：第一層 stepladders carry labels several inches long，第二層是 that warn that you might fall off，最後再看兩個插入的部分 among other things 和 surprise!。這句的意思是「現今梯子上都貼有數英吋長的標籤，警告爬梯子可能摔下去——驚！——等危險」。

三、分詞構句、獨立主格結構的干擾

分詞構句就是指用**現在分詞或過去分詞所引導的伴隨副詞**、原因副詞等；獨立主格結構有時由 with 引導，看似主詞－動詞結構，但實際上並沒有真正的動詞部分。由於這些成分的干擾，不僅增加了句子的長度，而且很容易使人錯把它們當成主句。在此，我們不想去研究它們的語法結構，我們所要探討的是，**在閱讀時如何分辨主句和這些從屬部分**。

應對之道：主句最重要的特徵就是有**完整的主詞－動詞結構**，尤其是獨立的動詞部分。什麼樣的詞能構成獨立的動詞部分呢？注意：do\does 和 is\am\are 的各種時態變化都可以做動詞，但 to do\doing\done 和 to be\being\been 等不定詞、動名詞或現在分詞和過去分詞，是不可以用作動詞的。一個看似句子的結構，如果沒有獨立的動詞部分，那它就不是句子了，而是分詞片語或是**獨立主格結構**。

例如：

"With as many as 120 varieties in existence, discovering how cancer works is not easy."

With 引導的是一個獨立主格結構，在這句中做原因副詞，意為「由於現存的癌症有 120 種之多，所以⋯⋯」。這句的主詞是由一個複雜的動名詞片語來擔綱，即 "discovering how cancer works"（要找出癌症的運作方式）。由於這個句子的副詞較長，主詞又是這樣一個複雜的結構，所以大家往往會覺得找不到這句的主幹。實際上，**只要抓住主動詞就很容易找到句子主幹**。由於是現在分詞或動名詞的形式，所以在這個句子中，**discovering** 絕不可能是主動詞。**它是一個動名詞**，相當於名詞的用法，因此**它是做主詞的**。works 雖然是動詞，但它是 how cancer works 這個子句中的動詞，而不是主句的動詞。所以，**主句的動詞只有 "is"**。

四、三合一的超複雜句子

然而，在實際的閱讀過程中，我們常常會碰到包含上面三種情況的超複雜句子，亦即一個句子中既有子句又有插入成分，還有**分詞構句**或**獨立主格結構**。

應對之道：閱讀這種句子的正確方法是，**由前向後，抓住獨立的動詞部分從而區別出主句和分詞構句**，再根據子句的連接詞（有時並無連接詞）來區分主句和子句，層層理解，插入語插在哪個層次就放在哪個層次中理解。例句：

"Declaring that he was opposed to using this unusual animal husbandry technique to clone humans, he ordered that federal funds not be used for such an experiment—although no one had proposed to do so—and asked an independent panel of experts chaired by Princeton President Harold Shapiro to report back to the White House in 90 days with recommendations for a national policy on human cloning."

這句相當長。主句在哪裡？首先我們應該在由前向後閱讀的過程中，根據獨立的主動詞找到主句。第一個動詞是 declaring，由於單純的現在分詞形式不能做動詞，所以它引導的是一個伴隨副詞。主句的主詞是第二行的 he，動詞是 ordered，後面的 that 所引導的名詞子句做 ordered 的受詞，這個受詞子句中還出現了一個插入語（用破折號標示）。

受詞子句的全部內容屬於下一個層次，可以暫時不看。再看破折號後面，又出現了一個獨立的動詞 asked，由於子句的主詞 federal funds（聯邦經費）不會做出 asked（要求）的動作，因此 asked 也是主句的動詞；這說明了主句的主詞 he 共做出了兩個動作 ordered 和 asked，用 and 連接，asked 的後面也有一個比較長的受詞片語。

在釐清了文章的第一層結構是 Declaring that..., he ordered that... and asked... 之後，現在就可以分別分析這三個動詞的受詞部分了。

(a.) **Declaring 後面是一個由 that 所引導的受詞子句**，表示其宣佈的內容是「反對利用這項不尋常的畜牧技術來複製人體」，而做 declaring 這個動作的人當然是 he（因省略相同的主詞而將 declared 變成 declaring）；

(b.) ordered 之後也是一個受詞子句，但其中又插入了一個成分：「他同時下令禁止動用聯邦經費來做這種試驗──儘管還不曾有人提出要這樣做」；

(c.) asked 這個動詞後面通常使用 **ask sb. to do sth.** 的結構。這一段比較複雜，但其主要結構仍是 asked an independent panel ... to report back，只不過每個主要成分又有限定和修飾語。這一段的意思是「要求一個由普林斯頓大學校長 Harold Shapiro 領軍的獨立專家小組在 90 天內向白宮彙報，對制定人體複製方面的國家政策提供建議。」

Unit 14　假主詞

必閃陷阱 非學不可

除祈使句 (imperatives) 外，英文的子句都要有主詞。有時當**動詞沒有主詞，因為真正的主詞位在句中某處時，我們必須使用形式主詞或假主詞** (preparatory subjects or anticipatory subjects or dummy subjects)。**英文所用的假主詞有二：There 和 it**。

There 在 There is (There's) 和 There are 結構中是**當作假主詞，真正主詞是 There is 或 There are 後面的名詞或名詞片語**。例如：

◆ **There's** a girl on the phone for you.（O）
（有個女生打電話找你。）

→ 這句的 There 是假主詞，真正主詞是 (a) girl。

◇ She's a girl on the phone for you.（✕）

◇ It's a girl on the phone for you.（✕）

◇ Is a girl on the phone for you.（✕）

◆ **There are** three foreigners in our community.（O）
（我們社區有三個老外。）

→ 這句的 There 是假主詞，真正主詞是 (three) foreigners。

◇ They are three foreigners in our community.（✕）

◇ Are three foreigners in our community.（✕）

It 在句中當假主詞時，真正主詞有三種型態：不定詞片語、動名詞片語

及 that 子句。例如：

◆ **It's very hard to believe** that he is an honest employee.（O）
（很難相信他是個誠實的員工。）

◇ Is very hard to believe that he is an honest employee.（✕）

→ 這句的 It 是假主詞，真正主詞是不定詞片語 "to believe that he is an honest employee"。所以，這句可改成 To believe that he is an honest employee is very hard.。

◆ **It's worth/worthwhile calling** him to clear up the misunderstanding between you and him.（O）
（值得打電話給他澄清你和他之間的誤會。）

◇ Is worth/worthwhile calling him to clear up the misunderstanding between you and him.（✕）

→ 這句的 It 是假主詞，真正主詞是動名詞片語 "calling him to clear up the misunderstanding between you and him"。所以，這句可改成 Calling him to clear up the misunderstanding between you and him is worthwhile.。

◆ **It is difficult (that)** they would finish their work in two days.（O）
（他們要在兩天內完成工作是有困難的。）

◇ Is difficult (that) they would finish their work in two days.（×）

→ 這句的 It 是假主詞，真正主詞是名詞子句 "that they would finish their work in two days"。所以，這句可改成 That they would finish their work in two days is difficult.。注意：若將真正主詞（即 that 所引導的名詞子句）置於主句的動詞之前，則 that 不能省略。）

Unit 15 補語

重要觀念 非學不可 🔍

補語 (complements) 是英文句子的四個構成要素之一，另外三個要素分別為主詞 (subjects)、動詞 (verbs) 和受詞 (objects)。不過，有人還將修飾成分（adjuncts，指在句中提供其他資料的副詞或副詞片語）列為第五個要素。

下列為吾人在學習英文過程中都會學到的**五大句型**：

1. S + V
2. S + V + C
3. S + V + O
4. S + V + O + C
5. S + V + O + O

從這五個基本句型可知，它們總共所含的就只有上述四個要素，即主詞 (S)、動詞 (V)、受詞 (O) 和補語 (C)，其中主詞與受詞必須是名詞、代名詞或名詞類 (如動名詞)，而補語通常是名詞或形容詞。在這些句型中，**補語只出現在 S + V + C 和 S + V + O + C 中，前者的補語為主詞補語，後者為受詞補語。**

主詞補語的作用係在**為主詞補充、添加更多資料，以使句子的意思完整**，它們通常位在連綴動詞後面──連綴動詞包括 BE 動詞、感官動詞 (smell、taste 等) 和狀態或靜態動詞 (appear、go、get、become、remain、seem 等)。主詞補語可以是名詞片語、形容詞片語、副詞片語或介系詞片語。例如：

1. Paul is an English teacher.
（保羅是英文老師。）
→ 名詞片語 an English teacher 當主詞補語。

2. He's a cousin of mine.
（他是我的一位堂兄弟。）
→ 名詞片語 a cousin of mine 當主詞補語。

3. Both her brothers became doctors.
（她的兩個哥哥都當了醫生。）
→ 名詞 (片語) doctors 當主詞補語。

4. Mary seems very happy with her new job.
（瑪麗對她的新工作似乎很滿意。）
→ 形容詞片語 very happy (with her new job) 當主詞補語。

5. That cake smells good.
（那蛋糕聞起來不錯。）
→ 形容詞（片語）good 當主詞補語。

6. The drink tastes of mint.
（這飲料有股薄荷味。）
→ 介系詞片語 of mint 當主詞補語。

7. Her hands smell of onions.
（她手上有洋蔥味。）
→ 介系詞片語 of onions 當主詞補語。

8. Peter remained outside while his sister went into the clinic.
（彼得的妹妹進入診所時，他留在外面。）
→ 副詞（片語）outside 當主詞補語。

9. All my books are upstairs.
（我的書全部放在樓上。）
→ 副詞（片語）upstairs 當主詞補語。

必須注意的是，**主詞補語與受詞截然不同**。例如：

1. She became an English teacher.
（她當了英文老師。）

→ became 為連綴動詞，an English teacher 為**主詞補語**，與主詞 she 是同一個人。（句型：S＋V＋C）

2. She married an English teacher.
（她嫁給一名英文老師。）

→ an English teacher 為動詞 married 的**受詞**，與主詞 she 為不同人。（句型：S＋V＋O）

必閃陷阱 非學不可 🔍

我們亦可在 **BE 動詞後面使用代名詞來做主詞補語**，但通常使用**受格代名詞**，即 me、us、him、her 和 them 等。例如：

1.

A: Who's that? Is that the girl you told me about?
(A：那是誰？是你跟我說過的那個女孩嗎？)

◆ B: Well, that's **her** over there. （〇）
◇ B: Well, that's she over there. （×）
（B：嗯，那邊那個女孩就是她。）

(Tom is in the room. Jack and John are knocking at the door.)
Tom: Who's **it**?
(湯姆：誰啊？)

2.

◆ Jack: It's **me** and John. （〇）
（傑克：是我跟約翰。）

◇ Jack: It's I and John. （×）
◇ Jack: It's John and I. （×）
（傑克：是約翰跟我。）

3.

◆ The dog knew it was **us** so he barked before we even came to the door. （〇）
◇ The dog knew it was we so he barked before we even came to the door. （×）
（狗知道是我們，所以我們還沒走到門，他就叫了。）

上面的 **it's ＋ 受格代名詞或 it is/was ＋ 受格代名詞**與強調成分為代名詞的分裂句 (cleft sentences) 結構看起來非常相似，但其實不然。在正式的上下文中，**分裂句中的強調成分若為人稱代名詞，一般都使用主格代名詞**，即 I、we、he、she 和 they 等。例如：

◆ It was they that cleaned the classroom yesterday.（O）
（就是他們昨天打掃教室。）

然而，在非正式情況中，**分裂句中的主格代名詞往往被寫成受格型態。**
例如：

◆ It is **us** who will come up with the solutions.（O）
（日後提出解決方案的人就是我們。）

受詞補語的作用就是為受詞補充、添加更多資料，以使句意完整。例如：

1. He will make her a good wife.
（他將使她成為好太太。）
→ 名詞片語 a good wife 當受詞 her 的補語。換言之，her = a good wife（注意：當受詞補語為名詞時，它和受詞是指同一人或同一物。）

2. Playing computer games always makes him very happy.
（玩電腦遊戲總是讓他很高興。）
→ 形容詞片語 very happy 當受詞 him 的補語。

3. Amy put her clothes in the cupboard.
（艾美把她的衣服放在衣櫥裡。）
→ 介系詞片語 in the cupboard 當受詞 her clothes 的補語。

在 S ＋ V ＋ O ＋ C 句型中，動詞係不完全及物動詞，除了需要受詞外，還需要補語才能表示完整意思。**上面三句若無受詞補語都無法單獨存在。**

Unit 16 過去分詞用作補語與被動態的區別

重要觀念 非學不可 🔍

過去分詞可以用作形容詞（亦即所謂的過去分詞形容詞），形成補語結構，但它也經常用於**被動語態**。因此，過去分詞可謂**靜態與動態結構**的混合體。靜態結構用來描述事物的**性質或狀態**，動態結構則是用來描述**動作及動作過程**。由於在表達形式上這兩種結構是一樣的，都由 "BE ＋過去分詞" 所構成，因此使我們在區別補語用法和被動語態用法時產生了困擾。現將幾種區別方法歸納如下：

從動詞的性質來區分

英文中的不及物動詞沒有被動態，但**不及物動詞的過去分詞可以用作形容詞**，放在 BE 動詞的後面作為**主詞補語**。在此結構中，過去分詞只表示動作已經完成，強調事物的狀態。常見的這種形式的不及物動詞包括 gone, come, arrived, fallen, retired, startled, vexed, mistaken 等等。這些不及物動詞都具有描述的性質。例如：

1. John was back to his hometown when he was retired.
（約翰退休後返回他的故鄉。）
2. His fever is gone, but he still feels weak.
（他已退燒，但身體仍感到虛弱。）
3. Winter is come.
（冬天來了。）

然而，如果過去分詞的動詞本身是**持續性動詞**，那就不表示動作的結果，而是**強調動作的持續性**，在這種情況下過去分詞大多是被動態。例如：

1. All the fruits were carried to the market.
（所有水果都被運送到市場。）

2. Several students were honored for their excellent performance in the final English exam.
（數名學生因英文期末考的優異表現而受到褒獎。）

從句子表達的內容來區分

被動態表示動作，**句子的主詞是動作的承受者**；補語結構中的**過去分詞**基本上已失去了動詞的意義，只有形容詞的作用，在句子中**作補語**，說明主詞的性質、所具有的特徵或所處的狀態。例如：

1. Their houses were beautifully decorated.
（他們的房子裝潢得很漂亮。）

→ 補語

2. Their houses were decorated and rented to several people.
（他們的房子裝潢後租給數個人。）

→ 被動態

3. The book is not illustrated.
（這本書沒有畫插圖。）

→ 補語

4. The book was beautifully illustrated by a famous artist.
（這本書由一位著名畫家畫上精美的插圖。）

→ 被動態

注意：在現代英語中，有一些是從古英語遺留下來的只能用作形容詞的過去分詞。這種**分詞形容詞特性顯著，完全作形容詞用**，如 amused, broken, closed, confused, crowded, covered, done, delighted, frightened, bent, blessed, bound, drunk, lit, melted, rotten, shaved, shrunk, sunk, believed, burnt, excited, faded, married, interested, pleased, satisfied, surprised 等等。

從過去分詞後所接的介系詞來區別

用作形容詞的過去分詞在個別情況下，**可以跟 by 以外的其他介詞連用**，如 about, at, in, on, with, over, to 等等。例如：

1. I'm interested in playing baseball, basketball, and table tennis.
（我喜歡打棒球、籃球和桌球。）

→ 補語

2. I was interested by what you showed me.
（我被你給我看的東西引發了興趣。）

→ 被動態

3. We are all really annoyed with his bad behavior.
（我們都對他不良的行為感到煩透了。）

→ 補語

4. I was much surprised by Mr. Lee's rudeness.
（我被李先生的粗魯無禮嚇了一大跳。）

→ 被動態

5. Her look was quite amused.
（她的神情相當愉快。）

→ 補語

6. The audience was amused by the performance.
（觀眾被這個表演逗樂了。）

→ 被動態

從修飾語來區分

在英文用法中，**過去分詞具有形容詞性質**，因此**可用程度副詞 more, quite, rather, very 等來修飾**。凡是能用這類副詞來修飾的過去分詞，大多為補語結構。例如：

1. Her look was quite amused.
（她的神情相當愉快。）

2. After working all day long, they were very tired.
（在工作一整天後，他們非常疲倦。）

倘若**過去分詞結構中是由時間副詞、地點副詞、原因副詞或方式副詞來修飾整個句子**，表示動作的持續性、重複性，那麼該句就是**被動態**。例如：

1. The work is completed.
（工作完成了。）
→ 補語

2. The work will be completed within two months.
（這件工作將在兩個月內完成。）
→ 被動態

3. He was wounded.
（他受傷了。）
→ 補語

4. He was wounded in the fight.
（他在打架中負傷。）
→ 被動態

利用時態來區分

補語結構中的 BE 動詞為連綴動詞，多用於簡單現在式和簡單過去式，有時在補語結構中也可見到簡單未來式和現在完成式。而**被動態結構中的 BE 動詞是助動詞，除了甚少用於完成進行式和未來完成式之外，**可以用於各種時態。例如：

1. I shall be much obliged if you can help me with my homework.
（如果你能幫我做家庭作業，我將會非常感激。）
→ 補語

2. The old house is being demolished.
（那棟舊房子正在被拆除。）
→ 被動態

必閃陷阱 非學不可

注意：英語是個「當省則省」的語言，也就是説，**省略 (ellipsis) 是英文的一個重要特色，但若省過頭了，就不是一件好事了──不合語法**。例如：The agreement was annulled.（這協議被取消了。）這個被動句中的 was 是助動詞，而 Its annulment was welcome.（協議被取消受到大家的歡迎。）這句中的 was 是連綴動詞。當我們把這兩句放在一起時，若寫成 The agreement was annulled and its annulment (was) welcome.（省略第二個 was），那就不合語法，因為**這兩個 was 的性質不同，所以第二個 was 不能省略**。

另外，從時態方面來考量，區分**被動態和補語結構時，可用「還原法」**來看能否**將 BE + 過去分詞形式還原為對應的主動態**。如果是**被動態，它的時態要與相應的主動結構一致**。如果是**補語結構，一般並無對應時態的主動結構**。例如：

1. The window is broken.
（窗戶破了。）

→ 此句是補語結構，沒有對應時態的主動句，**不能還原**為 Someone breaks the window.

2. A lot of employees have been sacked since the organizational reforms have been adopted.
（自採取組織改革以來，有許多員工已遭到解雇。）

→ 此句是被動態，可以還原為主動態：We have sacked a lot of employees since we adopted the organizational reforms.

從 BE 動詞能否被替代來區分

被動態一般是由**助動詞 BE + 過去分詞**所構成。**補語結構**除了與 BE 動**詞連用**之外，還可以用其他動詞來替換。能夠執行這項功能的動詞都是屬於連綴動詞，包括 become, get, turn, sound, rest, lie, look, keep, remain, seem, appear 等等。例如：

1. After working the whole morning, they looked very tired.
（在工作整個上午之後，他們看起來非常疲倦。）

2. He appeared confused about the future.
（他對未來似乎感到茫然。）

以上我們使用 **look** 和 **appear** 來替換 BE。我們可以認定該句**是補語結構。如果不能替換就是被動結構。**不過，還要注意 get 的用法。**Get ＋過去分詞既可作補語結構，**也可以作**被動結構**，究竟屬於那種結構，主要是看說話者強調的重點。如果強調的是**動作**，那麼該結構就是**被動結構**，反之，則是**補語結構**。例如：

The house will get painted next week.
（這棟房子下週要油漆。）
→ 此句強調動作，因此我們可以認定此句是被動結構。

Unit 17 與 hope 有關的幾個重要文法觀念

必閃陷阱 非學不可

Hope 可當動詞和名詞用，是個大家所熟知的字。然而，並非每個人都完全掌握它的正確用法。一個這麼常用的字，如果文法用錯了，委實說不過去。以下就來說明與 hope 有關的幾個重要文法觀念。

Hope 當動詞時經常後接省略連接詞 that 的名詞子詞，而在名詞子句中，我們經常**使用現在式來表示未來**。例如：

1. I hope my girlfriend comes today.
（我希望我女友今天來。）

2. We hope you pass your exam next week.
（我們希望你下週通過考試。）

3. We hope the train is on time tomorrow.
（我們希望明天火車準時。）

4. I hope that he will succeed.
（我希望他會成功。）

5. I just hope you will help me.
（我只希望你會幫助我。）

Hope 不可用於否定句。例如：

◆ We **hope** it doesn't rain.（○）
（我們希望不要下雨。）

◇ We don't hope it rains.（×）
（我們不希望下雨。）

◆ I **hope** you don't waste your time and energy on trifles.（○）
（我希望你別把時間和精力浪費在瑣事上。）

◇ I don't hope you waste your time and energy on trifles.（×）
（我不希望你把時間和精力浪費在瑣事上。）

Hope 可用作可數名詞。例如：

1. There is still a slim hope of success.
（仍有一線成功的希望。）

2. Our team's hopes of a championship are fading fast.
（我們這一隊獲得冠軍的希望正在快速消逝。）

Hope 亦可用作不可數名詞。但泛指時，hope 只能當不可數名詞用，其前不可有定冠詞 the。例如：

These young people are full of hope for the future.
（這些年輕人對前途充滿希望。）

◆ You must never give up **hope**.（○）
◇ You must never give up the hope.（×）
（你一定不要絕望。）

Part II
寫作用法精論

Chapter 2

字彙與片語

Chapter 2 | 字彙 & 片語

Unit 01　A lot、lots 和 plenty 的代名詞用法

> ### 重要觀念 非學不可 🔍
>
> **A lot、lots 和 plenty** 係用於非正式的上下文來表示數量、金額和程度等。**A lot** 和 **lots** 用作代名詞或名詞時，意思相當於 **much** 和 **many**，而 lots 又比 a lot 更加非正式。
>
> **Plenty** 當代名詞用時意為「**足夠 (enough)；夠多 (more than enough)**」。例如：

1. That's plenty.
（夠了。）

2. 500 US dollars will be plenty.
（500 美元夠多的了。）

3. A: How long will it take?
（A：那要花多久的時間？）

 B: Two hours should be plenty.
（B：兩個小時應該夠了。）

> **A lot、lots 和 plenty** 後面須有 **of** 才能接名詞；a lot of 和 lots of 意為「很多的」，而 plenty of 意為「很多的；充裕的；足夠的」。它們**都可接可數和不可數名詞**。例如：

1. A lot of people don't like the plan much.
（很多人都不太喜歡這項計畫。）

2. Mary eats a lot of fruit.
（瑪麗水果吃得很多。）

3. He has lots of relatives.
（他有很多親戚。）

4. He earned lots of money last year.
（他去年賺了很多錢。）

5. The students have plenty of ideas.
（這些學生有很多想法。）

6. They've always had plenty of money.
（他們總是有很多錢。）

◆ Don't hurry! We have **plenty of time**.（○）
◇ Don't hurry! We have plenty time.（×）
（別急！們有的是時間／我們有足夠的時間。）

> **必閃陷阱 非學不可**

如果 a lot、lots 和 plenty 後面的名詞不言可喻，那麼該名詞通常被省略。當它們後面沒有名詞時，**of 就不需要了**。例如：

1. A: Do you have any friends?
（A：你有任何朋友嗎？）

   B: Yes, I have a lot (of friends).
（B：有，我有很多（朋友）。）

◆ John didn't bring anything to eat but there's **lots (of food)** in the kitchen.（○）
◇ John didn't bring anything to eat but there's lots of in the kitchen.（×）
（約翰沒有帶任何吃的東西來，但廚房有很多（食物）。）
◆ This car cost me **plenty (of money)**.（○）
◇ This car cost me plenty of.（×）
（這部車花了我很多錢。）

在比較正式的上下文中，我們通常使用 **a good/great deal of（＋ 單數不可數名詞）**、 **a large number of（＋ 複數名詞）**或 **a large quantity of（＋ 單數不可數名詞或複數名詞）**來表示「很多的；大量的」意思。例如：

1. A good deal of research has been done already.
（已經做了大量的研究。）

221

2. He spent a great deal of time on the plan.
（他花了大量的時間在這項計畫上。）

3. A large number of letters of complaint have been received.
（已經收到大量的投訴信。）

4. A large quantity of imported American beef has been sold.
（已售出了大量的進口美牛。）

Unit 02　Across、over 和 through 的用法

重要觀念 非學不可

由於這三個介系詞或副詞的意思加起來少説也有幾十個之多（這還不包括它們用作其他詞類的意思），本文將僅重點式地説明其中一些相關的用法及其用法上的差異。

Across

Across 可當介系詞和副詞用，分別意為「穿過，橫過，越過（有明確邊緣、界線和範圍的地方，如鄉鎮城市、道路或河流），從一邊到另一邊；在……的對面，在……的對岸，在……的另一邊／另一頭；遍及，在……各處，在整個……」和「從一邊到另一邊，到對面，到對岸；寬（或直徑或對角線長度）」。例如：

介系詞用法

1. We walked across the field/street.
（我們穿過田野／橫過街道。）

2. I walked across the room.
（我走過房間。）

3. She took a boat across the river.
（她乘船過河。）

4. There are two bridges across the river.
（那條河上有兩座橋。）

5. The restaurant is just across the road.
（餐廳就在馬路對面。）

6. He stared at the girl across the table.
（他注視著坐在桌子對面的那個女孩。）

7. He stared across the room at his wife.
（他注視著房間另一頭的太太。）

8. *The Teenage Psychic* became popular across Asia.
（《通靈少女》在亞洲各國廣受歡迎。）

9 The company has branches across the world.
（那家公司在世界各地都設有分公司。）

10. The virus has spread across most of the country.
（病毒已蔓延到該國大部分地區。）

必閃陷阱 非學不可

當我們**要表達「從一邊到另一邊；遍及，在……各處，在整個……」**的意思時，**要使用 across，不可用 on**。例如：

◆ He divided the paper by drawing a red line **across** it.（○）
◇ He divided the paper by drawing a red line on it.（✕）
（他在紙上 [從一邊到另一邊] 劃一條紅線，將它分成兩半。）
◆ Newspapers were scattered **across** the floor.（○）
◇ Newspapers were scattered on the floor.（✕）
（報紙散落一地。）

副詞用法

1. She came across to talk with me.
（她走過來跟我交談。）

2. When they reached the river, they simply swam across.
（他們到河邊後便直接游了過去。）

3. The road is busy and it is hard for us to get across.
（這條路交通繁忙，我們很難穿越過去。）

4. The table is 120 cm long and 55 cm across.
（這張桌子長 120 公分、寬 55 公分。）

5. The lake is two kilometers across.
（湖面寬兩公里。）

美式英語經常使用 **"across from"** 來表示「**在……的對面**；在……的另一邊／另一頭」的意思。例如：

1. She's staying at a little hotel just across from the Guatemalan Embassy.
（她住在瓜地馬拉大使館正對面的小旅館。）

2. The post office is just across from the drugstore.
（郵局就在藥局的對面。）

3. His office is just across from hers.
（他的辦公室是在她的辦公室的另一頭。）

Over

Over 亦可當介系詞和副詞用，分別意為「在……上方，在正上方；（覆蓋）在……上面；越過……上方，從一邊到另一邊；在……對面，在……的另一邊／另一頭；在……期間」和「在上方；越過，從一邊到另一邊；在／到對面，在／到另一邊／另一頭」。**Over 所表示的某物處於另一物的正上方，往往指上面的物體從一邊移動到另一邊的情況**。例如：

介系詞用法

1. They live over a small restaurant.
（他們住在一家小餐館的樓上。）

2. I held the umbrella over my boss.
（我給我的老闆撐傘。）

3. A plane flew over the house.
（一架飛機飛過了房子。）

4. The sheep jumped over the wall.
（羊跳過牆。）

5. He looked over the wall.
（他從牆頭望過去。）

6. I walked over a bridge.
（我從橋上走過去。）

7. My mother frequently chats with our neighbor over the garden fence.
（我母親經常和我們鄰居隔著花園的籬笆閒聊。）

8. There's a nightclub over the road we could go to.
（我們可以去路那邊的一家夜店。）

9. He spread a carpet over the floor.
（他在地板上鋪了地毯。）

10. She pulled the blanket over her head and fell asleep.
（她把毯子拉上來遮著頭睡著了。）

11. My grandparents will stay over the Lunar New Year.
（我的祖父母在春節期間將待在這兒。）

副詞用法

1. A plane flew over and crashed into an apartment building.
（一架飛機飛過上空，然後墜毀撞擊一棟公寓大樓。）

2. You can come over any time; I'm always in.
（你隨時可以來家裡坐坐，我都在家。）

3. Who's that woman over there?
（那邊那個女人是誰？）

用作副詞時，over 與 across 在「從一邊到另一邊；到對面，到另一邊／另一頭」的意思上是同義詞。例如：

1. They walked over to the restaurant.
（他們走到 [馬路] 對面的餐廳。）

= They walked across to the restaurant.

2. Mary stepped over to the other side to avoid meeting Kevin.
（瑪麗走到街道的另一邊以避免跟凱文碰面。）

= Mary stepped across to the other side to avoid meeting Kevin.

Through

Through 同樣可當介系詞和副詞用，意思與 across 或 over 都有若干重疊之處，但下面將僅討論 through 與 across 或 over 的一些用法差異。

Across 還是 through 呢？

當我們從一邊移動到另一邊時，如果是位在某物的裡面或被某物所圍繞，譬如說在森林或長草中或在某個鄉鎮城市或其他地點中，那麼我們要用 **through 來取代 across**。例如：

◆ When I walked **through** the forest, I saw a grizzly bear.（○）
◇ When I walked across the forest, I saw a grizzly bear.（✕）
（當我穿過森林時，我看見一頭棕熊。）

◆ His dog ran **through** long grass and got lost the other day.（○）
◇ His dog ran across long grass and got lost the other day.（✕）
（幾天前他的狗跑進長草中就不見了。）

◆ I love cycling **through** the small fishing village Sundays.（○）
◇ I love cycling across the small fishing village Sundays.（✕）
（我喜歡每星期天騎單車經過那個小漁村。）

◆ She's travelling **through** Europe at the moment.（○）
◇ She's travelling across Europe at the moment.（✕）
（她目前正在周遊歐洲。）

在指**從開始到結束的一段時間**時，美式英語通常使用 **through**，而英式英語則使用 **from ... to / till ...**。例如：

1. The clothing store is open Monday through Saturday, 10 a.m.—6 p.m.
→ 美式英語
2. The clothing store is open from Monday to Saturday, 10 a.m.—6 p.m.
→ 英式英語
（這家服裝店營業時間為週一至週六，早上 10 點至下午 6 點。）

然而，**當從開始到結束的某段時間有明確的天數、週數、月數或年數等等時，我們須使用 over，不可用 through**。例如：

I was in Kaohsiung over the winter.
（我整個冬季都在高雄。）

◆ I haven't seen John **over** the last five months. （O）

◇ I haven't seen John through the last five months. （×）
（過去五個月期間，我都沒有見到約翰。）

◆ **Over** the last few years/over the last decade, we have seen a sudden increase in the number of cases of divorce. （O）

◇ Through the last few years/through the last decade, we have seen a sudden increase in the number of cases of divorce. （×）
（過去幾年間／過去十年間，離婚案例突然增加了。）

◆ Most hotels are fully booked **over** the holiday weekend. （O）

◇ Most hotels are fully booked through the holiday weekend. （×）
（大多數旅館在假日週末都被訂滿了。）

Unit 03　Age 的名詞用法

重要觀念 非學不可

Age 用作名詞時主要意為「年齡」。例如：

1. Robert looks a lot older but he is actually the same age as me.
（羅伯特看起來老很多，但他其實跟我同齡。）

2. The average age of the students was under 20.
（這些學生的平均年齡不到 20 歲。）

At the age of 意為「（某人）幾歲時」，是個常用的片語。例如：

1. His daughter started to learn the piano at the age of four.
（他女兒四歲開始學鋼琴。）

2. The two brothers became professional tennis players at the ages of twenty-four and twenty-seven.
（這兩個兄弟在 24 和 27 歲時成為職業網球選手。）

必閃陷阱 非學不可

At the age of 為固定用語，所以在指人的年齡時不可使用 in the age of。例如：

◆ **At the age of** 40, I started to learn English.（O）
◇ In the age of 40, I started to learn English.（×）
（40 歲時我開始學英文。）
◆ Kevin entered Parliament **at the age of** 25.（O）
◇ Kevin entered Parliament in the age of 25.（×）
（凱文 25 歲時成為國會議員。）

除了 at the age of 外，我們亦可使用下面幾種方式來**談及某人的年齡**。例如：

John will be 30 on October 10.
（約翰到 10 月 10 日就 30 歲了。）
John will be 30 years old on 10th October.
John will be 30 years of age on the tenth of October.
→（比較正式的用法）

在**詢問或談論某人現在的年齡**（今年貴庚）或某物存在的時間時，我們要使用 **How old ...?** 而**不用 What age ...?**。例如：

◆ **How old** are you, Tom?（O）
◇ What is your age, Tom?（×）
（你幾歲了，湯姆？）
◆ I'm not sure **how old** his sister is.（O）
◇ I'm not sure what age his sister is.（×）
（我不太確定他妹妹多大。）
◆ **How old** is your car?（O）
◇ What age is your car?（×）
(你的車子買多久了？)

然而，

◆ **What's the age** of that old building?（O）
（那棟古老的建築有多久的歷史呢？）

◆ Do you know **the age** of that old building?（O）
（你知道那棟古老的建築有多久的歷史嗎？）

What age ...? 係用來談論過去或將來某一時間某人的年齡。例如：

◆ At **what age** did you start playing tennis?（O）
（你幾歲開始打網球呢？）

◆ Have you decided **what age** you will retire at?（O）
（你已決定幾歲退休了嗎？）

好用 Tips 非學不可

在非正式場合或口語中，我們可以使用 **age** 的複數型 **ages** 來表示「**很長時間；很久**」。英式英語有時亦使用 **an age** 來表示相同的意思。例如：

1. She took ages to answer the door.
（她過了很久才應門。）

2. The party was planned ages ago.
（派對很久以前就計畫好了。）

3. It seems (like) ages / an age since we last saw Peter.
（我們似乎很久沒有看到彼得了。）

4. It's been ages / an age since we last spoke.
（我們好久沒有交談了。）

Age 當名詞用時還意為「年老；衰老；老化；陳年」，但此時 age 往往與介系詞 **with** 連用，以 with age 這個當副詞用的介系詞片語來表示隨著年齡或時間越來越年老、衰老、老化、陳年的意思。例如：

1. With age, our reactions get slower.
（隨著年齡的增長，我們的反應會變得越來越慢。）

2. My father's back was bent with age.
（隨著年齡的增長，我父親的背駝了。）

3. His temper hasn't improved with age!
（他的脾氣並未隨著年齡的增長而變好！）

4. Good wines improve with age.
（酒越陳越好。）

最後值得一提的是，**age 還意為「時代；時期」**。若指歷史上的特定時期，該時期經常被視為專有名詞，連同 age 都要大寫，如 the Ice Age（冰河時期）。例如：

1. We live in a materialistic age.
（我們生活在一個物質主義時代。）

2. We live in the Space Age.
（我們生活在太空時代。）

3. Life in the Middle Ages was very hard for most people.
（在中世紀，大多數人的生活都非常艱辛。）
→ 注意：別把 **the Middle Ages**（中世紀—西元 476 至 1453 年的歐洲歷史時期）寫成 the middle age（中年—通常指 40 到 60 歲。）

Unit 04 At all 的用法

必閃陷阱 非學不可

At all 是個副詞片語，意為「根本，到底，無論如何，絲毫，一點兒」，係用於否定句和疑問句（不可用於肯定句），表示強調。例如：

1. Our manager never laughed at all.
（我們經理從來不笑。）

2. It is not so much how much he leaked out the plans of the pay cuts; the question is whether he leaks at all.
（他洩漏多少減薪的計畫無關緊要；問題在於他到底有沒有洩漏。）

3. He hasn't been at all well recently.
（最近他的健康非常差。）

4. He'll propose tomorrow if he proposes to Mary at all.
（如果他真的要向瑪麗求婚的話，那麼他一定會在明天採取行動。）

5. Is there any possibility at all of snow tonight?
（今晚真的有可能下雪嗎？）

6. Is there any uncertainty at all about the way she committed suicide?
（對於她自殺的方式，有沒有任何疑點呢？）

好用 Tips 非學不可 🔍

At all 可以用在形容詞之前或之後。例如：

1. He was not at all surprised.
（他一點也不驚訝。）

= He was not surprised at all.

2. Her argument wasn't at all convincing.
（她的論據絲毫沒有說服力。）

= Her argument wasn't convincing at all.

3. Is it at all possible that John alone can drink ten bottles of beer?
（難道約翰真的能一個人喝十瓶啤酒嗎？）

= Is it possible at all that John alone can drink ten bottles of beer?

At all 經常用在問句的末尾來使問句聽起來更有禮貌。例如：

1. Would you like any desserts at all?
（您想要甜點嗎？）

2. Do you have any small change at all?
（你有零錢嗎？）

我們可以使用 **not at all（別客氣；一點都不）** 來對 Would you mind ...? 或 Do you mind (if) ...?（[如果]……你介意嗎？你反對……嗎？）這兩個常用問句以及別人對你說 thank you 的禮貌回答。例如：

1. A: Would you mind turning (= please turn) your ringtone down a little please?
（A：你介意將手機鈴聲調小一點嗎？／請你將手機鈴聲調小一點好嗎？）

  B: No, not at all.
（B：不，一點都不。）

2. A: Do you mind if I (= May I) use your computer?
（A：你介意我用你的電腦嗎？）

  B: Not at all.
（B：一點都不。）

3. A: Thank you for your help.
（A：感謝您的幫忙。）

  B: Not at all.
（B：不客氣。）

4. A: It's very kind of you to help me, thank you.
（A：承蒙惠助，不勝感激。）

  B: Not at all.
（B：別客氣。）

Unit 05 At、on 和 in 後接地點的用法

重要觀念 非學不可

At 可用來指位置或地點，意為「在……；在……裡；在……旁」。例如：

1. My girlfriend was already waiting at the gate when I got there.
（當我到達那裡時，我女朋友已在大門口等候了。）

2. Mary was sitting at her desk.
（瑪麗坐在她的書桌前。）

3. Gary's sitting at the table in the corner.
（蓋瑞坐在角落的一張桌子旁。）

4. There's a telephone booth/box at the crossroads.
（十字路口有個電話亭。）

→ 注意：crossroads 雖是複數型，但卻是個單數可數名詞。

必閃陷阱 非學不可 🔍

At 可用來指在某家公司上班或在某個工作場所工作，但在**某部門工作（任職於某部門）或在辦公室、辦事處、事務所等建築物工作，要用 in。**某家公司的承包商或顧問，由於不是員工，一般都用 **with**。例如：

1. She works at Google.
（她在谷歌上班。）

= She works for Google.

2. She works in the accounting department at Google.
（她任職於谷歌的會計部門。）

3. She works with Google as a consultant.
（她擔任谷歌的顧問。）

4. She should be at work by now.
（她現在應該在上班。）

→ at work（在上班）、go to work（去上班）或 off work（沒上班）中的 work 都意為「工作場所；上班的地方」。

At 可用來指提供美容美髮或醫療服務等的場所。在下面的例句中，**「各行各業從業人員 ＋ 's」是指各該從業人員的工作場所**，為可數名詞。這大多是英式英語的用法。例如：

1. My wife has got a six o'clock appointment at the hairdresser's (or salon or hairdressing salon).
（我太太約好了六點鐘到美容院。）

2. I've got a four o'clock appointment at the barber's (or barbershop).
（我約好了四點鐘到理髮店。）

3. Frank's at the dentist's (or dental clinic) –he'll be back soon.
（法蘭克去看牙醫──他很快就會回來。）

4. He was at the doctor's (or clinic) this morning for a check-up.
（他今天上午去診所做身體檢查。）

At 可用來指有一群人參與活動的場所。例如：

1. We were at the cinema/movies last night when you called.
（昨晚你來電時我們正在看電影。）

→ the cinema（英）/ the movies（美）在此指「電影院」。

但 He has worked in the cinema/movies all his life.（他一輩子都在電影業工作。）

→ the cinema / the movies 在此指「電影業」。）

2. Were you at Benjamin's birthday party?
（你有參加班傑明的生日派對嗎？）

3. Mrs. Jones isn't here; she's at/in a meeting.
（瓊斯女士不在這兒，她在開會。）

→ meeting 前面用 at 或 in 都可以。

4. We'll be at his concert on Sunday.
（我們週日要去聽他的演唱會。）

At 可用來指上課、上學、就學、教書的場所，即各級學校，尤其校名前面一定要用 at。例如：

1. The kids will be at / in school until 4:00 today.
（今天這些小孩要到四點才放學。）

2. Is Amy in / at school today?
（艾美今天有上學嗎？）

3. Paul always did well at school.
（保羅在學期間成績一向良好。）

4. Her daughter is still at school.
（她女兒還在就學。）

→ 學生上學或在學校上課可以用 at school 或 in school 來表示，但在學或就學中只能用 at school。「在課堂上」是 in class。

5. My son went to school with Peter.
（我兒子和彼得唸同一所學校。）（美）

= My son was at school with Peter.（英）

= My son went to the same school at the same time as Peter.

6. Which university are you at?
（你讀哪所大學？）

= Which university do you go to?

= Which university do you study at?

7. He studied at the University of Leeds.
（他曾就讀里茲大學。）

8. My wife and I met while we were at university.
（我跟我太太是在讀大學時認識的。）

9. I studied information engineering at college.
（我大學唸資訊工程。）

10. He teaches cookery at the local college.
（他在當地一所學院教烹飪。）

11. She teaches at the University of California, Berkeley.
（她任教於柏克萊加州大學。）

At 可用來指大多數的商店。例如：

1. I stopped at the butcher's (shop) on the way home from work to get some beef.
（我下班回家的路上到肉販買了些牛肉。）

2. Look what I bought at the supermarket today.
（看看我今天在超市買了什麼。）

At 可用來指地址。例如：

1. She lives at number 10 Downing Street.
（她住在唐寧街10號——英國首相官邸。）

2. He works at 1600 Pennsylvania Ave. Washington, DC.
（他在華盛頓特區賓夕凡尼亞大道 1600 號工作——美國白宮地址。）

On 可用來指任何表面上的位置，意為「在……上面；到……上面」。例如：

1. All my books are on the desk.
（我所有的書都放在書桌上。）

2. She's lying on the floor.
（她躺在地板上。）

3. There were several attractive posters on the wall.
（牆上有幾張引人注目的海報。）

但 There's a crack in the wall.
（牆上有條裂縫。）

4. I could hear the rain falling on the roof.
（我聽得到雨滴落在屋頂上的聲音。）

On 可用來指建築物的樓層。例如：

1. They live on the 39th floor.
（他們住在 40 樓（英）／他們住在 39 樓（美）。）

2. She works on the 51st floor.
（她在 52 樓工作（英）／她在 51 樓工作（美）。）
→ 英國的一樓是 the ground floor，二樓是 the first floor；美國的一樓是 the first floor，二樓是 the second floor。

On 可用來指道路或街道，意為「在……路上；在……街上」。例如：

1. My house is in/on Penghu Street.
（我的房子位在澎湖街上。）

2. There were a lot of people in/on the street.
（街上有許多人。）

→ 有關 in the street 和 on the street 之間的區別，端賴說話者從什麼角度來看。
如果說話者當時人在那條街上，那麼就用 in the street；如果說話者當時人在距
離不遠的另一條街上或在其他地方，那麼就用 on the street。

On 可用來指河海湖泊或邊界，意為「在（任何水域或邊界）旁；緊鄰著」。例如：

1. It's a small fishing village on the east coast of Taiwan.
（那是台灣東海岸的一個小漁村。）

2. They live in a town on the Mississippi.
（他們住在密西西比河邊的一座城鎮。）

3. There are two small towns on the frontier.
（邊境附近有兩個小鎮。）

4. Strasbourg is on the border of France and Germany.
（史特拉斯堡位在法德邊界。）

→ 緊鄰邊界。

5. They were stopped at the border.
（他們在邊界被攔下。）

→ 在邊界檢查哨。

On 可用來指任何地方、地區或土地，意為「在……地方」。例如：

1. The king is buried on a small island.
（國王被葬在一個小島上。）

2. Allen spent his childhood on a farm in Indonesia.
（艾倫的童年是在印尼的一個農場度過。）

3. They live in that log cabin on the hill.
（他們住在山上的那間小木屋。）

4. Who was the first man on the moon?
（第一個登上月球的人是誰？）

In 可用來指房間或建築物，意為「在……裡」。例如：

1. John is still in his room.
（約翰還在他的房間裡。）

2. The children are downstairs in the sitting room.
（孩子們在樓下客廳裡。）

3. His cellphone was lost somewhere in the post office.
（他的手機掉在郵局裡的某個地方。）

In 可用來指地區、城市、國家、洲或世界，意為「在……裡」。例如：

1. Roger lives in Kaohsiung.
（羅傑住在高雄。）

2. Tanzania is a country in Africa.
（坦尚尼亞是個非洲國家。）

3. That's the highest building in the world.
（那是世界最高的建築物。）

根據**在 at 中的敘述，在辦公室等建築物內工作或任職於公司某部門要用 in**，但在**農場工作**或在**收銀台工作**，則要用 **on**。例如：

1. Nina works in an open-plan office.
（妮娜在一間開敞式辦公室工作。）

2. I work in the company's Tokyo office.
（我在公司的東京辦事處上班。）

3. I hope I can work on a farm in the future.
（我希望將來能在農場工作。）

4. His sister works on the checkout at the local supermarket.
（他妹妹在當地超市的收銀台工作。）

但 Your fruit and vegetables will be weighed at the checkout.
（你的水果和蔬菜要在收銀台過磅。）

Unit 06　At、on 和 in 後接時間的用法

重要觀念 非學不可 🔍

幾點鐘（或幾時幾分幾秒）、一天當中的某個時間點、一週當中的某個時間點、特別的節日等時間詞的前面須使用 at。例如：

1. I'll pick you up at the airport at six o'clock.
（我六點鐘會到機場接你。）
2. I woke up from a dream at 4:30 a.m.
（我凌晨四點半從夢中醒過來。）
3. He was released/discharged from (the) hospital at midday.
（他中午出院。）
4. What are you doing at the weekend?
（你週末要幹什麼？）
→ 美式英語通常使用 on the weekend。
5. John works at (the) weekends.
（約翰每個週末都工作。）
→ 美式英語通常使用 on (the) weekends。
6. Mary will meet her pen pal at Christmas.
（瑪麗將在聖誕節和她的筆友見面。）
7. At the Lunar New Year, the Lion Dance is one of the most popular traditional performances.
（在農曆新年，舞獅是最受歡迎的傳統表演之一。）

在非正式情況中，**"What time ...?" 這個問句的前面通常不用 at**。例如：

1. What time do you collect the kids from school?
（你什麼時候去接孩子放學呢？）
2. At what time do you collect the kids from school?
→ 這句沒有上句來得自然，通常用在非常正式的場合。

日期、星期幾、特別的日子等時間詞的前面須使用 on。例如：

1. I moved to Kaohsiung on October 20, 2000.
（我在 2000 年 10 月 20 日搬到高雄。）

2. Kevin had a visit from his mother-in-law on Sunday.
（凱文的岳母星期天到他家作客。）

3. John works (on) Saturdays.
（約翰每週六都工作。）

→ Mondays、Tuesdays ... 意為「每週一」、「每週二」……，**其前的 on 可以且通常省略。**

4. They'll give a party for me on my birthday.
（他們將在我生日那天為我舉辦派對。）

5. They were married in two different cities on the same day last year.
（他們去年同一天在兩個不同的城市舉行婚禮。）

上午、下午、月份、年份、季節、世紀等時間詞的前面須使用 in。例如：

1. What time do you usually wake up in the morning?
（你早上通常幾點醒來？）

2. He'll do his homework in the evening.
（他將在晚上做作業。）

3. The company was established in October 2010.
（這家公司於 2010 年 10 月創立。）

4. The museum was built in 1643.
（這座博物館建於 1643 年。）

5. It was a cold, sunny day in early spring.
（那是早春裡寒冷而陽光燦爛的一天。）

6. We live in the twenty-first century.
（我們生活在二十一世紀。）

必閃陷阱 非學不可

At 還是 on 呢？

根據上述，at 是用在特別的節日和週末等時間詞之前，但**時間詞若是指某個特定的日子或特定的週末，那麼要使用 on**。試比較下面的例句：

1. At the Lunar New Year, the Lion Dance is one of the most popular traditional performances.
（在農曆新年，舞獅是最受歡迎的傳統表演之一。）

  On Lunar New Year's Day, we always play mahjong.
（在農曆新年，我們都會打麻將。）

2. We meet for lunch once in a while at/on the weekend.
（我們週末偶爾會見面吃頓午餐。）

3. The music festival is always held on the first weekend in February.
（這個音樂節都在二月的第一個週末舉行。）

In 還是 on 呢？

雖然我們使用 **in the morning**、**in the afternoon**、**in the evening** 和 **in the night** 來表示「（在）上午」、「（在）下午」和「（在）晚上」，但若是指**特定的上午、下午和晚上，則要使用 on**。試比較下面的例句：

1. The armed robbery took place at five in the morning.
（這起武裝搶案發生在清晨五點。）

2. His private jet took off on the morning of the tenth of December.
（他的私人飛機在 12 月 10 日早上起飛。）

3. He always gets home at seven in the evening.
（他總是在晚上七點回到家。）

4. I usually play basketball on Sunday evening.
（我經常在星期天晚上打籃球。）

5. In the afternoons, I like to listen to the radio.
（每到下午，我喜歡收聽廣播。）

6. Cindy always goes to see a movie on Saturday afternoons.
（辛蒂總是在星期六下午去看電影。）

At 還是 in 呢？

In the night 和 at night 都意為「（在）夜晚」，但前者通常指特定的夜晚，而後者則泛指任何夜晚。例如：

1. I woke up several times in the night.
（我夜裡醒來好幾次。）

2. It's not safe for a girl to walk alone at night.
（女孩子夜晚踽踽獨行並不安全。）

好用 Tips 非學不可 🔍

不使用 at、on 或 in 的時間詞

當時間詞的前面已有 each、every、next、last、some、this、that、one、any 和 all 等修飾語時，不可再使用 at、on 或 in。例如：

◆ She got married **last Christmas**.（O）
◇ She got married at last Christmas.（×）
（她去年聖誕節結的婚。）

◆ Is John coming **this weekend** or **next weekend**?（O）
◇ Is John coming at this weekend or next weekend?（×）
（約翰這個週末要來還是下個週末要來？）

◆ I play baseball **every Saturday**.（O）
◇ I play baseball on every Saturday.（×）
（我每週六打棒球。）

◆ Sarah is starting school **next September**.（O）
◇ Sarah is starting school in next September.（×）
（莎拉明年九月開始上學。）

Unit 07 Before 的用法

必閃陷阱 非學不可

Before 可當介系詞、副詞和連接詞用。在進入主題之前，必須再次強調一點：在寫作中，我們經常會用到 **as mentioned above**（如上所述，如上面所提及的）、**as noted above**（如上面所指出的）、**as demonstrated above**（如上所示）、**as shown above**（如上所示）和 **as stated above**（如上所述，如前所述）等片語來表示上文、上面或之前所提到的事物，但**在這些片語中，不可使用 before 來代替 above**。例如：

◆ **As stated above**, there is no shortcut for learning English grammar.（○）
◇ As stated before, there is no shortcut for learning English grammar.（×）
（如上所述，學習英文文法沒有捷徑。）
◆ **As noted above**, the government lacks efficiency.（○）
◇ As noted before, the government lacks efficiency.（×）
（如上面所指出的，這個政府缺乏效率。）

Before 用作介系詞時意為「在……之前 (earlier than)；在……前面 (in front of)」，其後最常接名詞片語來表示在（某個時間點、事件或行動）之前、在（某地點）前面、在（某人或某物）面前、（在列表或一系列物件中）在……之前。例如：

1. I regularly go for a run before breakfast.
（我經常在早餐前跑步。）

2. She got there before me.
（她比我先到那裡。）

3. Turn right about a kilometer before the railway station.
（在火車站前約一公里處右轉。）

4. A few miles before the border the refugees were stopped at an army checkpoint.
（難民在距離邊界數英里的一個軍事檢查哨被攔了下來。）

5. Before the library stood a bronze statue of Abraham Lincoln.
（圖書館前聳立一尊林肯銅像。）

6. John stood up before all his colleagues and asked Mary to marry him.
（約翰在所有同事面前站起來向瑪麗求婚。）

7. The letter U comes before V in the English alphabet.
（在英文字母表中，U 排在 V 前面。）

8. His name comes before mine on the list.
（名單上他的名字排在我的前面。）

Before 意為 in front of 是一種比較正式的用法，經常後接受格代名詞來表示**在某人「前面」的一段時間**，但這段時間可能是過去的時間，也可能是未來的時間。例如：

1. We have the whole weekend before us—what do you want to do?
（我們有整個週末的時間——你想做些什麼？）

2. Kevin was fifteen years old. He had his whole life before him.
（凱文得年 15 歲。這就是他身前的整個人生。）

3. Brian became a lawyer, like his father before him.
（布萊恩克紹箕裘，當了律師。）

Before 後接動名詞的結構也頗為常見，這也是一種比較**正式的用法**。例如：

1. Before leaving Tom said goodbye to each of us.
（湯姆離開前向我們每個人說再見。）

→ 比 Before he left, Tom said goodbye to each of us. 更正式。

2. You should seek legal advice before signing anything.
（在簽字之前，你應該徵詢法律專家的意見。）

→ 比 You should seek legal advice before you sign anything. 更正式。

Before, by, till/until

Before、by 和 till/until 後接某個時間點都是相當常見的結構。然而，由於 **before 和 by 的中文意思都是「在（某個時間點）之前」**，因此不少人誤以為它們是同義詞，非也！**它們所表示的時間含意並不相同。**同樣地，**till/until** 也有「在（某個時間點）之前」的意思，但它所表示的是**「（做某事）直到（某個時間點）」**。例如：

1. I have to get to the airport before five o'clock.
（我必須在 5 點之前到機場。）

→ 這句的含意是：5 點到機場就太遲了，必須在 5 點之前到達。

　 I have to get to the airport by five o'clock.
（我必須在 5 點之前到機場。）

→ 這句的含意是：最遲 5 點必須到機場，5 點是我到機場的最晚時間。

2. It must be done before next Friday.
（這件事必須在下週五之前完成。）

→ 這句的含意是：下週五完成就太遲了，必須在下週五之前完成。

3. It must be done by next Friday.
（這件事必須在下週五之前完成。）

→ 這句的含意是：最遲在下週五必須完成，下週五是完成這件事的最晚時間。

4. I'll be out of the office till/until 10th October.
（10 月 10 日之前我都不在辦公室。）

→ 這句的含意是：10 月 10 日當天我就會在辦公室。

→ 這句可視為 not ... until 的變形，意為「直到（某個時間點）（才做某事）」。所以，這句的意思相當於「我要到 10 月 10 日才會在辦公室。」

5. They'll stay in Taipei till/until Monday.
（他們會在台北一直待到星期一。）

→ 這句的含意是：他們最晚會在台北待到星期一，星期一過後他們就不在台北了。

Before 用作副詞時意為「以前」，經常放在 day、night、week、month、year 等時間名詞後面，構成 **the day before**、**the night before**、**the week before**、**the month before**、**the year before** 等片語來表示「前一天」、「前一天晚上」、「前一個禮拜」、「前一個月」、「前一年」等意思。但 **the day before yesterday（前天）和 the week before last（上上週）**等片語中的 before 為介系詞。例如：

1. Cindy mentioned a movie she'd seen the night before.
（辛蒂提到她前一天晚上看過的一部電影。）
2. A: Did you graduate in 2000?
（A：你 2000 年畢業嗎？）

   B: No, actually, I finished college the year before.
（B：不，其實我是在前一年完成大學學業。）
→ 前一年是指 2000 年之前一年，也就是 1999 年。

Before 和 ago 雖然皆意為「以前」，但前者指的是「現在之前的任何時間」（亦即指**過去某個不確定的時間**），而後者是指「**現在之前的某個確定的時間**」。所以，before 可以跟現在完成式連用，而 **ago 只能用於過去簡單式；但 before 也可用於過去簡單式**。例如：

◆ Have you two met **before**?（○）
◇ Have you two met ago?（×）
（你們兩人以前見過面嗎？）

◆ Your father phoned ten minutes **ago**.（○）
◇ Your father phoned ten minutes before.（×）
（你父親 10 分鐘前來電。）

◆ He was never late **before**.
（以前他從不遲到。）

Ago 所指的時間都是從現在開始往以前推算，但 before 所指的時間除了也是從現在開始往以前推算之外，還可指**從過去某個時間點往更早之前推算的時間**。所以，當我們要表示**比 ago 更早的時間時，我們只能用 before**，而不能用 ago。在這種句子中，**ago 用過去簡單式，而 before 用過去完成式**。例如：

1. My grandfather died five years ago; my grandmother had already died three years before.
（我祖父 5 年前過世，而我祖母在那之前 3 年就已經過世了。）
→ 亦即祖母是在 8 年前過世。

2. Two years ago he went back to his hometown that he had left ten years before.
（兩年前他回到睽違 10 年的故鄉。）
→ 亦即他在 12 年前離開故鄉。

Before 用作附屬連接詞時意為「在……之前」，其所引導的子句通常使用**過去簡單式**來表示 before 子句的動作緊接在主要子句的動作之後發生。**Before 子句可以放在句首或句末**。例如：

1. Before he left, Tom said goodbye to each of us.
（湯姆離開前向我們每個人說再見。）
2. Tom said goodbye to each of us before he left.

與 when、while、after、by the time、as soon as、if 和 unless 等附屬連接詞所引導的時間子句一樣，**before 子句的時間若指未來，該子句須用現在簡單式表示未來**，絕不能有表示未來的 will 或 be going to 等字眼。例如：

◆ Check it carefully **before you hand it in.** （○）

◇ Check it carefully before you are going to hand it in. （×）

（交來之前仔細核對一下。）

◆ **Before she goes** to work, she reads English poems aloud for about an hour. （○）

◇ Before she will go to work, she reads English poems aloud for about an hour. （×）

（上班之前，她都會朗讀約一小時的英詩。）

好用 Tips 非學不可 🔍

Just before、immediately before、long before

我們可以在 before 的前面使用 just、immediately、shortly 和 long 等副詞，以及含有 days、weeks、months、years 等詞的時間片語。Just/immediately/shortly before 意為「就在……之前」，而 **long before 意為「很久以前」（注意與 before long 的不同）**。例如：

1. His parents had got married just before the war.
（他的父母親就在戰爭之前結婚。）

2. I knew her long before she became famous.
（遠在她成名之前我就認識她了。）

3. It will be years before I earn that much money!
（我得好幾年才能賺到那麼多錢！）

Beforehand

我們可以**使用 beforehand（提前；預先，事先）來替代當副詞用的 before**，尤其是所指的時間比較不明確的時候。Beforehand 通常用於非正式的口語，比較少用於寫作。我們也可以在 beforehand 的前面使用 **just、immediately、shortly** 和 **long** 等副詞，以及含有 days、weeks、months、years 等詞的時間片語。例如：

1. We are going to get everything ready beforehand.
（我們將事先把一切準備好。）

2. We had seen them shortly beforehand.
（不久前我們見過他們。）

3. Months beforehand, John had bought three tickets for the concert.
（約翰已提前幾個月買了三張演唱會入場券。）

Before long

Before (very/too) long 意為「**不久，很快**」(after a short time, soon)，
大多用於寫作。例如：

1. Before long it will be winter.
（冬天很快就要到來了。）
2. They'll be home before very long.
（他們很快就要到家了。）
3. I hope to see you before long.
（我希望不久可以再看見你。）
4. My books will be published before long.
（我的書不久就要出版了。）

Unit 08 Blow up vs. blowup, pick up vs. pickup, take over vs. takeover 等等

必閃陷阱 非學不可

英文中有許多（數量可能有上百個或甚至更多）兩個字的**片語動詞**
(phrasal verb)，都可以結合在一起來**構成名詞或形容詞**，如 blow up/
blowup, burn out/burnout, left over/leftover, log in/login, look out/lookout,
pay back/payback, pick up/pickup, roll out/rollout, run away/runaway,
set up/setup, take over/takeover, work out/workout 等等，真是族繁不及
備載。

這些由**雙字片語動詞**結合在一起所形成的單詞或複合字，通常**當名詞或形容詞用**，或**兩者兼而有之**。它們的意思大多與各該片語動詞相近，但往往又發展或延伸出其他意思。這些單詞**通常已完全複合化，亦即沒有連字號**，但有時仍會見到加連字號的拼法，尤其是在英國出版品中。必須注意的是，這些**複合字在正式寫作或出版品中絕對不會被當動詞用**，但**在非正式的上下文中卻不時被用作動詞**，換言之，一個字和兩個字的差異只有在正式寫作或出版品中才會被遵循。

Unit 09　Bring、take 和 fetch 的用法

必閃陷阱 非學不可

這三個動詞都是用來表示拿著／帶著某物或帶著某人到某地的意思，但它們移動的方向並不相同，使用時必須搞清楚方向才能用最適切的字來表達最正確的意思。

Bring 意為「拿來，帶來」，移動的方向可以是從說話者到聽者所在的地方或是從聽者到說話者所在的地方。Bring 是個不規則動詞，過去式和過去分詞都是 brought。例如：

1. Bring your guitar when you come to visit me.
（你來看我時把你的吉他帶來。）

2. I'll bring my guitar to your house tonight.
（今晚我會把我的吉他帶去你家。）

3. Can I bring my sister with me tonight?
（今晚我可以帶著我妹妹一起來嗎？）

4. Please don't forget to bring your grammar books next time.
（下次請別忘記帶你們的文法書來。）

5. A: Shall I bring anything to your birthday party?
（A：我要不要帶些東西參加你的生日派對呢？）

  B: Oh, just a bottle.
（B：哦，帶瓶酒就好了。）

◆ Tony visited us and **brought** his sister with him.（〇）
◇ Tony visited us and took his sister with him.（×）
（東尼帶著他妹妹一起來看我們。）

◆ Can you **bring** me my grammar book I left on your desk the other day?（〇）
◇ Can you take me my grammar book I left on your desk the other day?（×）
(你能把我幾天前留在你書桌上的文法書帶來給我嗎？)

Bring 亦可表示拿著／帶著某物或帶著某人從另一地方移動到說話者或聽者所在的地方。例如：

A: Did Mary bring anything to your birthday party?
（A：瑪麗有帶些東西參加你的生日派對嗎？）

B: Yes, she brought me a bottle of wine and some chocolate.
（B：有，她帶了一瓶葡萄酒和一些巧克力給我。）

在上例中，瑪麗是另一人，她人位在與 A（說話者）或 B（聽者）所在地方不同的另一地方。她帶著東西到 B 所在的地方。

Take 意為「帶去」，移動的方向是從說話者或聽者所在的地方到另一地方。Take 也是不規則動詞，過去式和過去分詞分別為 took 和 taken。例如：

1. I'll take my guitar to her house tonight.
（今晚我會把我的吉他帶去她家。）

2. Dad took us to the museum last Saturday.
（上星期六爸爸帶我們去博物館。）

◆ Tony visited them and **took** his sister with him. （〇）
◇ Tony visited them and brought his sister with him.（×）
（東尼帶著他妹妹一起去看他們。）

在上面的例句中，說話者或聽者都不在「她家」、「他們所在的地方」或「博物館」。這些地方都是與說話者或聽者所在地方不同的另一地方。

然而，**有時在同一個句子中可以使用 bring 或 take，兩者都講得通**，端賴說話者是從動作執行者的角度 (take) 或動作接受者的角度 (bring) 來看事情而定，或者說端賴說話者是站在動作執行者的立場 (take) 或動作接受者的立場 (bring) 來看事情而定。例如：

1. Amy visits her husband in hospital every morning and she always takes him the day's newspaper.
（艾美每天早上都會探望她住院的丈夫，她每次都會帶著當天的報紙去給他。）
→ 站在動作執行者（艾美）的立場看事情。

2. Amy visits her husband in hospital every morning and she always brings him the day's newspaper.
（艾美每天早上都會探望她住院的丈夫，她每次都會帶著當天的報紙來給他。）
→ 站在動作接受者（艾美的丈夫）的立場看事情。

此外，我們也經常會見到**同一句子分別使用這兩個動詞來表示同一意思，但不同的方向概念**。例如：

1. I'll bring my girlfriend home today.
（我今天要帶女朋友回家。）
→ 現在你人在家，這是你對父母或其他家人說的話。

2. I'll take my girlfriend home today.
（我今天要帶女朋友回家。）
→ 現在你人在外面，這是你對朋友或其他人說的話。

Fetch 意為「（去）拿來，帶回來」，移動的方向是從說話者或聽者所在的地方到另一地方然後回來，把某物或某人帶回來。Fetch 為規則動詞，過去式和過去分詞都是 fetched。我們經常**可以用 get 來代替 fetch**。例如：

1. Fetch/Get your drinks yourself, Peter.
（彼得，你自己去拿飲料吧。）

2. Could you fetch me my smartphone/fetch my smartphone for me from the other room, please?
（你去另一個房間幫我把手機拿過來好嗎？）

3. Allen has gone to fetch her mother from the airport.
（艾倫已經去機場接他媽媽了。）

總而言之，

1. 當你人在台北，你就說：
Bring something/someone to Taipei.。

2. 當你人不在台北，你就說：
Take something/someone to Taipei. 。

3. 當你人不在台北而且不想把某物或某人留在台北，你就說：
Fetch something/someone from Taipei.。

Unit 10　Come 和 go 的用法（一）：如何正確使用 come 和 go

必閃陷阱 非學不可

大家都知道，come 是「來」，go 是「去」，兩者互為相反詞。一般的認知或中文的含意是，從說話者（我）往聽者（你）的方向移動是「去」，反之若從聽者往說話者的方向移動是「來」。然而，**在英文中，說話者與聽者之間的移動都可以且經常使用 come**。例如：

1. You can come to my office and discuss the matter.
（你可以來我辦公室討論這件事。）
→ 聽者移動到說話者。

2. Shall I come to your office at 10 a.m.?
（早上十點我「去」你的辦公室好嗎？）
→ 說話者移動到聽者。

從**另一地方**移動到說話者或聽者所在的地方也都可以使用 come。例如：

1. A salesperson came to my door last night selling shampoos.
（一名推銷員昨晚上門來推銷洗髮精。）

→ 另一人移動到說話者。

2. Julian is going to come to you on Wednesday if that's okay.
（可以的話，朱利安星期三會「去」找你。）

→ 第三人移動到聽者。

從說話者或聽者所在的地方移動到另一地方都是使用 **go**，這與中文的含意相當，殆無疑義。例如：

1. Can you wait here while I go back to the house to fetch my cellphone?
（我回去屋裡拿手機時你可以在這裡等一下嗎？）

2. Linda has gone to Japan.
（琳達去日本了。）

Unit 11　Come 和 go 的用法（二）：使用 come 或 go 都可以的情況

必閃陷阱 非學不可

當句中的人物另有其人（既非說話者亦非聽者）時，來或去的方向就會因人而異，此時使用 come 或 go 都可以的情況就出現了。至於要使用 come 或 go，則端賴說話者是從動作執行者的角度 (go) 或動作接受者的角度 (come) 來看事情而定，或者說**端賴說話者是站在動作執行者的立場 (go) 或動作接受者的立場 (come) 來看事情而定。**

在下面第 1 句中，我們是從**動作接受者（約翰的父親）的角度**來看事情，所以使**用 come**。在第 2 句，我們是**從動作執行者（約翰）的角度來看事情**，所以**用 go**。

1. John came to his father for help.
（約翰來找他父親幫忙／約翰來尋求他父親的協助。）
2. John went to his father for help.
（約翰去找他父親幫忙／約翰去尋求他父親的協助。）

下面兩句也是使用 come 或 go 都可以的情況，理解方式如上述。

1. Kevin came to Peter's help yesterday.
（凱文昨天來援助／幫助彼得。）
2. Kevin went to Peter's help yesterday.
（凱文昨天去援助／幫助彼得。）

在英文中，這類**使用 come 或 go 都可以的情況不在少數。有時他們與同一字連用時甚至會出現意思一樣的情況。**例如：

1. [董事長特助對一名在董事長室外面等候見董事長的幹部說]
Will you come in now, please.
（你現在可以進來了。）
2. [寒流天在一處泳池旁]
It's so cold! I don't want to go in the water.
（好冷啊！我不想下水。）

在上面的例句中，**come in** 和 **go in** 分別意為「進來」和「進去」。儘管它們的中文意思因語言差異看似不同，但**英文意思其實都是 "enter"**。同樣地，**come home** 和 **go home** 也為 come 和 go 與同一字連用時產**生相同意思**的情況提供了有力的證明。

Unit 12 Do 和 make 後接名詞片語當受詞時的用法差異

Do 和 make 當及物動詞時都有「做；製作」的意思，當它們後接名詞（片語）當受詞時，**do 著重於動作或做某事的過程**，而 **make 則強調動作的產物或結果**。例如：

1. Betty did a very good math paper, but she still made two mistakes.
（貝蒂的數學考卷答得很好，但還是有兩個地方錯誤。）

2. When I was doing the cooking course, I made two chocolate cakes.
（我在修烹飪課程時做了兩個巧克力蛋糕。）

下列為與 **do 和 make** 連用或固定搭配的一些常用名詞（片語）：

DO: activity, business, cleaning, cooking, course, damage, drawing, duty, exam(ination), exercise, favor, gardening, harm, homework, ironing, job, laundry, one's best, painting, shopping, task, test, washing (up), work 等。

1. My wife does her shopping on Wednesdays and Saturdays.
（我太太每星期三和星期六去買東西／購物。）

2. Mary hates to do the ironing.
（瑪麗討厭燙衣服。）

3. The divorce did a great deal of damage to his political career.
（離婚對他的政治生涯造成極大的傷害。）

4. I really should do/take more exercise.
（我真的應該多運動。）

MAKE: apology, assumption, bed, breakfast, cake, change, coffee, comment, complaint, dinner, effort, error, excuse, friends, guess, law, list, loss, love, lunch, mess, mistake, money, noise,offer, phone call, plan, profit, progress, promise, remark, sound, soup, speech, statement, tea 等。

1. John made an apology for his rudeness to me last night.
（約翰為他昨晚對我粗魯無禮道歉。）

2. He's made an offer on a mansion in downtown Taipei.
（他已出價購買台北市中心一棟豪宅。）

3. Amy's always making excuses for being late for school.
（艾美總是為上學遲到找各種藉口。）

4. He made a profit of five million dollars on his house.
（他賣掉房子獲利五百萬元。）

Unit 13　Else 的用法

重要觀念 非學不可

Else 是個副詞，可用在以 any-、every-、no- 和 some- 開頭的一群字後面來表示「其他；別的；另外」的意思。這群字包括 anybody、everybody、nobody、somebody、anyone、everyone、no one、someone、anything、everything、nothing、something 等不定代名詞以及 anywhere、everywhere、nowhere、somewhere（或美國口語的 anyplace、everyplace、no place、someplace）等副詞。例如：

1. Anybody else would have condemned his foolish behavior.
（換了誰都會譴責他的愚蠢行為。）

2. Owen stayed at work when everybody else had gone home.
（別人都回家了，歐文還在工作。）

3. No one else can do it.
（沒有其他人能做這件事了。）

4. Tracy married someone else.
（崔西嫁給別人了。）

5. Is there anything else I can do for you?
（我還能為你做什麼事嗎？）

6. There is nothing else on the desk except a sheet of paper.
（書桌上除了一張紙外沒有其他東西。）

7. Did you go anywhere else last night?
（你昨晚有沒有到別的地方？）

8. If we don't provide a good service, customers will go somewhere else.
（如果我們服務不好，顧客就會到別的地方。）

9. This animal is not found anyplace else in the world.
（這種動物在世界其他地方都沒有。）

10. You'll have to sit someplace else.
（你必須坐別的地方。）

Else 亦可用在 **how、what、where、who、why、whatever 和 whoever** 等疑問和關係代名詞後面來表示「**其他；別的；另外**」的意思。例如：

1. What else did Tom tell you?
（湯姆還告訴了你什麼？）

2. Who else is coming?
（還有誰要來？）

3. Where else did you go?
（你還去了什麼地方？）

4. Please focus on teaching grammar and whatever else the students need for the TOEIC tests.
（請集中教授語法及學生參加多益測驗所需的其他東西。）

5. Whatever else may be said of you, you should be humble, be humble and stay humble.
（無論別人還說了你什麼，你應該謙卑、謙卑、再謙卑。）

6. Whoever else you ask, the answer must be always the same.
（不管你問其他什麼人，答案肯定都是一樣的。）

7. Whoever else said that?
（到底還有誰那樣說？）

必閃陷阱 非學不可 🔍

然而，**else 不可以用在 which 之後**。例如：

◇ Which else do you want apart from a new smartphone?（×）

◆ **What else** do you want apart from a new smartphone?（O）

◆ What other thing(s) do you want apart from a new smartphone?（O）

◆ Which other thing(s) do you want apart from a new smartphone?（O）

（除了一支新智慧型手機，你還想要什麼東西？）

◇ Which else did you tell the secret to?（×）

◆ **Who else** did you tell the secret to?（O）

◆ What other person or people did you tell the secret to?（O）

◆ Which other person or people did you tell the secret to?（O）

（你還把這個秘密告訴過誰了？）

◇ Besides National Central Library, which else have you worked?（×）

◆ Besides National Central Library, **where else** have you worked?（O）

◆ Besides National Central Library, what other place(s) have you worked at?（O）

◆ Besides National Central Library, which other place(s) have you worked at?（O）

（除了國家圖書館，你還曾經在什麼地方工作過？）

好用 Tips 非學不可 🔍

Else 還可用在 little 和 much 後面來表示「其他；別的；另外」的意思。例如：

1. I have little else to give you.
（我幾乎沒有別的東西可以給你了。）

2. There is little else to mention.
（幾乎沒有什麼別的事情要提了。）

3. There's not much else left to say.
（沒什麼別的話要說了。）

4 There isn't much else to tell you.
（沒什麼別的東西要告訴你了。）

Unit 14　Enough 的用法

重要觀念 非學不可 🔍

Enough 可當限定詞、代名詞和副詞用，意為「足夠（的／地）」，其主要句型為 **enough for somebody/something**、**enough to do something** 及 **enough for somebody/something to do something**。**Enough 當限定詞時後接複數可數名詞或不可數名詞**。例如：

1. The conference room has enough seats for everyone.
（會議室有足夠的座位給每個人坐。）

2. We've seen enough television repeats.
（我們已看了夠多的電視重播。）

3. I usually don't get enough sleep.
（我經常睡眠不足。）

4. There was enough food for about five people.
（食物夠大約五個人吃。）

必閃陷阱 非學不可 🔍

Enough 當代名詞意為「足夠；太多」，其後經常接「of ＋ 受格代名詞或特指的名詞」（所謂特指的名詞，就是名詞的前面加上 the, that, this, these, those 或所有格，如 my, John's 等等）。例如：

1. [飯後]
A: Have you had enough?
（A：吃飽了嗎？）

B: Yes, thanks.
（B：吃飽了，謝謝。）

2. I have had enough to eat/drink.
（我已經吃／喝得夠多了。）

3. It's enough to make her cry for joy.
（這足以使她喜極而泣。）

4. I've got only 200 dollars—will that be enough?
（我只有 200 元，夠用嗎？）

5. Enough is enough.
（凡事要適可而止。）

6. That's (quite) enough! I don't want to eat food of this kind again.
（夠了！我不想再吃這種食物了。）

◆ There aren't **enough of** them to make up a team.（O）
◇ There aren't enough them to make up a team.（×）
（他們的人數還不夠組成一個隊。）

◆ I'm leaving. I've had **enough of** him/Peter's rudeness/all this nonsense!（O）
◇ I'm leaving. I've had enough him/Peter's rudeness/all this nonsense!（×）
（我要走了。我已經受夠了他這個人／彼得的粗魯無禮／這些廢話！）

◆ Sam hasn't eaten **enough of** his dinner.（O）
◇ Sam hasn't eaten enough his dinner.（×）
（山姆晚餐沒有吃飽。）

Enough 當程度副詞時意為「足夠地」，直接用在形容詞、副詞或動詞之後。例如：

◆ The table isn't **big enough**.（O）
◇ The table isn't enough big.（×）
（這張桌子不夠大。）

◆ They cannot walk **fast enough**.（O）
◇ They cannot walk enough fast.（×）
（他們走得不夠快。）

◆ I haven't **practiced enough**.（O）
◇ I haven't enough practiced.（×）
（我練習得還不夠。）

Strangely/Oddly/Funnily enough, no one seemed to notice that Robert was in his pajamas.（奇怪的是／可笑的是，似乎沒有人注意到羅伯特穿著睡衣。）
= It was strange/odd/funny that no one seemed to notice that Robert was in his pajamas.

好用 Tips 非學不可 🔍

從上述可知，**enough 當限定詞（有人稱為形容詞）用時其後一定有名詞**，若其後沒有名詞且位在 BE 動詞之後，那麼它是**代名詞而非限定詞（或形容詞）**。當副詞用的 **enough 則緊接在形容詞、副詞或動詞之後**。不過，enough 還有一項相當正式或文學上的用法，就是用在某些特定名詞之後，但這種用法不是很常見。例如：

1. Tom was fool enough to believe it.
（湯姆竟然傻到會相信這個。）
= It was foolish of Tom to believe it.

2. I had reason enough to be angry.
（我有充分的理由生氣。）
= I had a good reason to be angry.

 Unit 15 Even 的副詞用法

必閃陷阱 非學不可 🔍

Even 當副詞用時意為「（用來表示令人驚訝、非比尋常、出乎意料或極端的事物）竟然，甚至，連，即使」，通常位在句子的中間，亦即位在主詞和主動詞之間（即普通動詞之前），或位在語氣助動詞或第一個助動詞之後，或位在**當主動詞的 BE 動詞之後**。例如：

1. Mary left without even apologizing.
（瑪麗竟然沒有道歉就離開了。）

2. Some people never even read a newspaper, let alone a book.
（有些人從不看報紙，遑論讀書了。）

3. My mother hasn't even started making dinner.
（我媽媽竟然還沒開始做晚飯。）

4. Peter didn't even have enough money to get a Universiade ticket.
（彼得甚至沒有足夠的錢來買世大運門票。）

5. Tom doesn't even know who I am.
（湯姆甚至連我是誰都不知道。）

6. It's a really useful website if you're interested in online games. There's even a section on walkthroughs and cheats.
（如果你對線上遊戲有興趣，那麼它是個很有用的網站。它甚至有個教學和密技區。）

我們可以**將 even 或 not even 放在句中我們要強調的字詞或片語前面**。例如：

1. Everyone likes money--even a five-year-old does.
（每個人都喜歡錢——即使是五歲小孩也喜歡。）

2. Even the dog refused to eat it.
（連狗都不吃這東西。）

3. John never stopped working, not even on New Year's Eve/New Year's Day.
（約翰從未停止工作，連除夕／元旦都沒有。）

4. Don't tell anyone, not even your husband.
（別告訴任何人，連你先生也不要說。）

在非正式場合說話時，**even 有時用在它所修飾的字詞後面，或用在句末來表示強調或加強語氣。Even 位在其所修飾的字詞後面**，主要是在表示更準確或更詳細的說法，此時它意為「甚至可以說，更確切地說，其實」(more exactly)。例如：

1. New York is a huge city, larger even than Tokyo.
（紐約是個大城市，甚至比東京還大。）

2. The task might be difficult, impossible even.
（這項任務可能很困難，甚至可以說不可能完成。）

3. Most of us find some of his habits somewhat unpleasant, disgusting even.
（我們大多數人都覺得他的一些習慣頗令人討厭，甚至可以說是令人作嘔。）

4. I can't remember Professor Lee at all. I've forgotten that he'd been my grammar teacher even.

（我一點都記不得李教授了。我甚至忘記了他曾經是我的文法老師。）

→ 平常的位置：I can't remember Professor Lee at all. I've even forgotten that he'd been my grammar teacher.

好用 Tips 非學不可 🔍

Even 經常用來修飾形容詞和副詞的比較級以表示強調或加強語氣。

Even 在此意為「更加，愈加，甚至更」。 例如：

1. It's even hotter today than it was yesterday.
（今天甚至比昨天還要熱。）

2. Things were bad, but they are even worse under the current government.
（過去情況很糟，但在現任政府領導下情況更糟。）

3. The female singer has become even richer, and her concerts even more popular.
（這位女歌手已變得更有錢，而她的演唱會也更受歡迎。）

Even as

Even 可放在 as 所引導的子句前面來表示「正當，恰好在……的時候」 的意思。例如：

1. Even as we spoke, he ate his breakfast quickly.
（就在我們說話的時候，他匆匆地吃完了早餐。）

2. Even as I watched, the bus crashed into the house.
（正當我看著的時候，巴士就撞上了房子。）

Even if

Even 可放在 if 所引導的子句前面來表示「即使」的意思。 例如：

1. Even if you take a taxi, you'll still be late for school.
（即使搭計程車去，你還是上學遲到。）

2. I'm still going to eat out(,) even if it rains.
（即使下雨，我仍要外出用餐。）

Even though

Even 可放在 though 所引導的子句前面來表示「**儘管，雖然**」的意思。**Even though 與 although 或 in spite of the fact that 同義**，但比 although 更具強調作用。例如：

1. Even though Gary has a master's degree in business administration, he can't fill out his tax form.
（蓋瑞儘管擁有企管碩士學位，但還是不會填報稅表格。）
2. He rents his house(,) even though he's so rich.
（他雖然很富有，但還是租房子住。）

Even so

我們可以使用 **even so 來做對比**，意為「**即使如此，即使這樣；儘管如此，儘管這樣**」，與 **however 或 nevertheless 同義**。Even so 最常用在子句句首，但亦可用於句末。它**往往位在連接詞 but 之後**。例如：

1. Terrorist attacks are rare, but, even so, there should be stricter safety measures.
（恐攻是罕見的，但儘管如此，仍應有更嚴格的安全措施。）

2. I had a terrible headache, but even so I went to the Christmas party.
（我頭痛得要命，但儘管如此我還是去參加聖誕節晚會。）

3. I didn't understand what Cindy said completely, but it was interesting even so.
（我沒有完全聽懂辛蒂所說的話，但即便如此她所說的還是很有趣。）

Unit 16 Featuring / feat. / ft. / f.

必閃陷阱 非學不可

現今許多人，尤其是年輕人，經常上 YouTube 或其他著名影音網站觀看和聆聽歌手（或樂團）的音樂錄影帶 (Music Video, MV) 或現場演唱 (live concert or live performance) 影片。這些影片的上方或下方都會有歌名和歌手名稱，如果是中文，大家一看就懂，自是無庸筆者多言。但若是英文歌名和歌手名稱，倒是有個地方值得提出來討論並加以延伸說明。

讀者乍看本文標題可能會一頭霧水，心想這是什麼「碗糕」？事實上，這四個字是同一個字，**因為 feat.、ft.、f. 都是 featuring 的縮寫**，其中以 feat. 和 ft. 最常見。它們跟 MV 或現場演唱影片又有什麼關係呢？當然有，因為它們經常和英文歌名和歌手名稱結合在一起，形成**「A 歌手 ──《歌名》feat./ft./f. B 歌手」**的習慣寫法。**Featuring 在流行音樂中，意思相當於「由（某歌手）客串」**，亦即 A 歌手邀請 B 歌手在其主唱的單曲 (single) 或專輯 (album) 中演唱或來一段 rap，而客串的歌手叫做 guest artist。

現在就來看幾支有**歌手客串演唱**因而**使用 feat. 和 ft. 的 MV**：

1. Eminem—Love The Way You Lie ft. Rihanna
(http://www.youtube.com/watch?v=uelHwf8o7_U)

2. Pitbull—Rain Over Me ft. Marc Anthony
(http://www.youtube.com/watch?v=SmM0653YvXU)

3. 50 Cent—My Life (Feat. Eminem, Adam Levine) (Official Video)
(https://www.youtube.com/watch?v=UcSmypn_ObI)

4. Justin Bieber—Beauty And A Beat ft. Nicki Minaj
(http://www.youtube.com/watch?v=Ys7-6_t7OEQ)

上面第 1 支 MV 的歌名是《Love The Way You Lie》，由阿姆 (Eminem) 主唱，蕾哈娜 (Rihanna) 客串；第 2 支 MV 的歌名是《Rain Over Me》，由嘻哈鬥牛梗 (Pitbull) 主唱，馬克安東尼 (Marc Anthony) 客串；第 3 支 MV 的歌名是《My Life》，由五角 (50 Cent) 主唱，阿姆和亞當 (Adam Levine) 客串；第 4 支 MV 的歌名是《Beauty And A Beat》，由小賈斯汀 (Justin Bieber) 主唱，麻辣雞 (Nicki Minaj) 客串。然而，**影集、連續劇或其他電視節目的客串演出或友情演出，並不是 featuring，而是使用 guest appearance 來表示**；不過，guest appearance 亦適用於流行音樂的客串演唱，只是現**在幾已被 featuring 所取代**。電視劇的客串演出者叫做 **guest role** 或 **guest star**，後者特指明星或名流的客串演出，由於他們通常僅演出一集或數集，因此亦經常被叫做 **special guest star**，即特別客串演出（者）。

好用 Tips 非學不可 🔍

還有一些與流行音樂有關的字也值得學習。大家都知道，一首好歌一定會有人翻唱。**翻唱的英文叫做 cover**，可當動詞或名詞（可數）用，如 Our band mostly **covers** old Beatles classics.（我們樂團大多翻唱披頭四的經典老歌）；They did a brilliant **cover** of the old songs of that famous singer.（他們出色地翻唱了那位名歌手的老歌。）至於**翻唱別人歌曲的樂團或歌手**，則叫做 **cover band**。有人翻唱，也有人惡搞或 Kuso，如更改歌詞、翻拍 MV 等。相信許多人都想知道「**惡搞或 Kuso**」的英文，那就是 **parody**。最後要提的是「**幕後花絮**」的英文，叫做 **"behind the scenes"** 或 **"making of"**，可指 MV、電視節目、電影製作及其他所有藝術表演的幕後花絮，如 This footage is the **behind the scenes/making of** The Black Eyed Peas — I Gotta Feeling.（這段影片是黑眼豆豆《I Gotta Feeling》MV 的幕後花絮）。

Fish vs. fishes

Part 二 寫作用法精論

必閃陷阱 非學不可

Fish（魚）的複數可以是 fish 或 fishes，但大多用 fish。不過，fishes 也有若干不可或缺的用法。譬如說，**在生物學中，fishes 是用來指不同的魚品種**。所以，如果你說你在浮潛時看到 **five fish**，這表示你看到**五條魚**，但如果你說你看到 **five fishes**，那麼一般可能會認為你看到**不知數量的五種魚**。

Fish 的複數所有格是用 fishes' 來表示，如 These fishes' scales were green.（這些魚的鱗是綠色的。）當然了，當 fish（捕魚；釣魚）用作動詞時，fishes 是第三人稱單數動詞，如 John fishes in the river.（約翰在河裡捕魚。）

Fishes 也出現在黑幫電影慣用的 sleep with the **fishes**（與魚共眠）這個片語中，用來表示某人已被擊昏，可能被丟入海中。英文其他成語都是使用 **fish**，如 have other **fish** to fry（另有更重要的事情要處理）和 there are plenty more **fish** in the sea（天涯何處無芳草。）

Unit 18 Hear that, see that

Hear that 和 see that 經常被用來引導新的訊息或資訊，此時 **hear** 意為「**聽說，得知**」，而 **see** 意為「**知道；明白；瞭解**」。在這項用法中，hear 和 see 通常使用**現在簡單式**，而 **that** **有時會省略**。例如：

1. I hear (that) Teresa has a thing for Benjamin.
（我聽說泰瑞莎喜歡班傑明。）

2. I hear Mary's getting married in August.
（我聽說瑪麗八月要結婚。）

3. I see (that) John is going to move to Taipei next month.
（我知道約翰下個月將搬到台北。）

4. I see Professor Chen remarried.
（我知道陳教授再婚了。）

Gather（**瞭解，認為；推測，猜想**）、**learn**（**得知，獲悉，聽說**）和 **understand**（**明白，瞭解，聽說**）等動詞亦有相似的用法。例如：

1. I gather that he is the one in charge.
（我猜想他是負責的人。）

2. Peter loves his new job, I gather.
（我認為彼得喜歡他的新工作。）

3. I told them the secret yesterday and they understand the prime minister will reshuffle his cabinet soon.
（昨天我告訴他們這個秘密，他們都知道總理很快就會改組內閣。）

4. I understand you wish to see the president.
（聽說您想見總統。）

5. I learned from his email that he went on a business trip to Japan.
（我從他的電子郵件中得知他到日本出差。）

6. I later learned (that) you had never lent him any money.
（我後來聽說你都沒有借錢給他。）

綜上所述，在「聽說；知道」的意思上，我們可以**將 hear, see, gather, learn 和 understand 等動詞歸納為用法相似的一類**，其句型為「**動詞 + (that) 子句**」，而動詞在句中通常使用**現在簡單式**。

Unit 19　John Doe, Joe Bloggs, Fred Nerk

必閃陷阱 非學不可 🔍

John Doe 是美式英語對法律訴訟或刑事偵察中**需要保密或不知姓名（如無名屍）的當事人假設的稱呼**，相當於中文的某甲、路人甲、張三或李四。這個專有名詞**指的是男性，若是女性，則用 Jane Doe** 來表示。除 John Doe 外，美國一般男子的假設稱呼還可用 **Joe Blow**、**Joe Schmoe**、**John Q. Public** 或 **Joe Sixpack** 來表示，後者是指**藍領工人**。

英國一般男子的假設稱呼是用 **Joe Bloggs**、**John Smith** 或 **Joe Public** 來表示。澳洲一般男子的假設稱呼為 Fred Nerk、Joe Blow、Joe Bloggs 或 John Citizen。紐西蘭則使用 Joe Bloggs、Joe Blow 或 John Doe 來稱呼假設的普通男子。在加拿大，假設的普通男子被稱為 John Jones 或 Jos Bleau。

John Doe、Joe Bloggs、Fred Nerk 及其他名稱都是無名氏的稱呼。
現今有許多情況可能需要用到這種名稱，包括 1. 法律訴訟中原告或被告的身份需要保密；2. 無名屍；3. 指父母不詳的棄嬰；4. 談論美國、英國或澳洲的一般平民百姓、普通人時；5. 在指示如何填寫表格時，作為姓名的範例。

Unit 20 Long 的用法

必閃陷阱 非學不可

Long 用作副詞或形容詞，可用來指時間、距離和長度。然而，這個幾乎在我們一開始學英文就會學到的字，卻有一些用法可能讓人用錯而不自知。**Long 的用法陷阱主要存在於它用作副詞來指時間的時候。**本文將僅就此詳加說明，其他用法並無深究的必要，自是無庸贅述，或者礙於篇幅暫不予討論。

Long 用作副詞來表示時間「很久」時，只能用在疑問句和否定句。例如：

1. How long have you been here in Taipei?
（你來台北多久了？）

2. Will you be long, or shall I wait?
（你要很長的時間嗎，我要不要等你？）
→ "Be/take long" 意為「要很久；要很長的時間」。

3. Don't be long getting ready, please.
（請馬上準備好。）

4. I hope you haven't been waiting long.
（我希望你沒有等很久。）

5. John didn't stay long in the library.
（約翰沒有在圖書館待很久。）

Long 單獨一個字不可用在肯定句。我們通常使用 (for) a long time。例如：

◆ John stayed **for a long time** in the library.（O）
◇ John stayed long in the library.（×）
（約翰在圖書館待了很久。）

◆ It **took a long time** for me to write this article.（○）
◇ It took long for me to write this article.（×）
（寫這篇文章花了我很長的時間。）

◆ A: Will it **take long**?（○）
(A：那要很長的時間嗎？)

◆ B: No, it won't **take long**.（○）
（B：不，不要很長的時間。）或

◆ B：Yes, it'll **take a long time**.（○）
◇ B：Yes, it'll take long.（×）
（B：是的，那要很長的時間。）

不過，當 **long 與 too, enough 和 so 連用時可單獨用在肯定句**。例如：

1. Two weeks is too long to wait for an interview.
（等候面試要等兩個禮拜太久了。）

2. Mary stayed just long enough to meet her boyfriend's parents.
（瑪麗只待到和她男友的父母見了面。）

3. His father waited long enough for an appointment.
（他父親等候任命等得夠久了。）

4. Cindy asked her boyfriend why he took so long to call her.
（辛蒂問她男友怎麼這麼久才打電話給她。）

5. What took you so long?
（你怎麼這麼久？）

在談到實質的時間長度時，我們可以在肯定句（疑問句和否定句當然也可以）使用「**時間 + long**」以及 **all day/night/week/month/year long**（整天／整晚／整週／整月／整年）和**my whole life long**（我的一輩子）等片語（long 在這些片語中都是副詞）。例如：

1. The concert was four hours long.
（演唱會長達四小時。）

2. They worked all day long.
（他們整天都在工作。）

好用 Tips 非學不可

我們亦可在**肯定句中使用 a long time ago**（很久以前）、**long ago**（很久以前）、**long before**（在……之前很久）、**long after**（在……之後很久）和 **long since**（很久以前）。例如：

1. The hospital was established a long time ago.
（這家醫院建於很久以前。）

= The hospital was established long ago.

2. You should have ended the extramarital affair long ago.
（你早該結束這段婚外情。）

3. Kevin knew his wife long before they got married.
（凱文在結婚之前很久就認識他太太了。）

4. Allen left not long before you arrived.
（你抵達時艾倫剛離開不久。）

5. Jack was born long after his parents got married.
（傑克的父母結婚多年後才生下他。）

6. They've long since gone home.
（他們早就回家了。）

7. I learned my lesson long since.
（我早就學到教訓了。）

Unit 21　Luck 和 lucky 的用法

必閃陷阱 非學不可

Luck 是名詞，意為「運氣；幸運，好運」，其後往往接**介系詞 in 或 with 再接人事物**來表示在某人事物上或對某人事物的運氣；lucky 是形容詞，意為「幸運的，運氣好的」。例如：

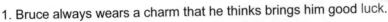

1. Bruce always wears a charm that he thinks brings him good luck.
（布魯斯總是戴著一個他認為會給他帶來好運的護身符。）

2. John seems to have had a lot of bad luck in finding a job.
（約翰找工作時似乎碰到許多倒楣的事情。）

3. My luck held/lasted and I found a gas station just in time.
（好運與我常相左右／好運一直伴隨著我，我即時找到一處加油站。）

4. A lucky person won the first prize in the competition.
（一位幸運兒贏得了這項比賽的首獎。）

5. You're lucky to work for such a nice company.
（你能在這麼好的一家公司工作真是幸運。）

6. A: I got promoted yesterday.
（Ａ：我昨天升官了。）

   B: Lucky you!
（Ｂ：你真是幸運！）

Luck 係不可數名詞，其前不可使用不定冠詞 a/an 且沒有複數型，但可以使用 **any, some, much, a bit of 或 a lot of 來表示運氣的程度**。例如：

◆ It was **pure/sheer luck** that they found the house.（○）
◇ It was a pure/sheer luck that they found the house.（×）
（他們找到那棟房子純屬運氣。）

◆ Their **luck** is bound to run out sometime.（○）
◇ Their lucks are bound to run out sometime.（×）
（他們的運氣終將用完。）

1. Have you had any luck with finding a job?
（你找到工作了嗎？）

2. He has had much luck with girls.
（他的女人緣極佳。）

3. With any luck (or with a bit/piece/stroke of luck), I'll be a dentist next year.
（幸運的話，明年我就當牙醫了。）

由於 **luck 為不可數名詞，因此泛指時，其前不可有定冠詞 the**。例如：

◆ Sometimes it's a matter of **luck** whether we are successful.（○）
◇ Sometimes it's a matter of the luck whether we are successful.（✕）
（有時我們能否成功要靠運氣。）

中文的「祝你好運」可用 Good luck, (The) best of luck 和 I wish you luck 來表示。這三句都很常用且是固定用語，有人將 **best of luck 說成或寫成 best luck 是錯的**。例如：

1. Good luck!
（祝你好運！）

2. I wish you luck!
（祝你好運！）

3. I wish you luck in your driving test!
（祝你通過駕照考試！）

4. I wish you all the best of luck!
（祝你一切順心如意！）

5. Good luck in your job interview!
（祝你求職面試順利！）

◆ The **best of luck** in/with your exams!（○）
◇ The best luck in/with your exams!（✕）
（祝你考試順利！）

◆ I think you're taking a big risk, but anyway, **best of luck**!（○）
◇ I think you're taking a big risk, but anyway, best luck!（✕）
(我認為你冒很大的風險，但不管怎樣，祝你好運！)

好用 Tips 非學不可 🔍

英文沒有 best luck 的說法，但（除 good luck 外）卻**有 better luck 和 worst luck** 的說法。例如：

1. Better luck next time!
（祝你下次運氣好一點！）

2. Worse luck!
（真倒楣！）

3. I've got to work on Sunday, worst luck!
（我星期天得加班，真倒楣！）

Unit 22 Many 的形容詞用法

必閃陷阱 非學不可

Many 是個大家所熟知的字，當形容詞時意為「（可數名詞）多的，許多的，很多的」，通常**用於否定句和疑問句**。例如：

1. How many sisters do you have?
（你有幾個姊妹？）
2. I don't have many relatives.
（我的親戚不多。）

Many 的前面可以加上 not 來表示 few（極少的）意思。例如：

1. Not many students (or Few students) like exams.
（喜歡考試的學生寥寥無幾。）
2. Not many people (or Few people) came to the meeting.
（與會者不多。）

所以，**在肯定句中，many 鮮少單獨用在名詞之前**。例如：

◆ There are **a lot of** books on the desk.（O）
◇ There are many books on the desk.（×）
（書桌上有許多書。）

然而，在正式的上下文中，我們有時可以**在肯定句中使用 many 或 many of （many 在此為代名詞）來代替 a lot of 或 lots of**。例如：

276

1. Many teachers are strongly opposed to the pension reform.
（許多老師強烈反對年金改革。）

2. Many of his students have become public servants.
（他的許多學生已成為公務員。）

→ 如果沒把握能準確地判斷正式或非正式，最保險的作法就是在肯定句中都使用 a lot of 或 lots of。

不過，在下面所述的情況中，many 可以用於肯定句：

Many ＋ 名詞後接修飾該名詞的**關係子句**時。例如：

1. Many people who voted for him in the last election will not be doing so this time.
（許多在上次選舉中投票給他的人這次不會那麼做了。）

2. There were many questions which were left unanswered after passage of the "one fixed day off and one flexible rest day" (or five-day work week) bill.
（「一例一休」法案通過後有許多問題未得到答覆。）

好用 Tips 非學不可 🔍

Many 前面使用 very、a good/great、so 和 too 等副詞來修飾時。例如：

1. There are still very many problems left to be resolved.
（還有很多問題留待解決。）

2. A good/great many students have complained to me about the food.
（許多學生向我抱怨伙食不佳。）

3. I've explained the difference between transitive and intransitive verbs so many times, but they still can't understand!
（有關及物和不及物動詞之間的差異，我已說明很多次，但他們還是不明白！）

4. Most people know the reason why so many young people want to leave the country.
（大多數人都知道這麼多年輕人想離開這個國家的原因。）

5. If there are only three of us going to the concert, then I've booked two too many seats (or two seats too many).
（如果我們當中只有三個人去聽演唱會，那我就多訂了兩張票。）

6. There is one too many chairs here. / There is one chair too many here.
（這裡多一張椅子。）

7. As many as 8,000 elderly people may have been infected with the disease.
（可能已有多達 8,000 名老年人染上此病。）

→ as many as 意為「多達」。

8. Amy has had five boyfriends in as many months.
（艾美五個月就交了五個男朋友。）

→ in as many 意為「（與前面提過的數目）一樣多的」。

= Amy has had five boyfriends in five months.

Unit 23 Might as well

必閃陷阱 非學不可

Might as well 是日常生活中常見的一個片語，意為「倒不如；不妨；做……也無妨」，如 We might as well celebrate our wedding anniversary at home.（我們倒不如在家裡慶祝結婚紀念日。）這個片語還意為「還不如」，如 The party was a complete waste of time. I might as well have stayed at time.（這場聚會完全是浪費時間，早知道還不如待在家裡好。）

Might as well 的起源不可考，可能來自英國成語 "someone might as well be hanged/hung for a sheep as a lamb"，最後將這個成語的後半部拿掉而變成現在的樣子。

這個成語意為「偷小羊還不如偷大羊，反正一樣要被處絞刑；一不做，二不休」（古時候，英國的偷羊者，不論是偷大羊還是偷小羊，均處以絞刑），且經常不用主詞，如 **Oh, might as well be hung for a sheep as a lamb, I suppose.（哦，我看乾脆一不做，二不休。）**

值得一提的是，有人可能認為 "someone might as well be hanged/hung for a sheep as a lamb" 中的 hung 用錯了，因為 hang 這個動詞有兩個主要意思，一為「懸掛；掛，吊」，另一為「絞死；吊死」，它們的過去式和過去分詞分別為截然不同的 hung, hung 和 hanged, hanged。然而，這是針對美式英語而言，在英式英語中，hung 亦不時被用作 hang 意為「絞死；吊死」時的過去式和過去分詞，本成語即是其中一例。不過，**考試時，建議還是嚴格遵守美式英語的區別**，以免被認為錯誤。

好用 Tips 非學不可 🔍

除了 **might as well** 外，我們亦經常見到和聽到 **might just as well** 和 **may as well** 的寫法和說法。事實上，**might as well、might just as well 和 may as well 的意思完全一樣**，如 For the little extra it'll cost, we might just as well stay for another night.（只要多花一點錢，我們不妨再住一晚。）若把 as 拿掉，變成 **might well** 和 **may well**，兩者均意為**「很可能」**，如 A small technical error might/may well result in a serious accident.（小小的技術失誤很可能導致嚴重事故。）

Unit 24　More or less 的用法

重要觀念 非學不可

More or less 是個略為非正式的片語，當副詞用，意為「**大約；幾乎，差不多；多少有些，大致上**」。在句中，它通常位在副詞慣常的中間位置，即主詞和主動詞之間、語氣助動詞或第一個**助動詞之後**，或當主動詞用的 **BE 動詞之後**。例如：

1. I've more or less finished reading the novel.
（我差不多已經看完這本小說了。）

2. His youngest son was more or less mentally retarded.
（他的么兒有點弱智。）

3. The plan was more or less a success.
（這項計劃大致成功。）

More or less 通常位在數字和測量單位之後。例如：

1. The alligator's 800 kilos, more or less.
（這隻短吻鱷大約有 800 公斤重。）

2. She can earn 10 US dollars an hour, more or less, as a waitress.
（她當服務生一小時可賺 10 美元左右。）

3. A sum of three million dollars, more or less, will be needed to carry out the plan.
（執行這項計畫需要大約三百萬元。）

必閃陷阱 非學不可

More or less 不可用在年齡之前。例如：

◆ His mother's about 40. （ O ）
◇ His mother's more or less 40. （ × ）
（他媽媽大約 40 歲。）

Unit 25 Most, the most

在 **most people, most of people, most the people** 和 **the most people** 這四個片語中，哪一個或哪幾個的文法正確或錯誤呢？現在我們就來說明 most 的用法及一般使用上可能發生的錯誤。

Most 為 many 和 much 的最高級，可當限定詞（或形容詞）、代名詞和副詞用。

Most 用作限定詞（或形容詞）時後面**緊接複數可數名詞或不可數名詞**，意為「大多數的；大部分的」，此時 **most 前面不可使用定冠詞 the**。例如：

1. Most people think that he is a good president.
（大多數人都認為他是好總統。）
2. I go swimming most weekends.
（週末我大多去游泳。）
3. Most information was useful.
（大部分資訊都是有用的。）
4. Most tap water is drinkable.
（大多數自來水都可飲用。）

當 most 後面的名詞不言可喻時，該名詞可以省略。例如：

A few of the students enjoy writing, but most (students) enjoy reading.
（有一些學生喜歡寫作，但大部分喜歡閱讀。）

若 most 前面有 the，則 **most 意為「（數量、金額等）最大的，最多的」**。例如：

1. Paul earns the most money in our family.
（保羅賺的錢是我們家中最多的。）

2. We'll try our best to help the most people.
（我們將竭盡全力幫助最多的人。）

同樣地，當 the most 後面的名詞不言可喻時，該名詞可以省略。例如：

Sam didn't tell the best jokes but he told the most (jokes).
（山姆說的笑話不是最好的，但他說了最多笑話。）

對於上述 **most 意為「大多數的；大部分的」而 the most 意為「最大的，最多的」二分法**，筆者可能會被打臉，因為國內一本頗多人使用的英漢辭典提供這樣的例句：The storm did (the) most damage to the houses on the cliff.（暴風雨破壞最多的是位在懸崖上的房屋）；換言之，**most 的前面沒有 the 也可表示「最大的，最多的」意思**。還好其他辭典都沒有提到這樣的用法。

由於「大多數或大部分」和「最大或最多」的含意並不完全相同，如果 most 可同時表示這兩種意思，那麼往往會造成意思混淆、模稜兩可的情況。譬如說，若按照該辭典的說法，Mary earns most votes. 這句就可以理解為「瑪麗囊括最多的選票」或「瑪麗囊括大多數的選票」。假設除了瑪麗外，還有另外兩位候選人艾美和辛蒂，如果瑪麗的得票率為 35%，而艾美和辛蒂的得票率分別為 33% 和 32%，那麼「瑪麗囊括最多的選票」講得通，但「瑪麗囊括大多數的選票」就不通了。這種講不通的情況所在多有，所以**若要表示「最大的，最多的」意思，務必使用 "the most"，the 不可省略**。

反過來說，若要表示「大多數的；大部分的」意思，則要使用 "most"，即 most 前面沒有 the。例如：

◆ The sun shines several hundred hours during June, July and August in Taiwan and on **most days** temperatures rise above 33 degrees.（○）
（台灣六月、七月和八月的日照時間有幾百個小時，白天氣溫大多會上升至 33 度以上。）

◇ The sun shines several hundred hours during June, July and August in Taiwan and on the most days temperatures rise above 33 degrees.（×）

◆ I go swimming **most weekends**.（O）

◇ I go swimming the most weekends.（×）

（週末我大多去游泳。）

→ 注意：**Most days/evenings/mornings/weekends** 等片語中的 most 一定意為「大多數的；大部分的」，前面不可有 the。

Most 用作代名詞時意為「大多數；大部分」。這是一種「特指」

（**"most + 名詞" 是泛指**），句型為 **"most + of + 受格代名詞**或特指的名詞"。所謂特指的名詞，就是名詞的前面加上 the, that, this, these, those 或所有格，如 my, John's 等等。由於這裡的名詞為複數可數名詞或不可數名詞，所以在此不可使用 this 和 that。在此句型中，無論是**缺少 of 或缺少名詞前面的 the, these, those 或所有格都是文法錯誤**。例如：

◆ **Most people** think that he is a good president.（O）

◆ **Most of the people** think that he is a good president.（O）

◇ Most of people think that he is a good president.（×）

◇ Most the people think that he is a good president.（×）

（大多數人都認為他是好總統。）

1. Most of them enjoy driving fast.

（他們大多數人都喜歡開快車。）

2. I spent most of my life in Kaohsiung.

（我一生大部分時間都是在高雄度過的。）

在地理名詞前面不用 the, these, those 或所有格。例如：

Most of Taiwan is hot throughout the day.

（台灣大多數地方整天都是炎熱的。）

Most 當副詞時，主要用來與有三個或更多音節的形容詞和副詞以及部分只有**兩個音節的形容詞和副詞連用，來構成這些形容詞和副詞的最高級**，此時 **most 的前面須有 the**，而 the most 是位在形容詞和副詞的前面，意為「最」。例如：

1. These companies are using the most advanced technology in the world.
（這些公司使用世上最先進的科技。）
→ 形容詞 advanced 的最高級。

2. Even the most carefully prepared plans sometimes go wrong.
（即使是最精心準備的計畫有時也會出錯。）
→ 副詞 carefully 的最高級。

當 most 的前面為所有格或其他所有格形式時，不可再使用 the，亦即在最高級形式的 most 前面，不可同時使用 the 和所有格。例如：

◆ My **most trustworthy** friend in my life is myself.（O）
◇ My the most trustworthy friend in my life is myself.（×）
（我一生中最值得我信賴的朋友是我自己。）

◆ Taipei is Taiwan's **most important** city.（O）
◇ Taipei is Taiwan's the most important city.（×）
（台北是台灣最重要的城市。）

Most 用作副詞時也經常與動詞連用來表示「最大程度地」意思，此時 **most 前面的 the 可有可無**。例如：

1. We all cried, but Cynthia cried the most.
（我們所有人都哭了，但辛西雅哭得最厲害。）

2. They all ate a lot, but Peter ate the most.
（他們所有人都吃很多，但彼得吃最多。）

3. He did the most he could.
（他已盡最大努力去做了。）

4. Grace looks the most like her mother.
（葛蕾絲長得最像她的母親。）

5. What I need most now is money.
（我現在最需要的是錢。）

6. What John wants most of all is to spend more time studying English.
（約翰最想做的是多花時間唸英文。）

有人認為在此 the most 中的 most 為代名詞，尤其是當 the most 位在及物動詞之後時。若從文法觀點來看，這種說法不無道理，站得住腳。

好用 Tips 非學不可 🔍

當**用來修飾形容詞和副詞的 most 前面沒有 the 時，這個 most 就不是最高級，意思也不是「最」，而是與 very 同義的「非常，很」**。這是一種正式的用法，但 most 與 very 之間並不能劃上等號，因為 **most 後面接的必須是表示個人感情或主觀看法的形容詞和副詞**。例如：

1. She is a most beautiful woman.
（她是個很漂亮的女人。）
→ 漂不漂亮有時純屬主觀的看法。

2. She is a very tall woman.
（她是個很高的女人。）
→ 身高高就是高，矮就是矮，比較沒有模糊空間。

3. It is really most unfortunate.
（這真的很不幸。）
→ 每個人對不幸的看法不盡相同。

4. It was a most amazing coincidence.
（那是令人驚奇的巧合。）
→ 你覺得驚奇，但我認為稀鬆平常。

5. He did all these things very quickly.
（他很快地做完這些事情。）
→ 這些事情別人要一個禮拜才能做完，他三天就完成了，你說快不快，任何個人感情或主觀看法都改變不了既定的事實。

Unit 26

Mother's Day 還是 Mothers' Day、Father's Day 還是 Fathers' Day、Manager's Meeting 抑或 Managers' Meeting 呢？

必閃陷阱 非學不可

母親節是 Mother's Day 還是 Mothers' Day 呢？所有格符號 (') 是位在 s 的前面還是後面呢。

根據文法，若**名詞為單數**，我們是**在名詞的後面加上所有格符號**，然後**再加 s** 來表示名詞的所有格（亦即所有格符號是位在 s 的前面）；若**名詞為複數**，則**所有格符號是加在 s 的後面**。這是一般的規則，但這規則也有例外。譬如說，美國退伍軍人節或退伍軍人紀念日既不是 Veteran's Day 亦不是 Veterans' Day，而是 Veterans Day。這是美國官方的正式名稱，是個聯邦假日，一個全國性節日。

所以，上述通則有時候還是會使不上力，尤其是當您不確定名詞是單數還是複數時，就無法正確地寫出它們的所有格。這種情況最常發生在下列名詞身上：

1. Mother's / Mothers' Day

2. Father's / Fathers' Day

3. Manager's / Managers' Meeting

4. Chief Executive's / Chief Executives' Meeting

現在筆者就來一一說明它們正確的寫法。

Mother's Day 還是 Mothers' Day 呢？

母親節的正式英文名稱是 Mother's Day，這是一個慶祝每個家庭的母親的日子。當然，從文法上來說，它也可以是 Mothers' Day，亦即一個慶祝全世界所有母親的日子。然而，**Mother's Day 是美國法律中所載的寫法**，該法律規定 Mother's Day 為美國國定節日。

Father's Day 還是 Fathers' Day 呢?

同樣地,**Father's Day 是美國國會**在 1913 年立法將父親節訂為美國國定節日過程中所用的名稱。

Manager's Meeting 還是 Managers' Meeting 呢?

對於 Manager's/Managers' Meeting 等用語,這要**視該會議是由一名經理所主持,抑或該會議是所有經理都得參加的會議而定**。換言之,

1. Manager's Meeting(經理的會議):指的是一名經理所召開的會議(譬如說,這可能是一場由該經理擔任主席的會議)。
2. Managers' Meeting(經理會議):指的是所有經理都得參加的會議。

Chief Executive's Meeting 還是 Chief Executives' Meeting 呢?

(Chief Executive 意為「政府最高行政首長」,如總統、州長、省長等)

如上述。換言之,

1. Chief Executive's Meeting(總統/州長/省長的會議):指的是該最高行政首長所召開的會議(譬如說,這可能是一場**由該最高行政首長**擔任主席的會議)。
2. Chief Executives' Meeting(州長/省長會議):指的是**所有州長/省長**都得參加的會議。

Unit 27　Nearby 的用法

必閃陷阱 非學不可

Nearby 可當形容詞和副詞用,前者意為「附近的」,後者意為「在附近」。例如:

1. My father lives in a nearby village.
（我父親住在附近的村莊。）→（nearby 為形容詞）

2. The gymnasium nearby can seat 50, 000 people.
（附近那座體育館可容納五萬人。）→（nearby 為形容詞）

3. My father lives nearby.
（我父親住在附近。）→（nearby 為副詞）

從上面的例句可知，當形容詞用的 nearby 可放在其所修飾的名詞之前或之後，但放在名詞之後的情況比較少見。

Nearby 不能用作介系詞，在需要用到介系詞的場合，我們必須使用 near。例如：

◆ John has been working in a restaurant **near** the park.（O）
◇ John has been working in a restaurant nearby the park.（×）
（約翰一直在公園附近的一家餐廳工作。）

Unit 28　Need 的用法

必閃陷阱 非學不可

Need 可當「半語氣助動詞」（marginal modal or semi-modal—dare、ought to 和 used to 也是屬於這類助動詞）和普通動詞用，前者與其他語氣助動詞一樣，後接原形動詞，但它幾乎都是用在**否定句**和（少部分用在）**問句**中。例如：

1. He needn't earn overtime.
（他不必賺加班費。）

2. You needn't take off your shoes.
（你不必脫鞋。）

3. Need I reply?
（我必須回覆嗎？）

當語氣助動詞用的 need 鮮少用於肯定句，除非是在正式的上下文中。但即使 need 後面未接 not，**句子中也幾乎都會使用 no one、nobody、nothing 等否定詞，使得句子仍屬否定句**。例如：

1. Nothing need be done about his birthday party till Saturday.
（週六之前有關他的生日派對，什麼事都不必做。）

2. Nobody need trouble about this.
（沒有人必須為這事操心。）

3. No one need write a report about this book.
（沒有人必須寫這本書的讀書報告。）

4. Not a thing need change on this document.
（這份文件不必做任何修改。）

當語氣助動詞用的 need 是直接在後面加上 not 來變成否定，即 need not（正式的寫法），但可縮寫為 needn't（非正式的寫法）。所以，我們不可在 need 的前面再加上 don't/doesn't/didn't。例如：

◆ You **need not** worry about this issue.（○）
◆ You **needn't** worry about this issue.（○）
◇ You don't need worry about this issue.（×）
（你不用擔心這問題。）

當語氣助動詞用的 **need 也很少用於問句，除非是在正式的上下文中。**
Need 用於問句時是直接挪到主詞的前面，句末加上問號。所以，我們不可在主詞的前面使用 Do/Does/Did。例如：

◆ **Need** you go so soon?（○）
◇ Do you need go so soon?（×）
（你需要這麼早走嗎？）

當語氣助動詞用的 need 不可再跟其他語氣助動詞連用。例如：

◆ **No one need** write a report about this book.（O）
◇ No one need must write a report about this book.（×）
◇ No one must need write a report about this book.（×）

當語氣助動詞用的 need 沒有過去型。所以，若要表示**過去的「必須，必要，需要」，要使用 didn't need to**（need 在此為普通動詞）或 **didn't have to**。例如：

◆ We **didn't need to** lend money to him.（O）
◆ We **didn't have to** lend money to him.（O）
◇ We didn't need lend money to him.（×）
（我們不必把錢借給他。）

Needn't have ＋ P.P. 和 didn't need to ＋ 原形動詞都是在表示過去發生的事件。**Needn't have done** 是表示**本來不必做或用不著做**，但卻做了；**didn't need to do** 則是表示**不必做或用不著做，但有可能做了，也可能沒做**。例如：

1. Mary needn't have taken her umbrella.
（瑪麗本來不用帶傘的。）
→ 但她卻帶了。
2. Mary didn't need to take her umbrella.
（瑪麗不必帶傘。）
→ 但實際上可能帶了，也可能沒帶。

好用 Tips 非學不可 🔍

當語氣助動詞用的 **need 和 need to 可以互換**，但**當普通動詞用的 need 須接帶 to 的不定詞**，而且有人稱、數和時態的變化。例如：

1. Need you study?
（你必須唸書嗎？）
Do you need to study?

2. He needn't study.
（他不必唸書。）

He doesn't need to study.
He needs to study.
（他必須唸書。）

→ 在肯定句中，need 幾乎都是用作普通動詞；主詞為第三人稱單數，動詞須加 s。

Need 後面若要接名詞片語或動名詞，則 need 只能用作普通動詞。例如：

◆ I don't **need** a jacket.（○）
◇ I needn't a jacket.（×）
（我不需要外套。）
◆ The room doesn't **need** painting.（○）
= The room doesn't need to be painted.
◇ The room needn't painting.（×）
（房間不需要粉刷。）

Unit 29 No longer, not any longer

重要觀念 非學不可 🔍

No longer 和 not any longer 均意為「不再」，一般視之為同義詞，但 no longer 比較正式。例如：

1. I could stand John's rudeness no longer.
（我無法再忍受約翰的粗魯無禮。）

2. I couldn't stand John's rudeness any longer.
（我不能再忍受約翰的粗魯無禮。）

No longer 和 not any longer 的反義詞為 still。例如：

1. She no longer works here.
（她已不在這裡工作。）
2. She doesn't work here any longer.
（她已不在這裡工作。）
3. She still works here.
（她仍在這裡工作。）

No longer 通常位在句子中間一般副詞的位置，亦即**位在主詞與主動詞（普通動詞）之間、位在語氣助動詞**或**第一個助動詞**之後，或者位在當主動詞的 **BE動詞之後**，尤其在比較正式的文體中更是如此。例如：

1. Jack no longer plays in the rock band.
（傑克已不在那個搖滾樂團演奏了。）
2. What I could no longer stand was that they were always complaining.
（我不能再忍受的是，他們老是抱怨東抱怨西的。）
3. Mary is no longer living in Taipei.
（瑪麗現在已不住在台北了。）

必閃陷阱 非學不可

在非常正式的文體中，我們可以**用倒裝句來強調 no longer**。此時**主詞和動詞的位置須對調**。例如：

No longer did I dream of winning the lottery a very long time ago. I know my life will be very ordinary.
（很久很久以前我就不再夢想中樂透。我知道我的生活將是平淡無奇。）

然而，在回答問話時，我們只能用 **not any longer，不可用 no longer**。例如：

A: Are you still living in Taipei?
（你還住在台北嗎？）

◆ B: **Not any longer.**（不再）（○）

◇ No longer.（✕）

◇ No, not still.（✕）

Unit 30 No more, not any more

必閃陷阱 非學不可 🔍

No more 和 **not any more** 均意為「**不再**」，可當限定詞和副詞用，但 **no more** 比較正式。例如：

No more, not any more 當限定詞

1. I will watch no more Korean dramas.
2. I won't watch any more Korean dramas.
（我不會再看韓劇。）
3. There's no more milk left. I'd better go and buy some more.
4. There isn't any more milk left. I'd better go buy some more.
（牛奶都喝完了。我最好去再買一些。）

No more, not any more 當副詞

1. All the problems have been solved. You should worry no more.
（所有問題都已解決。你應該不用再擔心了。）
2. Amy and Helen used to be good friends, but they don't like each other any more. (= any longer)
（艾美和海倫過去是好朋友，但現在已不再是了。）

No more than, not any more than

No more than 和 **not any more than** 均意為「**不過；只，僅 (only)**」（帶有令人驚訝的含意），但 **no more than** 比較正式。例如：

1. John is no more than a puppet.
（約翰只不過是個傀儡。）

2. John isn't any more than a puppet.

3. Tom makes no more than NTD 22,000 a month.
（湯姆每月竟然僅賺 22K。）

4. Tom doesn't make any more than NTD 22,000 a month.

5. No more than five people applied for the job.
（申請這份工作的竟然只有五人。）

No more ... than, not any more ... than

No more ... than 和 not any more ... than 均意為「與……同樣不；跟……一樣不」，但 No more ... than 比較正式。例如：

1. He is no more a god/a doctor than we are.
（他和我們一樣都不是神／醫生。）

　He isn't any more a god/a doctor than we are.

2. She is no more stupid than you are.
（她和你一樣不傻。）

　She isn't any more stupid than you are.

3. James can no more sing than Jack can.
（詹姆斯沒有比傑克更會唱歌。）

4. Flying to Taipei isn't any more expensive than getting the HSR.
（搭飛機到台北跟搭高鐵一樣不貴。）

Not more than, not more ... than

除 no more than 和 no more ... than 外，我們不時也會見到 not more than 和 not more ... than 的用法。Not more than 意為「不超過，大概不到，頂多，至多 (at most)」(基本上，與 no more than 同義)，而 not more ... than 意為「沒有（達到）……的程度」。例如：

1. There were not more than 50 people at his wedding.
（頂多 50 人參加了他的婚禮。）

2. It's no/not more than 500 meters to the MRT station.
（到捷運站不到 500 公尺。）

3. I am not more stupid than you.
（我沒有像你那樣傻。）

= I am not as/so stupid as you.

好用 Tips 非學不可 🔍

Any more 還是 anymore 呢？

英式英語通常將這個副詞寫成兩個字，即 any more，但美式英語通常寫成一個字，即 anymore；這就是當你在 Word 中寫一個含有副詞 any more 的句子時，any more 被認為錯誤、底下被畫線的原因。不過，當限定詞用時，只能寫成 any more，不可寫成 anymore。例如：

◆ My father doesn't work **any more**. （O）
◆ My father doesn't work **anymore**. （O）
（我父親不再工作了。）

◆ Do you have **any more** questions/problems? （O）
◇ Do you have anymore questions/problems? （×）
(你們還有什麼問題嗎？)

◆ I can't print **any more** documents. The printer isn't working. （O）
◇ I can't print anymore documents. The printer isn't working. （×）
（我不能再列印文件了。印表機掛了。）

Unit 31　Nowadays、these days 和 today 的用法

必閃陷阱 非學不可

Nowadays（注意這個字的拼法，不是 nowdays）、these days 和 today 都可用作副詞來表示相較於過去的「現今，當今，如今」。例如：

1. Most people think kids nowadays are lazy.
（大多數人都認為現在的小孩很懶。）
2. People nowadays live far more comfortable lives.
（現今人們過著比過去舒適很多的生活。）

These days 比較不正式一些。例如：

1. Young people these days don't respect their teachers any more.
（時下的年輕人不再尊敬他們的老師。）
2. These days you seldom see a young person give up their seat for an older person on the bus.
（現今在公車上你很少會見到年輕人讓位給年長者。）

Today 略微正式一點。例如：

1. People today are much more concerned about their health than they were in the past.
（現在人們比以前更關心自己的健康。）
2. Computers today are so advanced.
（現在的電腦很先進。）
= The computers of today are so advanced.

Today 還可當名詞用，而且可使用所有格 's 或 of today 結構。這是一項相當正式的用法，但 nowadays 或 these days 則無此用法，因為它們**皆不可當名詞用。**

再者，「today's + 名詞」前面不能有定冠詞 the，但「名詞 + of today」前面則須有定冠詞。例如：

◆ In **today's** rapidly changing **society** almost anything seems possible. （O）
◇ In nowadays' rapidly changing society almost anything seems possible. （×）
◇ In these days' rapidly changing society almost anything seems possible. （×）
（在當今變化快速的社會中，似乎任何事情都有可能發生。）

◆ She is one of the best-known novelists **of today**. （O）
◇ She is one of the best-known novelists of nowadays. （×）
◇ She is one of the best-known novelists of these days. （×）
（她是當今最負盛名的小說家之一。）

Nowadays、these days 或 today 皆不可當形容詞用。例如：

◆ Teenagers **nowadays/these days/today** are so sophisticated. （O）
（現在的青少年太世故了。）

= Today's teenagers are so sophisticated.

= The teenagers of today are so sophisticated.

◇ The nowadays teenagers / The these days teenagers / The today teenagers are so sophisticated. （×）

Unit 32 Once 的用法

必閃陷阱 非學不可

Once 可當副詞、連接詞和名詞用。

Once 當副詞時意為「一次，一回」，如 We've met only once.（我們只見過一次面。）在這項用法中，我們經常使用 **once a ＋ 單數時間詞 (once a week/month/year** etc. 一星期／一個月／一年等一次）及 once every ＋ 複數時間詞（once every two days/three years etc. 每兩天／三年等一次）來表示事情發生的頻率。例如：

◆ We go for dinner together **once a week.**（○）
◇ We go for dinner together once the week.（×）
（我們一個禮拜會共進晚餐一次。）

Tom visits his parents only once every two or three months.
（湯姆每兩三個月才探望他父母親一次。）

Once 當副詞時還意為「從前，曾經」。在這項用法中，**once 通常位在句子的中間**，亦即位在主詞和主動詞之間（即普通動詞之前），或位在**語氣助動詞**或第一個助動詞**之後**，或位在**當主動詞的 BE 動詞之後**。例如：

1. John once knew Mary, but they are no longer friends.
（約翰以前認識瑪麗，但他們已經不是朋友了。）

2. It was hard to believe that she had once been beautiful.
（很難相信她以前很漂亮。）

3. Egypt was once a great nation.
（埃及曾經是個偉大的國家。）

由**當副詞用的 once 所構成的片語**不在少數，其中之一就是大家所熟悉的 **once upon a time**。

這片語意為「從前，很久以前（童話故事的開頭）」，如 Once upon a time there was a little girl called Little Red Riding Hood...（很久很久以前，有個小女孩叫做小紅帽……），但它現在也不時用於口語中，意為「以前，過去」(long ago)，如 We used to go to nightclubs once upon a time.（我們以前常上夜店。）

Once 當連接詞時意為「**一旦，一…… 就……**」(as soon as)。例如：

1. Once I've picked Cindy up at the airport, I'll call you.
（一旦我在機場接到辛蒂，我就會打電話給你。）

2. Once you get into a bad habit, you'll find it hard to get out of it.
（一旦染上惡習，就很難改掉了。）

與 when, while, before, after, by the time, as soon as, if 和 unless 等所引導的時間副詞子句一樣，**once 所引導的時間子句亦不可使用表示未來的 will 或 be going to**。例如：

◆ **Once** I pass all these exams, I'll be fully qualified.（○）
◇ Once I will pass all these exams, I'll be fully qualified.（╳）
（一旦我通過所有這些考試，我就完全合格了。）

好用 Tips 非學不可 🔍

Once 當名詞時意為「**一次，一回**」，主要用於 **at once**（立即，馬上；同時）、**all at once**（突然，忽然）、**(just) for once**（僅此一次，就這一回，難得一次）、**(just) this once**（就這一次，就此一次）、**(just) that once**（就那一次）及 **(just) the once**（就這一次；就那一次）等片語中，或者說**主要用來構成這些片語**。例如：

1. Come at once!
（馬上過來！）

2. They met at my birthday party and became good friends at once.
（他們在我的生日派對上相識，並很快成了好朋友。）

3. Don't all talk at once!
（不要同時都說話！）

4. He can do two things at once.
（他可以同時做兩件事。）

5. She left all at once.
（她突然離開了。）

6. For once Jack was telling the truth.
（傑克就這一回說了實話。）

7. You can pay the bill just for once.
（你難得一次可以付帳。）

8. He only came the once.
（他只來過一次。）

9. Do it just the once.
（就做這一次吧。）

10. Sam did it just this once, but once is enough.
（山姆只做了這一次，但一次就夠了。）

11. We met just the/that once, but I still remember her very clearly.
（我們就見了那一次，但我仍很清楚地記得她。）

Unit 33 One, you, we, they

重要觀念 非學不可

One, you, we 和 they 都可用作泛指的 (generic) 人稱代名詞，亦即用來指所有人或非特定的任何人，而不是指特定的某個人或某些人。它們的意思相當於總稱的「任何人」、「人們」或「大家」。

One, you 和 we

當 **one, you 和 we** 用作泛指的人稱代名詞時，它們包括說話者或寫作者本身在內。例如：

1. One cannot learn English well unless one works hard.
（下苦功才能學好英文。）

= You cannot learn English well unless you work hard.
= We cannot learn English well unless we work hard.

2. One must try one's best.
（人人都要盡力而為。）

3. One has to trust one's family.
（大家都要相信自己的家人。）

4. It does make one think.
（這的確發人深省。）

5. You can never predict what the president would do next.
（誰也無法預料總統接下來會做什麼事。）

6. If you exercise every day, you'll feel much better.
（天天運動，你會覺得好多了。）

7. Our manager is a person who makes you feel very important.
（我們經理是個會使人覺得自己很重要的人。）

8. We all make mistakes.
（人人都會犯錯。）

9. We usually need a raincoat in Keelung.
（在基隆，人們經常需要雨衣。）

10. Why can we learn our mother tongue very easily?
（我們為什麼能輕易學會母語呢？）

必閃陷阱 非學不可

必須注意的是，**one 比 you 或 we 來得正式許多**，因此鮮少用在講話中。例如：

One would have thought that PM2.5 could be reduced effectively by adopting some measures.
（大家以為採取一些措施就可以有效降低細懸浮微粒濃度。）

They

They 用於泛指時，大多與 say, call, think 等動詞連用，亦即以 they say, they call, they think 等型態出現。例如：

1. They say a high-rise office building will be built here.
（人們說／據說這裡要興建一棟超高辦公大樓。）
2. They used to call her "the Iron Lady."
（大家過去稱她為「鐵娘子」。）

They 也可用來泛指一大群人，如政府、當局、組織、機構等。例如：

1. They've opened a new French restaurant in the city center.
（他們已在市中心開了一家新的法式餐廳。）
2. They've decided to hold local elections as soon as possible.
（政府已決定盡快舉行地方選舉。）
3. They're going to amend the Constitution to allow same-sex marriage.
（當局將修憲來允許同性結婚。）

好用 Tips 非學不可

我們亦可使用 **they 和 them 代替 he/she 和 him/her** 來指前文出現的 **someone, anyone, everyone 等不定代名詞**；由於這些不定代名詞的人數和性別皆未可知，使用 they 和 them 既可總稱亦可包含兩性。此外，我們還**可將泛指的 they 和 them 用於附加問句**。例如：

1. You cannot walk away just because someone tells you they don't want to buy.
（你不能只因有人告訴你他們不想買，就走開了。）
2. Everyone should have a chance to say what they think.
（大家應該要有機會說出自己的想法。）

3. If anyone comes with a parcel for me, can you ask them to take it next door?
（如果有人帶包裹要給我，你可以叫他們送到隔壁嗎？）

4. Someone wanted to borrow John's bike, didn't they?
（有人想要借約翰的單車，不是嗎？）

Only 的用法

必閃陷阱 非學不可

Only 可用作形容詞和副詞。

Only 當形容詞時意為「唯一的，僅有的」，其後須接名詞（當然了，only 和名詞之間可以插入數字或其他形容詞）或 one。 例如：

1. Mary is the only girl in the class.
（瑪麗是班上唯一的女生。）

2. There are only three books on the desk.
（書桌上只有三本書。）

3. That was the only off-the-rack T-shirt left in that color.
（那是那種顏色僅剩的一件均碼 T 恤。）

→ off-the-rack (adj.) 為美式英語，意為「（衣服）均碼的，標準碼的」；英式英語為 off-the-peg，澳洲英語叫做 off-the-hook。

◆ John is the **only** one who can speak Indonesian in the class.（O）
◇ John is the only who can speak Indonesian in the class.（✕）
（約翰是班上唯一會講印尼語的人。）

值得一提的是，在「one of ＋ 複數名詞 ＋ 關係代名詞 ＋ S ＋ V」的句型中，關代的先行詞是複數名詞、不是 one，所以**關係子句中的動詞要用複數動詞**。然而，若 one 的前面加上 the only，那麼關代的先行詞就變成了 one，亦即關代後面要用**單數動詞**。例如：

◆ Ted is **one of the students who are** absent.（O）

◇ Ted is one of the students who is absent.（×）

（泰德是缺席的學生之一。）

◆ Ted is the **only one of the students that is** absent.（O）

◇ Ted is the only one of the students that are absent.（×）

（泰德是唯一缺席的學生。）

Only 當副詞時意為「只，僅，才」。例如：

1. It's only four o'clock and dawn is already breaking.

（才 4 點，天就開始亮了。）

2. Amy only arrived fifteen minutes ago.

（艾美 15 分鐘前才到。）

3. I was only joking.

（我只不過是在開玩笑。）

4. Only an idiot would do that.

（只有白癡才會做那種事。）

5. Only Tom and I attended almost every lecture and seminar when we were college students.

（我們唸大學的時候，只有湯姆跟我幾乎參加了每一場講座和研討會。）

6. At present these bicycles are only available in Taiwan.

（目前這種腳踏車只有在台灣才能買到。）

在口說英語中，only 可與 just 連用來加強語氣。Only just 意為「剛剛，才；差一點沒，幾乎不」。例如：

1. I've only just moved to Taipei.

（我剛剛搬到台北。）

2. People were leaving and he'd only just arrived.

（人們都要離開了，而他才剛剛到。）

3. There were only just enough reference books to go round.

（參考書剛好夠每人發一本。）

4. She only just caught the bus.

（她差點沒趕上公車。）

5. I got there in time for my flight, but only just (= but I almost did not).

（我及時趕上了班機，差一點就錯過了。）

Only 當副詞時可放在句中不同的位置，視其所要強調的元素而定。若主詞是重點所在，那麼就把 **only 放在主詞的前面**。例如（援用上面的例句）：

1. Only an idiot would do that.
（只有白癡才會做那種事。）

2. Only Tom and I attended almost every lecture and seminar when we were college students.
（我們唸大學的時候，只有湯姆跟我幾乎參加了每一場講座和研討會。）

如果重點是句中其他元素，那麼 **only** 跟一般副詞一樣，通常**位在句子的中間**，亦即位**在主詞和主動詞之間**（即普通動詞之前），或位在語氣助動詞或第一個助動詞之後，或位**在當主動詞的 BE 動詞之後**。例如（援用上面部分例句）：

1. Amy only arrived fifteen minutes ago.
→（only 位在主詞和主動詞之間。）

2. Amy had only arrived fifteen minutes before I left for the airport.
（艾美在我動身前往機場之前 15 分鐘才到。）
→（only 位在第一個助動詞之後。）

3. It's only four o'clock and dawn is already breaking.
→（only 位在當主動詞的 BE 動詞之後。）

好用 Tips 非學不可 🔍

如果要強調的重點是整個子句，那麼 **only 就放在子句之前**。例如：

1. They want to have their first child only when they are ready.
（只有在他們準備好的時候，才會想要生第一個孩子。）

2. Only when his husband ends his extramarital affair will there be probably any improvement in their relationship.
（只有他先生結束婚外情，他們的關係才可能會有所改善。）
→ Only when 引導的副詞子句挪到句首時，主句要倒裝。

Unit 35 Other, others, the other, another

重要觀念 非學不可 🔍

Other 作限定詞用

Other 作限定詞用時後接不可數名詞和複數可數名詞，意為「另外的；額外的；更多的；別的；其他的；不同的」。例如：

1. In addition to Amy, Mrs. Smith has two other children.
（除了艾美，史密斯太太還有另外兩個孩子。）

2. There are other ways to perform this task.
（還有別的方法可執行這項任務。）

3. The company website has general information about its new products. Other detailed information can be obtained by calling the free phone number.
（該公司網站提供其新產品的一般性資訊。其他詳細的資訊可打這支免費電話取得。）

4. Some music is soothing; other music has the opposite effect.
（有些音樂具有撫慰作用；其他音樂則效果相反。）

Other 作限定詞用時，若後接單數可數名詞，則 other 前面必須要有另一限定詞或所有格。例如：

◆ Cindy doesn't like the blue one. She prefers **the other** color.（○）
◇ Cindy doesn't like the blue one. She prefers other color.（×）
（辛蒂不喜歡藍色的。她比較喜歡另一顏色的。）

1. I have only one other shirt.
（我只有另一件襯衫。）

2. We'll go there some other day.
（我們改天會去那裡。）

3. Jason is my other brother.
（傑森是我另一個哥哥。）

4. No other student in our school runs faster than David.
（本校沒有其他學生跑得比大衛快。）

必閃陷阱 非學不可

Other 作限定詞用時如同形容詞，沒有複數型。例如：

◆ John invited all his **other** relatives and friends.（○）
◇ John invited all his others relatives and friends.（×）
（約翰邀請了他的其他所有親戚朋友。）

Other 作代名詞用

Other 亦可作**代名詞用**。當代名詞用的 other 有**複數型 others**，意為

「其餘的人或事物」。例如：

1. This issue, more than any other (issue), has divided the new cabinet.
（主要是這個問題造成新內閣的分裂。）

2. Some apps are better than others (= other apps).
（一些應用程式優於其他應用程式。）

3. Some students are reading; others (= other students) are writing.
（有些學生在閱讀，有些則在寫作。）

The other 作限定詞用

The other 作限定詞用時，若後接單數名詞（the 可用所有格替代），意

為**「（兩者中）另一人的；另一個的」**。例如：

1. Mary was looking around for her other shoe.
（瑪麗在找另一隻鞋。）

2. This computer is new. The other computer is about six years old.
（這台電腦是新的。另一台電腦大約六年了。）

3. He held onto the rope with his other hand.
（他用另一隻手抓住繩子。）

4. One of the twin brothers was Roger. What was the other one called?
（這對孿生兄弟一個叫羅傑，另一個叫什麼？）

5. I saw Jim stand on the other side of the street.
（我看到吉姆站在街的對面。）

The other 作限定詞用時若後接**複數名詞**（the 可用所有格替代），意為「（一個群體中）其餘的」。例如：

1. There are five women sitting there. One of them is his wife and all the other women are his sisters.
（有五個女子坐在那裡。其中之一是他太太，其餘都是他的姊妹。）

2. Paul stayed until all the other students had gone home.
（保羅一直待到其餘的學生都回家為止。）

3. Both his other brothers will go abroad for further study next year.
（他的另外兩個兄弟明年將出國深造。）

4. Where are the other two summer travel brochures? I can only find three.
（另外兩本夏日旅遊指南在哪裡？我只能找到三本。）

The other 作代名詞用

The other 作代名詞用時，意為「（兩者中）另一人；另一個」。例如：

1. It is hard to tell the twin sisters one from the other.
（這對雙胞胎姊妹很難分辨。）

2. I have two puppies, one is white and the other is black.
（我有兩隻小狗，一隻是白色的，另一隻是黑色的。）

The others 作代名詞用時，意為「（一個群體中）**其餘的人或事物**」。例如：

1. One boy slipped on a banana skin and the others laughed.
（一個男孩踩到香蕉皮滑倒，其餘的孩子都笑了起來。）

2. I have some photos for you this time. I'll attach two photos to this email and I'll send the others tomorrow.
（這次我有一些照片要給你。我會在這封 email 附上兩張，明天我會把其餘照片寄出。）

Another 作限定詞用

Another 作限定詞用時，後接單數可數名詞，意為「**再一的；另一的**」。

例如：

1. Can I have another drink?
（我能再來一杯嗎？）

2. Tom's mom is expecting another baby in September.
（湯姆的媽媽九月份又要生孩子了。）

3. They're doing a big concert tonight and another one on Friday night.
（他們今晚將舉辦一場大型演唱會，星期五晚上還有一場。）

4. That's quite another matter.
（那完全是另一回事。）

◆ After a week in Bangkok, the official was ready to visit **another** city.（○）
◇ After a week in Bangkok, the official was ready to visit other city.（✕）
（在曼谷待了一個禮拜後，這位官員準備訪問另一城市。）

Another 作代名詞用

Another 作代名詞用時，意為「**再一（個）；另一（個）**」。例如：

1. Would you like another?
（想再來一份嗎？）

2. I don't like this one, please show me another or others.
（我不喜歡這個，請給我看另一個或另外幾個。）
→ 不帶 the 的複數型 others 是代名詞 another 的複數。

3. I lent my bicycle to John, and he lent it to another of his friends.
（我把腳踏車借給約翰，他又轉借給他的另外一個朋友。）

Unit 36 Own 的用法

Own 可當形容詞、代名詞和動詞用。**Own 用作形容詞時意為「自己的，本人的」**，其句型為：**「所有格代名詞（my、his、our、their 等）或名詞的所有格（名詞 + 's）+ own + 名詞」**。例如：

1. Mary grows all her own vegetables.
（瑪麗的蔬菜全都是自己種的。）

2. You'll have to make up your own mind what to do next.
（你下一步要做什麼須自己做決定。）

3. He has his own room.
（他有他自己的房間。）

4. It's the president's own fault.
（那是總統自己的過錯。）

Own 用作代名詞時意為「自己，本人」，其前須有所有格代名詞（my、his、our、their 等），但其主要句型為：**「名詞 + of + 所有格代名詞 + own」**。例如：

1. This is my husband's cellphone. My own got lost yesterday.
（這是我先生的手機。我自己的昨天弄丟了。）

2. Monica has three small children of her own.
（莫妮卡有三個自己的小孩。）

3. He has a room of his own.
（他有他自己的房間。）

無論用作形容詞或是代名詞，own 的前面都可用 very 來加強語氣，意為「完全屬於自己的」。例如：

I'd like to have my very own apartment.
（我想要一間完全屬於自己的公寓。）
= I'd like to have an apartment of my very own.

必閃陷阱 非學不可

然而，必須注意的是，**own 的前面須使用所有格代名詞，不可使用冠詞**（a/an 或 the）。例如：

◆ John would like to have his **own** car.（O）
◇ John would like to have an own car.（×）
◇ John would like to have the own car.（×）
（約翰想要有自己的車子。）

由用作形容詞或代名詞的 own 所構成的數個片語和成語都頗為常見，請大家查閱字典或參考相關書籍，在此就不再贅述。但其中之一的 **(all) on one's own** 值得加以討論。這個片語意為「**單獨地，獨自地 (alone)；獨力地，無援地 (without any help)**」，其中 **all** 是用來加強語氣。例如：

1. I live all on my own in a tiny apartment.
（我獨自一人住在一間小公寓。）

2. The suitcase is too heavy. She can't carry it (all) on her own.
（手提箱太重。她自己一個人提不起來。）

Own 用作動詞時意為「擁有」（尤指具有合法權利的擁有）。例如：

1. We own our house.
（我們擁有自己的房子。）

2. Who owns this book?
（這本書是誰的？）

由用作動詞的 own 所構成的 **own up to**（to 為介系詞）也值得學起來。
這個片語動詞意為「**承認、坦白**（過失、罪刑、錯誤等）」。例如：

1. No one owned up to breaking the window.
（沒有人承認打破窗戶。）

2. Nobody has owned up to stealing the money.
（沒有人承認偷了那筆錢。）

3. Sam and his brother later owned up to the prank.
（山姆和他弟弟後來承認了這起惡作劇。）

Unit 37　Please 的用法

Please 是個大家所熟知的字，幾乎每天都會用到。它主要**用作感嘆詞，用來使請求或要求更有禮貌**。在此用法中，**please 意為「請，好嗎」**。
例如：

1. Can I borrow your bicycle, please?
（請把腳踏車借給我，好嗎？）

2. Please follow the instructions to install the driver.
（請按照指示安裝驅動程式。）

Please 的詞序

我們通常將 **please** 放在由 could、can 和 would 所引導的請求句的句
末。但我們亦可將 **please** 置於句首或句子中間。句子中間位置的 please
可使請求更為強烈。例如：

1. Could you say your name again, please?
（請再說一次您的名字，好嗎？）

2. Can you tell me how much this car costs, please?
（告訴我這部車要花多少錢，好嗎？）

3. Would you help me with these bags, please?
（請幫我提這些袋子，好嗎？）

4. Can we invite John over, please?
（我們邀請約翰到家中作客，好嗎？）

這是 **please** 在請求句中最常見的位置。句首位置的 **please** 使請求聽起來比較強烈，就跟命令一樣。

1. Please could you say your name again?

2. Please can you tell me how much this car costs?

3. Please would you help me with these bags?

4. Please can we invite John over?

句子中間位置的 please 使請求更為強烈。這個位置的 **please** 通常要重讀。

1. Could you please say your name again?

2. Can you please tell me how much this car costs?

3. Would you please help me with these bags?

4. Can we please invite John over?

小孩對大人或學童對老師講話時，當他們**提出請求或要求許可時**，通常**將 please 置於句首**。例如：

學童對老師：

◆ **Please** could I leave early today, Sir?（O）
（老師，我今天提早離開／放學好嗎？）

員工對老闆：

◆ Could I leave early today, **please**?（○）

◇ Please could I leave early today?（×）

（我今天提早離開／下班好嗎？）

Please 與祈使句連用

Please 可與祈使句連用來表示禮貌性請求或命令，或者說用來強調請求或命令。這種情況常見於教室情境、禮貌性公告／通知或書面請求。在這種情況中，我們通常**將 please 置於請求**——尤其是書面請求以及公告／通知——**的開頭**。在此用法中，please 意為**「請」**。例如：

1. Please turn to page 101. / Turn to page 101, please.
（請翻到 101 頁。）

2. Please note that there will be no class next Friday.
（請注意下週五不上課。）

3. Please note that credit cards are not accepted.
（請注意不可以刷卡。）

我們亦可**使用 please 來強調陳述**或**比較強烈地請求某人做某事**。在此用法中，please 意為**「請」**。例如：

1. Please believe me.
（請相信我。）

2. A: Do you mind if I come in?
（A：你介意我進來嗎？）

　B: Please do.
（B：請進。）

講話時，我們經常**使用 please 來使命令顯得不是那麼直接**或**緩和語氣**。例如：

Pass the salt, please.
（請把鹽巴遞過來。）

我們經常使用 **please** 來表示禮貌地接受某物，尤其是食物和飲料。在此用法中，please 意為**「謝謝」**。例如：

1. A: Would you like another cup of coffee?
（A：要不要再來一杯咖啡？）

 B: Yes, please.
（B：好的，謝謝。）

2. A: What would you like to drink?
（A：你想喝什麼？）

 B: Orange juice, please.
（B：柳橙汁，謝謝。）

3. A: Do you want a ride home?
（A：你想搭便車回家嗎？）

 B: Oh, yes, please. That would be great.
（B：哦，好的，謝謝。那再好不過了。）

我們可以**單獨使用 please** 來表示對某人或某事不信、驚訝或惱怒。在此用法中，please 意為**「拜託，少來」**。例如：

1. A: Why don't you join the army?
（A：你為什麼不去從軍？）

 B: At my age? Oh, please!
（B：我這把年紀？哦，拜託！）

2. A: He does 500 push-ups and 500 sit-ups every day.
（A：他每天做 500 下伏地挺身和 500 下仰臥起坐。）

 B: Oh, please. I can't believe that.
（B：哦，少來。我不信。）

3. Children, please.
（孩子們，別鬧了。）

好用 Tips 非學不可 🔍

一、Please 用作動詞

Please 當動詞（及物或不及物）**用時**意為「**取悅；討好；使高興；使滿意；願意**」。例如：

1. Mary's anxious to please her husband.
（瑪麗急於取悅她的先生。）

2. As a child, he'd always been eager to please.
（他還是小孩的時候，就處處想要討人歡心。）

3. You can't please everyone.
（你不可能讓每個人都滿意。）

二、以下為 please 當動詞用時常用的一些片語：

Hard/difficult to please（難伺候）

Those customers are very difficult to please.
（那些顧客很難伺候。）

As you please（隨你的便；隨意）

1. Our party is very informal, so you can dress as you please.
（我們的聚會很隨便，你愛怎麼穿就怎麼穿。）

2. A: I'm going now.
（A：我要走了。）

B: As you please.
（B：隨你的便／你想走就走吧。）

If you please（煩請）用來強調要求

Come this way, if you please.
（請這邊走。）

Please God（但願；上帝，求求祢）用來表達強烈願望

1. Please God Gary comes!
（但願蓋瑞能來！）

2. Let my sister be alive, please God!
（老天爺求求祢，讓我妹妹活下來！）

Unit 38　Quite 的用法和意思

必閃陷阱 非學不可

Quite 為程度副詞，視其後所接的字詞而定，它有兩個意思：1.「相當，尚可，頗，有幾分」(rather, fairly, to some degree)；2.「很，非常，完全，十分」(very, totally or completely)。例如：

1. Laura had been quite good at drawing when she was at school.
（蘿拉求學時頗為擅長繪畫。）

2. We were quite excited about buying a new car.
（我們對買了新車都感到相當興奮。）

3. His life has been quite different ever since his wife died.
（從他太太過世起，他的生活就完全不一樣了。）

4. The victim remembered those rogues quite clearly.
（受害者十分清晰地記得那些流氓。）

Quite ＋ 可分等級的形容詞和副詞

Quite 與**可分等級的形容詞或副詞**（有比較級和最高級形式的形容詞或副詞）**連用時**，通常表示**「相當，尚可，頗，有幾分」**的意思。例如：

1. It's quite cold/warm today.
（今天相當冷／相當暖和。）

→ Quite ＋ 形容詞。

2. Duke ran quite fast until they were already out of sight.
（杜克跑得相當快，直到他們都已看不見了。）

→ Quite ＋ 副詞。

3. Mary comes to visit her parents quite often.
（瑪麗頗常探望她的父母親。）

→ Quite ＋ 頻率副詞。

Quite ＋ 不可分等級的形容詞和副詞

Quite 與不可分等級的形容詞或副詞（極限形容詞或副詞，即通常沒有比較級和最高級形式的形容詞或副詞）**連用時**，通常表示**「很，非常，完全，十分」**的意思。例如：

1. You're quite right/wrong.
（你完全正確／完全錯了。）
2. The professor is quite clearly fond of flowers.
（很顯然這位教授喜歡花。）
3. The scenery was quite incredible.
（風景很美。）

注意：在口語中，這項用法的 quite 跟它所修飾的形容詞和副詞一樣都要唸重音。

好用 Tips 非學不可 🔍

Quite ＋ 名詞

Quite ＋ a/an/some ＋ 名詞具有強調該名詞的作用；quite a/an/some 意為**「相當」**。例如：

1. Joyce's quite a girl.
（喬伊絲可不是普通的女孩。）
2. It was quite a/some party.
（那是一場頗為特別的聚會。）

3. It was quite an/some idea.
（那是個相當棒的想法。）

4. I've been working for that company for quite some time.
（我為那家公司工作已經相當久了。）

Quite + a/an + 形容詞 + 名詞亦是在表示「**相當，尚可，頗，有幾分**」的意思。例如：

1. He was quite a good actor.
（他是個相當優秀的演員。）

2. They had to wait for quite a long time.
（他們得等相當長的一段時間。）

3. It's quite a big company. Around 200 staff.
（那是一家還算大的公司。約有 200 名員工。）

Quite a bit, quite a few, quite a lot

Quite 經常與 **a bit**、**a few** 和 **a lot** 連用來構成 **quite a bit**、**quite a few** 和 **quite a lot**。這三個相當常用的片語為同義詞，意為「**大量，許多**」。例如：

1. We should ask Paul for some advice. He knows quite a bit about skateboarding.
（我們應該要求保羅給我們一些意見。他很懂滑板。）

2. Quite a few (of) people has signed for this dating app.
（不少人已經在這款交友應用程式上註冊。）

3. His sisters spent quite a lot of money on clothes.
（他的姊妹花了許多錢買衣服。）

Quite a bit 和 quite a lot 亦可表示「**經常，常常**」的意思。例如：

1. I used to go swimming quite a bit.
（我過去常游泳。）

2. Does Bruce come here quite a lot?
（布魯斯常來這裡嗎？）

Quite a bit/a lot ＋ 比較級

Quite a bit 和 quite a lot 經常與比較級形容詞或副詞連用來表示「非常，很大程度上」(much, very much) 的意思。例如：

1. It's quite a bit colder/warmer today.
（今天冷得多／暖和得多。）

2. We went to Thailand when I was quite a bit younger.
（在我很年輕時，我們去了泰國。）

3. The new smartphone is quite a lot lighter than the old model.
（這款新智慧型手機比舊機型輕很多。）

= The new smartphone is much lighter than the old model.

Quite ＋ 動詞

在非正式的講話中，我們經常使用「**quite ＋ like, enjoy, understand 或 agree**」來表達自己的看法或偏好。視上下文而定，**quite** 可能意為「**相當**」、「**非常**」或「**完全，十分**」。在句子中，這種用法的 **quite** 通常位在副詞慣常的中間位置，即**主詞和主動詞之間、語氣助動詞**或**第一個助動詞之後**，或**當主動詞用的 BE動詞之後**。例如：

1. I quite like watching basketball games.
（我相當喜歡看籃球比賽。）

2. I quite like seafood.
（我相當喜歡吃海鮮。）

3. I quite enjoy going to weddings, but I don't want to go to theirs.
（我很喜歡參加婚禮，但我不想參加他們的。）

4. I quite agree. You're absolutely right.
（我完全同意／十分贊同。你對極了。）

5. I can quite understand why you are angry.
（我完全能理解你為什麼生氣。）

Not quite = not completely

我們經常使用 **not quite** 來表示 **not completely** 的意思，即「**不太；不完全是；不是全部**」，其後可接形容詞、副詞、名詞、動詞、分詞片語、介系詞片語和 wh- 子句。例如：

1. The door was not quite closed.
（門沒有全部關上。）

2. There were not quite as many/interesting/expensive as last time.
（沒有像上一次那麼多／那麼有趣／那麼貴。）

3. I don't quite know why Eunice didn't come.
（我不是很清楚尤妮絲為什麼沒來。）
= I don't know quite why Eunice didn't come.

4. I couldn't quite remember where she lived.
（我不太記得她住在哪裡了。）
= I couldn't remember quite where she lived.

5. Cindy hesitated, not quite knowing what to do.
（辛蒂猶豫了，不太清楚要做什麼。）

6. That's not quite what I meant.
（那不完全是我所要表達的意思。）

Not quite 亦可用作簡答。例如：

A: Are you ready, Kevin?
（A：你準備好了嗎，凱文？）

B: No, not quite.
（B：沒有，還沒。）

Unit 39 　Reason 的用法

必閃陷阱 非學不可

Reason for

Reason 後接介系詞 for（不是 of）再接名詞或動名詞片語，意為「**某事的原因或做某事的原因**」。例如：

◆ I don't know the **reason for** her bad mood.（O）
◇ I don't know the reason of her bad mood.（×）
（我不知道她心情不好的原因。）
◆ There were several **reasons for** his cruelty to animals.（O）
◇ There were several reasons of his cruelty to animals.（×）
（他虐待動物是出於幾個原因。）
◆ Could you tell me your **reason(s) for** marrying such an ugly woman?（O）
◇ Could you tell me your reason(s) of marrying such an ugly woman?（×）
（你能告訴我你娶這樣一個醜女人的原因嗎？）

Reason 後面可以使用 of 的情況只出現在 **by reason of**（因為或由於某事）和 **for reasons of**（基於……原因）這兩個正式場合使用的片語中（請注意這兩個片語中 reason 的單複數）。例如：

1. He escaped caning by reason of his youth.
（他因為年輕，得以免除鞭刑。）
2. The government has taken these measures for reasons of economy/national security.
（政府採取這些措施是出於經濟上的原因／基於國家安全考量。）

Reason why

Reason 後面可接 why 所引導的子句，但 why 經常省略，尤其是在直述句中。例如：

1. The reason (why) so many people had food poisoning is still not clear.
（這麼多人食物中毒的原因仍然不明。）

2. The reason (why) Benson didn't contact you was that he was only in Taipei for a few hours.
（班森沒有跟你聯絡的原因是，他在台北僅待了幾小時。）

Reason 不可跟 because 連用。例如：

◆ Is there any **reason** why Mary's usually late for class?
◇ Is there any reason because Mary's usually late for class?（ × ）
（為什麼瑪麗上課經常遲到？）

Reason that

Reason 後面可接 that 所引導的子句，但 that 經常省略，尤其是在直述句中。**Reason that 比 reason why 略微正式一些**，但不若 reason why 來得常用。例如：

1. The reason (that) these cars are so expensive is that they are completely built by hand.
（這些汽車如此昂貴的原因是，它們完全手工打造。）

2. One reason that Wesley decided to move to Kaohsiung was that his mother didn't get along well with his wife.
（衛斯理決定搬到高雄的一個原因是，他母親和他太太婆媳不和。）

然而，**當 reason 為複數時，reasons 只能與 why 子句連用，不可跟 that 子句連用。**例如：

◆ There are several **reasons why** she quit after only three months in the job.
◇ There are several reasons that she quit after only three months in the job.
（ × ）
（她只工作三個月就辭職有幾個原因。）

Reason ＋ 不定詞

Reason 後面可接不定詞。例如：

1. I see no reason to refuse the job offer.
（我沒有任何理由拒絕這項聘用通知。）

= I see no reason for refusing the job offer.

= I can't see any reason to refuse the job offer.

= There is no reason for me to refuse the job offer.

→ see no reason / not see any reason (to do sth or for doing sth) 意為「沒有任何理由（做某事）」。

2. There was every reason to accept her invitation.
（有充分理由接受她的邀請。）

= There was every reason for accepting her invitation.

= There were very clear reasons to accept her invitation.

→ there is every reason (to do sth or for doing sth) 意為「有充分理由（做某事）」。

3. I had every reason to accept her invitation.
（我有充分理由接受她的邀請。）

= I had every reason for accepting her invitation.

4. I had no reason to accept her invitation.
（我沒有理由接受她的邀請。）

5. This result gives us all the more reason to learn English.
（這項結果讓我們更有理由學英文了。）

= This result gives us all the more reason for learning English.

→ all the more reason (to do sth or for doing sth) 意為「更有理由（做某事）」。

Unit 40 — Same、similar 和 identical 的用法

必閃陷阱 非學不可

Same 可當形容詞和代名詞用，前者意為「同一的；相同的；一樣的」，後者意為「相同的人；相同的事物」，指的是兩個或多個人事物完全相同。**當我們使用 same 來比較人事物時，其前須有定冠詞 the。**例如：

◆ John and I went to **the same** school.（○）
◇ John and I went to same school.（✕）
（約翰和我曾在同一所學校唸書。）

◆ These two tables are not **the same**.（○）
◇ These two tables are not same.（✕）
（這兩張桌子並不一樣。）

The same as

The same 後面是接 as 不是 that 或 than。例如：

◆ I treat daughters exactly **the same as** sons.（○）
◆ I treat daughters exactly the same that sons.（✕）
◆ I treat daughters exactly the same than sons.（✕）
（我對女兒和兒子完全一視同仁。）

◆ My new jacket is **the same** model **as** my old one.（○）
◇ My new jacket is the same model that my old one.（✕）
◇ My new jacket is the same model than my old one.（✕）
（我新外套的款式與舊外套一樣。）

The same ＋ 名詞 ＋ 子句

當 the same 與名詞連用時，其後可接 that 引導的關係子句，亦可接比較**少用的 who 或 which 引導的關係子句**。但我們通常**省略這些關係代名詞**。例如：

Chapter 2｜字彙 & 片語

1. He's the same person (that) John fought with at that restaurant last night.
（他是昨晚在那家餐廳和約翰打架的人。）

2. Is Linda still going out with the same boyfriend (who) we knew when we were at college?
（琳達還在和我們唸大學時認識的同一個男朋友交往嗎？）

我們經常在 **the same 前面使用 exactly/just、much 和 very 等副詞來修飾或加強語氣**，但它們所在的位置並不完全相同。Exactly/just 和 much 係位在 the same 的前面，即 **exactly/just the same**（完全一樣的；一模一樣的）、**much the same** (= almost the same)（幾乎一樣的；幾乎一模一樣的），而 very 係位在 the 和 same 之間，即 **the very same（正是同一個）**。例如：

1. Mary was wearing exactly/just the same skirt as I was.
（瑪麗所穿的裙子和我的一模一樣。）

2. My opinion on this subject was much the same as theirs.
（我對這一主題的看法與他們幾乎一樣。）

3. It was the very same day that my grandfather died.
（那正好是我祖父過世的同一天。）

4. That very same day, he got married and died in a car accident.
（就在同一天，他結婚並在車禍中喪生。）

好用 Tips 非學不可 🔍

Similar 和 identical

Similar 和 identical 這兩個形容詞分別意為「相似的，相像的，類似的」和「同一的，完全相同的」。 它們的句型為 **similar to、a similar ＋ 名詞**或 a similar ＋ one 以及 **identical to、an identical ＋ 名詞或 an identical ＋ one**。我們不可使用 a same。例如：

1. My purse is similar to yours.
（我的錢包和你的相似。）

2. His bicycle is identical to mine.
（他的腳踏車和我的一模一樣。）

3. These two words are identical in pronunciation.
（這兩個字的發音完全一樣。）

◆ We had **a similar problem**, so the solution could be the same.（O）
◇ We had a same problem, so the solution could be the same.（×）
（我們有類似的問題，所以解決辦法可能是一樣的。）

◆ The salesclerk first showed me a red skirt. Then she showed me **an identical one**, but they were produced by two different companies.（O）
◇ The salesclerk first showed me a red skirt. Then she showed me a same one, but they were produced by two different companies.（×）
（店員先讓我看一件紅裙。然後她又讓我看一件完全一樣的紅裙，但它們是由兩家不同的公司所生產。）

Unit 41 So 和 not 與 expect, guess, hope, suppose, think 等動詞連用

必閃陷阱 非學不可

我們可以在一些**動詞的後面使用 so 來避免重複受詞子句**，尤其是在簡答。這些動詞中最常用的是 **appear, assume, be afraid, believe, expect, guess, hope, imagine, presume, reckon, seem, suppose** 和 **think**。例如：

1. Denise thinks iPhone 7 is too expensive, and Diana thinks so too.
（丹妮絲認為 iPhone 7 太貴，而戴安娜也認為是這樣。）
→ 原句為 ... and Diana thinks iPhone 7 is expensive.。

2. A: Do I have to finish writing my composition by Saturday?
（A：我一定要在週六之前寫好我的作文嗎？）

  B: I'm afraid so.
（B：恐怕是的。）
→ 原句為 I'm afraid you have to finish writing your composition ...。

3. A: Do you think Mary will get married to you some day?
（A：你認為瑪麗將來有一天會嫁給你嗎？）

　B: I hope so.
（B：希望如此。）

→ 原句為 I hope Mary will get married to me some day.。

4. A: He must have missed the train.
（A：他必定是沒趕上這班火車。）

　B: Yes, I suppose so.
（B：是的，我猜想是這樣。）

→ 原句為 I suppose he must have missed the train.。

我們可以在 **be afraid, guess, hope 和 suppose** 的後面使用 **not** 來避免重複否定的受詞子句。例如：

1. A: Did you pass your exam?
（A：你考試過關了嗎？）

　B: I'm afraid not.
（B：恐怕沒有。）

→ 原句為 I'm afraid I didn't pass my exam.。

2. A: Will you be coming tomorrow?
（A：你明天會來嗎？）

　B: I guess not.
（B：我想不會。）

→ 原句為 I guess I won't be coming tomorrow.。

3. Gordon thinks he might fail in physics, but he hopes not.
（戈登認為他的物理可能不及格，但他希望不會。）

對於 believe, expect 和 think，我們通常使用「**助動詞 do + not + 主動詞 + so**」的句型。例如：

1. A: Did Barbara go to church on Sunday?
（A：芭芭拉星期日有上教堂做禮拜嗎？）

　B: I don't believe so.
（B：我想沒有。）

2. A: Will you be late?
（A：你會遲到嗎？）

  B: I don't expect so.
（B：我想不會。）

3. A: Do you think Mr. Chen is a good guy?
（A：你認為陳先生是個好人嗎？）

  B: I don't think so.
（B：我認為不是。）

雖然在古典文學及非常正式的情況中，我們會見到 **believe not, expect not** 和 **think not** 的用法，但在**日常生活使用的現代英語中，它們並不常見**。例如：

A: May I go to the movies?
（A：我可以去看電影嗎？）
B: No, I think not.
（B：不，我看不行。）

必須注意的是，**不可將 so 與受詞子句連用**。例如：

A: Will Teresa be coming Wednesday?
（A：泰瑞莎星期三會來嗎？）
◆ B: I don't think so.（O）
（B：我認為不會。）
◇ B: I don't think so Teresa will be coming Wednesday.（×）

在簡答中，我們**不可把 so 漏掉而只說 I think 或 I don't think**。例如：

A: Do you think Miranda is a pretty woman?
（A：你認為米蘭達是個美女嗎？）
◆ B: Yes, I think so.（O）
◇ B: Yes, I think.（×）
（B：是的，我認為是。）

Chapter 2 字彙 & 片語

Unit 42　Some odd

重要觀念 非學不可

Odd 這個形容詞可用在數字（尤其是可被 10 除盡的數字）之後來表示「略高於（該數字）」(little more than) 的意思，數字和 odd 之間都會加上連字號，如 Benjamin's about 40-odd－maybe 45.（班傑明大約 40 多歲——也許 45 歲）。這種用法被認為不適合用在正式的上下文中，尤其是論文，因為這表示你的研究做得不夠，無法提供確切的數字，因此顯得不夠權威。

在一些新聞報導中，**數字和 odd 之間有時還會加上 "some"，而數字、some 和 odd 之間也都加上連字號**。這種寫法的意思與上述並無二致，但它的含意是確切的數字並不重要，如 There were 500-some-odd people gathering in front of the presidential palace last night.（昨晚聚集在總統府前面的民眾超過 500 人）。

必閃陷阱 非學不可

然而，**some odd** 不只用在數字之後而已，更常見的是用在 "some odd reason" 這個片語中。由於 odd 的主要意思是「奇怪的；古怪的」，有人可能會直覺地將之譯為「一些奇怪的原因」，錯了！**由於 reason 是單數，所以 some 的意思是「某個」而不是「一些」**，但它真正的意思也不是「某個奇怪的原因」，而是**「某個不明或未知的原因」**，亦即事情或事件發生的原因不明（至少對寫作者來說是如此）。例如：

1. The computer is not working for some odd reason.
（電腦因某個未知的原因無法運作。）

2. For some odd reason, the video can't upload on YouTube.
（影片因某個不明原因無法上傳 YouTube。）

Unit 43　Supposed to, suppose to

重要觀念 非學不可

Supposed to 意為「**應該（是／有）；一般認為；是要；允許**」，其中 supposed 是形容詞，而這個相當常用的形容詞片語都用在 BE 動詞之後，例如：

1. You're **supposed to** be at the meeting on Wednesday.
（你應該出席週三的會議。）
2. The company **is supposed to** make excellent smartphones.
（一般認為那家公司製造的智慧型手機很棒。）
3. The new law **is supposed to** increase penalties for telecom fraud offenses.
（新法是要提高電信詐騙罪的刑罰。）
4. You're **not supposed to** smoke in the classroom.
（不准在教室裡抽菸。）

必閃陷阱 非學不可

由於在講話時，**supposed to** 的發音是英文所謂的「**子音的重複**」或「**複音**」（見文末附註），亦即 **supposed** 的最後一個字母 d 並**不發音**，因此一些人在寫 supposed to 時往往就寫成 suppose to。由於 suppose to 的寫法過於普遍，吾人認為，至少在非正式的書寫中，suppose to 是可以被接受的，因為它不會造成混淆。譬如說，在下面的例句中，相信**不會有人只因 supposed to 被寫成 suppose to 就誤解了句子的意思。**

1. You're suppose to visit your parents.
（你應該去探望你的父母親。）
2. It's suppose to be a good restaurant.
（那家餐廳口碑不錯。）

然而，必須注意的是，一定會有為數可觀的人認為 suppose to 是錯誤的。在正式的上下文中，或在用字遣詞要求嚴謹的地方，**supposed to 是比較安全的選擇**。在其他地方，使用 suppose to 並非嚴重的錯誤。

附註：**「子音的重複」**或**「複音」**（germination 或 sound twinning），是指當一個字的最後一個字母是子音，而下一個字的第一個字母也是相同的子音或**同組的子音**時，它們**只發一個音**而不是發兩個音——所謂同組的子音是指**發音方式相同的有聲音和無聲音**，如 / d / 和 / t /、/ b / 和 / p /、/ g / 和 / k /、/ v / 和 / f /、/ z / 和 / s / 等。

Unit 44 Then 在口語中的用法

重要觀念 非學不可

Then 可當形容詞和副詞用，前者意為**「當時的」**，僅用在名詞前面。例如：

1. The then president/governor/owner/landlord etc.
（當時的總統／州長或省長／所有人或物主／房東等等。）
2. The then mayor of Taipei was Ma Ying-jeou.
（當時的台北市長是馬英九。）
3. The government sold the then state-owned steelworks to his father.
（政府把那家當時國有的鋼鐵廠賣給他父親。）

Then 當副詞用時有多個不同的意思。

Then 可表示過去的**「當時，那時」**，代表性片語為 **since then**、**from then on**；**then 亦可表示未來的「屆時，到時候」**，代表性片語為 **before/by/until then**。就此用法而言，then 通常位在句末。例如：

1. I was living in Pescadores then.
（那時候我住在澎湖。）

2. A lot of things have changed in Taiwan since then.
（從那以後台灣許多事情都發生了變化。）

3. From then on, Tom studied harder.
（從那時起，湯姆更加用功了。）

4. If you come to my house at 10:30, you will meet Mary then.
（如果你十點半來我家，屆時你就會遇見瑪麗。）

5. Give your report to me next Monday—I won't have time to read it before/until then.
（下週一才把你的報告給我——我只有到那時才有時間看。）

6. I will let you know by then.
（屆時我會讓你知道的。）

Then 可用來表示「然後，接著，後來」的意思。例如：

1. She was a journalist, then a singer.
（她當過記者，後來當了歌手。）

2. Then came the big news.
（接著傳來了重大消息。）

3. First he will be sworn in as president. Then comes the international news conference.
（他將先宣誓就任總統，隨後舉行國際記者招待會。）

4. Cindy opened the door, then the lights came on and everybody shouted, "Happy Birthday."
（辛蒂打開門，然後所有燈都亮了，每個人都大聲說出「生日快樂」。）

Then 與 **if** 連用來構成表示因果關係的 **If ... then ...** 句型，意為「**如果、若……那麼……、則……**」。例如：

1. If x = 3 and y = 5, then x + y = 8.
（若 x = 3、y = 5，則 x + y = 8。）

2. If you love him very much, then you should be very willing to do anything for him.
（如果妳很愛他，那麼妳應該很願意為他做任何事情。）

必閃陷阱 非學不可

然而，在口語中，then 不僅用法與上述有別，意思亦不盡相同。

在口語中，**then** 可用來表示「**另外；而且；還有；再者**」(also, besides, in addition) 的意思。例如：

1. You must ask Amy to my birthday party, and then there's Mary—don't forget her.
（你一定要叫艾美來參加我的生日派對，另外還有瑪麗──別把她忘了。）

2. Here's my new house and then I have two more houses in the country.
（這是我的新房子，此外我在鄉下還有兩棟房子。）

在口語中，**then 經常用於問句句末**，來表示你認為某人剛剛說過或提到的事情是真的，意為「**這麼說（來），那麼說，既然如此**」。例如：

1. You'll be selling your iPhone 7, then?
（這麼說你要賣掉你的 iPhone 7？）

2. You're not angry with me, then?
（這麼說你不生我的氣啦？）

3. Is it all arranged then?
（那麼說一切都安排好了？）

4. They're working for the same company. They know each other then?
（他們在同一家公司上班。這麼說他們互相認識嘍？）

在口語中，**then 經常用於談話結束時表示同意**，通常位在子句句末，意為「那麼，就」。例如：

1. You don't want anything to eat? Okay. So I'll just get you a coffee then.
（你不想吃東西？好的。那麼我就給你弄杯咖啡。）
2. So that's agreed then—You lend me ten thousand dollars tomorrow.
（那就這麼說定了——你明天借我一萬塊。）

此外，**(all) right then, now then** 和 **okay then** 這幾個片語經常在口語中用來引起注意，意為「喂，聽著，聽我說」。例如：

1. Okay then, let's go to the movies tonight.
（聽我說，我們今晚去看電影吧。）
2. All right then, who'd like some coffee?
（喂，誰想喝咖啡呢？）
3. Now then, what's all this?
（喂，這是怎麼回事呢？）

Unit 45　Very 能否修飾分詞形容詞的判斷法

必閃陷阱 非學不可

Very 是個副詞加強語，可修飾某些**現在分詞**和**過去分詞形容詞** (participial adjectives)，但卻不能修飾其他分詞形容詞。在此，筆者提供 3 個**判斷 very 是否能修飾分詞形容詞的方法**讓大家參考，準確度相當高。

判斷方法之一：**若分詞形容詞為可置於名詞之前起修飾作用的形容詞，則 very 可以修飾這些分詞形容詞**。例如：

He had a very surprised expression on his face.
（他臉上露出非常驚訝的表情。）

判斷方法之二：**若分詞形容詞為極限形容詞，則 very 不可以修飾這些分詞形容詞**。例如：

He is terrified of his wife, so he is a hen-pecked husband.
（他很懼內，所以他是個妻管嚴或怕老婆的先生。）

判斷方法之三：這方法比較傾向於經驗法則，**當 very 被用來修飾某個特定分詞形容詞時，若聽起來或看起來蠻熟悉和流暢的，那麼這樣用應該沒錯**，否則就不要用。

英語純正人士傾向於**嚴格限制可用 very 來修飾的分詞形容詞的數量**，所以當心中有疑惑時，我們**可使用 much 或另一副詞加強語來代替 very**，如 much astonished（非 very astonished）（非常驚訝）或 absolutely disgusted（非 very disgusted）（討厭至極）。

Unit 46　Wish 的動詞用法

必閃陷阱 非學不可

Wish 接不定詞

當 **wish** 後接不定詞時，wish 與 want 同義，意為**「想要；希望」**，但 wish 比較正式。在此用法中，**wish 不可用進行式**。例如：

◆ I **wish** to be a famous singer and make a lot of money.（○）
◇ I'm wishing to be a famous singer and make a lot of money.（×）
（我想成為名歌手，賺很多錢。）

◆ She **wishes** to make a complaint.（O）
◇ She's wishing to make a complaint.（×）
（她想投訴。）

在此用法中，wish 不可接 that 子句。例如：

◆ I **wish** to become a lawyer in the future.（O）
◇ I wish that I become a lawyer in the future.（×）
（我將來想當律師。）

跟 want 和 would like 一樣，**wish 與其後的不定詞之間可以插入名詞片語**（或受格代名詞）**來當它的受詞**。例如：

1. I do not **wish my daughter** to marry such a mama's boy.
（我不希望我女兒嫁給這樣一個媽寶。）
2. We don't **wish you** to talk about it.
（我們不希望你談論這件事。）

然而，必須注意的是，在此用法中，**wish** 與其他所有後接不定詞的動詞一樣，主動詞與不定詞**擁有共同的主詞**，譬如説，在 I wish to become a lawyer in the future. 這句中，**wish 和 become 的主詞都是 I**。
但當 wish 與其後的不定詞之間**插入了名詞片語或受格代名詞**，那麼該**名詞片語或受格代名詞**就變成了不定詞的主詞，此時 **wish 與不定詞的主詞並不相同**，譬如説，在 I do not wish **my daughter** to marry such a mama's boy. 這句中，wish 的主詞是 I，但 marry 的主詞是 my daughter（做 marry 這個動作的人是 my daughter 不是 I）。

綜上所言，**當主動詞與不定詞之間沒有名詞片語或受格代名詞時，那就表示主動詞與不定詞擁有共同的主詞**（由於主詞相同，而將不定詞的主詞省略）；反過來説，**主動詞與不定詞之間的名詞片語或受格代名詞一定是不定詞的主詞**。

瞭解了這項重要的文法觀念之後，那麼下面這兩種不時可見的錯誤將得以避免。例如：

◆ I don't **wish to be** recognized.（O）
（我不想被人認出來。）
◇ I don't wish people to be recognized.（×）
（我不想人們被認出來.。）
→ to be recognized 的主詞是 I 不是 people，因為是 I 不想被認出來，不是 people。

◆ I wish **to have** a desk in my room, please.（O）
◇ I wish a desk to have in my room, please.（×）
◇ I wish a desk in my room, please.（×）
（我想要在我的房間放一張書桌，謝謝。）
→ wish 與不定詞之間不可插入無生命的事物，亦即 **wish 後面不可直接接無生命的事物當受詞**，該受詞須放在不定詞的後面。

然而，**want 或 would like**（注意：在英式英語中，禮貌的請求不用 want，而是用 would like）都**可直接接無生命的事物當受詞**。例如：

◆ I **want a desk** in my room, please.（O）
◆ I **would like a desk** in my room, please.（O）

Wish 接雙受詞（間接受詞 + 直接受詞）
Wish 後面可接雙受詞（**間接受詞 + 直接受詞**），意為「**祝願，祝福**」。例如：

1. I wish **you every success** in the future.
（我祝你將來事事順利成功。）

2. I wish **you (a) happy birthday**.
（祝你生日快樂。）

3. May I wish **you all a very Merry Christmas**.
（祝大家聖誕快樂。）

4. Wish **you good luck**!
（祝你好運！）

5. We wish **you good health**.
（我們祝你健康。）

6. We came by to wish **you many happy returns**.
（我們來此祝你生日快樂。）

7. I wish **you a long life**.
（我祝你壽比南山。）

8. I wish **you good health** and a long life.
（我祝你健康長壽。）

9. We wish **you the very best of luck** with the exam!
（祝你考試很順利！）

Wish 接 that 子句

Wish 後面可接 that 子句，意為**「但願，希望」**。這是一種**假設語氣句型**，that 子句可以是與現在事實相反的條件句、與過去事實相反的條件句或與未來事實相反的條件句（指未來不太可能發生的事情或不太可能實現的願望）。在非正式情況中，**that 通常省略**。注意：與未來事實相反的條件句型跟與現在事實相反的條件句型長得一模一樣。

與現在事實相反的句型為「wish ＋ (that) ＋ S ＋ **過去簡單式**（或比較少見的**過去進行式**）」，這是對現在存在的某事或某種情況**表示遺憾**。與**未來事實相反的句型亦同**，但是在指**未來不太可能發生的事情或不太可能實現的願望**。例如：

1. I wish I **was/were** rich.
（但願我很有錢。）

2. I wish Mary **was** playing this game with me.
（瑪麗要是和我一起玩這個遊戲就好了。）

3. Evelyn wished that she **could** think of a way of solving the problem.
（伊芙琳希望她能想出一個解決這問題的辦法。）

→ Wish 亦常用於禮貌性說法，亦即用過去式指現在的時間。

4. I wished I **was/were** a bit more handsome.
（我要是再帥一點就好了。）

與過去事實相反的句型為「**wish ＋ (that) ＋ S ＋ 過去完成式**」，這是對過去發生的某事或某種情況表示懊悔。例如：

1. Arthur wishes he'd never married.
（亞瑟真希望他沒有結婚。）

2. I just wish I hadn't drunk so much last night.
（我真希望昨晚我沒喝那麼多。）

3. Now he wished that he had studied very hard.
（現在他真希望當時很用功唸書。）
→ Wish 的禮貌性說法，用過去式指現在的時間。

I wish (that) ＋ S ＋ would ＋ V ……也是一種頗為常見的句型，意為「**我希望……**」。這種句型是在表示對現在正在發生（或沒有發生）的某事或未來會發生（或不會發生）的某事感到厭煩。**在非正式情況中，wish 可以用進行式**。例如：

1. I wish Amy would stop talking for a minute.
（我希望艾美能閉一下嘴。）

2. I just wish you'd stop going on about all your problems!
（我真希望你不要再談論你那些問題了！）

3. He's embarrassing me with his compliments. I'm just wishing he would go away!
（他奉承的話使我很不好意思。我真希望他走開！）

必閃陷阱 非學不可

最後值得一提的是，在**非假設語氣的情況**中，亦即當我們希望未來某事**會發生**而且**極有可能發生**，或者希望過去某事會發生而且已經發生時，我們要**用 hope，不可用 wish**。例如：

◆ I **hope** you (will) visit us again in the near future.（○）
（我希望不久的將來你能再度來訪。）
→ 將來再度來訪的可能性非常大。

◇ I wish you (will) visit us again in the near future.（×）

◆ I **hope** my wife didn't miss her flight.（○）

（我希望我太太沒有錯過她的班機。）

→ 事實上也沒有錯過班機。

◇ I wish my wife didn't miss her flight.（×）

Unit 47 後置形容詞

重要觀念 非學不可 🔍

大多數**形容詞都可放在名詞之前來修飾名詞**，亦**可放在 BE 動詞之後來描述當主詞用的名詞**，前者叫做**定語形容詞** (attributive adjectives)，後者叫做**表語形容詞** (predicative adjectives)。例如：

1. The red apple
（那個紅色的蘋果）

   The apple is red.
（那個蘋果是紅色的。）

2. The old woman
（那個老婦人）

   The woman is old.
（那個婦人是年老的。）

3. The happy students
（那些快樂的學生）

   The students are happy.
（那些學生是快樂的。）

不過，**有一小部分形容詞的位置卻是固定的，亦即只能當定語形容詞或表語形容詞**。

舉例來說，**main 只能當定語形容詞**，如 the main reason，不能用作表語形容詞，因此 the reason is main 是錯的。相反地，**afraid 只能當表語形容詞**，如 the child was afraid，不能用作定語形容詞，因此 an afraid child 是錯的。

必閃陷阱 非學不可

必須注意的是，**表語形容詞並非緊接在名詞之後，而是緊接在 BE 動詞之後**。然而，有些**形容詞卻是緊接在名詞之後**，尤其是在一些**約定俗成的用語中**。例如：

1. The Governor General
（總督→英國派駐大英國協會員國或殖民地、代表女王或國王的官員）
2. The Princess Royal
（大公主，長公主→英國授予女王或國王長女的封號）
3. Times past
（過去的時光；往昔）

我們稱這些形容詞為**「後置形容詞」**(postpositive adjectives or postnominal adjectives)，它們也是**定語形容詞**，只是位在它們所修飾的名詞或代名詞之後。當形容詞修飾代名詞時，後置是強制性的，亦即**形容詞必須位在代名詞之後**。例如：

1. Something useful
（有用的東西；某個有用的東西）
2. Everyone present
（在場或出席的每個人）
3. Those responsible
（負責的人；那些該負責的人）

後置形容詞經常跟**最高級的定語形容詞**連用。例如：

1. The shortest man possible in the world
（可能是世上最矮的男子）

2. The tallest building possible in the world
（可能是世上最高的建築物）

3. The best hotel available in Taiwan
（台灣目前最好的旅館）

4. The cheapest TV set available in Taiwan
（台灣目前所能買到最便宜的電視機）

5. The worst conditions imaginable
（人們能夠想像到的最糟的情況）

6. The most humiliating circumstances imaginable
（人們所能想像最屈辱的情況）

7. The least humane way imaginable
（人們所能想像最不人道的方式）

在某些語言中，如法文、西班牙文、義大利文和羅馬尼亞文，形容詞後置是一種正常的語法，但在英語中則顯得不自然，因此比較少見，大多侷限於古文和詩詞的應用（如 **creatures unseen**，看不見的生物）、某些傳統片語（如 **heir apparent**，法定繼承人）以及某些特定的文法結構（如 **those anxious to leave**，那些急切想要離開的人）。

好用 Tips 非學不可 🔍

在這些**後置形容詞**中，以**順序固定的傳統片語**數量最多，除 heir apparent 外，還有 **accounts payable**（應付帳款）、**attorney general**（美國司法部長或檢察總長）、**battle royal**（激戰，混戰）、**body politic**（政治實體）、**court martial**（軍事法庭）、**notary public**（公證人）、**poet laureate**（桂冠詩人）、**postmaster general**（郵政總長；郵政大臣）、**time immemorial**（無法追查的過去時間）、**words unspoken**（未說出口的話）等等。

英文**有些名詞**似乎比較**常接後置形容詞**，其中 **matters** 和 **things** 可能是其中犖犖大者，如 **matters unknown**（未知的事情）、**things innumerable**（數不清的東西）。認識英文的後置形容詞對於決定這種「**名詞 ＋ 形容詞**」片語的正確複數至關重要。我們通常在**名詞的末尾加 s 來使這些片語變成複數**，如 **attorneys general**、**courts martial**、**poets laureate**，但有些寫作者則把它們視為複合名詞，直接在整個片語末尾加上 s，如 attorney generals、battle royals，不過這畢竟是少數且被絕大多數文法學者視為錯誤。

Unit 48 限制性修飾語

重要觀念 非學不可 🔍

限制性修飾語 (limiting modifiers) 會對它們所修飾的字詞產生限制作用。英文中最常見的限制性修飾語為 **almost, hardly, nearly, just, only** 和 **merely**，而被它們修飾的單字或片語通常緊接在這些修飾語之後。例如：

1. Eugene knows hardly anybody.
（尤金幾乎不認識任何人。）
2. He hardly knows anybody.
（他幾乎不認識任何人。）
3. Only Justin drinks coffee.
（只有賈斯汀喝咖啡。）
4. Justin drinks only coffee.
（賈斯汀只喝咖啡。）

必閃陷阱 非學不可

限制性修飾語在句中的位置會對句意產生重大的影響。講話時，錯置的限制性修飾語往往不著痕跡地就一閃而過，但在正式寫作中，白紙黑字，不容出錯，所以在使用這些修飾語時必須稍作思考它們適當的位置。限制性修飾語最常見的錯誤發生在使用 only 時。例如：

1. Only John eats lollipops.
（只有約翰吃棒棒糖。）
（傑克、彼得等人都沒吃棒棒糖；only 限制了人。）

2. John only eats lollipops.
（約翰只吃棒棒糖。）
（約翰是「吃」棒棒糖而不是「丟掉」棒棒糖；only 限制了動作。）

3. John eats only lollipops.
（約翰只吃棒棒糖。）
（約翰只吃棒棒糖而沒有吃甜點、麵包等；only 限制了食品。）

由於中英文語法的差異，上面第 2 句和第 3 句的中文翻譯都一樣。大多數人都會將第 2 句和第 3 句視為同義，尤其是在講話時。然而，若就「約翰只吃棒棒糖而沒有吃其他東西」這項意思而言，第 2 句是錯的。所以，下面兩句也是錯的：

◇ Carl only visits his parents once a year.（✕）
（卡爾一年僅探望他父母親一次。）
→ 應該是
◆ Carl visits his parents only once a year.（O）
◇ Their marriage only lasted (for) three months.（✕）
（他們的婚姻只維持三個月。）
→ 應該是
◆ Their marriage lasted **only** three months.（O）

Unit 49 當副詞用的 pretty 不可用於否定句

必閃陷阱 非學不可

Pretty 當副詞用時意為「相當，頗，很，非常」，可放在形容詞或另一副詞前面當修飾語。它是個**非正式用字**，通常用於口語及非正式場合，不可用於較正式的場合；**正式場合須使用 quite 或 fairly**。例如：

◆ Professor Smith comes from a **fairly** poor country but he is not poor.（○）
◇ Professor Smith comes from a pretty poor country but he is not poor.（✕）
（史密斯教授來自一個相當貧窮的國家，但他並不窮。）

如標題所述，**pretty 不可用於否定句**。例如：

◆ This type of smartphone isn't **very** good, really. I don't think I'll use it again.
（○）
◆ This type of smartphone isn't **so** good, really. I don't think I'll use it again.（○）
◇ This type of smartphone isn't pretty good, really. I don't think I'll use it again.
（✕）
（這款智慧型手機的確不是很好。我想我不會再用它了。）

好用 Tips 非學不可

Pretty 與 much 和 well 固定搭配所形成的 **pretty much** 和 **pretty well**，是兩個不時可見的副詞片語，但意思與其字面相去甚遠，值得學起來。它們與另一片語 **pretty nearly** 都是**同義詞**，意為「差不多；幾乎」(almost)。例如：

1. I can pretty much guarantee that he'll be back in time.
（我幾乎可以保證他會及時回來。）

2. It's pretty well impossible for us to guess what he thinks.
（我們幾乎不可能猜出他的想法。）

3. The work is pretty nearly finished.
（這項工作差不多要完成了。）

隱含比較級

必閃陷阱 非學不可

英文中有 6 個形容詞有時被稱為**「隱含比較級」**(implicit comparatives)，它們是：**major、minor、junior、senior、inferior 和 superior**。這 6 個字（原本在拉丁文中都是比較級形容詞）**均具比較級型態，但缺乏原級和最高級型態。**

雖然它們**隱含比較的功能**，但在作用上其實就跟原級形容詞一樣。在現代英語用法中，major 和 minor 並不跟 than 搭配做比較，而 **junior、senior、inferior 和 superior** 雖可做比較，但**其後的介系詞是接 to** 而不是 than。例如：

1. This restaurant is superior to the one we usually go to.
（這家餐廳比我們常去的那家好。）
2. She is senior to everyone else in the company.
（她在公司裡的年資比其他人都長。）

然而，事實上，由於在作用上就跟原級形容詞一樣，**junior、senior、inferior 和 superior 有時仍可接 more 和 most 來形成比較級和最高級。**例如：

John is more senior than me.
（約翰比我資深。）

Part II
寫作用法精論

Chapter 3

拼字

Chapter 3 | 拼字

-able, -ible

重要觀念 非學不可

這**兩個形容詞字尾 (suffixes) 均意為「能……的，可……的；具有……性質的」，但兩者卻有極大的差異**。最重大的差異是，**-able 是個活字尾**，意謂我們不用連字號，就可以在**幾乎任何動詞的後面加上 able**，但 **-ible 不會被用來創造新字，**它主要存在於幾百年或上千年傳承下來的舊字中。

倘若不理會拼字檢查的「打臉」，那麼我們可以興之所至隨時創造出如 sanctionable, overthrowable, redoable 等新字而不用連字號。在創造 -able 新字時，我們處理動詞的方式與創造 -ing 新字的方式如出一轍。譬如說，我們將 move 的 e 去掉後加上 ing 來創造出 moving（動人的，感人的；活動的，移動中的）這個字；所以，若要創造 move 的 -able 形容詞，我們也是將 move 的 e 去掉後加上 able，而創造出 movable（可動的，可移動的）。

必閃陷阱 非學不可

然而，最重要的是，**在創造新的 -able 形容詞之前一定要先確定是否已經有對應的 -ible 形容詞存在**。譬如說，convertable 是多餘的、不必要的，因為已經有 convertible 的存在。所有公認的 -ible 形容詞都已列在字典中，不會再有其他 -ible 字了，因為如上述，-ible 這個字尾不會被用來創造新字，它們僅存在於幾百年或上千年傳承下來的舊字中。

茲將若干目前最常用的 -ible 形容詞臚列如下，供大家參考：

accessible	defensible	exhaustible	invincible	possible
admissible	digestible	fallible	legible	reprehensible
audible	discernible	feasible	ostensible	susceptible
convertible	dismissible	flexible	perceptible	terrible
controvertible	edible	gullible	permissible	visible
credible	eligible	horrible	plausible	

許多 -ible 形容詞都有對應的 -able 字,但它們大多隨著時間的演進而發展出不同的意思。舉例而言,forceable 和 forcible 的意思並不相同,儘管前者無法在任何一本字典中找到,但在 Fowler's Modern English Usage 以及 Bryan Garner 的 Modern American Usage 這兩本英語用法指南中皆有著墨,它意為「可用力打開的」,如 The door is forceable.(這個門是可用力打開的——破門而入),而 forcible 意為「強行的,用暴力的;強迫的,強制的」,如 forcible entry(強行進入)。再者,contractable 意為「(疾病、習慣等)易感染的」,而 contractible 意為「(橡皮筋等)可收縮的」;infusable 意為「(茶等)可沖泡的」,而 infusible 意為「(鑽石等)不可熔解的」。事實上,infusable 和 infusible 並無對應關係,因為前者是動詞 infuse 加上 -able 的結果,而後者是形容詞 fusible 加上字首 in- 所形成的反義字。

好用 Tips 非學不可 🔍

然而,其他 -able 和 -ible 並存的形容詞,意思則完全一樣,只是其中一個比另一個來得常用。下列為若干字尾 -able 和 -ible 意思完全相同的形容詞,左邊的形容詞為目前比較常用者:

collapsible	collaps**able**
collect**able**	collectible（在北美比較常見）
condens**able**	condensible
confus**able**	confusible
connectible	connect**able**
deductible	deduct**able**
discussible	discuss**able**
extendible	extend**able**
extract**able**	extractible
gullible	gull**able**（19 世紀以後就不用了）
ignit**able**	ignitible
indetect**able**	indetectible
prevent**able**	preventible

Unit 02　Bi-, semi-, biannual, biennial, semiannual

必閃陷阱 非學不可

當我們**在時間名詞前加上字首 bi- 時，bi- 意為「每兩個」**，所以 **bimonthly** 意為**「每兩個月（的）；兩個月一次（的）」**(every two months)，biweekly 意為「每兩週（的）；兩週一次（的）」(every two weeks)。當我們在時間名詞前加上字首 semi- 時，**semi- 意為「一半」**，所以 semimonthly 意為「每半個月（的）；一個月兩次（的）」(every half month or twice a month)，semiweekly 意為「每半個禮拜（的）；一週兩次（的）」(every half week or twice a week)。

然而，事情並沒有這麼簡單。Bisect 意為「一分為二；二等分」；此外，還有許多以 bi- 作開頭的字，其 **bi- 的意思是「一分為二」而非「每兩個」**。

所以，bimonthly 還有一個少見，但一直令人唉聲嘆氣的意思是「一個月兩次（的）」(twice a month)。因此，良心的建議是：**在使用字首為 bi-和 semi- 的字時，最好藉助於上下文來加以界定**，即使因此會造成一些累贅 (redundancy)，亦在所不惜。

最後，讓我們來探討標題中 biannual, biennial, semiannual 這三個字的意思。Biannual 中的 bi- 是「一分為二」的意思，所以這個字通常意為「每年兩次的；每半年的」。Biennial 來自一個字首 bi- 的意思是「二」的拉丁字，所以這個字意為「兩年一次的」，如 biennium 意為「兩年期間」。Semiannual 的意思是「每半年的；半年期的；半年生的；一年兩次的」。總而言之，不管使用哪個字，最重要的是一定要**確保句意的清晰明確。如果發現可能會有模稜兩可、混淆不清的情況發生，那麼使用half-yearly（每半年的）和 two-yearly（兩年一次的）**可能會比上述任何一個字都要來得好。

Unit 03　-ce, -cy / dependence, dependency

必閃陷阱 非學不可

我們**使用 -ce 和 -cy 這兩個字尾 (suffixes) 來取代以 -ant 或 -ent 做結尾的形容詞的最後一個字母 -t，使其變成名詞**：brilliant 變成 brilliance 或 brilliancy；lenient 變成 lenience 或 leniency；virulent 變成 virulence 或 virulency。這些成雙成對的名詞都是同義字，但以 -cy 做結尾的名詞使用頻率較低，甚至看起來有些賣弄的意味。然而，有些類似的成雙成對名詞並非完全同義，最明顯的例子之一就是我們常用的 dependence 和 dependency。

Dependency 有個特殊的意思是 dependence 所沒有的，那就是「**附屬國，附屬地**」，如 Those three small islands are dependencies of Japan.（那三個小島是日本的屬地。）**Dependence** 意為「**依靠，依賴，信賴**」或「**毒癮；酒癮**」。例如：We need to reduce our dependence on oil as a source of energy.（我們必須減少仰賴石油做為能源）；It is very hard to get rid of his dependence on the drug.（要戒除他的毒癮很不容易。）Dependency 也有這些意思，如 drug dependency（毒癮），但可能有點比較少用。在此類用法中，這兩個字是同義字，且是標準英語用字。此外，要記得的是，無論是形容詞 dependent 或名詞 dependence, dependency，其後慣用的介系詞都是 on 或 upon。

Unit 04 Co-

必閃陷阱 非學不可

這個字首 (prefix) 經常會產生三個用法上的問題：**(1) 當 co- 與 worker 和 pilot 連用形成 coworker 和 copilot 等字時**，它的意思是「**（職位）相等的**」(equal to) 還是「**隸屬的**」(subordinate to) 呢？答案是：可能是其中之一或兩者兼而有之，一般而言，上下文會告訴我們是那個意思。Coworker（同事）通常是指職位不低於也不高於其他 worker，但 copilot（副駕駛）的職位一定低於 pilot（正駕駛）。

(2) 使用這個字首的新字新詞一開始都是俚語嗎？或者這些字如 cohost （共同主持人）和 co-agent（合夥人，合作者）一開始就是標準英語呢？ 答案是：只要**意思夠清楚**，這些字以及亦**使用字首 co-為特殊需要臨時造出來的字 (nonce words) 幾乎一開始就是標準英語**，如 sled-dog driver（雪橇犬駕駛人）及其 codriver（副駕駛）可能跟 pilot 和 copilot 一樣都是伙伴關係，任何時候都只有一人處於掌控的地位，另一人是他的伙伴。**(3) 字首 co- 與字根或基本字 (base word) 結合時需不需要加連字號呢？** 答案是：**通常不加連字號且中間沒有空格**（如 coincidence, coordinate），但**當字根的第一個字母為 o 時，有時會用連字號**，如 co-opt（拉攏，籠絡；吸收），co-own（共同擁有）；或**當某個字太新，看起來怪怪的且有被讀錯之虞，那麼此時通常也會加連字號**，如 co-anchor （共同主播），co-belligerent（共同作戰國；戰爭中之同盟國）。

這個**字首意為「共同；（和⋯⋯）一起」**，如 co-owner（共同擁有者）；「相等；同樣；互相」，如 coextensive（有共同空間的；共同擴張的），cooperative（合作的）；「和⋯⋯一起做；以相同程度做某事」，如 coauthor（共同執筆者；合著者），coproducer（聯合製片人）或 to cosign（共同簽署；連署）；「輔助⋯⋯做；副」，如 coadjutor（助手；助理主教）。上述 (1) 的職位相等或隸屬問題有時會引發歧義，如 cohost 和 coanchor 等。在數學三角函數中，co- 意為「補；餘」，如 cosine（餘弦），cotangent（餘切）。co- 還有另外三種型態：col-（在 l 之前，如 collaborate「合作；勾結」）；com-（在 b, p, m 之前，如 combine「結合」，companion「同伴，伴侶；朋友」，commiserate「憐憫；同情」）；con-（在其他字母之前，如 contaminate「污染」）。

E-book, ebook, eBook

必閃陷阱 非學不可

電子書的英文全名叫做 electronic book，但簡寫為 **e-book**、**ebook** 或 **eBook**。eBook 逐漸過時或幾近走入歷史，至少平面出版品都已經不用。自 2012 年初以降，美國、加拿大和澳洲那些有發行網路版的新聞出版品一律使用**加連字號、沒有大寫的 e-book**。與此同時，英國大多數有網路版的新聞出版品則使用拼成一個字的 **ebook**。**一個字的拼法很有可能成為放諸四海皆準、全世界普遍使用的標準拼法，就如同 email 和 website 等字的發展一樣。**然而，美國一些刊物仍抗拒使用科技名詞較新的拼法。譬如說，深具影響力的《紐約時報》(New York Times) 一直不動如山，迄今仍使用 20 世紀的拼法，即 e-mail、Web site 等，因此吾人可能還是不要期待他們會很快捨棄 e-book 而改用 ebook。此外，**ebook 尚未通過拼字檢查**，Microsoft Word 會在其下標示紅線，這對 e-book 有利。所以我們現在只能拭目以待這個字最後演變的結果。

當 ebook 和 e-book 位在句子開頭的第一個字時，它們跟其他任何字一樣也要大寫，如 Ebooks on English learning are popular.（關於英文學習的電子書現在正夯）；E-books of this kind are free.（這種電子書是免費的。）**如果你堅持使用 eBook，那麼最好改寫句子以避免它出現在句子的開頭。**

註：若干編輯方針保守的刊物仍然偏愛 e-mail 而不用 email，但大多數英語系國家都已採用沒有連字號的拼法。在 Google News 的搜尋中，email 和 e-mail 出現的比例至少都是 6 比 1，與幾年前的情況大異其趣。在新聞寫作以外的領域，沒有連字號的拼法甚至更常見。

Unit 06 -er, -or?

必閃陷阱 非學不可

我們都知道，**一個動詞加上字尾 -er 或 -or 後就變成名詞，意為「執行該動詞所表示之動作的人」**，但我們何時該使用 -er，又何時該使用 -or 呢？

老實說，這沒有規則可循。理論上，-er 可加到英文現有的任何一個動詞的後面。但實際上，雖然有許多字是以 -er 做字尾（其中常用的字約有 100 個之多），但另外一些字則以 -or 做字尾；還有一些字則是兩者都可以（意思有時不同）。一般而言，**以 -er 做字尾的名詞，拿掉 -er 後還是英文的動詞**，如 **doer, driver, enquirer, eraser, player, runner, steeplechaser**。而 -or 通常用在由拉丁字根所構成的名詞中——換言之，**就是那些把 -or 拿掉後就不是英文動詞的字**，如 **doctor, author, mentor, sponsor**；但情況並非總是如此，如 actor, conductor, exhibitor, investigator, sailor 等字拿掉 -or 後還是不折不扣的英文動詞。此外，**有些動詞兼容並蓄，可加上 -er 或 -or，意思相同**，如 adapter/adaptor, adviser/advisor, vender/vendor，但有時意思不同，如 sailer/sailor (sailer 為「帆船」，而 sailor 為「水手，船員」)。不過，我們可以掌握一個大原則，那就是：**最近創造的名詞以及那些沒有拉丁字根的字通常使用 -er 做字尾。**

亦值得一提的是，當 **-er 被加到最後一個字母是 y 的動詞時，若 y 前面的字母為子音，則 y 通常變成 i**，如 **carrier, occupier** 等等；若 y 前面的字母為母音，則 y 維持不變，如 buyer, employer, player 等等。不過，有時兩種型態都可以，如 drier/dryer（乾燥機，烘乾機），flier/flyer（飛行員，飛行物；廣告傳單）——目前 flyer 要比 flier 來得常用許多，尤其是意為「廣告傳單」(leaflet) 時。

Unit 07 -ic, -ical

必閃陷阱 非學不可

目前並無規則或一貫的模式來規範以 -ic 和 -ical 結尾的形容詞的構詞法。有些 -ic 字比同形的 -ical 字更受到青睞（如 ironic 比 ironical 更討喜）；反之，有些 -ical 字則比同形的 -ic 字更常用（如 alphabetical 比 alphabetic 來得常用，而 metaphorical 比 metaphoric 更常用。）

然而，**有些 -ic 和 -ical 字組隨著時間的演進和變遷**漸行漸遠，最後分道揚鑣，**現在的意思已經不同**，如 classic 和 classical、economic 和 economical、electric 和 electrical、historic 和 historical 以及 periodic 和 periodical 等。

當您不確定某一 -ic 和 -ical 字組中哪個比較常用，或者它們是否已演變成不同的意思時，唯一可以確知的方式就是查閱字典或其他參考資料。不過，在此有一點是可以確定的：無論是**以 -ic 結尾還是以 -ical 結尾的形容詞，若變成副詞，它們的字尾一定都是 -ically**，亦即它們的副詞型態或拼法完全一樣（-ic 字加上 -ally，而 -ical 字加上 -ly）。

Unit 08　Inter-, intra-

必閃陷阱 非學不可

字首 **Inter- 意為「在……之間」**(between; among)，如 interdepartmental（各部門之間的；各系之間的）；interstate（州際的，州與州之間的）；intermarriage/intermarry（[不同群體、種族或宗教之間的] 通婚；近親結婚）。**Intra- 意為「在……之內」(inside; within)**，如 intradepartmental（部門內的；系內的）；intrastate（[尤指美國] 州內的）；intracranial（顱內的）。

Inter- 和 intra- 可以加到任何普通名詞而不用連字號，但許多寫作者並不是很有自信這麼做。拼字檢查軟體可能認為不加連字號所創造的 inter-/intra- 新字新詞拼寫錯誤，若是如此，那麼拼字檢查軟體就是弄錯了！

Unit 09　-ish, -y

重要觀念 非學不可

在非正式的上下文中或講話時，我們可以**在一些字的後面加上 -ish 和 -y 這兩個字尾來故意「含糊其辭」，表示「大約，大概」的意思。**-ish 通常加在數字、時間或數量的後面，例如：

1. A: How old do you think our manager is?
（A：你認為我們經理幾歲？）

 B: Fortyish. Possibly younger.
（B：四十歲左右。可能更年輕。）

2. I'll call you at sevenish and then we can discuss that matter.
（我會在大概七點左右打電話給你，到時候我們可以討論那件事。）

-ish 可以加到形容詞、副詞和介系詞後面。例如：

1. A: Is he tall, Amy's new boyfriend?
（A：他，艾美的新男友，個子高不高？）

 B: Well, tallish.
（B：嗯，還算高。）

2. A: Is it far from the shopping mall?
（A：它離購物商場遠不遠？）

B: No, but it's near the MRT station, well, nearish to the MRT station.
（B：不遠，但靠近捷運站，嗯，蠻靠近捷運站的。）

必閃陷阱 非學不可

必須注意的是，**-ish 和 -y 通常不能互換。-ish 比 -y 來得常用，-y 大多跟顏色連用，但 black 和 white 除外，亦即不可將 -y 加到 black 或 white 的後面**。例如：

What color tie do you think goes with this shirt? The blue one? Or should it be the greeny one?
（你認為什麼顏色的領帶跟這件襯衫搭配呢？藍色的這條嗎？還是應該是略帶綠色的這一條呢？）

Unit 10 -ize, -ise?

必閃陷阱 非學不可

在英式英語中，許多動詞字尾的 [-aiz] 音可能拼成 -ize 或 -ise，如
baptize/baptise（給……施洗禮），organize/organise（組織；籌辦），
realize/realise（瞭解；意識到），recognize/recognise（認出；承認；
認可）等等。然而，由於美國的國際影響力，現代大多數字典都將 -ize
列為優先的拼法，而 -ise 是公認的變體。事實上，**大致來說，-ize 和
-ise 在英式英語中都一樣常用。**這兩種拼法都有詞源依據，它們經由法
文的 -iser 導源於拉丁文的 -izare 和希臘文的 -izein。

不管那種拼法較受青睞，重要的是，在一篇作文或其他寫作中，我們
必須**保持用字的一致性**，無論是選用其他 -ize/-ise 字或選用任何以
-zation/-sation, -zer/-ser, -izable/-isable 等做字尾的衍生字，都要從頭至
尾一以貫之。換言之，整篇文章不是全部使用 -ize 字就是全部使用 -ise
字，不要混合使用。

Capsize（翻船）是兩個音節或兩個音節以上的 -ize 動詞中唯一沒有
-ise 拼法的字。然而，沒有 -ize 拼法的 -ise 動詞則不在少數，其中最常
見者包括 advertise（做廣告），advise（勸告，忠告），chastise（懲
戒，責罰），circumcise（為……行割禮；割包皮），comprise（組
成；由……組成），compromise（妥協），despise（鄙視），devise
（設計；策劃），enfranchise（給予……選舉權），excise（切除），
exercise（練習；運動），franchise（給予加盟權），improvise（即興
創作；即興表演），merchandise（推銷；促銷），revise（修訂），
supervise（監督），surmise（推測；猜測），surprise（使吃驚），
televise（播送電視節目）。

以 -yse 做字尾的動詞，如 analyse（分析）和 paralyse（使癱瘓），在英式英語中都沒有 -yze 的拼法。在**英式英語中有 -ize 和 -ise 兩種拼法的動詞**，在**美式英語中都拼成 -ize**，但 advertise … televise 這些字通常維持 -ise 的拼法。Analyse 和 paralyse 等字在美式英語中都拼成 analyze, paralyze ...。

有些人反對現代創造新動詞的趨勢，即在名詞或形容詞後面加上 -ize/-ise，如 pedestrianize/pedestrianise（使成為行人專用道；步行），hospitalize/hospitalise（使……住院治療），prioritize/prioritise（按優先順序處理），finalize/finalise（敲定，完成）等等。**當有較簡易的型態或同義詞可用時，這些動詞最好避免，如 to martyrize（使殉道；使成為烈士）可用 to martyr 來代替，而 to finalize 通常可用 to finish 來取代。**然而，對於既沒有較簡易型態又沒有同義詞的 -ize/-ise 動詞（及其衍生字）來說，它們的作用可就大矣，如 to computerize the stock control system（使庫存控制系統電腦化）；the decimalization of British currency（英國貨幣改為十進制）。

Unit 11　-ness, -ty

必閃陷阱 非學不可

由於英文中有許多形容詞同時擁有以 -ty（包括若干以 -ety 和 -ity 為字尾的抽象名詞）和 -ness 為字尾的名詞，有人或許想知道這兩種名詞之間有何不同，所代表的意義為何，以及該如何使用。本文將就此作一說明。

首先，我們必須要知道的是，**由 -ness 和 -ty 字尾所構成的名詞，都是衍生自形容詞**。英文的任何形容詞都可**加上 -ness 來變成名詞，但這種型態的名詞目前仍有在使用的數量**，比起衍生自拉丁文形容詞而以 **-ty、-ety 或 -ity 為字尾的名詞要少了許多**。因此，除了特殊用途，如在英文論文中的應用，我們可能從 one, loyal 和 various 等形容詞創造出 oneness, loyalness 和 variousness 等名詞外，一般大多使用 unity, loyalty 和 variety 等。

在現行以 -ty 為字尾的名詞中，絕大多數在所有應用中都比相對應的 -ness 名詞來得常見。這些 -ty 字俯拾即是，如 ability, honesty, notoriety, prosperity, sanity, stupidity，因此我們實在沒有必要、實際上也沒有令人信服的理由一定要使用 ableness, honestness, notoriousness 等名詞來代替之。再者，目前比 -ty 字來得常用的 -ness 字相當罕見——現在能想到的只有 acuteness 和 conspicuousness 分別比 acuity 和 conspicuity 來得常用。

總體而言，-ty 字大多比相對應的 -ness 字來得常用，除非它們的意思和用法已經完全不同或有部分不同。意思完全不同者包括 ingenuity（創意，發明才能；足智多謀；心靈手巧）和 ingenuousness（天真；坦率）、casualty（死者；傷者；傷亡人員）和 casualness（隨便）以及 sensibility（感覺力，感受力，鑑賞力）和 sensibleness（合理；明智）。部分不同者則是肇因於 **-ty 字比較常用而發展出具體的意思**，因此許多 -ty 字現在除了能表示原有之抽象意思外，也能表示具體的意思，而**大多數的 -ness 字**因為少用並未發展出具體的意思，**一直只有抽象的意思**。換言之，**這兩種名詞都具有各該形容詞所表示之性質或特性的抽象意思，但許多 -ty 字現在除了當抽象名詞外，亦可當具體名詞，而大多數的 -ness 字則僅能用作抽象名詞。**

Semi-, hemi-, demi-

必閃陷阱 非學不可

Semi-、hemi- 和 demi- 這三個字首或前綴 (prefixes) 都意為「半」，但它們使用在不同的領域。

Semi- 除了「半」的意思外，還意為「部分的（地）」及「（一段時期中）發生兩次的」。這個字首源自意思也是「半」的拉丁文 semi-。英文字通常使用同一基礎語言的字和字根來構成。由於 semi- 係拉丁文字首，因此它往往也與源自拉丁文的字用在一起。

在有關**技術、科學及數學**的領域中，semi- 經常被用來表示「半；部分的（地）」的意思。英語人士在創造**意為某事物之半的字詞時，最常用的字首就是 semi-**。例如：semiconductor（半導體）、semi-autobiographical novel（半自傳體小説）、semiannual plant（半年生植物）；The gun is semiautomatic.（這把槍是半自動的）。

Hemi- 也意為**「半」**。這個字首源自意思也是「半」的希臘文 hemi-。Hemi- 通常與**化學、數學、生物學**和**醫學**領域的字詞用在一起。例如：hemisphere〔（尤指地球的）半球——the northern/southern hemisphere（北／南半球）、hemiplegia（半身麻痺；半身不遂）、hemicellulose（半纖維素）、hemifacial spasm（半面痙攣——美式英語有時拼成 haemifacial spasm）。

Demi- 亦意為**「半；部分的（地）」**。這個字首源自意思也是「半」的古法文 demi。Demi- 不像 semi- 和 hemi- 那麼常見。例如：demigod（半神半人）——Some football players become like demigods to their fans.（有些足球運動員在球迷心目中似乎被神化了）(Cambridge Dictionary)；demisemiquaver（三十二分音符）—— quaver（八分音符）加上 semi- 後變成 semiquaver（十六分音符），再加上 demi- 後變成 demisemiquaver（三十二分音符）。

Unit 13 -ward, -wards

必閃陷阱 非學不可

這兩個字尾與 back, down, up 或 on 等所構成的字幾乎隨處可見。但 **-ward 所構成的字可當形容詞和副詞用**，而 **-wards 所構成的字只能當副詞用**；換言之，若是形容詞，則只能使用 -ward 所構成的字，若是副詞，則可使用 -ward 或 -wards 所構成的字——就副詞而言，美國大多使用 –ward（或者說美式英語使用 -ward 和 -wards 當副詞）而英國大多使用 –wards（或者說英式英語僅用 -wards 當副詞）。例如：

1. He is a backward child.
（他是個遲鈍的小孩。）

2. She looked backward/backwards when she heard someone calling her.
（當她聽見有人叫她時，她向後看了一看。）

3. There is a downward trend of share prices.
（股價下滑的趨勢。）

4. He looked downward/downwards to avoid my eyes.
（他低著頭看，以避開我的目光。）

5. We can see the forward part of the ship.
（我們可以看見船的前部。）

6. He hurried forward/forwards to meet her.
（他趕緊走上前去迎接她。）

7. The plane's onward movement was slowed by adverse winds.
（飛機前進的速度因逆風而減慢。）

8. Miss Lee hurried onward/onwards.
（李小姐匆匆向前走去。）

→ forward 和 onward 都意為「向前（的）」。

9. There is an upward movement of prices.
（物價上漲。）

10. The bird flew upward/upwards.
（鳥兒向上飛去。）

然而，**當副詞用時，並非所有 -ward 和 -wards 所構成的字都可以互換**，如 **step forward**（向前跨步）是正確的英文，**而 step forwards 則是錯誤的**；不過，move backward/downward/upward（向後／向下／向上移動）和 move backwards/downwards/upwards 都是毫無疑問的標準美式英語，只是**一般通常比較喜歡沒有 s 的字**。

最後要討論的是 **toward** 和 **towards**。務必記住：這兩個字的詞類與上述完全不同，它們並非形容詞和副詞，**而是介系詞。美式英語兩者都用，但使用 toward 比較多，而英式英語通常使用 towards**。

Unit 14　年份的說法

重要觀念 非學不可

年份的說法是一項英文基本功，但有些事情可能使其變得複雜，而英式英語和美式英語的說法又有一些差異。

現在就讓我們從簡單的開始。對於像 1456、1832 或 1791 這樣的年份，我們都是將**前面兩個數字**和**後面兩個數字**分開來唸，猶如它們是單一數字：fourteen fifty-six；eighteen thirty-two；seventeen ninety-one。**若第三個數字是 0，那麼有兩種說法**。例如：

1.
1508：fifteen oh eight 或 fifteen hundred and eight
2.
1903：nineteen oh three 或 nineteen hundred and three

不過，第二種說法比較少見且聽起來略顯過時，尤其對美式英語來說更是如此。

對於**結尾是兩個 0 的年份**，慣例是：1600：sixteen hundred

至於**結尾是三個 0 的年份**，說法是：1000：(the year) one thousand

我們**經常在開頭先說 "the year"** 來明確表示這數字指的是年份。

必閃陷阱 非學不可 🔍

從 2000 年開始，年份的說法變得比較複雜。2000 年都是說成 "(the year) two thousand"，但 2000 年之後的年份則有兩種說法，視您說的是英式英語還是美式英語而定。例如：

1.

2008：**twenty oh eight**（英式英語和美式英語）或 two thousand and eight（英式英語）／two thousand eight（美式英語）──2008 年北京奧運只有單一說法，都是說成 **"the twenty eight Olympics"**。

2.

2016: **twenty sixteen**（英式英語和美式英語）或 two thousand and sixteen（英式英語）/two thousand sixteen（美式英語）──2016 年里約奧運只有單一說法，都是說成 **"the twenty sixteen Olympics"**。

對於 1000 年之前的年份，我們通常將第一個數字和後面兩個數字分開來唸。例如：

653：six fifty-three

（英式英語也可以說成：(the year) six hundred and fifty-three）

對於數字非常低的年份，我們通常會加上 AD。AD 可以置於年份之前或之後，但傳統派人士比較喜歡將 AD 置於年份之前。例如：

13：AD thirteen 或 (the year) thirteen AD

根據基督教的年份說法，**AD（西元；公元）**為拉丁文 Anno Domini（英文意思為 "in the year of the Lord"）的縮寫。**1 AD 據說是耶穌誕生的那一年。該年之前的年份會被標示為 BC。BC（西元前；公元前）**為 Before (the birth of) Christ 的縮寫，須置於年份之後。沒有 0 AD 或 0 BC 這樣的年份。

儘管自大約 1800 年以來，AD 和 BC 一直都是當前的用法，但**現今有許多人偏愛使用 CE**（Common Era 或 Christian Era）和 **BCE**（Before the Common Era 或 Before Current Era 或 Before Christian Era），尤其是在學術文章中。**CE 就是 AD**，而 **BCE 就是 BC**，但避免了提及基督教。

好用 Tips 非學不可 🔍

1 AD/CE（西元／公元 1 年）之前的年份都要在其後加上 BC/BCE（西元前／公元前）；BC/BCE 之前的數字越大，表示年份越久遠。例如：

240 BC：two forty BC
——對於這些年份，我們不必說 "the year"，因為 BC 已清楚地表示那是年份，不過有些人仍會這樣做，尤其是在英式英語中。

Unit 15 否定的字首

必閃陷阱 非學不可

否定字首或前綴 (negative prefixes) 是在表示「否定」、「相反」或「不足」之意，即「不，非，無」(not)。 英文中**最常用的否定字首為 in-, un-, non-, de-, dis-, a-, anti-, il-, im- 和 ir-**，但它們的區別往往在於**所指事物的相反性（而非否定性）程度**的不同。雖然這些字首有些在若干用法中可以互換，但它們之間仍有些微的差異。

a-, anti-, de-, dis-

A- 係加到以 -al 結尾的形容詞來表示**「非；沒有」**的意思，如 amoral（非道德的；無道德觀念的；沒有是非觀念的）、atypical（非典型的；不合規則的）。

Anti- 係表示：1. 反（對），如 antinuclear（反核的）、anti-American（反美的）；**2. 與……對立（相反）**，如 antimatter（反物質）、antipathy（反感）；**3. 防（止）**，如 antibiotic（抗菌的；抗生素）、antidote（解毒劑）、antiseptic（抗菌的，防腐的；防腐劑）。

De- 通常加到動詞前面來表示：**1. 相反的動作**，如 deactivate〔使（炸彈）不能爆炸；使（警報器及其他裝置）失靈或沒有作用〕、declassify（解密）；**2. 去除，（使）脫離**，如 debone（去骨頭）、deice（除冰）、defrost（除霜）、dethrone（廢黜）；**3. 降低，貶低**，如 degrade（使降級；降低……的地位、品格等）、devalue（使……貶值）。

Dis- 有部分用法與 **de-** 相似，另有部分用法與 **un-** 相似。它係表示：
1. 相反的動作或否定的意思，如 disapprove（不贊成，不同意）、dishonest（不誠實的）；**2. 使中斷，消除**，如 disconnect〔使分離，分開，斷開；切斷（電話、電源等）〕、disinfect（為……消毒）；**3. 去除，移去，拿走**，如 dismantle（拆除，拆開）、disqualify（取消……資格）。

in-, il-, im-, ir-
若從以否定字首創造新字的觀點來看，in-（及其衍生的字首 il-, im- 和 ir-）是這些否定字首中最沒用的，因為它 1. **只跟某些衍生自拉丁文的詞幹 (stem) 連用**，如 inarticulate（口齒含糊不清的）、intolerant（不能容忍的，無法忍受的）、impenetrable（無法穿透的，無法通過的）；2. **高度規則化，亦即 il- 只加到開頭字母為 l 的單詞、im- 只加到開頭字母為 b、m 或 p 的單詞、ir- 只加到開頭字母為 r 的單詞**，如 illegal（非法的）、imbalance（不平衡）、immobilize（使不能行動）、impossible（不可能的）、irregular（不規則的）；3. **與非否定詞的意思相同，因此加了這些否定字首反而造成混淆**，如 inflammable 和 flammable 的意思完全一樣，都意為「易燃的」、irradiate 和 radiate 都有（X 光、紫外線等）輻射、照射、放射的意思。

un-
Un- 通常加到字尾為 -ed 和 -able 的拉丁衍生字以及其他形容詞和副詞，如 unbounded（無限的）、unfounded（沒有根據的）、unbelievable（難以置信的）、unbreakable（不會破的，打不破的）、unfair（不公平的）、unhappy（不快樂的）、unfortunately（不幸地）。此外，這個**字首還可與動詞連用來表示相反的動作或否定的意思**，如 unblock（除去……堵塞物，疏通；解除封鎖）、undress（脫衣服）。

non-

Non- 是最有用的否定字首，因為它可以加到幾乎任何名詞、動詞、形容詞或副詞，且不會與其他常見的非否定詞產生混淆。與 in- 和 un- 這兩個往往創造出非絕對否定詞的字首不同的是，non- 大多被用來產生意思與其非否定型態完全相反的單詞。譬如說，nonconformist（不墨守成規的人）一定是 conformist（墨守成規者，遵奉習俗者）的相反詞。如果我們也創造了 inconformist 和 unconformist，它們的意思不會相同。

Non- 加到詞幹時無須使用連字號，除非該詞幹為專有名詞，如 nonalcoholic（不含酒精的）、nonfiction（非小說）、nonproliferation（防止核武或化武擴散）、non-Catholic（非天主教的；非天主教徒）、non-Western（非西方的）。拼字檢查軟體可能會在你創造的一些未加連字號的 non- 字底下劃紅線，但這並不表示你創造的字不正確。

Part II
寫作用法精論

Chapter 4

其他寫作／口說
須注意事項

Chapter 4 | 其它寫作／口說須注意事項

Unit 01 A.k.a., aka

必閃陷阱 非學不可

A.k.a. 為 also known as 的縮寫，意思是**「又名，亦稱（為），又叫做」**，係用在真實姓名的後面來指一個人的化名、別名、假名、外號或綽號。不過，**a.k.a. 亦可用在地方或事物的後面來表示該地方或事物的其他名稱。**

Also known as 最初在 1940 至 1945 年被縮寫時，每個字母後面都加上句點以示它本身是縮寫，並不是字。但**隨著 a.k.a. 被廣泛地使用，句點被拿掉了，變成 aka。現今這兩種拼法都很常用**，不過《牛津英語大辭典》(The Oxford English Dictionary, OED) 僅列出 aka 的拼法，顯示 **aka 受歡迎的程度略高於 a.k.a.**。有趣的是，即使 aka 的句點已被拿掉，但它還是以個別唸出三個字母的方式來發音，而不是把它當成一個字來發音。**書寫時，這三個字母可以全部小寫或全部大寫、加句點或不加句點**。例如：

1. That man who is talking to Mary is Kevin, a.k.a. "the lady killer."
（那個正在跟瑪麗談話的男子是凱文，外號「女性殺手」。）

2. James Brown, aka the "Godfather of Soul", died on December 25, 2006.
（有「靈魂樂教父」之稱的詹姆士•布朗，逝於 2006 年 12 月 25 日。）

3. Tomatoes, A.K.A. love apples, can be eaten raw.
（英文名稱又叫 love apple 的番茄可以生吃。）

4. According to police records, Tony Chen, AKA "Baby Face Tony" in the underworld, is very fierce and violent.
（根據警方記錄，黑社會人稱「娃娃臉東尼」的陳東尼非常兇暴。）

Unit 02 Cos, cos of

必閃陷阱 非學不可

Cos 是 because 的簡寫，發 /kəz/ 的音，也可以拼成 'cause。它可用來取代 because，而 **cos of** 則**可取代 because of**。我們經常在講話、電子郵件和簡訊中，尤其是在非正式情況中，使用 cos 和 cos of。

Cos 和 cos of 的用法與 because 和 because of 一樣。換言之，cos 後接子句，而 cos of 後接名詞、動名詞或名詞片語。當 cos 引導的原因（附屬）子句位在主要子句的前面時，其後**通常使用逗點**來與主要子句隔開。然而，儘管 because of 這個介系詞片語可放在句首或句末，**但 cos of 卻不常用在句首**。例如：

1. Mary is absent cos she is ill.
（瑪麗因病缺席。）

2. Cos he was so tired, he went to bed at 8 p.m.
（由於很疲憊，他八點就上床睡覺了。）

3. John cannot go to work cos of sickness.
（約翰因病不能上班。）

4. Because of the storm I canceled the business trip to Taipei.
（因為暴風雨，我取消了到台北出差。）

= Because of the storm, I canceled the business trip to Taipei.

= I canceled the business trip to Taipei because of the storm.

= I canceled the business trip to Taipei cos of the storm.

Unit 03 Coulda, shoulda, woulda, dunno, gonna ··· wanna

必閃陷阱 非學不可

英文口語為了**達到「省話」的目的**，以符合言簡意賅的要求，往往將兩個字合成一個字來說，既省話又省力，不亦快哉。雖然一般認為標題所列這些口語合成詞都是錯誤或非正規 (nonstandard) 的拼法，但**這些拼字反映了實際的發音，何錯之有！**茲將英文口語最常用的合成詞臚列如下供大家參考，並輔以適當例句讓大家加深印象，豈不快哉：

Coulda（= could have：原本可以）

Justin coulda gone to your birthday party but he had to go to Taipei to sign an important contract.

（賈斯丁原本可以去參加你的生日派對，但他必須去台北簽訂一份重要合同。）

Shoulda（= should have：原本應該）

You shoulda helped him but you just sat on your hands.

（你本來應該幫助他的，但你卻袖手旁觀、坐視不管。）

Woulda（= would have：原本會；原本想要）

I woulda said yes to lending my new car to Jack but my wife woulda killed me!

（我本來想把我的新車借給傑克，但我太太會把我給宰了！）

Dunno（= don't know：不知道）

"How long has Professor Smith been living here in Taipei?"

（史密斯教授在台北住多久了？）

"I dunno, maybe over 10 years."

（我不知道，也許超過 10 年了。）

Gonna（= going to：會，將）

This kind of problem isn't gonna get easy solution.

（這種問題不會輕易獲得解決。）

Gotta（= have/has got to：必須，要，得）

I gotta go now.
（我現在要走了。）

Hafta（= have to：必須，要，得）

We don't hafta let John know the secret of where his ex lives.
（我們不必讓約翰知道他前妻／前女友住那裡的秘密。）

Kinda（= kind of：有點，有幾分）

I kinda hate my new colleague Teresa because she looks prettier than me.
（我有點討厭我的新同事泰瑞莎，因為她看起來比我漂亮。）

Outta（= out of：沒了；走了）

1. We're outta cigarettes. You go get them!
（我們的香菸抽完了。你去買吧！）

2. This activity's kinda boring. I gotta get outta here.
（這項活動有點無聊。我要走了。）

Sorta（= sort of：有點，有幾分）

That new guy in our office is sorta arrogant.
（我們辦公室那個新來的傢伙有點傲慢。）

Wanna（= want to：想要）

I wanna go see a dentist tomorrow.
（我想明天去看牙醫。）

Unit 04 You know, you see

必閃陷阱 非學不可

在**說話或交談時**，我們很常使用 **you know** 和 **you see** 這兩個詞。它們的用法和意義說明如下：

You know

You know 意為「你知道的」，在交談時主要用來提醒對方或補充資料。此時說話者心中係認為聽者**也知道**他們所講的人事物。例如：

1. Guess who I've just seen? Professor Lee! You know—he was highly critical of the president's energy policy yesterday!
（你猜猜剛才我看見誰了？李教授啊！你知道的，他昨天尖銳地批評總統的能源政策！）

2. Jessica's expecting a baby. You know, the woman next door!
（潔西卡懷孕了。你知道的，就是隔壁那個女人啊！）

You know 有時也用於話語的銜接，讓說話者有時間思考接下來要說的話，意為「**你知道嗎**」，但無實際的意義。例如：

1. My whole body fell down and was, you know, soaked in blood.
（我整個身體都倒下了，你知道嗎，倒臥血泊中。）

2. The professor was angry at Judy for cheating in the exam, so he walked up to her and, you know, slapped her in the face twice.
（教授對茱蒂考試作弊很生氣，所以就走向前去，你知道嗎，打了她兩記耳光。）

You see

You see 意為「你看；要知道」，在交談時用於解釋。此時說話者心中係認為聽者**並不知道**他們所講的人事物。例如：

1. You see, Mary's coming tomorrow, so I can't come.
（你看，瑪麗明天要來，所以我就不能來了。）

2. You see, David is the only one of the students that is absent.

（要知道，大衛是唯一缺席的學生。）

3. You see, I think she's shy so I don't think she'll go to your birthday party.

（你看，我認為她很害羞，所以我才認為她不會參加你的生日派對。）

4. We'll solve the problem but, you see, the service is free of charge, so just be patient!

（我們會解決問題，但要知道，這項服務是免費的，所以耐心點！）

Unit 05　正式用語與非正式用語

重要觀念 非學不可

在學習英文的過程中，無論是研讀書籍或查閱字典，我們經常會看到某些文法或字彙被解釋或標註為**「正式」**(formal) 或 **「非正式」**(informal)。**正式用語**通常用在**正經、嚴肅、要注意禮貌**或**所牽涉的人士跟我們並不熟或跟我們有階級、長幼、輩分之分的情況或場合。非正式用語**則大多用**在比較輕鬆、比較生活化（口語或俚語）**或**所牽涉的人士跟我們相當熟識**或**頗為麻吉的情況或場合。**說得白話一點，正式用語通常用於作文、論文、合約、協議等場合或與您的老闆、教授、父母親等長輩的溝通；非正式用語則大多用於朋友、同學或兄弟姊妹之間的溝通。

正式用語比較常見於書寫，而**非正式用語則比較常見於口說**。然而，並非所有書寫都使用正式用語，有時英文書寫也會很「非正式」，如寫明信片，寫信給朋友或同學、寫電子郵件、發簡訊等。同樣地，口說英語有時也會很「正式」，如演講或授課。不過，英文的使用大多是「中性的」，亦即既非「正式」亦非「非正式」。

正式用語與非正式用語的形成與**特定文法和字彙**的選擇有關。一般而言，**縮寫 (contraction)**、**沒有關代的關係子句**及**省略 (ellipsis)** 比較常見於**非正式用語**。例如：

1. She does not know where her salary goes!
（她不知道她的薪水花到哪裡去！）→（正式）

　She doesn't know where her salary goes!
→（非正式──doesn't 為縮寫）

2. He has gone on a business trip to Singapore.
（他已經去新加坡出差）→（正式）

　He's gone on a business trip to Singapore.
→（非正式──He's 為縮寫）

3. The foreigner whom I talked to in the library yesterday was a tourist from Honduras.
（昨天在圖書館與我交談的那位老外，是一名來自宏都拉斯的觀光客。）→（正式）

　The foreigner I talked to in the library yesterday was a tourist from Honduras.
→（非正式──沒有關代 whom 的關係子句）

4. We went to Taipei to hold a meeting with clients. We want to update you on a lot of things.
（我們去台北和客戶開會。我們想提供你許多事情的最新資訊。）→（正式）

　Went to Taipei to hold a meeting with clients. Want to update you on lots (of things).
→（非正式──省略主詞及其他字。不過，這樣的句子比較可能出現在書寫或簡訊，較不可能出現在口說。）

較正式的字彙通常是比較長的字或源於拉丁文和希臘文的字，而**較非正式的字彙通常是比較短的字**或源於盎格魯-薩克遜 (Anglo-Saxon) 古英語的字。大多數字典都會指出非常正式或非正式的字。例如：

1. 正式字彙 (formal vocabulary)：

Commence（開始）、terminate（終止；結束）、endeavor（努力；試圖）

2. 非正式字彙 (informal vocabulary)：

Start（開始）、end（終止；結束）、try（努力；試圖）

我們亦經常**使用某些語氣助動詞來使句子變得比較正式且有禮貌**。例如：

1. Can I come in?
（我可以進來嗎？）→（中性）
2. May I come in? →（較正式）
3. Might I come in? →（非常正式）

Unit 06　用過去式指現在的時間

重要觀念 非學不可

在英文中，**為了表示禮貌或使語氣比較沒有那麼直接，有時會使用過去式來指現在的時間**。我們通常使用 hope、think、want 和 wonder 等動詞來達成這項目的。在這種句子中，**動詞可能是過去簡單式**或是**過去進行式**，後者更有禮貌。例如：

1. I was hoping you had a job.
（我希望你有工作。）
→ 沒有 I hope you have a job. 那麼直接。
2. I was having problems with my computer and I was just wondering if you could fix them for me.
（我的電腦出了問題，我只是想知道你是否能幫我修復。）
→ 沒有 I have a problem with my computer and I wonder if you could fix it for me. 那麼直接。**I was just wondering if ...** 這個句型經常可見，宜牢記。

3. Would you give this book to Simon, please?
（請你把這本書拿給賽蒙，好嗎？）

→ 沒有 Will you give this book to Simon, please? 那麼直接，而且比較有禮貌。

4. I wanted to ask you a question.
（我想問你一個問題。）

在**正式的上下文**中，我們**有時會在現在時態的問句、邀請和請求中使用過去簡單式或過去進行式，來使句子聽起來更有禮貌**。例如：

1. Did you want another coffee?
（想再來一杯咖啡嗎？）

2. I thought you might like to know that Peter has bought a mansion in downtown Taipei.
（我想你可能想知道彼得已買下台北市中心的一棟豪宅。）

3. We were rather hoping that you'd stay for a cup of coffee.
（我們很希望你能留下來喝杯咖啡。）

在**商店及其他服務情況中**，服務人員經常使**用過去式來表示禮貌**。例如：

1. Clerk: What was the name please?
（店員：請問貴姓？）

Customer: Deborah, D-E-B-O-R-A-H.
（顧客：黛柏拉，D-E-B-O-R-A-H）

2. Clerk: Did you need any help, madam?
（店員：夫人，要幫忙嗎？）

Customer: No, thanks. I'm just looking.
（顧客：不用，謝謝。我只是隨便看看。）

必閃陷阱 非學不可

一般而言，動詞過去式係表示**動詞的動作發生在過去、亦結束在過去**，現在不再發生，抑或動詞所表示的狀態存在於過去，但現在已不復存在。然而，**有時我們可用過去式來指現在仍然存在的狀態**。例如：

1. John had an interview for a foreign trade job with a big company the other day but he didn't get in because his spoken English wasn't good enough.

（約翰幾天前參加一家大公司的外貿職缺面試，但未被錄取，因為他的英文口語不夠好。）

→ 約翰英文口語不夠好這一事實或狀態現在還存在，不會幾天光景就突然改變。

2. The two armed men who were caught trying to rob a jewelry store yesterday were Vietnamese.

（昨天企圖搶劫一家珠寶店時被捕的那兩名武裝分子是越南人。）

→ 那兩名武裝分子是越南人這一身份或國籍，現在還是，短期內不太可能因為時空而改變。

Unit 07 完成式不定詞

重要觀念 非學不可

我們有時會在 be、claim、expect、hate、hope、like、love、prefer、pretend 和 seem 等動詞後面使用完成式不定詞（perfect infinitive，即 **to + have + P.P.**）來表示**該完成式動作比這些動詞還要早發生**，但完成式不定詞的動作**可能是過去的事實**，也可能是**過去的非事實**（與過去事實相反）。

完成式不定詞的動作係過去的事實。例如：

1. Peter claims to have met the president, but most of us don't believe him.
（彼得聲稱見過總統，但我們大多不信。）

→ 至於彼得是否真的見過總統並不重要，也不影響它在英文中被視為「過去的事實」這一事實。

= Peter claims (that) he has met the president, but most of us don't believe him.

2. I seem to have lost my way.
（我好像迷路了。）

= It seems to me that I have lost my way.

3. He seems to have gone out.
（他似乎已經出門了。）

4. John hated to have quarreled with his wife.
（跟太太吵了一架，約翰感到遺憾。）

完成式不定詞的動作係與過去的事實相反。這種**過去的非事實**主要用在下列句型：

Be to + have + P.P.

→ **這是表示過去計畫好或安排好的事情沒有實現或發生**，所以這裡的 BE 動詞只能用 was/were。這相當於在口語上用得比較多的 **was/were supposed to**。例如：

1. Jack was to have gone on holiday with Miss Chen, but she couldn't get time off work.
（傑克原本要和陳小姐去度假，但她無法請假。）
= Jack was supposed to go on holiday with Miss Chen, but she couldn't get time off work.

2. They were to have met me in the library, but they didn't get there.
（他們原本要跟我在圖書館見面，但他們沒有到。）
= They were supposed to meet me in the library, but they didn't get there.

Would like/love/prefer to + have + P.P. 或 **wanted + to + have + P.P.**（注意：這裡 want 必須用**過去式**）。例如：

1. My brother would like to have studied abroad.
（我弟弟本來想出國留學——但事實上並沒有出國。）
= My brother wanted to have studied abroad.
= My brother would have liked to study abroad.
→ 我們亦可用 would like 的過去式 would have liked ＋ 現在式不定詞（to ＋ 原形動詞）來表示過去的非事實。

2. I would like to have gone to Pescadores for the weekend.
（我本來想去澎湖度週末 ──但事實上並沒有去。）

= I wanted to have gone to Pescadores for the weekend.

= I would have liked to go to Pescadores for the weekend.

3. I would prefer to have worked for a small company than a big multinational conglomerate.

（我寧願在小公司工作，而不是在大型跨國企業集團──但事實上他並非任職於小公司。）

Pretend to + have + P.P. 也是**完成式不定詞的動作與過去事實相反的句型**。例如：

She pretended to have just broken up with her boyfriend.
（她假裝剛與男朋友分手。）

= She pretended that she had just broken up with her boyfriend.

→ 這句 pretended 為過去式，所以比過去（簡單）式更早的動作要使用過去完成式。

必閃陷阱 非學不可

完成式不定詞除了可以表示**該完成式動作比主動詞還要早發生**之外，亦可表示**該完成式動作比主動詞還要晚發生**（指將在**未來某個時間點**完成的事情）。例如：

1. I hope to have got a doctor's degree in physics from MIT by the end of July.
（我希望在七月底之前取得麻省理工學院物理博士學位。）

2. Salary growth has been weak for 2017 and is not expected to have changed significantly for 2018.

（薪資成長在 2017 年一直處於疲軟狀態，預料在 2018 年也不會有重大變化。）

現在式不定詞（**to + 原形動詞**）可以用作名詞來當句子的主詞；同樣地，**完成式不定詞 (to + have + P.P.)** 亦可用作名詞來當句子的主詞，而且可藉由主動詞的時態變化，讓**完成式不定詞**的動作可以是**過去的事實**，也可以是**過去的非事實**。例如：

1. To have got a doctor's degree in physics from MIT was a great achievement.
（取得麻省理工學院物理博士學位是一項重大成就。）
→ 此人已取得該學位。

2. To have got a doctor's degree in physics from MIT would have been a great achievement, but that was just a dream.
（取得麻省理工學院物理博士學位會是一項重大成就，但那只是個夢想。）
→ 此人並未取得該學位。

Unit 08 英文寫作的正式文體

必閃陷阱 非學不可

英文寫作經常採用正式文體。英文有多種不同的正式文體，所以**文法和字彙的選擇至關重要。正式文體通常少用人稱代名詞，但多用名詞片語和被動態。文體越正式，越不帶感情、越去人稱化！**
少用人稱代名詞
人稱代名詞被 it 或 there 的非人稱結構所取代。例如：

1. 一般文體：I suggest that you apologize to your teacher for coming to school late.
（我建議你應該為上學遲到向老師致歉。）
正式文體：It is suggested that you make an apology to your teacher for coming to school late.
（建議你應該為上學遲到向老師致歉。）
→ 這句用非人稱代名的的 it 開頭。

2. 一般文體：We would like to donate a large number of books to the library.
（我們想把大量的書捐贈給圖書館。）

正式文體：There are a large number of books to donate to the library.
（有大量的書要捐贈給圖書館。）

名詞片語

在**不帶感情、去人稱化的正式文體**中，我們**經常使用名詞片語**而不用動詞片語。這種**動詞（或形容詞）的名詞化**，英文叫做 nominalization。例如：

1. 一般文體：The plan was implemented successfully and this brought immense profit to the company.
（該計畫已成功地執行，而這帶給這家公司巨大的利潤。）

正式文體：The successful implementation of the plan brought immense profit to the company.
（該計畫之成功執行帶給這家公司巨大的利潤。）

2. 一般文體：He is due to retire as chief executive officer in January next year.
（他預計明年一月從執行長職位退下來。）

正式文體：His retirement as chief executive officer is due to be in January next year.

被動態

被動態在不帶感情、去人稱化的正式文體中很常用，尤其是在學術寫作中。被動態讓寫作者得以**專注於文章寫作的過程**，而非專注在**主詞（人）的動作上**。例如：

一般文體：In this thesis I explore and analyze the translation strategies of neologisms in the English-to-Chinese news translation.
（在本論文中，我探討和分析英翻中新聞翻譯之新字新詞的翻譯策略。）

正式文體：In this thesis the translation strategies of neologisms in the English-to-Chinese news translation are explored and analyzed.

特別收錄

精選易混淆
文法練習題

精選易混淆文法觀念練習題

學習了一連串的正確文法觀念之後,接下來,就利用下面的試題來驗收一下學習的成果,並溫故知新吧!(請先作答,再看後面正確解答)

下列哪一句是對的?請勾選。

1 □ **a.** Neither of these shirts is dry yet.
　　□ **b.** Both (of) these shirts aren't dry yet.
（這兩件襯衫都還沒乾。）

2 □ **a.** Blanche likes you more than who?
　　□ **b.** Blanche likes you more than whom?
（布蘭奇喜歡你更甚於誰?）

3 □ **a.** It is a gift from my husband and me.
　　□ **b.** It is a gift from my husband and I.
（那是我先生跟我送的禮物。）

4 □ **a.** Cindy earns her living by sell insurance.
　　□ **b.** Cindy earns her living by selling insurance.
（辛蒂靠賣保險為生。）

5 □ **a.** Neither Tracy nor Gina do as they are told.
　　□ **b.** Neither Tracy nor Gina does as they are told.
（崔西和吉娜都沒有按照指示去做。）

6 □ **a.** They both need some money.
　　□ **b.** Both they need some money.
（他們兩人都需要一些錢。）

7 ☐ **a.** I don't like either color.
☐ **b.** I don't like either colors.
（這兩種顏色 [中任何一種] 我都不喜歡。）

8 ☐ **a.** Phil suggested to go in his car.
☐ **b.** Phil suggested going in his car.
（菲爾提議坐他的車子去。）

9 ☐ **a.** We can eat either now or after the concert.
☐ **b.** We can either eat now or after the concert.
（我們可以現在吃飯，也可以在演唱會後吃。）

10 ☐ **a.** The specialist suggests parents that they should adopt a different way of bringing up their children.
☐ **b.** The specialist suggests to parents that they should adopt a different way of bringing up their children.
（這位專家建議父母應採取不同的教養子女方式。）

11 ☐ **a.** From my point of view, the president hasn't done enough to deal with tricky problems.
☐ **b.** On my point of view, the president hasn't done enough to deal with tricky problems.
（在我看來，總統在處理棘手問題方面做得還不夠。）

12 ☐ **a.** My data are being collated by three professionals.
☐ **b.** My data is being collated by three professionals.
（我的資料正由三位專業人士核對校勘中。）

13
☐ **a.** Sandy ate a whole bag of potato chips all by himself!
☐ **b.** Sandy ate all a bag of potato chips all by himself!
（桑迪一個人把一整包洋芋片全吃光了！）

14
☐ **a.** I've got a shirt just as that.
☐ **b.** I've got a shirt just like that.
（我有一件和那件一模一樣的襯衫。）

15
☐ **a.** The whole equipment has been checked.
☐ **b.** All the equipment has been checked.
（所有設備都檢查過了。）

16
☐ **a.** My room was situated at the end of the corridor.
☐ **b.** My room was situated in the end of the corridor.
（我的房間位在走廊的盡頭。）

17
☐ **a.** This type of schoolbag was just under two kilos, so they could not hinder development in schoolchildren.
☐ **b.** This type of schoolbag was just below two kilos, so they could not hinder development in schoolchildren.
（這款書包重量不到兩公斤，所以它們不會妨礙學童的發育。）

18
☐ **a.** The waiter asked if we were all together, so I said that we were two separate parties.
☐ **b.** The waiter asked if we were altogether, so I said that we were two separate parties.
（服務生問我們是不是一起的，我說我們是不同的兩組人。）

19 ☐ **a.** This film's adult contents are not suitable for young children.
☐ **b.** This film's adult content is not suitable for young children.

（這部電影的成人內容對兒童不宜。）

20 ☐ **a.** More and more fans moved onto the concert.
☐ **b.** More and more fans moved on to the concert.

（越來越多的粉絲往演唱會移動。）

21 ☐ **a.** The traffic accident happened in May, i.e., three months ago.
☐ **b.** The traffic accident happened in May, e.g., three months ago.

（這起車禍發生在五月，亦即三個月前。）

22 ☐ **a.** Disappointed almost to the point of tears I have decided not to talk politics at all from now on.

☐ **b.** Disappointed almost to the point of tears, I have decided not to talk politics at all from now on.

（失望到幾近落淚的程度，我已決定從此完全不談政治。）

23 ☐ **a.** Miranda's so-called "boyfriend" got married to another girl a few days ago.

☐ **b.** Miranda's so-called boyfriend got married to another girl a few days ago.

（米蘭達所謂的男友幾天前和另一名女子結婚了。）

24 ☐ **a.** Did you manage to get the Bruno Mars tickets?
☐ **b.** Did you manage to get the Bruno Mars Tickets?

（你成功買到「火星人」布魯諾・馬爾斯的門票了嗎？）

25 ☐ **a.** Never will we give up the struggle for freedom and peace.
☐ **b.** Not ever will we give up the struggle for freedom and peace.
（我們絕對不會放棄為自由與和平而奮鬥。）

26 ☐ **a.** Mary prefers coffee to tea.
☐ **b.** Mary prefers coffee than tea.
（瑪麗喜歡咖啡更勝於茶。）

27 ☐ **a.** They have rather some expensive wine.
☐ **b.** They have some rather expensive wine.
（他們擁有一些相當昂貴的葡萄酒。）

28 ☐ **a.** I'd rather you didn't phone after 10 o'clock.
☐ **b.** I'd rather not you phoned after 10 o'clock.
（我寧願你 10 點之後不打電話。）

29 ☐ **a.** Upon entering the classroom, a big balloon caught my eye.
☐ **b.** Upon entering the classroom, I immediately noticed a big balloon.
（一進入教室，我就注意到一個大氣球。）

30 ☐ **a.** The thing you need to remember is that you've lent James 50,000 dollars.
☐ **b.** The thing you need to remember is you've lent James 50,000 dollars.
（你必須記住的是，你已借給詹姆斯五萬元。）

31 ☐ **a.** Newspapers were scattered across the floor.
☐ **b.** Newspapers were scattered on the floor.

（報紙散落一地。）

32 ☐ **a.** At the age of 40, I started to learn English.
☐ **b.** In the age of 40, I started to learn English.

（40 歲時我開始學英文。）

33 ☐ **a.** She got married at last Christmas.
☐ **b.** She got married last Christmas.

（她去年聖誕節結的婚。）

34 ☐ **a.** There aren't enough of them to make up a team.
☐ **b.** There aren't enough them to make up a team.

（他們的人數還不夠組成一個隊。）

35 ☐ **a.** The sun shines several hundred hours during June, July and August in Taiwan and on most days temperatures rise above 33 degrees.
☐ **b.** The sun shines several hundred hours during June, July and August in Taiwan and on the most days temperatures rise above 33 degrees.

（台灣六月、七月和八月的日照時間有幾百個小時，白天氣溫大多會上升至 33 度以上。）

36 ☐ **a.** John invited all his other relatives and friends.
☐ **b.** John invited all his others relatives and friends.

（約翰邀請了他的其他所有親戚朋友。）

37 ☐ **a.** It took a long time for me to write this article.
　 ☐ **b.** It took long for me to write this article.
（寫這篇文章花了我很長的時間。）

38 ☐ **a.** Sometimes it's a matter of the luck whether we are successful.
　 ☐ **b.** Sometimes it's a matter of luck whether we are successful.
（有時我們能否成功要靠運氣。）

39 ☐ **a.** His mother's about 40.
　 ☐ **b.** His mother's more or less 40.
（他媽媽大約 40 歲。）

40 ☐ **a.** John has been working in a restaurant near the park.
　 ☐ **b.** John has been working in a restaurant nearby the park.
（約翰一直在公園附近的一家餐廳工作。）

41 ☐ **a.** I can't print any more documents. The printer isn't working.
　 ☐ **b.** I can't print anymore documents. The printer isn't working.
（我不能再列印文件了。印表機掛了。）

42 ☐ **a.** I wish to be a famous singer and make a lot of money.
　 ☐ **b.** I'm wishing to be a famous singer and make a lot of money.
（我想成為名歌手，賺很多錢。）

43 ☐ **a.** Carl only visits his parents once a year.
　 ☐ **b.** Carl visits his parents only once a year.
（卡爾一年拜訪他的雙親一次。）

44 ☐ **a.** This type of smartphone isn't so good, really. I don't think I'll use it again.

☐ **b.** This type of smartphone isn't pretty good, really. I don't think I'll use it again.

（這款智慧型手機的確不是很好。我想我不會再用它了。）

- -

45 ☐ **a.** This restaurant is superior to the one we usually go to.

☐ **b.** This restaurant is superior than the one we usually go to.

（這家餐廳比我們常去的那家好。）

- -

46 ☐ **a.** We go for dinner together once the week.

☐ **b.** We go for dinner together once a week.

（我們一個禮拜會共進晚餐一次。）

- -

47 ☐ **a.** Once I pass all these exams, I'll be fully qualified.

☐ **b.** Once I will pass all these exams, I'll be fully qualified.

（一旦我通過所有這些考試，我就完全合格了。）

- -

48 ☐ **a.** John would like to have an own car.

☐ **b.** John would like to have his own car.

（約翰想要有自己的車子。）

Answer Key

1. (a) 2. (b) 3. (a) 4. (b) 5. (b) 6. (a) 7. (a) 8. (b) 9. (a)

10. (b) 11. (a) 12. (b) 13. (a) 14. (b) 15. (b) 16. (a) 17. (a)

18. (a) 19. (b) 20. (b) 21. (a) 22. (b) 23. (b) 24. (a) 25. (a)

26. (a) 27. (b) 28. (a) 29. (b) 30. (a) 31. (a) 32. (a) 33. (b)

34. (a) 35. (a) 36. (a) 37. (a) 38. (b) 39. (a) 40. (a) 41. (a)

42. (a) 43. (b) 44. (a) 45. (a) 46. (b) 47. (a) 48. (b)

語言力 _E027_

一本掌握易混淆英文文法：
文法常見錯誤與用法精論

快速提升閱讀、口說、寫作實力。

作　　　者	俞亨通
顧　　　問	曾文旭
統　　　籌	陳逸祺
編輯總監	耿文國
主　　　編	陳蕙芳
執行編輯	翁芯俐
封面設計	吳若瑄
內文排版	吳若瑄
法律顧問	北辰著作權事務所

印　　　製	世和印製企業有限公司
初　　　版	2020年07月
	（本書改自《非學不可的易混淆英文文法：閱讀、口説、寫作高分養成班》一書）
出　　　版	凱信企業集團-開企有限公司
電　　　話	（02）2773-6566
傳　　　真	（02）2778-1033
地　　　址	106 台北市大安區忠孝東路四段218之4號12樓
信　　　箱	kaihsinbooks@gmail.com

定　　　價	新台幣399元／港幣133元
產品內容	1 書

總 經 銷	采舍國際有限公司
地　　　址	235 新北市中和區中山路二段366巷10號3樓
電　　　話	（02）8245-8786
傳　　　真	（02）8245-8718

國家圖書館出版品預行編目資料

一本掌握易混淆英文文法：文法常見錯誤與用
法精論 / 俞亨通著. -- 初版. -- 臺北市：開企，
2020.07
　　面；　公分
ISBN 978-986-98556-9-3(平裝)

1.英語 2.語法

805.16　　　　　　　　　　　　109008763